CITY OF RANCHO MIRAGE ©

PUBLIC LIBRARY

Presented By:

Marcia Justice
Memorial Book Fund

FORM 4(6/95)

A TIME OF PEACE

A TIME OF PEACE

Beryl Matthews

This first hardcover edition published in Great Britain 2005 by
SEVERN HOUSE PUBLISHERS LTD of
9–15 High Street, Sutton, Surrey SM1 1DF,
by arrangement with Penguin Books Ltd.
This title first published in the USA 2005 by
SEVERN HOUSE PUBLISHERS INC of
595 Madison Avenue, New York, N.Y. 10022.

British Library Cataloguing in Publication Data

Matthews, Beryl
    A time of peace
    1.   Nineteen sixties - Fiction
    2.   London (England) - Social life and customs - Fiction
    I.   Title
    823.9'2 [F]

ISBN 0-7278-6221-9

Typeset by Palimpsest Book Production Ltd.,
Polmont, Stirlingshire, Scotland.
Printed and bound in Great Britain by
MPG Books Ltd., Bodmin, Cornwall.

To every thing there is a season,
And a time to every purpose under the heaven:

A time to weep, and a time to laugh;
A time to mourn, and a time to dance;

A time to rend, and a time to sew;
A time to keep silence, and a time to speak;

A time to love, and a time to hate;
A time of war, and a time of peace.

Ecclesiastes 3: 1, 4, 7, 8

I

May 1960

This was it!

Kate Freeman stood on the pavement in Fleet Street and gazed at the building in front of her. She was nervous, but at the same time so elated that she couldn't stop smiling. The *World Explorer* was a newspaper renowned for its foreign coverage and respected for the way it presented the news without the sensationalism that you saw so much of these days. She'd wanted to be a part of it for some time. And this was the day the dream was about to come true.

She had arrived early and intended to savour the moment, so she turned in a slow circle to look up and down the busy street.

'Are you lost?'

Kate grinned at the middle-aged man who had stopped to see if she needed help. 'Oh, no, I know *exactly* where I am!'

'Good for you.' He gave a rueful smile at her obvious excitement and continued walking, lifting his hand in a wave as he disappeared into the crowd.

She felt like doing a little jig of delight but managed to resist the temptation and retain her dignity in the crowded street. It was still hard to believe she had actually got the job, but she had the letter in her bag to prove it.

She was about to become a photographer for the *World Explorer*!

With one more glance at the gold lettering over the door, Kate walked into the foyer and up to the front desk.

'Hello, I'm Kate Freeman and I'm starting work here today.'

The receptionist gave her a friendly smile. 'Take a seat, Miss Freeman, someone will be right down for you.'

She was too nervous to sit, so she wandered around the foyer, examining the many photographs on the walls. They were good – very good – and she hoped to be as expert herself one day. Photography was her passion, but she was well aware that she still had a lot to learn. And this was the place to do it!

She looked up to see a man in his early thirties striding towards her with a smile on his face.

'You must be Miss Freeman.' He shook her hand. 'I'm Terry Jenkins, the paper's senior photographer, and you'll be working with me.'

'Please call me Kate.' He was tall and reed-thin, with brown hair and wide-set grey eyes. She liked him at once and hoped everyone was going to be this friendly.

He glanced at the bag on her shoulder as they walked to the lift. 'I see you've brought your own camera. May I have a look at it?'

She handed it over when they reached the next floor, and, while he examined it, she glanced down the long room to the office at the end where she'd had her interview. She could see through the windows that it was empty, and she was relieved about that; she wasn't sure she liked the man who had interviewed her.

'That's a beauty, a top-of-the-range Leica. They'll give

you one here, but it won't be as good as this.' He gave the camera back to her.

'My parents bought it for me when I left college.'

'A lovely gift.' Terry studied her carefully. 'And what have you been doing since then?'

Kate's smile was wide. 'You mean do I have any experience?'

'Well, the chief hasn't told me much about you,' Terry admitted.

'Ah.' That didn't surprise Kate. Andrew Stevenson had been quite hostile during the interview, so it had come as a complete surprise when she'd received a letter saying she'd got the job. 'In that case I'd better explain. I'm twenty-three years old. After taking a course in graphic design at art college, I worked for a professional photographer for a year, and then spent another year on a local newspaper.'

'And what do you hope to achieve now you're working for us?' Terry leant on the edge of a desk and folded his arms, obviously wanting to find out as much as he could about her.

Kate became serious. 'I've been very lucky in my life, with a wonderful family around me. I would like to try and help those who are less fortunate than myself. This is supposed to be a time of peace, but there's still too much fighting going on, and it's the ordinary citizens of those countries who are suffering. Pictures can be very powerful, and I'd like the chance to bring their plight to everyone's notice.'

'A woman with passion.' Terry pushed himself upright and smiled. 'Welcome to the *Explorer*, Kate Freeman. I think it's going to be interesting to work with you.'

'My mother says that if you want something bad enough, you've got to get off your backside and fight for it.' Kate gave a quiet chuckle. 'If you want to meet someone with real passion and determination, then you ought to meet my mother, Rose Freeman.'

'You must introduce me one day.' Terry led her to the far end of the office. 'Come on, I'll show you the darkroom we use.'

He took her to a well-equipped but untidy room. 'You'll be doing mostly developing and printing at first, but you'll soon be given assignments. We're in desperate need of another photographer.'

'I know I'll have to start at the bottom,' she told him. She was aware that she was going to have to prove herself, but failure was not something Kate was prepared to contemplate. From her mother, Rose, Kate had inherited not only her dark hair and eyes but also a desire to uncover injustice and suffering, and this was something she took very seriously.

'There's a pile of films there with instructions for what is needed in the way of prints. Start on those and I'll come and help you later. Then I'll introduce you to everyone, and we'll grab some lunch.'

Kate sang the Elvis song 'It's Now or Never' as she worked. In her darkroom at home she had a gramophone and a stack of the latest records, but she would have to make her own music here. She loved her own darkroom. It was a place she could spend hours experimenting with printing techniques, and very often her mother had to thump on the door to make her come out to eat. Time meant nothing to her when she was immersed in her passion, photography. When her brother, James, had told them two years ago that he was buying a house on Richmond Green, Kate had immediately claimed his room; and, with her father's help, she soon had a lovely place to work in at home.

Her easy laugh echoed around the *Explorer*'s darkroom as she remembered her brother's protest that she couldn't wait to get rid of him. That wasn't true, of course, but he had always teased her. He would still ruffle her hair and call her a stubborn, weird kid. But she didn't agree with that, preferring to think of herself as determined!

She was happy and the time passed quickly.

'You sound bright.' Terry came to find her a couple of hours later and pulled the curtain back in place. 'How have you been getting on?'

Kate grinned at him in the gloom of the developing light. 'I'm thrilled to have been given this chance.'

'There's no accounting for tastes.' Terry shook his head ruefully. 'You'll be worked like a slave, and the Chief, Andrew Stevenson, isn't the easiest of men. His temper can be volcanic.'

'He interviewed me and wasn't very friendly, so I was staggered when I received the letter telling me I'd got the job.'

Terry studied her thoughtfully. 'To be honest, so am I. He's anti-women and says he doesn't like them littering up the newsroom.'

'I'll have to be careful, then.' Kate pulled a face, knowing that was going to be difficult for her. Although she thought things through carefully before taking any action, once she had made her mind up she wouldn't budge. Her mother said she had a stubborn streak a mile wide. Kate smiled to herself as she remembered the tussles they'd had while she'd been growing up, but she'd always been encouraged to speak her mind by her parents and she was incredibly grateful to them for that.

'You know your job; this is excellent work.'

She was relieved Terry approved. That was a good start, but she was going to have to watch her step around Mr Stevenson and try not to upset him, because if she did she'd be out. And that thought might curb her tongue because she wanted this job quite desperately.

Terry switched on the main light. 'Leave the rest, Kate. Most of the staff are in now, and I'll introduce you before we have some lunch.'

I'll never remember every name, she thought, as she went from desk to desk. They were all men except for the woman on the switchboard, and that made her appointment even more puzzling. She hoped she was a competent photographer with some artistic flair, but she still had a way to go before she became as good as she intended to be. But this was a step in the right direction, and she'd learn a lot here.

She listened to the banter in the busy newsroom with a smile on her face. After Terry had made the introductions, some of the men had gathered round her, and she didn't miss the gleam of appreciation in their eyes. Without being vain, she knew she was pretty – beautiful some people said – but in her eyes there was only one real beauty in her family, and that was her mother.

Her gaze swept around the newsroom again, looking for one person, but it was unlikely she'd recognize him anyway, because the only picture she'd seen of him had been a grainy newspaper one. He was the *Explorer*'s most-respected war correspondent, and she had followed his career avidly. She devoured his regular reports from many of the world's trouble spots. If there was a war or uprising anywhere, Jon Devlin would be there. He had a wonderful way with words, and you got the impression that he really cared for the people he was writing about. How she'd love to do something like that one day.

'Is there any chance of meeting Mr Devlin? Or is he still abroad somewhere?' she asked when the introductions were over.

'Jon – what on earth do you want to meet him for?' A reporter named Mike Bowles snorted in disgust, but couldn't hide his smile.

In fact everyone was grinning. She glanced back at Terry, puzzled. 'He's a marvellous reporter.'

'Can't deny that, but he's an unreliable sod.' Terry pulled a face. 'Excuse my language.'

'Don't worry about that,' she said, laughing. 'I've heard worse when my mother's annoyed. So what's he done?'

Mike perched on the edge of his desk, eyes glinting with amusement. 'He was supposed to get married last week. We were all at St George's Church in Mayfair, wearing our best suits. Terry had set everything up for the photographs, and Jon never turned up.'

'Where was he?' She could picture the scene and felt sorry for the poor bride. What a terrible thing to happen.

'Still in the Congo. A note arrived an hour before the wedding to say that he couldn't get back.' Mike shook his head, obviously still amused.

In that case Kate was prepared to give him the benefit of the doubt. 'Things are very tense out there – '

'Nah. If you ask me he got cold feet. I bet that's the first sign of cowardice he's ever shown.'

Terry was nodding. 'The only thing that frightens Devlin is commitment, and one thing's for sure, Jane – that's his fiancée – has finished with him. The message came just in time or she'd have been left at the altar. She's not the kind of girl to stand for that.'

Everyone in the newsroom had an opinion to venture, and they were still chatting a few minutes later.

When a voice spoke from behind her, the men dived for their desks, and Kate was left standing alone in the middle of the room.

'So you've arrived, then.'

Kate turned round with a bright smile and looked into the glowering face of Andrew Stevenson, editor of the *Explorer*. 'Yes, sir, and I'm looking forward to working here.'

His expression was one of contempt as he spun on his heel and started to walk away, calling over his shoulder to Terry, 'Keep a sharp eye on her. Damned woman!'

Kate was stunned by his rudeness. As silence reigned in the newsroom, she watched his retreating figure until he reached his office, slamming the door so hard she expected the glass to shatter. She gave Terry a startled look. 'I haven't been here long enough to do anything wrong, so what's he going to be like if I do make a mistake?'

'If I were you,' he said with a puzzled frown, 'I wouldn't want to find out.'

'Do you have to replace the glass in his door very often?' she asked, making a joke of the episode, determined not to let one man spoil her pleasure in her new job.

'He never usually closes it.' Terry guided her out of the office.

'Oh, dear, I don't like the sound of that.' She shrugged as if shaking off something unpleasant, that remark about 'damned woman' had sounded personal, as if he were talking just about her and not about his dislike of women in general. That thought was quickly dismissed. She was imagining things; he'd employed her. So perhaps he was in a *very* bad mood today? She smiled at Terry. 'Where do we have lunch? I'm starving.'

'In the Hare and Hounds just down the road.'

Lunch consisted of a ham sandwich and half a pint of beer with Terry and the reporter Mike Bowles. They were easy going, and Kate really enjoyed their company. After they wandered back to the office, Kate finished the printing, studying each picture carefully to see what kind of thing the paper was looking for. Of course she did this every day when the newspaper was delivered to their house, but it would be interesting to see what was used and what was rejected.

She was clearing up when there was a tap on the door and Mike looked in. 'Bring your camera,' he ordered. 'There's trouble in Charing Cross Road.'

Kate hurried after him and only just managed to shut the car door as Mike roared off along the road. She held on to the dashboard in alarm. Her father had taught her to drive last year, but he was a placid man and drove in a calm and controlled way. This was unbelievable: Mike was driving like a maniac.

He gave her a quick glance. 'Don't look so scared. If we don't get there soon, the action will be all over.'

'We'll be making headlines ourselves,' she muttered under her breath, 'if you drive like this.'

Mike didn't seem at all put out by her concern and accelerated as a gap appeared in the traffic. They arrived just as the crowds were dispersing. 'Damn, looks like we're too late, but shoot off a few pictures anyway,' he said, jumping out of the car and hurrying off to see what it had been about.

Kate followed and began taking pictures of Mike talking to a group of people and a policeman, who seemed to be the focus of everyone's anger. She snapped away. This was her first job, and it was hard to contain her excitement.

Mike made his way back, tucking his notebook into his pocket. 'Don't waste your film, Kate, there isn't much of a story here.'

'What was it about?' she asked.

'It was a protest about the introduction of traffic wardens in September. Can't say I blame them.'

She knew that the proposed system for penalizing motorists for illegal parking in London was not popular. They went back to the newsroom without a story, but Kate didn't mind. She'd been taken out on a job on her first day and even got to take some pictures. That promised well for the future.

Later that evening, Kate, sitting on the train home, felt tired, but she was bursting to tell her parents about her first day on the paper. She watched the passing scenery with a smile on her face. Her father had designed two houses in Roehampton for the Freemans, Kate's family, and the Websters, her mother's family, to live in. Her smile spread as she remembered him telling her how he'd had them built before he'd managed to persuade her mother to marry him. Rose Webster, as she had been then, had been driven by the desire to get her family out of the slums of London, believing that education was the key to open the door to a better life. Through great hardship and determination she had managed to go to university and become a solicitor. After that she had fought for a better deal for women, for improved housing and for anyone suffering injustice. Kate knew what a special woman her mother was. Although she no longer worked as a solicitor, having retired from business five years ago, Rose Freeman was still battling with injustice wherever she found it. And woe betide anyone who got in her way!

'She only has to fix her dark gaze on any man to make him want to run for cover,' Kate's father had told her, his gentle eyes sparkling with respect and amusement.

Ah, how she loved them both. But it was her father who had an extra special place in her heart. The second she'd been born, her mother told her, she'd looked at her dad, and the bond had been forged at that moment.

The train arrived at Roehampton and Kate got out, her mind still mulling over the memories as she walked home. She considered herself one of the luckiest people she knew, for her family was the most important thing in her life. The things they had all done were incredible. Was it any wonder she was so proud of them!

Their charming Roehampton house was detached with bay windows in the front, and so full of love it was a joy to walk into. They hardly ever used the front door, so Kate walked up the path to the side gate and into the well-kept garden at the rear. As soon as she entered the kitchen, her parents, who were longing to hear about her first day, greeted her. Her mother had timed the meal just right, and it was being dished up just as she was removing her coat.

'How did you get on today?' her mother asked, as they sat down to eat.

Kate explained every detail of the work she'd been asked to do, waving her arms as she excitedly told them about being taken out by Mike on her first day. She rolled her eyes. 'You ought to see the way he drives!'

'You've worked hard for this chance and you'll make a success of it,' her father said. 'Won't she, Rose?'

Kate leaned forward and spoke with passion. 'If I can prove to the paper that I'm a good photographer, then they might send me abroad to some of the trouble spots. The world needs to be shown tragedies like the Sharpeville massacre in South Africa last March. There's a revolt going on in Algeria that is only going to get worse. The Belgian Congo is unstable.' She ground to a halt when she noticed her father's pained expression. 'There's so much happening. Pictures can be very powerful, and I'd like the chance to do something useful.'

Her father's sigh was heartfelt. 'I thought having one crusader in the family was enough. I still can't stop your mother getting involved in every worthy cause.'

Rose laughed. 'You're exaggerating, Bill, I'm not taking on quite so much these days.'

'Really? I hadn't noticed.' Bill's tone was amused, but the look he gave his wife was one of pure love and respect.

Kate took hold of her father's hand and smiled wryly. 'It's in the blood, I'm afraid.'

'I know,' he said with a resigned tone, 'but this is a great time for you youngsters. You've got a freedom undreamt of in our youth, so enjoy it.'

'I'm going to,' she laughed, wrapping her arms around his neck and kissing his cheek affectionately. 'Chris Barber and his jazz band are at the Hammersmith Palais all this week. I'm going with Beth tonight.'

Rose chuckled. 'Who might they be?'

'They're the top jazz band,' said Kate.

Bill smiled at his daughter. 'Your mother was obsessive about work, and I don't want to see you doing the same thing. Have a good time, relax and enjoy yourself.'

'I will,' Kate assured her father, smiling fondly at him.

'How's Beth?' her mother asked. 'We haven't seen her for a while.'

'That's because she's found herself a steady boyfriend, but we still meet up a couple of times a week, even if it's only for a quick gossip in a coffee bar.' She stood up. 'Thanks for a lovely supper, Mum. Now I must get ready.'

After a quick bath, Kate rummaged through her wardrobe for something to wear. She really ought to go out shopping for some of the latest fashions, but she'd never been interested in following the trends. She pulled out a red dress with a slash neck and full gathered skirt. That would have to do, but she knew that Beth would say the skirt was too long. They had met at art college, and, although they were complete opposites, they soon became firm friends. Beth Upton was short with fair hair and baby blue eyes; Kate was quite tall with black hair and dark brown eyes. Her friend was bubbly and excitable;

Kate was quieter, more thoughtful. Beth had always been interested in fashion and was now working as an assistant window dresser in a trendy shop in Kensington, but Kate had wanted to be a photographer for as long as she could remember.

After a final brush of her hair and a touch of lipstick, she called to let her parents know she was leaving, and set off for Hammersmith, looking forward to an evening of good music and laughter.

2

Over the next few weeks, Kate discovered that the newsroom, with its constantly changing moods, was an exciting place to work. At times it was quiet, almost peaceful; and at others noisy, frantic. It was the frantic times she watched in fascination, wondering how a newspaper was ever produced from such chaos and uproar. She couldn't help being sorry for the errand boy, Pete, as he tried to cope with voices shouting at him from all directions. He ran from place to place, his dark greasy hair falling into his eyes and his face red from the exertion. When she had time herself, she would pitch in and help him, receiving a smile of gratitude from him.

Kate learnt a lot from Terry, who had taken her with him a few times. She was now going out with a couple of the reporters on a regular basis, and she loved the work.

The man who had interviewed her, Mr Stevenson, was still making his dislike of her plain. It was almost as if he could hardly bear to speak to her, but it didn't bother Kate. His hostility towards her was puzzling, but she was not one to let a thing like that upset her. Everything was going well, and she was happy. They'd used a few of her photographs, and she had been praised for their quality. It was all very encouraging.

'Quick!' Mike peered around the door of the darkroom

one sunny Tuesday morning. 'We've got a student demonstration at Marble Arch.'

Kate grabbed her camera and tore after him; she was in for another hair-raising ride, but she kept her eyes shut most of the time now and, thankfully, the journeys were always short.

They couldn't get close because of the police and crowds, so Mike left the car and they ran towards the noisy gathering of about 200 scruffy and boisterous girls and boys. They were all shouting and yelling, making it difficult to understand what they were saying.

'What's this all about?' Kate gasped, as they pushed their way to the front. She followed Mike as he skirted around the police cordon until he was right in front of the students.

'They're demanding independence for the Belgian Congo and all other countries under oppression.' He gave her a sideways grin. 'This is right up your street. Can't you hear what they're shouting? This is a time of peace. Peace for everyone!'

Kate didn't answer; she was too busy taking pictures. She'd never made a secret of her views on world affairs. Everyone at the paper was friendly towards her – except for one of course – and they often had lively discussions. They had included her from the very beginning, which had surprised her. The paper was a man's world, so she felt privileged to be asked to join them after work. The Hare and Hounds was their favourite haunt. Terry didn't often stay behind for a drink, as he was newly married and eager to get home, but Mike was always there. He was around forty, Kate guessed, not married, which she thought a shame because he was a really nice man. He had a sharp sense of humour and was a good, dedicated reporter. He wasn't bad-looking either, with dark hair and hazel eyes.

Mike tugged her arm. 'That's enough. Things are getting out of hand and we'd better get behind the police lines for safety.'

She continued taking pictures until Mike dragged her to the other side of the police cordon. They had just made it when the crowd surged forward. She was still snapping away as fast as she could. These were going to be the best action pictures she'd ever taken.

'Run!' Mike yelled at her, as she continued to stand there with the camera up to her eye.

He pulled her urgently, and, after one more photo, she turned, then tripped and fell flat. As the crowd rushed over her, yelling at the top of their voices, she curled into a tight ball to protect herself and her camera from what seemed like hundreds of feet thudding around her.

When the crowd had passed, she opened her eyes and was horrified to see Mike on the ground, blood running down his face. She scrambled over to him. 'Are you all right?'

He gave a groan and sat up, flexing his arms and legs to see if anything was broken. 'Why the hell didn't you run when I told you? We could have been killed.'

A policeman came and helped them up. 'You'd better be off to hospital,' he told Mike, 'you might need stitches in that gash. Charing Cross will be your best bet. Are you hurt, miss?'

'I'm all right, I think.' A sharp pain shot through her foot. 'I've twisted my ankle, that's all.'

'Better have that seen to as well, then.' He gave her a

stern look. 'And next time don't get so close. You never can tell what a crowd is going to do, even if it does appear to be good-natured.'

She helped Mike to the car and insisted on driving, even though her foot was throbbing badly. 'I'm so sorry,' she apologized, feeling upset that she'd been the cause of his injury.

'Didn't you see they were turning nasty?' He groaned as they went over a bump. 'I couldn't believe it when you stayed there taking your damned photos.'

'When I'm looking through a viewfinder I'm oblivious to everything else,' she admitted.

Mike remained silent with his eyes closed as they drove through the hospital gates. The Accident and Emergency Department was crowded. They weren't the only people who'd been injured that day, but they were seen quickly and she led Mike back to the car an hour later. He'd had three stitches in his head; she'd had her ankle bound up.

'Do you want to go home and rest?' she asked.

'No, better take me back to the paper. I've still got a story to get out. I hope your photos are brilliant, after all the trouble they've cost us.'

Kate hoped so too. She gave him a sideways glance and was pleased to see him looking better. She was dreadfully upset about this incident, and decided there and then that she would have to be more careful in the future. It wasn't going to do her career much good if she gained a reputation for being reckless. 'I couldn't help it, Mike, I tripped over something or someone.'

'Don't worry about it, Kate.' He dredged up a smile, obviously trying to make light of his injuries. 'No great harm done, eh?'

She chewed her lip and worried. Mike had always been so kind to her, treating her as an equal, regardless of her sex. She was so upset that he had been hurt because of her. The policeman had been mild with his censure, but she knew it would be a different story back at the paper. Now Mr Stevenson really had something to shout at her about!

They had been back for half an hour, and Mike had been in with Andrew Stevenson the whole time. Kate waited in trepidation, knowing she was in real trouble. When Mike finally walked out of the Chief's office, he lifted his hands in a helpless gesture.

'Sorry, Kate, I tried to tell him it was an accident.'

'Kate!'

She winced at the bellow from Andrew Stevenson. After today's débâcle, she knew she would be lucky to keep her job. Bracing herself, she walked into his office.

'Yes, sir.'

The expression on his face did not augur well for her. He was furious. 'Haven't you learnt anything over the last two months? What the hell did you think you were doing out there today?' he exploded.

'Taking pictures, sir.' Kate groaned inwardly for that unguarded remark. She really must be careful what she said, because she wanted to keep this job very much.

The Chief stood up with a growl of irritation. 'Don't you act the innocent with me. You know damned well what I'm talking about. Mike Bowles has been hurt trying to rescue you. He's a reporter with twenty years' experience, and when he told you to run, you should have run.'

Kate desperately wanted to defend herself but didn't dare, so she remained silent as the tirade continued, although she almost bit her tongue with the effort.

'You are there to assist a reporter. How can Mike, or anyone else, do their job if they're worried for your safety?'

'I'm sorry, sir. I tripped and fell – '

'I don't want to hear your excuses! You left it too late and now Mike's hurt.'

She was finding it difficult to keep the words from spilling out and shifted painfully on her twisted ankle. It had been a group of boisterous students, and when they'd burst through the police lines nothing could stop them. They hadn't meant to hurt her or Mike, she was sure of that. It was a struggle not to explain what had happened, but she was wise enough to know that her future was at stake, and the Chief wasn't interested in what *she* had to say. He hadn't even asked her if she had been hurt in the scramble.

His eyes narrowed. 'You wanted to say something?'

She paused for a fraction of a second, and then shook her head. 'No, sir.'

He grunted. 'Very wise of you.'

Kate had never been in the habit of keeping her opinions to herself, but nor was she a fool. There was a time to speak and a time to remain silent – and this was a time to keep her mouth shut.

'I should never have employed a woman photographer.'

That was something Kate had not been able to work out. He obviously didn't like women around and he never missed a chance to demean her. But this time she could understand his anger. She *had* left it rather late to run. Yet if she hadn't tripped they would have got away, she was sure. It had been an accident, and it looked as if it were going to cost her this job. All the studying and planning were going to be for nothing. She could get another position, of course, but this was the one she wanted. She was so happy here.

'I'm consigning you to the fashion pages from now on, but this is the only chance you're going to get. One more mistake and you're out! Is that understood?'

Kate tried not to show how upset she was. Working on the fashion section was the last thing she wanted to do, but he hadn't dismissed her, and that was a relief. If she did her job well, then she would probably be able to work her way back . . .

'Well, is it?' he thundered when she didn't answer.

'Yes, sir.'

'Right, and take Pete Sheldon with you. I don't know what to do with him. He's always tripping over his own feet and everyone else's, so you should suit each other. Now go and develop your photos and let's see if you've got anything worth using.' He glowered at her. 'That's if you haven't smashed the camera as well.'

'No, sir, it's undamaged.'

'You're lucky, then, because you would have had to replace it at your own expense.'

'It's my own camera,' she pointed out, keeping her voice quiet.

'Why are you using your own equipment? Have you lost our camera?'

'No, it's in the darkroom, but mine's a better one, and I prefer to use that.' She turned and walked out before he had time to respond to that piece of information. It was an effort not to limp but she was determined to walk properly.

It was only when she had closed the door of the darkroom behind her that she allowed her frustration to show. She hobbled up and down the small room. *The fashion pages!* She couldn't imagine anything more boring – a complete waste of time! How the blazes was she going to learn anything doing that! But it was no use raging about it; this was only a temporary setback. However, that assurance didn't ease her anger for acting so foolishly; she *had* been in the wrong, there was no getting away from that.

She flicked on the DO NOT ENTER light outside and gave vent to her anger and humiliation by using some of her mother's repertoire of swear words. If this job hadn't been so important to her she would have handed in her notice right then, but she didn't want to leave and so had allowed the Chief to shout like that. It had been loud enough for everyone in the newsroom to hear, and she hadn't missed the smirks as she'd come out of his office. In this instance she had deserved a telling-off, but that still didn't excuse the Chief bawling her out in public.

Kate ground her teeth and wondered how her mother would have handled it. That thought brought a fleeting smile to her face. Andrew Stevenson would now be nursing a black eye, or worse, if he'd tried that with Rose Freeman. But although Kate had inherited her mother's dark looks, and the same determination, she was different in temperament. Her mother stormed in to put right an injustice; Kate would achieve her aims in a quieter way. She would wait for the right time.

Putting on the red light, she started to work on the pictures she'd taken today. Kate Freeman never balked at a challenge, and she wasn't going to let today put her off.

As the pictures came to life in the developing tray, she could see they were good, and she felt a twinge of pleasure. She chose two of the best and took them back to Andrew Stevenson.

'Are these any good?' she asked, holding them up for him to see. 'Don't touch, they're still wet.'

After examining them carefully he nodded. 'Give them both to Mike and he can include them with his report, if he wants to.'

Without another word, Kate went over to the reporter's desk. 'The Chief said you might want to use these.'

Mike took the nearly dry prints from her and laid them carefully on his desk. 'Thanks, these are excellent, Kate. Almost worth it!'

She gave him a tight smile and apologized once again. 'I'm sorry about this afternoon.'

He grimaced and rubbed his right arm. 'A few bruises. I think the student who jumped on me was wearing hob-nailed boots, but the head feels better. Are you all right?'

'I'm fine.' Everyone in the room was staring at her, knowing she'd had a severe telling-off, and Mike looked as if he were going to prolong the conversation. Her feelings were raw at the moment, so she beckoned to Pete and took him to her darkroom, relieved to get away from the censure she could see in their faces. Because of her, one of their colleagues could have been seriously injured.

*

Kate's mood lifted on her way home that evening. Her father was retiring today, and they were going to have a huge party. For the last two years they'd been urging him to stop work, and now, at sixty-seven, he'd finally been made to see sense. Her brother, James, was more than capable of taking control of Grant Phillips, their building firm business. At six foot two, James was almost as tall as their father, with his quiet nature too, while both the Freeman children had inherited their mother's dark hair and eyes.

She was delighted to see that her Aunt Annie and Uncle Reid had already arrived, and hugged them enthusiastically. They lived in Thatcham, Berkshire, and she didn't see nearly enough of them. 'Are you staying long?'

'Just for tonight,' Annie told her. 'We're leaving for France in the morning for a holiday and then we're going to stay with Sam and his family for a few days.'

'Oh, lucky you.' Sam, Maria and their son, Jacques, were as close as family to the Freemans. They had met during the war, when Annie had been working with the Frenchman. He had escaped to Britain when France had been invaded, believing his family had been killed. Against all the odds he had found Jacques first, bringing him back for Rose to look after, and then Maria. They had been firm friends ever since. Kate grinned. 'Give Jacques my love.'

'You sure you want us to do that?' Reid didn't hide his amusement. 'He's loved you ever since he arrived in this country during the war.'

A moment of sadness clouded Kate's eyes as she remembered Sam's traumatized little boy, who had been plucked out of France by a father he hadn't known. Then her expression cleared. 'He's growing into a fine man, isn't he?'

Annie nodded. 'And at nineteen he's the image of his father.'

'Hi, Kate.' Annie and Reid's two sons erupted into the room. Paul at thirteen was like his father, strong and confident, with dark brown hair and blue eyes. He'd been named in memory of Reid's brother, who had also been a fighter pilot and had been killed in the war. David was eleven and took after his mother, with her fair looks. Paul was doing a business course at college, intending to take over his father's engineering firm when he was old enough. David hadn't made up his mind what he wanted to do yet.

Kate turned to say hello and then lunged to rescue her precious camera from them, gasping as a pain shot through her injured foot. 'Be careful!'

Paul hid it behind his back. 'We're only looking.'

'Give it to me,' Kate demanded. 'It isn't a toy.'

'Stop teasing your sister,' their mother ordered.

David took the camera away from his brother and handed it back to Kate. 'I don't know why you keep saying that, Mum, she isn't our sister.'

'Yes, she is.' Reid put his arm around Kate's shoulder and smiled affectionately at her. 'She offered to be our pretend daughter before you were born, and that's how we think of her.'

'That's right.' Kate inspected the camera lens for finger marks, and, finding it undamaged, she grinned at the boys. 'So don't argue with your elder sister.'

'We wouldn't dare!' Paul feigned horror. 'You're too

much like Auntie Rose, and no one crosses her if they've any sense.'

She watched the boys disappear into the garden and smiled at Annie and Reid. Annie was her mother's younger sister, and her husband Reid was a wonderful man. She loved them both very much.

'Talking of Mum' – Kate glanced around the spacious kitchen of their Roehampton house – 'where is she?'

'Gone to collect your father from the office,' Reid told her. 'She'll be back any minute.'

'I'm so relieved he's retiring. James has already taken on most of the responsibility, so there's no need for him to stay any longer.' Kate loved her father dearly and she had been worried about him lately.

'He knows that but he's been reluctant to give up the work he loves,' Annie told her with a wry smile. 'He can be just as determined as your mum when he wants to.'

'I know.' Kate went upstairs to put her precious camera in her chest of drawers. If the boys were staying for the night then she didn't want to put temptation in their way.

She heard a car pull up and went to the window to watch her father get out. Although he insisted that he was fit, Kate knew better. From a child their closeness meant that she'd been able to tell if he was troubled or not well, and he might deny it now, but she had a strong feeling there was something wrong. It was a huge relief to know he was giving up work at last. Their building firm of Grant Phillips would be in secure hands with her brother.

Their sitting room was packed, and, as it was a lovely warm evening, their guests were spilling out into the garden. The table in the kitchen was groaning from the amount of food on it, and in the background the old Glenn Miller tune, 'In the Mood', was playing on their gramophone. The room was really swinging, and Kate perched herself on the windowsill to watch everyone enjoying themselves. Her parents and brother were laughing over something Uncle Reid was saying; Aunt Annie was telling the boys to help collect the empty glasses. Rose had two brothers, Charlie and Will: Charlie and his wife, Madge, were living in Scotland now and couldn't be at the party; Will and his wife, Dora, still lived next door and were both here. Beth and her boyfriend Steve had come from Putney, and Steve seemed a nice, steady sort. Kate was very pleased for her friend, as she was definitely the settling-down kind. She gazed at the room filled with family and friends. She was lucky, and she knew it. Perhaps that was why she felt so strongly for those less fortunate than herself.

Suddenly her brother stopped the record playing, dived behind the settee and emerged with Grandpa Wally's old accordion. The whole room began to vibrate as James played 'Knees Up, Mother Brown'. Kate laughed, joining in and hanging on to Reid and Annie as they danced. Her brother couldn't play the instrument anything like as well as their grandpa had been able to.

When James stopped playing, they all collapsed on to the nearest chairs, out of breath.

'Where did you find that?' Rose asked her son.

'I've held on to it ever since Grandpa Wally died. He did love a party.'

'He certainly did,' Bill said.

Kate was alarmed at how old her father looked at that

27

moment. Thank goodness he was going to take life easier at last.

'I can't believe it's just over a year since Wally and Marj died,' Reid said, shaking his head in disbelief.

'Neither can I.' Annie's expression softened as she remembered. 'He was our stepfather, but we couldn't have wished for a better dad, could we Rose?'

'You're right there. He was a good husband to Mum. And the first thing Mum would have done after a knees-up would have been to put the kettle on.' She headed for the kitchen as everyone agreed.

Kate propped herself on the windowsill, still thinking about her grandparents.

Wally had been Marj's second husband; the first one had been a brute, Annie had told Kate. When he'd been killed in the First World War, Marj had married Wally. They had been very happy together. So happy in fact that they'd died within a few weeks of each other. She looked up as Dora came over to her.

'Beth seems happy,' she said pointedly. 'Have you got yourself a nice boyfriend yet?'

'No,' Kate laughed, knowing Dora's desire to see everyone as happily married as she was. 'I don't want one at the moment.'

'Well, you ought to. You're twenty-three now and James is almost thirty-one. It's time you had families of your own.'

'He's quite happy, Aunt Dora, and so am I.'

'Leave my niece alone.' Annie appeared beside them. 'Don't take any notice of her, Kate. She was continually badgering me when we were in the WAAF, and she hasn't changed much.'

'Well, I was right, wasn't I?' Dora gave Annie a satisfied smile.

'You were, but that's no reason to try to arrange everyone's life. Come on, let's give Rose a hand with the tea.'

Kate watched them walk towards the kitchen, laughing over something. They had been good friends since they'd served together in the war, when Dora had been a fun-loving typist. From what Kate had been able to find out, they'd had a hilarious time in the WAAF; even though life had been hard and dangerous, Dora had kept everyone laughing through it.

Kate wandered upstairs to get her camera and take pictures of the party. She found her nephew Paul sprawled across her bed, turning the pages of a scrapbook. When she arrived, he shut the book with a thud.

'Just looking. I'm not doing any harm, Kate.'

She sat beside him and picked up the scrapbook. It fell open at the photograph of a man, one that Kate knew well. Its subject looked tough and uncompromising, but he'd have to be like that to do the job he did.

Paul gave her a thoughtful look. 'Do you know him?'

'I know *of* him. His name's Jon Devlin and he's a war correspondent.'

'I noticed those cuttings are all about wars and things in other countries. Are you interested in that sort of thing?' he asked.

'Yes, I am.' She closed the book and tossed it on to a chair beside the bed.

Paul was puzzled. 'Why do you bother yourself with things going on a long way away? We've had our war, and our teacher said that for us this is a time of peace.'

'In a way he's right, but that isn't the case for everyone,' Kate explained. Paul was a thoughtful boy, and she was always happy to talk to him. 'There's still too much suffering in the world. Many are homeless, hungry or living in fear under brutal regimes.'

Paul slid off the bed and pulled a face. 'You sound just like Auntie Rose.'

'Well, I am her daughter.'

When Kate came down to breakfast the next day, she was surprised to see her father at the table reading his newspaper. She slipped her arms around his neck and kissed his cheek. 'What are you doing up? I thought you'd still be in bed after that riotous party last night.'

'Force of habit, I'm afraid. It'll take me a while to get used to not going out to work.'

'You'll soon get the hang of it. What do you think of my photo?' she asked, seeing that the photograph on the front page was hers.

'Excellent, Kate.' Her father smiled at her. 'Making your mark already.'

'Hmm, but there's been a hitch to my plans.' As this was the first time she'd been able to talk to them alone, she explained about the student demonstration and how Mike had been injured. 'So the Chief has exiled me to the fashion pages!'

'You won't let that stop you for long,' her mother remarked.

'Not if I can help it.' Kate sat down. Last night's party had swept away all her concerns about the job, and even her ankle was feeling easier. It must have been all that dancing last night, she thought with amusement.

Rose placed a cooked breakfast in front of her husband and daughter. 'We'll nip over to France and see Jacques before the autumn sets in.'

'Good idea.' Bill started to tuck into his eggs and bacon. 'It must be a year since we've been over there, and the boy's growing fast. I'd like to see him again.'

'Me too.' Rose gave a faint smile. 'Where have the last fifteen years gone?'

'Don't ask me.' Bill sighed, then glanced at his daughter. 'Why don't you come with us, Kate?'

'I might do that,' she told him. 'If I'm still taking fashion photographs, I'll need a break.' She pulled a face at the thought of doing that for the next two or three months.

Her father's eyes glinted with laughter at her disgusted expression 'Should be an interesting job.'

'Dad!' she exclaimed. 'I didn't join the paper to waste my time like that.'

He chewed thoughtfully on a piece of bacon. 'Just what do you want to do?'

'Oh, I've got some wild scheme, but it will probably come to nothing, so I think I'll keep it to myself,' she told them.

There wasn't time to pursue the subject further, as Annie and Reid appeared in the kitchen, with the boys hovering in the doorway.

'Thanks for putting us up for the night,' Annie told Rose.

'Give our love to Sam and his family,' Bill said. 'And tell them we'll be over to see them in September. We might bring Kate with us if she can drag herself away from glamorous models.'

'That will please Jacques,' Annie said.

Kate hugged them both and turned to Paul and David to do the same. They nipped behind their father for protection. 'Cowards,' she muttered.

'Pretend sisters don't kiss their brothers,' David protested.

'You always want to kiss people,' Paul told her with a look of disgust on his face.

They were all laughing as they left.

'Whoops!' Kate picked up her camera bag and slipped it on to her shoulder. 'I'd better get going. Mustn't be late or I'll be in for another telling-off.'

She waved and set off to spend her first day as a fashion photographer, determined to prove herself worthy of a more responsible job.

3

Standish House Children's Home in Wandsworth made Rose furious every time she stepped through the door. She'd just come from another row with the council, and still nothing had been done. For months now she'd been trying to improve the conditions for these kids. The children ranged in age from newborns to five-year-olds. It was clean enough and the staff did their best, but they just couldn't cope with the huge number of toddlers and babies. The answer would be to move the toddlers to new smaller units, a solution that was deemed too expensive.

Rose sighed in exasperation. Things hadn't changed much; that was the same argument she'd battled with when she'd been a councillor in Bermondsey. How could you relate the welfare of these poor little things to numbers in a ledger?

She swept one three-year-old off his feet and away from a small girl he was tormenting. 'Stop that or I'll put you in a cage!'

'No, you won't,' the boy chortled, not at all upset by the threat.

A young girl called Hetty came and took the child from her. 'You can't frighten him, Mrs Freeman, he knows you're too kind.'

'I am?' Rose said in disbelief. 'How did I ever give him that impression?'

The boy giggled again as Rose walked away, declaring that something had gone seriously wrong with her image.

A deep masculine laugh caught her attention. Sitting on the floor was a man she'd never seen before, nursing a baby on his lap and trying to play snakes and ladders with a four-year-old girl. He had fair hair and vivid green eyes – good-looking in a rugged way.

Miss Palmer, the woman in charge of the home, came to greet her. 'I've just heard that they won't be sending us any more babies for a while, as we're overcrowded already.'

'That's a start, I suppose.' Rose glanced at the man again.

'That's Jon,' Miss Palmer explained. 'He started life here and comes to play with the children when he can. Jon, this is Mrs Freeman. She's just been banging a few heads together, trying to improve our overcrowding problem.'

He clambered to his feet, holding the baby in the crook of his arm, and smiled at her. 'I'm pleased to meet you, Mrs Freeman. Someone needs to do that.'

She shook hands with him and then pointed to the child on the floor. 'The little girl has just sneaked your counter down a snake, I think.'

'She does like to win.' He grinned, sat down again and carried on playing.

The next morning Jon walked the short distance from his Wandsworth flat to another children's home, Wilkins House. Smaller than Standish House, it took boys from the ages of five to ten, and it was the one he devoted most of his time to. These boys were old enough to know that they didn't have any family and, in his experience, they were the most vulnerable.

Jon strode along, enjoying being home again after another stint abroad. He loved London – it had a special atmosphere all its own. He'd travelled widely but never found anywhere he liked as much. He took a deep breath: it even had a unique smell. Not that everyone liked it, but he thought it was wonderful. Some of the places he'd found himself in were disgusting. And with that thought, the memories of his early life came flooding back. He had been only a few days old when he'd been dumped on the orphanage doorstep. The overriding impression he had of that time was one of loneliness, but it wasn't until he went to the infants' school that he realized how different his life was from that of the other children. The mothers used to wait at the gates, smiling, when they saw their children, but he was ushered on to an old bus with the name STANDISH HOUSE on the side in big black letters. He'd begun to ask questions then, becoming angry and rebellious, resulting in the loss of many a meal in punishment.

But there was worse to come. At six, he had been transferred to Wilkins House and found himself in the care of a brutal man. That made him even more difficult to handle, and for years he fought everyone in sight. The anger was still there when he remembered the thrashings and the long dark hours shut in the cupboard under the stairs. Oh, that man really knew how to punish small boys! Some of the other poor little devils hadn't coped as well as he had, and he could remember sitting outside that cupboard talking to the terrified child inside to stop him feeling so alone. Jon clenched his hands, wanting to hit that brute, even after all these years. He had got out as soon as he'd been old enough and had been working ever since. Ten years ago he'd got the job as war correspondent because he had a fluency with words and didn't care where he went. And he was damned good at his job.

He was still fighting, really, and didn't dare let himself become too fond of anyone – except when he thought he would marry Jane and have a family of his own. He gave a snort of disbelief. What a crazy idea that had been, but he honestly had tried to get back in time for the wedding. Still, he had been on his own all his life and that's how he would remain. It was for the best. He was not good husband material.

As soon as he walked in the front door of Wilkins House, he noticed the neglect. He wiped a finger over a small table and left a mark in the dust. Knowing the children would be having their lessons, he charged up the stairs, taking them two at a time, and inspected each bedroom. The sheets didn't look as if they'd been changed for weeks, and the whole place was filthy. What the hell had happened here?

He thundered back downstairs and into the housekeeper's room. There was a scruffy man sitting with his feet on a table and smoking a cigarette. Jon waved his hand to clear the air. 'Where's Mrs Green?'

The man looked up. 'Been sacked, mate.'

'What for?' he demanded.

'Don't ask me. Happened before I came.' One fag was stubbed out and another one lit.

'And what's your job here?' He was having the utmost difficulty holding his temper in check.

'I'm Gus, the odd-job man.'

'Well, from what I've seen of this place there's plenty to keep you busy, so why don't you get off your bloody backside and do some work!'

That certainly got a reaction. Gus stumbled to his feet. 'Who do you think you are, coming in here and giving me orders?'

Jon stepped up to the belligerent man, his temper at breaking point, and at six foot two he towered over the disgusting odd-job man. He'd struggled for years to see these poor kids had a better life than he'd had, and as soon as his back was turned, this happened! 'It's my bloody money keeping this place going. Now who's in charge?'

Gus moved back when faced with Jon's fury. 'New bloke's been brought in. He's in the office at the end of the hall.'

He strode up to the door and threw it open, then stopped in disbelief when he saw who was there. 'What the hell are you doing here?'

The elderly man frowned at him, and then gave a harsh laugh. 'Well, well, Devlin.'

'I asked what you're doing here?' he repeated.

'I'm running the place again, and you can leave or I'll have you thrown out. You always were a nasty kid, and I don't expect you've changed much.'

A feeling of icy calm swept through Jon, the way it always did when he was faced with a dangerous situation. His mind cleared, and he knew he had to get this man out of here. 'You're a bit old to be taking on this job again, aren't you?'

'I'm quite capable of handling twelve brats.'

'Not for much longer,' he told him in a quiet voice,

keeping his fury under control by a thread. This was the very man he'd just been thinking about. 'And you won't be getting any more money from me, Dawson.'

'Yes, I will,' he sneered. 'This is the only pathetic family you've got, and you won't desert them.'

'You're right about that, but I'll help the boys by having you chucked out of here.' He turned and strode out of the room, through the corridor and out of the building, his long legs taking him with great speed towards the bus stop. Within half an hour he was banging on a door in Primrose Street, Stepney. This was where the housekeeper's sister lived, and he was banking on Mrs Green being there.

'Oh, Mr Devlin,' she cried when she saw him, 'I'm so relieved to see you. Have you been to the home?'

'Yes, I have, Mrs Green.'

'Please come in.' She showed him into a comfortable front room and settled her ample body in an armchair.

He sat opposite her. 'Tell me what happened.'

'Mr Jenks took ill and left about two weeks after you'd gone away. The council gave the job to Mr Dawson because they couldn't find anyone else at short notice. As soon as he arrived, he sacked all the staff.' Mrs Green dabbed her eyes with a handkerchief, then screwed it into a tight ball. 'We was just starting to make a nice home for the boys with your help, Mr Devlin.'

It tore at Jon's heart to see this kindly woman so upset. She was a widow in her forties and childless. She'd taken the boys to her heart, and in the two years she'd been in the job conditions had improved a great deal. Now all that hard work had been swept aside.

She began to cry. 'Those poor little mites, they don't

understand why this has happened. They're so miserable.'

'What happened to the money I gave you before I left for the Congo?'

'I put it in the cash box as usual and that horrible man took it. I told him it was your gift and it was to buy the children extra food and fruit. He laughed, put it in his pocket and told me I wasn't needed any more.' She looked at him with red-rimmed eyes. 'We can't leave the boys at the mercy of that terrible man. What can we do?'

'I don't know yet.' He closed his eyes for a moment, trying to think. Could he get Dawson for stealing? No, that idea was instantly dismissed. The man would say he'd used the money for the boys, and no one could prove otherwise.

'I've tried complaining to the council, but they won't listen to me.' Mrs Green mopped up her tears.

'I'll see what I can do.' He stood up. 'Are you all right for money, Mrs Green?'

She nodded. 'My sister says I can stay here as long as I like, and I've got a bit put by.'

He left and walked along the street, deep in thought. He'd visit the Wandsworth Borough council offices first.

After two days of complaining and arguing, Jon was in despair. No one would listen to him. They thought he was trying to get revenge on the man he'd had trouble with in his youth. The two solicitors he'd consulted hadn't held out any hope of success, and quite honestly he didn't know what else to do. He found a seat by the Thames and stared at the water, willing his mind to stop racing; water always had a soothing effect on him. There had to be a solution to the problem. Dawson was unfit to be in charge of children: he was brutal, unfeeling and much too handy with a strap. He could almost feel the force of it across his backside as he remembered.

He must have drifted off to sleep, because it was an hour later when he opened his eyes to find his mind had suddenly cleared and he knew what he must do. He'd have to try to find the woman he'd met at Standish House, Mrs Freeman. She obviously cared for the children and might be able to help.

Jon stood in front of a lovely house in Roehampton and hesitated. What right did he have to bring his troubles to the woman he'd met briefly three days ago? He nearly turned away, but, if he did, where else could he go? Concern for the boys drove him up to the front door. He knocked and waited, listening to footsteps coming towards him.

When the door swung open, Jon found himself looking into dark eyes alive with intelligence. The breath caught in his throat as he gazed at her. The impact of her presence was even stronger at the second meeting. She was wearing a plain navy and white frock and had aged with grace.

She didn't say anything, but he knew he was under intense scrutiny.

'Mrs Freeman, my name's Jon Devlin. We met at Standish House a couple of days ago. I need your help,' he said. 'I'm sorry to bother you, but I have a problem and don't know what else to do.'

After a brief hesitation, she stepped aside. 'You'd better come in.'

She led him into a large kitchen. 'Sit down, young man. We'll have a cup of tea while you talk.'

And for the next hour that's what he did, pouring out details of his appalling childhood in a large orphanage and then in Wilkins House, and his worry for the young boys now there. He was staggered at how easy it was to tell her things he'd never mentioned to anyone else: the beatings, dirt, hunger and humiliation. Dawson had a large repertoire of ways to subdue children. Not him, though. It had made him grow up stubborn and determined, but that kind of treatment could damage a sensitive boy for life. As he talked, he knew, without a shadow of a doubt, that she understood his worry about the boys he considered as family.

'Can you get some photographs of the place?' she asked, when he finally ground to a halt.

'No,' he shook his head. 'I tried that yesterday, but Dawson's put an ex-boxer on the door and he wouldn't let me in. I was tempted to use force, but I didn't think it would help my case if I got into a fight with him.'

'Describe Dawson to me.'

'Average height, florid complexion, must be about seventy by now . . .'

Rose stood up suddenly and called out of the kitchen door. 'Bill, I'm going out for a few hours.' Then she turned back to Jon. 'Come on. Show me this place.'

They went in her car and were soon at the house in Wandsworth. After getting out of the car, Rose Freeman swept up to the front door, only to be confronted by the doorman.

'Out of my way,' she ordered.

Jon was right behind her, and he was sure he saw the man flinch at the authority in her voice.

'You can't come in here.' The man pointed to Jon. 'And he certainly isn't welcome.'

'Mr Devlin is with me.' Rose stood hands on hips and fixed her dark gaze on the man. 'Now, are you going to move your body, or do I have to do it for you?'

Jon watched in wonder, in no doubt that she would carry out her threat. Even though she must be in her late fifties, he guessed, she was tall, still strong and very determined.

She brushed past the doorman, who had lost the urge to fight with this fierce woman, and, as she stepped inside, she turned her head. 'Come on, Jon, let's sort this bloody mess out!'

Dawson had come out of his office to see what the commotion was. Rose stormed up to him, and began talking to Dawson as if she knew him. And perhaps she did, for the man was clearly agitated; but Jon didn't ask any questions, he was more than happy to follow her around and watch her in action.

The next three hours were like a dream to him. After she'd inspected the home, there was a visit to the local council offices. Even though she had given up her work as a solicitor, she'd obviously kept in touch with things going on in the less well-off areas of London. He was also delighted to hear her tell them that ten years ago Dawson had served five years for a violent crime and remonstrated with them for not checking on him properly. This was all news to Jon, for he hadn't seen the man for nearly fifteen years.

Rose was like a tidal wave, sweeping through the

problem. Dawson and his men were immediately sent packing. Mrs Green and the other helpers were reinstated, and the young boys were soon laughing in relief. Jon was stunned by the rapid action, which Rose directed with military skill, pushing aside all objections.

Once harmony had been restored, he felt as if he'd just escaped after being under fire. He was shattered, but happy beyond belief.

'I can't thank you enough,' he told Rose. 'What do I owe you?'

The dark eyes fixed on him and he could feel the strength of her character in that steady look.

'I don't want your money, young man. I've already got more than I know what to do with. Give it to the boys. I think some sweets would be in order, don't you?'

He watched her stride away. He met many people in his job, some of them in high positions, but he'd never come across anyone he respected and admired as much as Rose Freeman. It had been a privilege to see her in action.

4

When the last of the film was finished, Kate closed her eyes for a moment in relief. She'd received a few unfriendly glares on the first day, but when the models had seen how good she could make them look, they had accepted her. Two of them were even demanding that she take their photos all the time, but this wasn't what she wanted to do. She'd been taking fashion pictures for only three weeks, and was already bored. It wouldn't be so bad if she was interested in the latest fashions, but she wasn't, and this was not what she'd joined the paper to do. There had been more variety in the photographs she'd taken at the local newspaper she had worked at. There were things going on out there in the world, and she wanted to be a part of them. Even if she wasn't good enough to work abroad yet, there must be something useful she could do here.

'Come on, Pete, let's go back to the newsroom.' She handed him the undeveloped films to put in the bag and slung the camera over her shoulder.

He collected the equipment, then hurried to catch her up. 'Would you let me try to do a couple of prints today?'

'Would you like to?' Kate watched his animated face and smiled. The Chief had given her Pete to get rid of him, but he was turning out to be an excellent assistant, and she liked him. He was eager to learn, and she could leave the developing with him now. It would be helpful if he could do some of the printing as well. She had been surprised when he'd told her that he had just turned eighteen, for he looked younger than that.

'Yes, please, Miss Freeman.' He nodded until a strand of greasy hair fell over his eyes. 'I'd like to learn everything I can. You're so patient and don't mind explaining how to do the printing and developing. I've told my mum and dad what fun it is working with you.' Pete gave an amused chuckle. 'It's good the models and designers can't hear what you think of their latest fashions.'

'Aren't they awful?' Kate's grin was wide. 'My dad would be horrified if I started wearing skirts that short.'

'Oh, but you'd look better in them than the models do. They're too skinny, but you've got lovely long legs . . .' He turned bright red. 'I didn't mean to be rude, Miss Freeman.'

'Call me Kate.' She laughed to put him at his ease. 'And thanks for the compliment, but I'll still keep my skirts just below my knees.'

They were both laughing as they walked into the building. While Pete hurried off to get everything ready in the darkroom, she headed for the Chief's office.

He was alone, so she tapped on the door and waited for him to look up.

'Yes?' He scowled up at her.

'I've finished the fashion shoot for today. Is there anything else you'd like me to do?'

Before Andrew Stevenson could reply, Mike poked his head around the door. 'There's been a robbery at a jewellers in Bond Street, Chief. Shall I cover it?'

'Of course.'

'I'm going to need a photographer and Terry's already

out, so can I take Kate with me?' Mike gave her a sly wink.

'I wouldn't have thought you'd want her anywhere near you again, but if you're willing to risk it . . .'

Mike towed her out of the office. 'Quick, before he changes his mind.'

She ran into the darkroom, left Pete with instructions on what to do while she was out, grabbed her camera and film, then hurried after Mike. He was waiting outside for her. 'Thanks, Mike.'

'Don't get too excited,' he told her with a grin. 'It's a simple job, but I know you're fed up with what you're doing, and I thought a look at what's going on in the streets might cheer you up.'

'You're right about that,' she told him. 'I feel as if I've been banished from the real world.'

He chuckled as they got into his car and sped off towards Bond Street. And for once, she didn't take any notice of his driving.

Kate was much happier during the next week, and even the chore of attending fashion shows and taking pictures of models couldn't wipe the smile from her face. The Chief had allowed her to do a small job for Mike, and she was hopeful it would lead to others.

'Let's get this lot developed, Pete,' she said, as they returned to the newsroom after taking photos of a large department store's new collection.

He gazed at her shyly. 'I'd like to be a photographer one day.'

'Would you?' Kate wasn't surprised. He had been taking a great interest in the work.

He nodded and then sighed. 'But I don't suppose there's much chance of that happening.'

She stopped, her heart going out to him. 'Don't ever believe that something is impossible. You can achieve anything if you try hard enough.'

He looked at her hopefully. 'Do you think so?'

'Positive.' She smiled in encouragement and continued walking, determined to see what she could do for him. They got on well together, and whenever she'd been frustrated with the work she was doing, Pete had been there for her in support. Although she was about five years older than him, as the weeks went by she could see he was very mature for his age. Being away from people yelling at him all day was allowing the sensible, intelligent side of him to surface. She was lucky to have him as an assistant.

'Kate!' the Chief bellowed as soon as she opened the door.

'Oh,' she said, pulling a face at Pete, 'now what have I done? Wait here. I hope I won't be long.'

She headed for Andrew Stevenson's office and walked in through the open door. 'You called, Chief?'

'Yes, about time you got back,' he grumbled. 'This is Robert Sinclair. He's just joined us and needs a photographer for the afternoon.'

Kate smiled at the tall man, making a quick assessment. He was around thirty-five, dark blond hair and hazel eyes. He was outwardly attractive, but the deep lines around his mouth hinted at a man who was a stranger to laughter.

She watched him look her up and down, and when his gaze returned to her face she lifted her head slightly.

His expression said that he disapproved of her dark brown trousers, cream blouse and flat shoes.

'You can't come with me in trousers. I'm meeting an important man this afternoon,' he snapped.

'I keep a skirt here,' she told him.

'Change at once. We haven't much time. And I hope you know your job – I don't want to have to keep telling you what to do.'

'You won't even know I'm there,' she told him sweetly. Then she turned to Andrew, who was viewing the scene through narrowed eyes. 'Can I take Pete with me?'

'Whatever for?' he asked.

'I'd like him as my permanent assistant. He's very good at changing films and carrying equipment.'

'Good Lord, is he?' The Chief looked astonished. 'He's always dropping things.'

'He's eager to please, that's all. So can I have him?'

'Pete!' Andrew bellowed through the open door.

The boy came scuttling in. 'Yes, sir?'

'You've just been promoted to Kate's permanent assistant.'

Pete looked as if he were going to pass out with joy. 'Thank you, sir.'

'We'll be with you in five minutes,' Kate told the reporter, who was beginning to scowl at the delay. She towed the stunned boy out of the office. 'Right, Pete, you go and collect six rolls of film and my tripod for me while I change into a skirt.'

He beamed before hurrying off to carry out her orders.

In exactly five minutes they were in Robert's car. 'Andrew assures me that you are competent, so I hope he's right.' The reporter cast her a sideways glance. 'I'm interviewing an interesting man today. It's taken me months to persuade him to talk to me and I want some good pictures.'

'You'll get them,' she told him with confidence. 'Who is he?'

'I don't suppose you'll have heard of him,' was the curt reply.

Kate sat back and didn't bother to ask any more questions. In fifteen minutes they stopped outside an imposing building in Knightsbridge, older and more elegant than many of the newer business premises. She looked at Robert in surprise. 'What are we doing here?'

'I'm interviewing the new MD of Grant Phillips.'

'Really?' Kate pretended to be checking to see she had everything with her, but it was to hide her amusement. She felt like howling with laughter. Did Andrew Stevenson have a sense of humour after all? He must have, because he'd sent her on this job without saying anything to the reporter.

'Hurry up,' Robert ordered as he got out of the car.

Kate and Pete followed him into the reception area. She whispered to Pete, 'Stick close to me. This is going to be fun.'

They were taken up to the top floor and shown into a spacious and comfortable office. The man behind the huge oak desk stood up and his gaze fixed on Kate, one eyebrow raised in query. She gave a quick shake of her head, and the corners of his mouth twitched; he then turned it into a smile as he shook hands with Robert.

'It's good of you to spare me the time, Mr Freeman. I hope you don't mind if my photographer takes a few pictures while we talk?'

'Of course not, Mr Sinclair, please sit down. Would you like coffee?'

'Thank you.'

'What about your photographer and her assistant?' the managing director asked, a look of polite inquiry on his face.

'That won't be necessary. They'll be too busy,' the reporter said dismissively.

The owner of Grant Phillips called his secretary. 'Coffee for two, please, Janet, and . . .' He paused and looked across at Kate, who hung her tongue out, indicating she was thirsty. ' . . . two teas for the photographers.'

Kate grinned at him from behind Robert's back and set about making ready to take the pictures.

The men talked politely while they drank their coffee, and Kate gulped her tea. She'd been on the go all morning without a chance to stop for a break, and she was gasping for a drink. She and Pete devoured the plate of biscuits the secretary had given them. Janet knew Kate, but she was well trained and showed no sign of recognition.

As soon as the interview started, Kate went into action, being as unobtrusive as the flash would allow. Her concentration was total and she took little notice of what was being said. It was only when she handed the camera to Pete for him to reload another film that she listened.

'Why is a prestigious company like Grant Phillips building cheap homes in the suburbs?' Robert waited, pen poised in readiness. 'Not the sort of high-quality development associated with this firm.'

The man behind the desk frowned slightly. It was an

expression Kate knew well. If the reporter had any sense, he would watch his words.

'Just because it's affordable housing doesn't mean it's inferior. We build to the highest standards, whether it's a manor or a small two-bedroom house.'

'I wasn't inferring that they were of poor quality,' Robert hastily assured him. 'I was just wondering why you had taken on such a project.'

'This company was involved in slum clearance as far back as the 1920s,' he said. 'My mother has always had a keen interest in providing homes for the less well off, and she likes us to take on schemes like this.'

'Ah, yes, your mother is Rose Webster, daughter of Sir George Gresham.' Robert looked pointedly at the man sitting on the other side of the desk, making it obvious that this was of great interest to him.

'Illegitimate daughter, Mr Sinclair.'

The pride in his voice made Kate smile broadly at him. There was no shame in their family about their mother having been born out of wedlock and brought up in the slums – quite the reverse in fact. The way she had fought and dragged herself and her family out of appalling conditions was an inspiration to them all. And after the devastation of the war, housing had been of prime concern to her mother. Over the last fifteen years she'd had many a battle with councils and unscrupulous landlords. He winked back at her when Robert turned his attention to his notebook.

'Your mother was a remarkable woman in her youth.' The reporter gave him a broad smile. 'Would she allow me to interview her?'

'She *still* is a remarkable woman, Mr Sinclair.' It was

a rebuke. 'To this day my mother works tirelessly for the underprivileged. And she never gives interviews.'

'That's a pity.' Robert Sinclair was obviously disappointed. 'Would you contact me if she ever changes her mind?'

The man behind the desk merely nodded.

'I think you've taken enough photos,' Robert told Kate curtly when the flash lit the room again.

She beckoned to Pete, indicating that he should sit with her on a sofa by the window. He looked at her strangely, then at the man being interviewed. He seemed to be intrigued and was much more observant than the reporter, she noted.

They waited patiently until the interview was over and then stood up when the men did. After shaking hands with the reporter the managing director held his hand out to Kate. She went over and kissed his cheek, much to the consternation of the reporter.

He swore under his breath. 'What's your surname, Kate?'

'Freeman,' she told him, and her grin broadened as he groaned.

'Andrew should have introduced us properly. You're clearly related.'

'She's my sister, Mr Sinclair,' James told him.

Robert viewed her with anger simmering under the surface. 'That's obvious now that I look.'

As Robert left the office, Kate slung her camera on her shoulder, gave James a wave and saucy wink, then hurried after the reporter and Pete. She could hear her brother's deep chuckle as she left.

Once outside, Robert turned on her. 'Why the hell didn't you tell me when we arrived?'

'You didn't give me a chance.'

'You should have made me listen.' Robert Sinclair opened the car door and she slid in; Pete had already settled himself in the back. When they were on their way, he said in a friendly way, 'It's nearly five o'clock, so would you like me to drop you home?'

'No, thanks, we still have our fashion photos to develop.' Kate hid a smile. He didn't think she was going to fall for that one, did he? 'My parents are on holiday this week.'

'Ah.' He shot her a glance. 'You can't blame me for trying.'

'Was it my brother you really wanted to interview, or was he to be the gateway to my mother?'

'No, I wanted to talk to your brother. He's a very shrewd businessman but it would have been a bonus to have a follow-up about his mother. Last year I was doing some research about the slums of London just after the end of the First World War, and I came across your mother's name. I've been trying to get close to your family ever since, and to Rose Webster in particular.'

'Well, you're wasting your time, because she'll never speak to reporters; nor will my father.'

'I know. I've tried to interview him several times, but he wouldn't see me.' Robert Sinclair sighed. 'You've an interesting family, but your brother is the first one I've been able to get near.'

'James is more outgoing. Our parents have never courted publicity.'

'So I've found out.' He paused while they waited at traffic lights. 'Tell me about your mother.'

Kate snorted inelegantly. 'Do you ever give up?'

'Never. I wouldn't be much of a reporter if I did, would I? Tell me what *you* want to achieve in life.'

'I haven't done anything yet.' Kate laughed at his persistence.

'No, but if you're anything like the rest of your family, you're going to.'

'I hope you're right, but that remains to be seen.'

When they arrived back, Kate promised Robert his photos by lunchtime the next day, then she went with Pete to catch up on their work.

'I don't know how that reporter didn't recognize you were related to Mr Freeman,' Pete said. 'You're so like each other.'

'We have the same colouring, but to Robert Sinclair I was just the paper's photographer; I don't think he looked too closely. We're photographers, Pete, and we see things other people miss.'

He smiled proudly at her in the gloom of the darkroom light. Calling him a photographer had obviously been a huge compliment, and he'd loved it. She was even more determined to do something for him now. He had handled himself quietly and efficiently today. He was showing a great deal of promise.

5

The next week passed quietly for Kate and she managed to stay out of trouble. Robert had written a complimentary article on her brother and Grant Phillips. He didn't appear to have mentioned his anger at not being told who she was, not even to the Chief. However, Kate was sure that Andrew Stevenson had known, and she couldn't help wondering if he'd tried to cause trouble for her and embarrassment to Robert. If so, then it hadn't worked. In fact Robert was now very friendly with everyone, and often joined them in the Hare and Hounds for a drink after work.

When she arrived home on the Friday evening, she was delighted to see her parents there. 'Hello, I didn't expect you back yet.' Kate hugged her father and smiled at her mother, who was busy preparing a meal for them. 'Couldn't stay away, eh?'

'Two weeks in strange beds was enough for me,' her father complained as he rubbed his back.

Rose chuckled. 'You're getting soft in your old age, Bill.'

'You might be right.' He pulled a face at his daughter. 'I'd better make the most of the next few days because I'm being uprooted again.'

'Where are you going this time?' Kate asked.

'Wales,' her mother said. 'We're going to get the

Haven ready for the school holidays. Annie and Dora are taking the kids up there for a couple of weeks.'

'Wish I could come with you.' The Haven had been their home for most of the war and held fond memories for Kate. It had always been full of people and laughter, but there had been worry and sadness as well. She knew memory played strange tricks and was inclined to select only the good times of childhood, but the Haven, as its name suggested, would always deserve a fond place in her heart. Grandpa George had bought it at the start of the war as a safe place for her and James, and anyone else who wanted to stay there. James had inherited the house after their grandpa had been killed by a flying bomb. It was still used by the family for holidays.

'We'll be back by early September,' her father told her, 'and then we're going to France for a week.'

'Are you coming with us, Kate?' her mother asked.

'I haven't been at the paper long enough to have holiday time, but I'll see what I can do.'

'You can tell that tyrant that you've got to keep your poor old dad company.'

Kate chuckled and settled down to enjoy her own meal. 'I think you're already getting used to being a man of leisure.'

'I must admit that it's pleasant to wake every morning and know I don't have to rush off to London,' said her father. 'But James is keeping me up to date with what's happening, of course.'

'Of course.' Rose and Kate smiled knowingly at each other.

The frantic hammering on the front door of his flat had

Jon tumbling out of bed. Who the hell was that at seven in the morning?

'Mr Devlin!' a young voice bellowed.

He wrenched open the door and saw Tom, a nine-year-old boy from Wilkins House, hopping about on the step.

'You've got to come quick.' Tom grabbed hold of his arm and tried to pull him through the door.

'Hold on a minute,' he ordered. 'Let me get some clothes on first. Come in and tell me what this is all about.'

Tom scuttled in and followed him to his bedroom. 'Mrs Green said to fetch you, urgent like.'

'Will you stop prancing about and tell me what's happened?' Jon pulled on the first pair of trousers he could lay his hands on.

'Ed's run away again and we've got babies.'

He stopped in the middle of dressing. 'Babies?'

'Yeah, two left on the step and bawling fit to wake the dead.'

'And how long has Eddie been missing?'

'Don't know. He was in his bed last night, but he'd gone when we woke up. He left a note saying he was going to look for his mum. At least that's what we think it said; his writing's awful.'

Jon swore so vehemently that Tom's eyes opened wide.

'Don't you dare repeat any of those words,' he told the boy sternly. At his age he was likely to think it was big to cuss like that.

Tom smirked but said nothing.

Jon's Wandsworth flat was only a fifteen-minute walk from Wilkins House. So he grabbed his jacket, and, with the boy trotting beside him, hurried to the home to find out what was going on. Mrs Green looked relieved when he appeared.

'Oh, thank you for coming. I shouldn't be worrying you with this, but it's too early to get hold of anyone else. Eddie's run away again and – '

Jon stopped her. 'Tom told me. Now what's this about babies?'

'Come with me.' She took him into her own room. A drawer had been emptied out and lined with a blanket. Sleeping peacefully in it were two tiny babies with identical tufts of fair hair sticking up.

'Good Lord,' he breathed. 'How old are they?'

'I would guess not more than a week,' Mrs Green whispered. 'They're boys and look like twins.'

As Jon gazed at them, fury raged through him and his hands clenched into fists. How could anyone do this? How could a mother abandon her babies?

'As soon as the council offices open, I'll take them there. I suppose they'll put the poor little things in Standish House . . .'

'No!' Jon exploded. 'Christ, no, Mrs Green.' He shuddered. This is just what had happened to him, and he'd never forgotten the awful sense of loneliness. The institution was too big and impersonal. It wasn't the staff's fault; there were just too many children and not enough helpers.

'But what are we going to do with them? The council would never let us keep them here. We're not equipped to deal with babies.'

'Then get equipped,' he growled, 'and leave the council to me. I'll threaten them with a visit from Mrs Freeman if they give me any trouble. But first I'll have to go and report this to the police.'

Mrs Green shook her head sadly. 'Of course, I forgot about that. I'd love to keep them, but we'll need more help and our budget won't run to that.'

He took all the money from his wallet and handed it to Mrs Green. 'Take this for the moment. I'll get you more today.'

'Well . . .' She gazed at the banknotes. 'My sister's girl is out of work and she loves babies.'

'Get her and I'll pay her wages.'

The housekeeper's eyes filled with tears. 'You're a good man.'

'No, I'm not; I'm a bloody furious one.' He ran a hand distractedly through his hair. 'Now, about Eddie, I think I know where he'll have gone. I'll find him first, then deal with the authorities.'

There wasn't a bus in sight, so he jogged to Wandsworth Common. The last time Eddie had run away he'd come here, and Jon was banking on him doing the same again. A forlorn little figure was sitting hunched under a tree, just as he'd expected.

He went and sat beside him. 'Hello, Ed.'

The five-year-old turned a dirty tear-stained face towards him, looking utterly dejected. 'I don't know where to look for her.'

'Neither did I.' Jon wanted to hug the boy but felt it wouldn't be the right thing to do at the moment, so he talked as if this were a casual meeting.

Eddie wiped his hand over his face, leaving another streak of dirt across his wet cheeks. 'Did you try to find your mum as well?'

'Oh, yes, until I saw what a waste of time it was. I realized she didn't want to be found.' He smiled down at Eddie, who was now listening intently. 'At least you've got a proper name: it was pinned to you, but my name's made up.'

'Is it?' Ed rose up on his knees. 'Do you mind?'

'No, it isn't a bad name. Now, you've got a home and family with Mrs Green and the others. They're worried about you.'

'Are they?'

'Tom came hammering on my door at seven this morning, frantic because you'd gone.' Jon stood up and held out his hand. 'Shall we go back and show them you're all right?'

Eddie nodded and took hold of his hand. 'I won't run away again.'

'Good.' He smiled at him. 'I'm starving, aren't you?'

Ed trotted beside him, seeming quite bright now. 'Yes, I only brought a chunk of bread with me and I gave that to the dicky birds. Mrs Green gives us boiled eggs for breakfast on Friday.'

The council officer listened to Jon and then shook her head. 'We can't allow that.'

'Why not?' He was determined not to lose his temper, but it was damned hard. 'Standish House is full to capacity, and Mrs Green is willing to take responsibility for the twins.'

'Wilkins House is only for boys from five to ten years of age.'

He clenched his jaw in irritation. He bloody well knew that! 'Can't you bend the rules just this once? Didn't you promise Mrs Freeman that no new children would be sent to Standish? I'll have to bring her here again. She'll soon sort it out,' he threatened.

'I'm sure that won't be necessary, Mr Devlin,' the woman said with an offended expression. 'I'm only trying to do my job. We want what's best for all the children. As you have rightly pointed out, we do have a problem placing children at the moment, and I'm sure they will be well looked after at Wilkins House, for the time being. I'll send someone round to check that the babies are in good health, and then prepare the papers for Mrs Green to sign.'

Once outside he gave a delighted chuckle. The woman had capitulated easily. Do you know that people in local government tremble at the mention of your name, Mrs Freeman? You really are something to behold.

The next stop was his bank, and he withdrew enough money to pay the new girl's wages for a month. He would have some more by the time it was needed. As long as he had enough to pay his rent and other expenses, then he would be fine. He spent most of his time abroad and lived simply when he was in London. Whenever he returned from a trouble spot, all he wanted to do was rest and spend time with the boys.

It was ten o'clock when he arrived back at the house to find Mrs Green in a state of high excitement.

'Look at this!' she exclaimed. 'Mrs Freeman's sent us a cheque for fifty pounds. This will cover our expenses for the babies. The police and the welfare have been round and said we can keep them until they can find a home for them.'

'That's wonderful.' Rose Freeman went up another notch in his estimation – if that was possible. He handed over the money he'd drawn out. 'Take this as well. Buy the boys some sweets and a couple of baby toys for the twins.'

'I'll do that.' Mrs Green gave him an affectionate pat on the arm. 'What are we going to call them?'

'I leave that to you.'

He left the home and jumped on a bus heading for Fleet Street. He'd had a lot of holiday time due him, but now he'd taken it all. It was time to get back to work.

Andrew Stevenson was in his office when he arrived at the newsroom.

'Ah, there you are, Jon. I've been trying to get hold of you. We've just heard that the army are taking over power in the Belgian Congo.'

'And you want me back there?' Jon raised a brow in query.

'Yes, I've already made your travel arrangements.' Andrew handed him an envelope.

He took it and stood up. 'Right. I'm on my way.'

6

It had taken Kate two days to pluck up the courage to ask Andrew Stevenson for some time off, but all he'd done was tell her she wasn't entitled to any yet.

She wandered back to the darkroom, sat on a stool and stared gloomily at Pete. 'The Chief won't let me have any holiday yet,' Kate grumbled.

It was the middle of September and she was still taking fashion photos. It didn't look as if he was ever going to give her anything interesting to do. She'd been patient and willing to do the work with a smile on her face, but if she didn't get taken off it soon she'd explode. Watching models glide along showing clothes no one in their right mind would wear seemed pointless to her. She'd never been very fashion conscious and she was even less so now, even though trendy shops were springing up all over London. Youngsters with more money in their pockets were eager for anything new. Beth's skirts were getting shorter every time she saw her. She had teased her friend, saying that she was embarrassed to go out with her, but Beth had only laughed, hitched her skirt higher and told her she was too old-fashioned.

Pete gave her a sympathetic look. 'I'd let you have some of mine if I could, but the Chief would never let me do that.'

She smiled at him. 'I wouldn't take it from you, even if I could. You need your holiday, Pete. Haven't you got a girlfriend you can take out for the day now and again?'

'I haven't got time for that,' he laughed. 'I want to be as good a photographer as you one day.'

Kate didn't doubt that he would be quite soon. He'd been an enthusiastic student from the beginning, with a real flair for photography. They had a good working partnership now, and her respect for him grew and grew.

Just then there was a sharp rap on the door and Terry came in.

'Are my prints ready, Kate?'

'Yes. You've taken some really terrific ones.' She handed him the photos. 'Pete's done a first-class job with them.'

He shuffled through them and gave the boy a slight smile. 'You're getting good at this.'

'Thank you, sir.'

The bellow that came from outside was so loud it penetrated their room. Kate looked at the photographer in amusement. 'The Chief's calling for you.'

Terry sat on a stool. 'Well, I don't want to be found. He's looking for someone to go out to the Congo in a week's time to assist Jon Devlin, and I bloody well don't want to go!'

Kate knew Terry had only been married about six months, and she could understand his reluctance to leave his new wife.

'Tell the Chief you don't want to go,' she suggested.

The look he gave her was incredulous.

'Perhaps not,' she conceded. Andrew Stevenson ruled the paper and its employees like a dictator. If you valued your job, you didn't argue with him. Still . . . Kate chewed her lip and came to an unusually hasty decision. 'I'll go and volunteer for the job,' she announced, and was on her way before Terry could stop her.

Andrew didn't have anyone with him, so she knocked on the open door and waited for him to look up.

'Yes?'

She stepped inside and took a steadying breath. 'I understand you're looking for a photographer to go out to the Congo. I'd like to do the job.'

The Chief glared at her. 'Terry's going.'

'I know he would be your first choice, but I'm willing to go in his place.'

There was a tense silence, broken only by the tap of his pencil on the desk. Kate understood that this had been a foolhardy thing to do, but she was never going to get anywhere if she didn't start being more assertive. And she really wasn't prepared to take much more of his rudeness.

Andrew tossed the pencil down. 'Get out of here before I lose my temper!'

For some reason her feet wouldn't move, but her mouth did. 'I'm quite capable of doing the job.'

He surged out of his chair. 'What gave you the idea that you could work in a dangerous place like the Congo?'

'I'd like the chance to do – ' The thunderous expression on his face stopped her in mid sentence.

'I wouldn't dream of sending a woman. Especially you. Haven't you heard that a car was fired on, killing two innocent people? So stop wasting my time,' he snapped. 'And send Terry in here. I know he's hiding in the darkroom.'

Kate kept her head high. The remark, 'especially you', had made her position clear. He obviously had a low opinion of her and would never let her do anything but photograph models. What she couldn't understand was why he had employed her in the first place. There were plenty of competent photographers around who could do this kind of work. She needed something more challenging. She was wasting her time here. That realization hurt. This was the best newspaper on the market, and she'd worked hard to become a part of it. She'd never settled for second best in her life, but it looked as if she was going to have to now. And she was damned if she was going to put up with him any more. She wanted some answers.

'Tell me, Mr Stevenson, you obviously think I'm not any good, so why did you employ me?'

'Because I didn't have a choice,' he shot at her. 'You were foisted on me.'

Kate was stunned. What on earth did he mean by that?

'You have friends in high places.' He gave her a contemptuous glance. 'And you may not understand this, but I don't particularly like being told who to employ!'

She was angry now, but relieved in some way that she now had a reason for his hostility towards her. 'I haven't the faintest idea what you're talking about, but if you object to me so much, why don't you just sack me?'

'Because I can't!' He was shouting in frustration now. 'I bloody well can't get rid of you.' He leant towards her and moderated his tone. 'If you don't like the way you're treated here, then you can always give in your notice. That's the only way I can see the back of you!'

Oh, no, thought Kate, all her stubbornness coming into force. So he'd been treating her like dirt to make her leave. Well, he was wasting his time, because she wouldn't give him that satisfaction. She glared at him, spun on her heel and stormed out of the office.

Terry and Pete were waiting anxiously for her when she reached the sanctuary of her darkroom.

'I'm sorry,' she told the photographer, 'I tried but it's hopeless. The Chief believes I'm incapable of doing anything responsible.' It was a bitter disappointment and one she couldn't hide as her dark eyes glittered with anger. She was deeply hurt to find out that someone had ordered Andrew Stevenson to give her the job. Who the hell could that be? But the realization that she hadn't won this job on her own merit as a photographer was like a needle piercing her heart. It was damned painful.

Terry squeezed her shoulder. 'Thanks for trying. I've got a week to see if I can find someone else to take my place.'

'Do you think you'll be able to?'

'I'll have a damned good try,' he muttered.

Kate gave him a rueful smile as Andrew Stevenson bellowed again. 'The Chief's getting impatient.'

'He's never anything else.' Terry walked away looking despondent.

'Terry,' Kate called after him, 'remember to duck.'

He gave a reluctant smile. 'If it gets rough, I'll spend my time flat on my face. They'll only get photographs of people's knees.'

'It's a pity we can't go out there together, Kate. We'd do a good job for the Chief,' Pete said when Terry had left.

'I know we would. You ought to have a camera of your own. It's amazing how much you've learnt already.'

Pete accepted the compliment with obvious pride. 'We make a good team.'

'We certainly do.' Kate pulled a camera out of the cupboard and handed it to him. 'This is the camera I used at college. You can have it now.'

Pete looked as if all his birthdays had come at once. He caressed the camera. 'Gosh, do you mean it?'

'Yes, and as you improve we'll see about putting a portfolio together for you.'

He tore his eyes away from his precious gift and frowned. 'Why do I need that?'

'So you can show it to editors when you go for a job as a photographer.'

Pete gave her a nervous grin. 'Do you think I could one day?'

'I wouldn't lie to you, Pete.' Some of the hurt she was feeling from the Chief's scathing words lifted when she saw the look of happiness on his face.

On the way home her natural optimism reasserted itself. There were always setbacks in life, and this one had made her more determined to succeed. She might have to change course and drop her cherished plans. It would need a great deal of thought, though, as she never made hasty decisions. And she wasn't going to lose her temper and play right into Andrew Stevenson's hands, even if the knowledge that he'd been ordered to give her the job was sitting like a lead weight in her stomach.

As it was Saturday, Kate didn't get up until ten. She'd had a restless night and only dropped off to sleep when the birds started to sing outside her window. She felt heavy-eyed and no nearer to deciding the best way to go, but she recognized that that was probably her stubborn nature unwilling to let go of the job she had longed for. When she got downstairs, she found her mother alone in the kitchen with a cup of tea in front of her, completely absorbed in a book. She couldn't remember a time in this house when a book wasn't within easy reach. Her mother still had an insatiable appetite for knowledge.

Rose looked up and smiled at her daughter. 'I thought you were going to stay in bed all morning. Do you want some breakfast?'

'Just tea, please.' Kate sat opposite her mother at the large kitchen table. 'Where's Dad?' she asked.

'He's taken the car to the garage. He said it's developed a rattle and it's driving him mad.' Her mother gave her a penetrating look. 'Are you all right?'

Kate pulled a face. 'Things aren't going well, Mum. Can I talk it over with you?'

'Of course.' Rose closed her book and poured her a cup of tea.

Kate started to tell her about her disappointment that the job on the paper wasn't working out. 'I don't want to do anything rash just because things aren't going the way I planned,' she told her mother.

'What do you really want to do in your career? I know you love photography, but I think you have specific plans you've never discussed with us.'

Kate sipped her tea and gazed at her mother over the rim of the cup. 'I've never talked about it because I might be aiming too high, but I'd just love the chance to work abroad and do something useful. Words are all very well, Mum, but pictures can bring a situation to life.' She pulled a face. 'I was fooling myself because it isn't going to happen.'

'Why?'

'The Chief doesn't think it's a woman's job.'

'Rubbish!' Rose sat back and studied her daughter. 'It wasn't considered a woman's job when I became a solicitor.'

'I know. This is supposed to be the age of liberation, but it doesn't seem as if things have changed all that much over the years.' Kate stirred her tea and watched it swirl in the cup. 'There's still a lot of prejudice against a woman taking on a man's job.'

'Then convince them they're wrong,' her mother told her firmly.

Kate looked up when she heard the vehemence in her mother's voice. 'If I kick up too much fuss, I'll get the sack.'

Rose's dark eyes smouldered. 'I rolled up my sleeves and fought every step of the way for what I thought was right, and still do. I took the knocks and disappointments in my stride and carried on, no matter what anyone thought about me. I hurt a lot of people along the way, and I'm sorry about that, but nothing stopped me.'

'Are you saying that I should stay at the paper and try to get them to give me a more responsible job?'

'No, I'm not suggesting that.' Her mother shook her head. 'This is your life and you must do what you feel is right, but if you think you're wasting your time there, then move on. Find another way. Don't give up your ambition and don't believe it depends on a particular paper. It doesn't. It depends on *you*, what you have inside you and how determined you are. When I was a young girl I believed that because I came from the slums of London, all doors to a better education and life were closed to me.' Rose's eyes took on a faraway look. 'I tried to kick open those doors, but do you know, Kate, they were open all the time and I just didn't see it. What I'm trying to say is that if the route you've planned seems blocked, then turn aside and find another door, for I'm sure there is one just waiting for you to step through.'

Kate had been holding her breath as she listened to her mother's impassioned words. She breathed out as her thoughts cleared. Of course, she had been approaching this in entirely the wrong way. She'd pushed her practical nature aside and been weaving dreams.

'Ah,' Rose said, smiling. 'I can see from your expression that you understand me.'

'Thanks, Mum. I'm not going to let Andrew Stevenson bully me any more. I've got to find my own way.'

Her mother nodded in agreement. 'You may realize that the path you've chosen isn't the right one. Be willing to change.'

'I will.' She put her head on one side and gazed at her mother. 'You're very wise, aren't you?'

Rose grimaced. 'I wish I'd had this much sense when I was your age. I learnt my lessons the hard way.'

Kate had one burning question she'd hesitated to bring up, but she knew she could talk openly with her mother. 'Andrew Stevenson told me yesterday that he was ordered to give me the job. He said I had friends in high places. Do you know what he was talking about, Mum?'

'I haven't the faintest idea.' Her mother frowned and studied her closely. 'You don't think we pulled any strings, do you?'

'No, of course not, Mum. You've been there for James and me, guided and advised us, but I know you and Dad never interfere with our lives.' Kate hadn't entertained that thought for a moment. She knew her parents and they would never do anything underhand like that. 'I just wondered if you had some idea what all this is about.'

'I'm sorry, I'm afraid not, but I shouldn't let it worry you too much. Your boss sounds like a vindictive man and probably gets pleasure from hurting people. If what he says is true, then we'll find out eventually.'

At that moment Bill walked in. 'Hello, you two, you're looking very serious,' he said, kissing his wife and hugging Kate.

'We've been having a good talk.' Kate grinned at her father. She wasn't going to worry him about this. 'Have you cured the rattle?'

'Yes, the car is purring along now.'

'Are you taking it with you tomorrow?' Kate asked.

'No. Sam's meeting us at Calais, then driving us to Saint-Omer, where we're meeting Maria and Jacques for lunch before going home with them.'

'I was so looking forward to coming with you. Give Jacques my love and tell him I'll come as soon as I can squeeze a holiday out of the Chief.'

'He's going to be disappointed.' Her father's grin widened. 'I wouldn't be surprised if he asked you to marry him, when he's finished at university.'

She tipped her head to one side and gazed at her father. 'Are you trying to get rid of me?'

'Of course not. I just want you to be happy, that's all.'

She stood up and wrapped her arms around him. 'I

am happy, Dad. A wonderful family has surrounded me all my life. And I've got the best parents in the world.'

Feeling more content than she had for some time, Kate went to Beth's that evening to play records and have a good gossip. With the song 'Cathy's Clown' by the Everly Brothers playing softly in the background, Kate told her friend about her talk with her mother.

'Your mum's right,' Beth said, when Kate had finished talking. 'Don't let it worry you so much. You're brainy and could get a job anywhere.'

Kate pulled a face. 'Sometimes I think I should have become a solicitor like my mother. The trouble is I want this job too much. I'm afraid to open my mouth when the Chief's around!'

Beth chuckled. 'That must be hard for you.'

'Oh, it is!' Kate sat cross-legged on the floor and began to sort through the records.

'This Pete you're working with,' Beth said, 'do you fancy him?'

'Not in a romantic way, but we are becoming good friends. He's a very nice boy, and I believe he's going to make an excellent photographer, if he only gets the chance.'

'And you're going to give him that chance?' Beth stopped the record player and joined Kate on the floor.

'Yes, I am!' Kate grinned at her friend. 'And how are you getting on with Steve?'

'Wonderful!' Beth pretended to swoon. 'I think I've found the man of my dreams. But what about you, isn't there anyone at the paper you could fall for? What about this Robert whatever his name is?'

'Sinclair. Well, we didn't get off to a very good start, but he's asked me out a couple of times.'

'You should go,' Beth urged.

Struggling to keep a straight face, Kate shook her head. 'I'd never be sure if he was interested in me . . . or my mother.'

Both girls roared with laughter at the suspicion that he might just be using Kate to get close to her mother. Then Beth stood up. 'I must admit that your mother's a stunning-looking woman. Come on, I'll make you a cup of cocoa before you go home.'

Kate's earlier gloom had completely disappeared after her talk with her mother, and then a chatty evening with Beth. It had been just what she needed to put things in their proper perspective.

Rose and Bill left early the next morning. The weather was windy with a steady drizzle coming down, and Kate hoped the crossing to Calais wouldn't be too rough. Not that it would bother her father. He was an ex-sailor, but her mother had no love of water. Her thoughts turned to the last war and how proud she had been of her father in his captain's uniform. But he'd disappeared for long periods at a time, and, being only a child, she had found that hard to understand. Not that she loved her mother less, but there had always been a special relationship between herself and her father. Kate considered herself very lucky indeed to have such wonderful parents. She could always talk her problems over with her mother and knew she would get sound, sensible advice.

When she'd made her bed, she picked up the scrapbook. After thumbing through it for a few minutes, she began to tear out the pages and rip the cuttings to shreds. The articles went back more than three years, when she'd been dreaming of working abroad as a photographer for the *World Explorer*. Well, that wasn't going to happen now. There must be a right place for her, and she would find it.

It was Sunday morning and she was just wondering what to do with her day when someone shouted up the stairs.

'Are you there, Kate?'

She looked over the banister and waved. 'You've just missed Mum and Dad, James.'

'I know. I thought I'd come and let you cook me a huge breakfast.'

'Didn't you have an overnight guest who could do that for you?' She ran down the stairs laughing. 'Or can't any of your girlfriends cook?'

'Not as well as my sister,' he teased. 'And if I had as many girls as you make out, I'd be too tired to work, let alone come round and pester you. So get cooking!'

Laughing together, they went into the kitchen. Kate put the frying pan on the stove. They'd both have a good breakfast.

James propped himself up against the sink and watched her at work. 'Have you got any plans for today?'

She broke four eggs into the pan and shook her head. 'The light's too bad for taking photos.'

'It might clear up later. Let's have a run out to the New Forest and go for a long walk, shall we?'

'I'd like that.' She checked the bacon and sausages under the grill. 'Do you want fried bread as well?'

'Please.'

★

By the time they'd parked the car, the rain had stopped, and the sun was trying to filter through the clouds. They walked in companionable silence, enjoying the different birdsongs and the flash of scuttling squirrels. It wasn't often they had the time to spare like this, as they were both very busy. Although James was almost eight years older than her, they had always been close, and with maturity had come a close friendship. She also knew her brother well enough to know this wasn't a casual visit.

'Is something wrong?' she asked, when they'd been walking for about half an hour.

His sigh was deep and troubled. 'We think someone is defrauding the firm, Kate.'

She stopped and faced him. 'Does Dad know?'

'No, and I don't want to bother him with this yet. The accountants are checking, but it's taking time.'

'Do you know who it is?'

'A suspicion only. The accountants are working evenings and weekends, as we don't want to alert whoever is doing this. We don't want them to disappear before we have proof.'

Kate started walking again, very uneasy. 'Is it going to put Grant Phillips in financial trouble?'

'Oh, no, Kate. It isn't as bad as that, but it's uncomfortable knowing there is a viper in the nest.'

She slipped her hand through his arm, being aware just how much her brother would hate something like this. 'You'll deal with it all right. Dad always says you're twice the businessman he is.'

James looked down at her with a gleam of amusement in his eyes. 'I doubt that, but thanks for the vote of confidence.'

They walked for another hour and she listened to James talk about the business, his tone becoming lighter all the time, until they were both laughing about how difficult it had been to get their father to retire.

'Ah, a café,' James said, leading her to a seat by the window.

As they enjoyed their tea and toasted teacakes, James reached across and squeezed her hand. 'Thanks, Kate, you always were the one to soothe in times of trouble. I'll always remember that awful time when Sam went behind enemy lines in France to rescue Jacques. When Sam brought him to the Haven, the poor little thing was terrified and huddled in the corner of the sofa. He wasn't quite three and had never seen his father, as Sam had been hunted by the SS and had had to get out of France quickly. You were only a child yourself, but you reached out with love and he responded. He adored you then and he still does now. You haven't lost your touch.'

'All I've done is listen,' she said.

'That was all I needed.'

Suddenly she couldn't understand why she was worrying about her job. It was so unimportant compared with the responsibility James had. It had been foolish to believe that one paper held the answer to her dreams. By accepting that, she was limiting her options. Her mother and Beth kept telling her that, but it had taken James's troubles to finally open her eyes.

When they left the café, she gave her brother a hug. 'You've helped me today as well.'

There was a whole wide world out there just brimming with opportunities, she thought, as they strolled back to the car.

7

Kate's parents had returned from holiday the previous night, and her father was in the garden making sure his plants had survived without him. He was whistling happily, and, as Kate watched him, she knew her brother was right not to worry him about the trouble at work until they had all the facts. Her mother was busy in the kitchen.

'Can I help?' she asked.

'You can peel the potatoes if you like.' Rose smiled at her daughter. 'That break was just what we needed. Your dad looks ten years younger.'

Kate scraped away at the potatoes. 'I think he's beginning to enjoy his retirement.'

Rose watched her husband through the window for a few moments. 'It was a struggle to get him to hand over the reins to James, but he knows it was the right thing to do.'

'Are you going to ease up as well, Mum?' Kate knew that her mother had never lost her drive to ensure that people had a decent life. She was still well known in London, and people were continually coming to her for advice. And decent housing was always her concern, so she kept an eye on the most needy areas of London.

'I will, but there's one more thing I'd like to do.'

'What's that?' Kate popped the last potato into the pot.

'It's something in Wandsworth that I've been involved in recently.' Her mother looked at her thoughtfully. 'Have you got any plans for tomorrow?'

Kate dried her hands. 'No.'

'Would you come with me and bring your camera with you?'

'Of course.' She was surprised and touched. This was the first time her mother had asked for her help. 'I'd love to.'

'I want to visit two places, and, as it will be Sunday, everyone should be there.'

'Will Dad be coming as well?' Kate asked.

'No, he's going to have a game of golf in Richmond Park with Will tomorrow. I might get him involved later when I've had a chance to see what conditions are like.'

They left at ten o'clock the next morning. Kate still didn't know what this was all about, but she guessed it was something that concerned her mother very much by the look of determination in her eyes.

Within an hour they were pulling up outside a large and forbidding structure, with a sign saying STANDISH HOUSE CHILDREN'S HOME nailed on a rickety gate.

'What a dreadful-looking place,' Kate said, as they got out of the car.

Rose gazed at it in silence, an expression of distaste on her face. 'This used to be a workhouse, and there hasn't been much attempt made to improve it.'

Kate took a barrage of pictures, soon realizing it was a good job she'd brought loads of film. Then she followed her mother inside.

The woman in charge greeted Rose with obvious

respect. 'Is it all right if I show my daughter the home?'

'Of course you can, Mrs Freeman.'

Kate was appalled. The place was clean enough, but the smell of cabbage water, Jeyes fluid and nappies that needed changing assaulted her. It was crowded with small children all under the age of five, who watched their progress with large, solemn eyes. She'd been brought up within a loving family but these poor little things didn't know what that was like. It was so impersonal and she wanted to hug every one of them. She took photographs until her eyes were misted with tears and she couldn't see through the viewfinder.

Every minute of their visit was torture for Kate. She'd been concentrating on things happening in other countries, when she should have been looking nearer home. It was then she really understood her mother's obsession – for that was what her father called it – with fighting for the underprivileged. She'd been tied up in her own dreams and plans, never giving the plight of children like this a thought. These children needed someone to kick open a few doors for them. Her mother was doing what she could, and Kate was determined to see if there was any way she could help as well. At that moment she really didn't care what Andrew Stevenson thought of her, or why he had employed her. There were more important things in life!

She wiped the mist from her eyes, loaded another film, clenching her jaw in determination. Her mother appeared untouched, but Kate could see the anger burning in her eyes.

After nearly two hours they left, and when they reached the car Kate rested her hands on it and bowed her head.

'Don't let pity swamp you,' her mother told her firmly. 'Get mad.'

'I am, Mum.' She lifted her head. 'I knew these places existed, but it's not until you go inside and see those children with no one to love them that it hits home.'

'I've seen worse,' her mother said, 'but it's over-crowded and understaffed.'

'What can we do?' Kate asked.

Rose gave her a grim smile. 'I was hoping you could persuade your newspaper to do an article on it and include some of your photographs. The most urgent need is for visitors who would be willing to give the children some attention, play with them for a while and make them feel wanted. Then a lick of paint would work wonders, inside and out. I've battled with the council and have come to the conclusion that the only way to get anything done is to do it ourselves.'

'If the Chief won't run the story, I'll take it to another paper. I'll even write it myself.'

They got back in the car, and her mother drove the short distance to the next place. Kate was relieved to see that Wilkins House, although shabby and in need of repair, was smaller and not as grim on the outside. Nevertheless she braced herself as they went inside.

'Mrs Freeman!' A woman hurried towards them. 'It's such a pleasure to see you. I can't thank you enough for the gift – '

'That's all right, Mrs Green,' Rose stopped her: she wasn't one for displays of gratitude; that wasn't why she helped others. 'How are things?'

'We're going along nicely now.' Mrs Green smiled at Kate. 'This must be your daughter.'

Kate stepped forward and shook her hand. 'Do you mind if I take some photos?'

'Please do. The children would love to have their pictures taken, and' – she turned to Rose – 'we've got two new little ones.'

Mrs Green took them to a large room filled with children. They all stopped whatever they were doing to gaze at the newcomers with interest. Kate saw that they ranged in age from about five to ten, except for two babies in a cot yelling at the top of their voices. A young girl was trying to amuse them, without much success. Kate and her mother went over and picked up one baby each.

'They're fretful today,' Mrs Green told them.

'What are you doing with children this young?' Rose asked.

As Kate listened to Mrs Green explain how they'd been left on the step, she felt emotion well up in her. She kissed the downy head of the baby in her arms and smiled when it gazed up at her and stopped crying. The one her mother was holding was now sleeping peacefully and there was silence in the room. The babies tugged at Kate's heart, as did the anguish a young mother must have felt. She must have been in a terrible situation and very frightened to believe there was no choice but to abandon her babies. What a sad business.

'They're twins. We haven't named them yet.' Mrs Green gave Rose a hesitant smile. 'Would you give them names, Mrs Freeman? They're both boys.'

Rose looked down at the one she was holding, thought for a moment, then said, 'This one will be George and the other Jack.'

'We need a surname as well,' Mrs Green said.

'What about Webster, Mum?' Kate spoke softly in case the baby woke again.

'I think we can do better than that. You can call them George and Jack Gresham.' Rose smiled at her daughter. 'What do you think, Kate?'

'That's perfect. Grandpa George would have liked that.'

Mrs Green was busy writing the names down and nodding her head with pleasure. 'I'll see to this at once. If they're adopted, they'll take on the name of their new family, but for the time being we need to call them something.'

'Would you mind if I visit now and again?' Kate asked.

'You'll always be welcome here.' Mrs Green beamed. 'Would you like to take their pictures?'

The next hour was fun as Kate tried to herd the children together for a group photograph. Some were unruly and told her they weren't going to have their picture taken; some were interested and tried not to show it in case the others sneered at them. But after a stern word from Mrs Green they all fell into line. Although the living conditions were spartan, the children were lively and the helpers were obviously trying to make it like a proper home. While her mother was inspecting the bedrooms, Kate settled down on the floor to play a game of snakes and ladders with two of the younger boys. Another child of around five sneaked up, then plonked down beside her, smiling shyly.

'I've never had my picture took before,' he said.

'Haven't you?' Kate picked up her camera and focused

on his face. 'You'd better have a special one, then.' The shutter clicked just as he giggled.

'Will I be able to see it?' he asked in excitement.

'I'll bring you copies as soon as they're printed,' she assured him. 'What's your name?'

'Eddie.' He was now kneeling up and gazing at her with interest. 'I want to give one to my friend.'

'And who's that?' Kate glanced around the room.

'He doesn't live here any more but he'll come back soon.'

'I'll do a nice large one for him, shall I?'

Eddie shuffled towards her on his knees, then leaned forward and gave her a hasty kiss, missing her cheek and planting it on her ear. 'You're nice.'

'Thank you; so are you.'

The boy looked around furtively, obviously uneasy in case anyone had noticed him kissing Kate; then, seeing that none of the boys was sneering at him, he grinned, scrambled to his feet and tore off to tell the others about his special picture.

'We must be going, Kate,' her mother said.

They talked all the way home, discussing what they'd seen and what improvements were needed.

That evening Kate's father joined her in the darkroom as she worked on developing and printing all the photographs she'd taken that day.

When they were ready, Bill studied the buildings through a magnifying glass, with the expert eye of an architect and builder. 'These places are in desperate need of renovation, but they appear to be solid enough. I'll send a surveyor round to have a proper look, though.'

Kate sat on a stool and sighed. 'The smaller house wasn't too bad, but the other one was horrible. I wish it was possible to do away with the large places and keep the children in smaller homes.'

'Let's hope they will one day. However, look on the bright side. At least the children are being cared for.'

'I know, Dad, but it's so impersonal. How do you think we can help?'

'Well, they're council run, so you can leave your mother to deal with them. She knows how to get things done.' Her father leant against the bench. 'But if you can get some publicity going, it might help.'

'I'm determined to,' she told him. 'Mum said there are probably lots of women who could spare a few hours a week to talk and play with the children. It would give the little ones individual attention for a while.'

Her father pushed himself away from the bench and smiled at her. 'You see what you can do about that. I'll arrange for the outsides to be cleaned and brighten the places up with a lick of paint.'

'And we can leave Mum to shake up the authorities.'

'She'll do that all right,' he said.

Kate listened to him chuckling as he went down the stairs.

Pete was working in the darkroom when Kate arrived at work on Monday morning. He was making prints of some photos he'd taken over the weekend with his camera.

The prints he showed her were competent, except for one of a tree with watery sunlight filtering through the branches. She held it up. 'This is excellent.'

'Thanks.' His eyes were glowing with a sense of achievement.

'Well done,' she praised. Then she studied him thoughtfully. He was going to make a photographer and it gave her enormous pleasure to know she had helped him. 'I'm just going to see the Chief. I have something here I think he might be interested in.'

She headed for Andrew Stevenson's office. In her head was the distressing memory of the overcrowded children's homes, and in her hand photographs and an article. She'd laboured over it until two in the morning and was determined to have it published.

Andrew glanced up when she tapped on his door. 'What do you want?'

Kate ignored the irritated expression on his face and stood in front of his desk. 'I've got a story for you.'

'Turned journalist now?'

Kate had just about had enough of this man; he never had a civil word for her. She put the photographs and article in front of him. 'I used to write a bit when I worked on the local paper. At least have a look at it.'

He shuffled through the prints, glanced through her typed pages, then handed them back to her. 'Not our kind of thing.'

'I'll take them to another paper, then.' She moved towards the door.

'You can't do that, you work for me,' he snapped.

That was the last straw for Kate. He wouldn't run the story and he was denying her the chance to give it to another paper, effectively killing the article. Well, she wasn't going to let that happen! Whatever the cost to her she would see it was printed in any daily she could persuade to take it. The only thing that mattered was the welfare of these children.

'You'll have my resignation in writing within the next fifteen minutes,' she told him. 'You've got your way and finally driven me out, so you can tell that shadowy figure *in high places* how clever you are!'

Taking a deep ragged breath, she looked him straight in the eyes, and then without another word left his office for the last time. She didn't have to put up with this!

She was halfway across the newsroom when he called her name. Kate made herself turn and face him.

'Let me see that article again. Now that you don't work for me I'll buy it from you.'

Ignoring his offer, she headed for her darkroom to collect her equipment. All she wanted to do was get out of there as quickly as possible.

Pete had obviously heard everything and was waiting for her, ashen-faced. 'Don't leave,' he pleaded. 'I've been so happy working for you. Once you've gone, they'll make me an errand boy again.'

'No, they won't.' She tried to assure the unhappy boy. 'You've proved yourself in this job and they won't move you.'

'They will, they will! I'll be running around after everyone, being shouted at and insulted, and I couldn't stand that again.' He looked ready to burst into tears. 'I've had a decent education, I'm not a fool, but they make me feel like one. It isn't right. You've never made me feel like that. I won't do it again . . .' He ran out of breath and had to stop. 'I'll give in my notice as well.'

Kate made him sit down on the stool. 'You mustn't

do that, Pete. This is a good job and you'll work your way up.'

He shook his head vigorously and began to write out his notice. 'I won't stay here without you. Please take me with you.'

'But I don't know what I'm going to do.' She chewed her lip anxiously, not wanting him to make a rash move, but she could see his point. From what she'd seen when she first came to the paper, they had treated him like dirt.

'Then I'll get a job somewhere else.' His head came up proudly. 'I deserve better than this, and so do you! You won't make me change my mind.'

'All right, if you're sure?'

'I'm positive.'

'Give in your notice, then, and come with me. If I can get another job, I'll try to take you with me.' She watched the relief on his face and decided that she would pay his salary every week out of her own savings until they found another position. There was a lot of potential in Pete, but he would never be given a chance at the *Explorer*. And he *was* right, they both deserved better.

8

'You're home early,' Rose said when she walked into the kitchen.

'I've left my job.' She kept her tone bright as she pulled Pete into the room. The decision was made now and she wasn't going to let the disappointment drag her down. 'This is Pete.'

'Hello, Pete.' Her father pulled a chair out from the table, totally unperturbed. 'Sit down and have a cup of tea with us.'

The boy eased himself into the chair, never taking his eyes off Kate's parents.

'Have you left as well, young man?' Rose asked.

He nodded shyly. 'I want to stay with Kate. She's taught me such a lot.'

'And what are your family going to say about your handing in your notice?' Bill asked.

'Er . . .' Pete looked as if he hadn't thought about this before. 'I don't suppose they'll be very pleased.'

'I'm going to pay his salary myself, Dad,' Kate assured him. 'Until we get another job of course.'

Her father nodded approval, then smiled at the worried boy. 'Where do you live?'

'Fulham, sir.'

'Well, you stay and have dinner with us, and then I'll drive you home and explain to your family, shall I?'

'Oh, thank you, sir.' He looked very relieved.

'I'm not sure you've done the right thing, Pete,' Kate told him. 'Mr Stevenson obviously doesn't think I'm a good photographer.'

'That's nonsense,' her father reprimanded.

She pulled a face to hide the hurt she was feeling. Her father would jump to her defence: they were very close and he would be more than a little prejudiced where she was concerned.

'Tell us what happened.' Her mother, as expected, went straight to the point.

Kate explained, and then told her mother, 'But don't worry about the article. I'll get another paper to run it.'

Pete had been sitting quietly drinking his tea, and then his cup clattered back into the saucer. 'The Chief shouldn't have spoken to Kate like that. She's the best photographer on the paper.'

'We know she is.' Rose smiled, refilled his cup and then looked pointedly at her daughter. 'What are you going to do now?'

'First I'm going to sell the orphans story to another paper, and then we'll have to find a job. Or I could open my own studio.' Kate didn't know where that idea had come from, it had just popped into her head, but it might be the solution. 'Then I could work freelance for any paper who would buy my pictures.'

'It's a good idea, but it would be hard work starting up your own business,' her father said. 'Still, I'm sure you'd soon have plenty of clients.'

She turned to her assistant. 'What do you think, Pete? Do you reckon we could make a go of it?'

He nodded vigorously. 'I'm sure we could.'

'You'll need premises in London,' her father said. 'That could be expensive.'

Kate chewed her lip as she tried to work out if she was going to have enough money for this step, then she nodded slowly. 'I've still got the money Grandma Marj left me, and some savings of my own. Then there's the money Grandpa George put in trust for me.'

'That isn't due out until you're twenty-five, or marry.' Her father looked concerned. 'And as you don't seem to have any intention of marrying yet, can you manage?'

'Yes, I can.' Kate sat up and smiled at her parents. She knew her father was eager to help her out, but her mother had always insisted that they make their own way, and mistakes, in life. She was incredibly lucky to have this money, and she wanted to do something brave with it, not fritter it away over the years. She would have to ask if she wanted their help, but she wasn't about to do that. And they would both understand her need to do this on her own.

'As soon as we've sold the story, we'll start looking for a shop.' The idea was growing on her all the time. Her mother had told her not to be afraid to change course if it seemed right.

'Haven't you spent any of the money Marj left you?' her father asked.

'Not a penny.' Kate looked at the cup of tea in front of her, knowing that her dear grandma would be happy for her to use the money in this way.

At that moment someone knocked on the front door, and Rose went to see who was there. She returned with Andrew Stevenson. 'Kate, Mr Stevenson wants to talk to you. Take him into the sitting room.'

'I'd rather stay here, Mrs Freeman.' Andrew glanced at everyone in the kitchen. 'I have some explaining to do and I'd like you all to hear.'

'Sit down, then,' Bill told him.

Kate couldn't believe he'd taken the trouble to come to her home, and Pete was amazed.

'Shall I leave?' he whispered to her.

She shook her head, and he slid down in his chair, trying to make himself as unobtrusive as possible.

'I have treated Kate badly,' Andrew said as soon as he was seated. 'But I was ordered to take her on by the head of the paper and I resented it.'

'Why would he do a thing like that?' Rose asked.

'He said he'd met you both and he owed you, so if your daughter wanted a job with us, then we would give it to her.'

Bill, usually placid, was clearly angry. 'Who is the man? He had no right to do that without consulting us first.'

'His name's Perkins, and he only took charge a year ago.'

Rose looked into space as if trying to bring the man to mind, and then she frowned at her husband. 'We don't know anyone by that name, do we, Bill?'

'No, we don't. Tell me why this man would insist that you employ our daughter.'

Kate could see her father was not at all pleased about this, and neither was her mother. They had never interfered in her life, and they obviously didn't like anyone else doing it.

Andrew Stevenson seemed to diminish in size under the combined glares of Rose and Bill Freeman. 'He wouldn't tell me anything else.' He shrugged. 'I assumed it was because of your connections.'

'What *connections*?' Rose was losing her patience.

'Well, there's Grant Phillips, and it's no secret about your father – '

'Sir George Gresham is dead, Mr Stevenson,' Rose said sharply. 'And as I was his illegitimate daughter, the title went with him. And I fail to see why our family history should be so important to the owner of your paper.' She sounded exasperated and suspicious. 'You're talking nonsense, Mr Stevenson. What is the real reason for your visit?'

'I've explained this because I want Kate and Pete to come back.'

'No! I can't answer for Pete, but I won't work for you again.'

'Neither will I,' Pete told him without hesitation.

As she saw Andrew Stevenson's dismay, Kate felt a wave of pity for him. He was in a difficult position. After having been ordered to employ her, he now had the unpleasant task of telling his boss that he'd lost her. He must have realized how much she wanted the job and been sure she wouldn't resign, no matter how badly he treated her. 'You must understand how I feel,' she told him. 'I believed I'd won that job because of my skill as a photographer, but I now know differently. I couldn't possibly come back to the paper.'

'Kate.' Andrew leant towards her, an earnest expression on his face. 'I admit I didn't want to employ you, and when you took my abuse without a word of protest, I thought even less of you. I knew who your mother was and I expected more fire from you.'

'I was brought up to respect and obey my elders,' Kate told him, 'and not to answer back. I wanted that job very much and was afraid of losing it.'

'You can still have it – '

Kate stopped him with a shake of her head. 'I would never have been taken on without Mr Perkins's orders. I wouldn't be able to forget that. I know now that I've got a lot of work to do before I'm good enough for the *World Explorer*.' It hurt her to admit that, but it was a fact that had to be faced.

'I never gave you a chance, but you've proved to have potential as a photographer.'

'I hope you're right, but I think I set my sights too high too soon.' Feeling inadequate was not something she was used to, but she would redouble her efforts to become the best there was. If she wasn't good enough yet, she would make damned sure she soon would be!

'I'm sorry.' The Chief rested his head in his hands for a moment, then he looked up at Kate again. 'Will you at least let me print the story about the children's homes?'

She glanced at her mother.

'It's your article,' Rose said. 'You're free to do what you like with it.'

Kate thought about it. The *World Explorer* was a respected paper, and it would be hard to find a better one. They needed wide coverage for the story, so it would be mean-spirited of her to turn down the chance just because she'd been hurt. Her feelings mustn't come into this – the children must come first.

'Very well, you may have it, but I shall expect the same payment you give your other freelance reporters.'

'Of course.' Andrew looked relieved. 'Can I take it with me? I'll run it in tomorrow's edition.'

Kate opened her bag and took out the papers.

The Chief slipped them into his case and stood up. 'If you ever change your mind, Kate, come and see me.'

She gave a slight nod and watched as her father saw him to the door. 'I didn't want to take the money,' she told her mother, 'but I'm in business now. I suppose I have to think about the future.'

'You did the right thing,' Rose assured her. 'It would have been wrong to let him have it for nothing. The labourer is worthy of his hire, Kate.'

Her father came back and sat down again. 'You're certain you're doing the right thing?' he asked.

'No, I'm not, but I can't go back there, Dad.' She looked at Pete. 'We don't have to sell the story now, so we'll start looking for a shop first thing in the morning.'

He nodded eagerly, giving a shy smile. 'It will be better than taking fashion photos.'

'It will.' She looked at her parents and pulled a face. 'You should see some of the clothes they're making now. They look all right on the models but most ordinary girls couldn't wear them. I think the designers make outrageous creations just to gain attention and put on a show for the catwalk.'

Her father laughed. 'Don't you be too sure. It seems as if anything goes with dress these days. The clothes are becoming as outrageous as the music. If you can call all that wailing music! Whatever happened to the wonderful bands of the war?'

'This is a new era, Dad.' She gave him a mock stern

look. 'I hope you're not calling Elvis and Cliff Richard wailers?'

'What do you call them, then?'

'Singers,' she said together with Pete.

'Really.' Bill struggled to keep from smiling. 'You could have fooled me.'

'Oh, Dad,' Kate gurgled. 'You know you like them. I've heard you whistling their tunes.'

Over dinner they discussed plans for her studio, and Pete, now looking more relaxed and at ease with her family, surprised them all with some very good suggestions for advertising. Kate decided she was going to put him in charge of that side of things.

'Where are you going to look for a shop?' her father asked.

'I don't know . . .' She fiddled with the pepper pot.

'If you're going to do this, then do it properly,' her mother said.

'I'll start with Kensington, shall I?' Kate outlined her plans as far as they went, but a heavy feeling in her stomach was making it difficult to eat. Pete, however, did not appear to be suffering from such an affliction; his face was animated with enthusiasm as he tucked into his meal. She felt as if she were taking a backward step. She wasn't, she told herself firmly. She'd always had a positive attitude to life, and she was damned if she was going to let this change her. Mr Stevenson and this shadowy figure of Perkins, whoever he was, were not going to destroy her confidence. She just would not allow it!

After they'd finished their meal, Kate arranged to meet

Pete in Kensington the next day. Then her father drove him home.

She helped her mother with the dishes, and when the last was put away she tried to read, but the words were meaningless to her. Her mind kept going over and over what had happened today. Opening a studio of her own was a big step. Was she doing the right thing . . .?

She leapt to her feet when her father returned. 'What did Pete's family say?'

'They were very concerned. His father's in poor health and out of work, and it appears that his mother relies on his salary. She couldn't understand why he'd given up a secure job.' Bill frowned at his daughter. 'I assured them that he would be paid the same as he's been getting at the paper. You shouldn't have let him give in his notice.'

It was a rare censure from her father, and Kate knew he was right. 'I did ask him to think about it carefully, Dad, but he'd made up his mind that he wanted to stay with me.'

'The lad idolizes you, and you ought to have taken that into account. However, it's done now, but he's your responsibility and you must see that his family don't suffer.'

'I will, I promise.' She chewed her lip anxiously, wondering just how long her money would last. They would have to set up the business as quickly as possible . . .

'You know we're here for you if you need us,' her mother said. 'But you're old enough to make your own decisions, and I think you're sensible enough to get over this disappointment.'

Kate gave a grateful smile. That was high praise from her mother, and she felt more hopeful about the future.

But later that night, as she watched the bedroom curtains rippling in the slight breeze, worry and doubt assailed her. Had she done the right thing? Should she have stayed at the paper? Could she make a success of her own business? And what about Pete? Her father was right, she should have persuaded him to keep his job. He'd given up safe employment for an uncertain future with her, and she did feel responsible for him. It was obvious that his family needed his salary, and she would make sure they didn't suffer, even if it took every penny she had.

She buried her head in the pillow and tried to shut out the worries, but they wouldn't go. Even as a young child she'd always been so sure of herself; sure she could handle anything. She'd longed to work on the *World Explorer* and had been delirious with happiness when they'd taken her on, but it had all been a sham. That was a great blow. This man Perkins had employed her against Andrew Stevenson's wishes. Her parents didn't seem to know him, so why had he done that?

Kate slid out of bed and shut the window. It was the beginning of October, and there was a nip of autumn in the air. She dived back under the covers. There wasn't any point in torturing herself like this, she must move on. Tomorrow would be a new beginning and it was time to let go of this particular dream. It obviously hadn't been right for her.

Exhaustion overcame her and she drifted off to sleep, determined to make a success of this new venture.

Downstairs Rose watched her husband enjoying his late-night brandy. He would normally be talking away, but tonight he was silent, staring at the golden liquid in his glass. 'What do you make of all this, Bill?'

'Damned if I know. I've been racking my brains, but I can't think of anyone we know by the name of Perkins.' He tossed the drink back. 'I think I'll go and see him tomorrow and ask him what the devil he thinks he's playing at.'

'You mustn't do that,' Rose told him. 'We've brought the children up to be independent and think for themselves; we mustn't go poking our noses in now. Kate's a grown woman and will sort this out herself.'

'I know she will, but this job meant a great deal to her. All it's done is dent her confidence.'

'She'll soon bounce back. You know Kate. Nothing's ever kept her down for long.'

Bill stood up, draped an arm around her shoulders and gave a tired smile. 'You're quite right, but I can imagine just how disappointed she must be feeling. Let's get some sleep and perhaps we'll be able to remember who this man is when we're more refreshed.'

Rose slipped her arm through Bill's, and they walked up the stairs together. 'I shouldn't worry too much – it will all come to light one day.'

9

To his credit, Andrew Stevenson did an excellent job with Kate's article and photographs. The whole of the fourth page of the newspaper was taken up with the story, and he'd included the most poignant pictures.

Kate's mother read it slowly and nodded approval. 'This is really good. You've pointed out the shortcomings without criticizing the council or those in charge.'

Kate breathed a sigh of relief. This was the first time her mother had seen the article. She'd told her to write it in her own way, and that's what she'd done, pouring out her distress at the plight of the children.

Rose handed the paper to her husband. 'That should provoke a response. If the words don't, then the photos certainly will. They're excellent, Kate.'

'I'll say they are,' her father murmured. 'Don't you dare believe anyone who says you're no good.'

Kate began to feel the hurt and disappointment fade. She had been silly to take it so much to heart. Things like this happened in life, and often they turned out for the best. 'I must admit they do show the conditions very vividly.'

'More than that,' her father said. 'What comes across is the emotion you felt while taking the pictures. Look at the little girl – you've captured the loneliness and hopelessness the child feels. You couldn't have done that if you hadn't felt it yourself.'

'Your dad's right. Your sensitivity is apparent in every word and image.' Rose gave her daughter a rueful smile. 'When I was your age I dealt with far worse cases than this, but I rolled up my sleeves and fought for what I felt was right. You can do it in a quieter and, I believe, a more effective way with your camera.'

Her mother never wasted words, and Kate knew she was being told the truth. Her parents had just spelt out her dreams – dreams she had believed a short time ago to be unattainable. But they weren't, and, like her mother, she'd fight anyone who tried to stop her!

She lifted her head and said softly, 'Do you think I've found my vocation?'

'You might have, but only you can answer that.' Rose poured them all another cup of tea. 'And after we've done what we can for these two homes, I'm definitely retiring, so you can take over as the crusader in this family.'

Bill smiled broadly. 'Do you know, Rose, I've waited more than thirty years to hear you say that?'

She retrieved the newspaper from him and folded it up. 'One more visit to a local council and I'm finished.'

Bill raised his eyebrows. 'Poor sods!'

Kate watched her parents laughing, and once again counted her blessings. They knew, in a way she never could, about the hardships and dangers of life. Her problems were *very* small in comparison to the things they had faced. She drank her tea and stood up. 'I'm off to meet Pete.'

She left the house with a spring in her step and a smile on her face. It had been silly to let Andrew Stevenson hurt her like that. She was far too sensitive – had been from a child. She would have to learn to curb that if she were going to achieve anything worth while in this life. It was time she showed some of her mother's toughness and her father's courage.

Bill listened to the front door closing and his laughter turned to a deep frown.

'Don't worry about her,' Rose told him. 'She's got a good head on her shoulders.'

'I know, but if I ever come face to face with this Perkins, I'll be tempted to wring his bloody neck.'

'I believe Kate's over it already. She must learn to cope with a few knocks in life.'

He looked at his wife with troubled eyes. 'Do you think we've protected her too much?'

Rose stopped clearing the breakfast table and sat down again. 'You know she's had an independent streak from the time she was born and wasn't easy to bring up. She would sum up a situation; calculate the advantages or disadvantages before taking a certain action. Although that isn't so evident now, I believe it's still there. If things haven't turned out as she planned, she still knows exactly what she's doing.'

'I'm sure you're right, Rose, but she isn't like most women of her age. She isn't interested in fashion, doesn't have loads of boyfriends, and with her beauty she ought to have. She appears to be interested only in photography.'

'She loves it and is completely absorbed with becoming as good as she can, but she isn't obsessive. One day she'll discover there's more to life than the scenes she sees through the viewfinder of a camera.'

Bill sighed. 'I hope you're right.'

'It surprised me when Andrew Stevenson said she'd

let him rage at her without saying a word.' Rose chuckled. 'That must have been a struggle for her.'

They were both laughing now, and Bill stood up. 'As she's going into business for herself, she'll need a car. I'll go and see what I can find for her.'

Rose listened to Bill whistling as he walked up to the garage on the corner of the road. She was well aware that her husband loved and respected James, but he adored Kate. There had been a bond between them from the moment of her birth, but Rose knew her daughter well. She wasn't foolhardy, taking her time making decisions. She was also a determined young woman, and once her mind was made up, it took a lot to stop her. That was why she wasn't worried about her. A few disappointments wouldn't do her any harm. Her daughter was very loving and sensitive to other people's moods, but underneath there lurked a stubborn nature. And in that way she was like her mother.

Rose walked into the Wandsworth council offices, and the chairman, Mr Marston, met her all smiles. 'Mrs Freeman, thank you for having that spread in the paper for us. We've already had two women come in with offers to help, and the bus company has said they'll take some of the toddlers out for the day to Southend.'

'That is good news.' Rose was delighted; this was just the kind of response she'd been hoping for. It wasn't possible to do much about the homes themselves; the council was doing the best it could. But perhaps they could improve the children's lives a little. She hoped the new contraceptive pill they were talking about would cut down on the unwanted births.

A man was struggling to get through the door with a large box, so Rose went to hold it open for him.

'Thank you.' He dumped the container on the counter. 'Saw the newspaper this morning and we had these in the loft, so thought you might like them for the little ones.'

The box was full of good-quality toys, and Rose smiled at the man. 'Thank you so much, the children will love them.'

'That's all right, ma'am. Glad to put them to some use. Our children are too old for them now.' He gave a slight bow and then left.

'I can see the children are being taken care of,' Rose told the chairman. 'That leaves the condition of the buildings. My husband has offered to have the outsides repaired and painted and the insides spruced up. Would the council accept this as a gift from us?'

Mr Marston looked quite overcome. 'That is most generous of you both, Mrs Freeman. We would be very grateful indeed for such a gift. We try to make the best use of the money we're allotted, but it isn't easy.'

'I know that only too well, Mr Marston. I was a councillor once myself; a long time ago of course, but I don't suppose things have changed that much.'

She really was going to ease up now, Rose decided as she drove back to Roehampton. She could spend more time with Bill, and prayed that they had many more years ahead of them.

It took Kate and Pete most of the day to find suitable premises. There wasn't anything available in Kensington High Street, and it was too expensive anyway. She was going to have to spend wisely or her money would run out before they'd started. They'd finally found a small shop only five minutes' walk from the high street.

'Let's get something to eat,' she groaned to Pete. 'I'm starving.'

'There's a café a few shops along.' He grinned happily at her. 'This is a busy street too, so we should get a lot of trade. Isn't it exciting!'

Kate had to admit that it was. She was glad to have Pete with her because his enthusiasm was rubbing off on her. This was going to be an adventure.

They sat at a table by the window, and, as it was too late for lunch, ordered scrambled eggs on toast and a pot of tea.

When they'd eaten, Kate sat back with a sigh. 'That's better. We won't be able to get into the shop until next week, so could you come over to my house tomorrow?'

'Sure. What we going to do for the rest of the week?'

'We'll spend tomorrow printing photos to put on the walls and in the window of the shop, then we'll roam London looking for pictures we can sell to the papers and magazines.'

Pete's eyes were gleaming with interest.

'I intend to take on as much freelance work as we can handle, so I'm going to need your help to run the shop.'

'You show me what you want doing and I'll manage it.' He spoke with confidence. 'What are we going to call the shop – Freeman's?'

'No, I thought I'd use my mother's maiden name of Webster for the business. She does so much good for people in need that I'd like to name it in honour of her. Webster's. What do you think?'

'That's a great idea. Are you going to use Webster for your business name as well?'

'Yes, why not? A fresh name for a fresh start, eh?'

Kate noticed his clean plate and asked for some toasted crumpets. He proceeded to demolish them as soon as they arrived. In the few months he'd been with her he'd shot up and was now slightly taller than her. At five foot nine she was above-average height for a woman, and Pete still had some growing to do. He would probably top six feet by the time he'd finished. He'd also lost a lot of his awkwardness.

She had to make a success of this. He trusted her, and she didn't want to let him down. 'How old are you now?' she asked.

He offered her the last crumpet and she shook her head. 'I've had enough.'

He took a bite, swallowed, and then answered her question. 'I was nineteen last week.'

'I wish I'd known. I'd have given you a card.'

'You've already given me a wonderful present.' He patted the camera that was always slung over his shoulder. 'I've been practising taking pictures in Hyde Park and I think I might have some quite good shots of the trees.'

'Wonderful. Bring the film over tomorrow and we'll see what you've got. Perhaps we'll be able to put some in the shop.'

He looked so pleased and proud that it touched Kate. Her father had told her his family were living in a poor area and times were clearly hard for them. If she could help to improve his lot in life, then it would be something *she* could be proud of.

'Have you had enough to eat?'

'Yes, thank you, Kate.' He put his hand in his pocket to pull out some money.

Kate stopped him. 'You work for me now. I'll pay for our snack. You can tell your family that you'll receive your salary as usual, with an increase of two and six-pence.'

'Thank you.' The shy smile was back. 'That will help my mum.'

'You're worth it,' she told him as she paid the bill. 'We can finish for the day. Come about ten o'clock tomorrow. Do you think you can find our house again or would you like me to meet you at the station?'

'I know where it is.' He waved and ran for his bus.

Kate headed for Wandsworth and Wilkins House. The children had just finished their tea when she arrived, and Mrs Green welcomed her with a broad smile of pleasure.

'I've brought the photos for you.' Kate took them out of her bag as the children clustered round her, laughing when they saw themselves in the pictures.

'These are wonderful!' Mrs Green and the other helpers were obviously thrilled.

'I've mounted some in cardboard frames so that you can stand them up.' She showed them how to do it.

There was a tug on her trousers and she looked down at Eddie, his face alight with expectancy. 'Did you bring my special one?'

'Of course.' She squatted down to his level and gave him two prints in the frames. 'One for you and one for your friend.'

He gazed at them in silence for a few moments. 'Is that me?' he asked, squirming with pleasure.

'Yes, that's just how you look when you laugh.'

He clutched them to his chest, turned to run away, then spun back, nearly toppling over his own feet in his haste. 'Have you got any babies?' he asked.

'No, I'm not married.'

Ed thought about this, then said quietly, 'You're nice. When you get married, will you be my mum?'

Kate felt emotion well up in her as she looked into his earnest little face. How these children must yearn to belong to someone, but she couldn't lie to him. 'I haven't any plans to marry yet, Eddie, but if you haven't been adopted by the time I find myself a husband, then I promise to think about it.'

He seemed happy with that and gave her a quick kiss before tearing off to show his photos to someone called Tom.

Kate arrived home in rather a sombre mood.

'Didn't you have any luck?' her mother asked.

'Oh, yes. We found an ideal shop and it's ours from next Monday.'

'That's great news, Kate. Why the long face, then?'

'I've just come from Wilkins House and one of the boys asked me if I'd adopt him when I get married.'

'And what did you say?'

Kate explained to her mother, who nodded. 'Go and visit him now and again, and when he sees you're not married he might forget about it.'

'I'll do that, Mum.'

'How were the twins?'

'Doing fine and they've grown even in this last week.'

'Mrs Green will look after them well, she's a good woman, and I expect they'll soon be adopted. They have more chance of finding homes for the babies than for those who're older.' Rose then explained about volunteers already coming forward as a result of the newspaper article, and the gift of toys. 'Your dad's going to arrange to have the places done up.'

'That's wonderful.' Kate's mood lifted at once. 'And this is only the first day. I'll see if Mr Stevenson will do a follow-up next week, just to keep things moving.'

'That's a good idea.' Her father walked into the kitchen. 'There's something in the garage for you, Kate.'

'Oh?'

He was looking very pleased as he handed her some keys. 'You'll need these.'

'Come on,' her mother said. 'I haven't seèn it yet.'

When they reached the garage, Kate stopped and gasped in delight. Standing there was a brand-new dark blue Mini. They'd only been launched last year and were fast becoming the thing to own.

'I hope you like the colour.' Her father slipped his arm around her shoulder. 'It was the only one they had in stock.'

Kate ran her hand over the gleaming car. 'Blue is perfect. Is this really for me?'

'You're going to need a car of your own for the new business.' Bill opened the door. 'Sit inside and see how it feels.'

Before getting in, she gave him a hug and her mother a tearful smile. 'Did you know he was going to do this?'

'Yes. You've always insisted that you only have things you can afford to pay for yourself, but there is a time to accept help, Kate.'

Her mother had never been outwardly demonstrative,

but Kate knew that she loved her family dearly. She rushed over and hugged her as well.

'Let's take it for a spin around Richmond Park.' Bill was rubbing his hands in anticipation. 'You get in the back, Rose.'

'I'll never get in there,' she said, looking at the small car.

'Yes, you will – there's bags of room.' Bill tipped the front seat forward.

Rose examined the space inside, shrugged and clambered in. She was tall but didn't look too uncomfortable. Bill eased himself into the passenger side, and, after Kate had adjusted the driver's seat, they headed for the park.

Kate fell in love with it at once. It was nippy and easy to drive, so she went round the park several times until she felt confident driving the little car. It really was a beauty and a very unexpected but welcome gift.

'It's just wonderful,' Kate told her parents over dinner. 'Thank you so much.'

'Glad you like it.' Her father couldn't hide his pleasure at being able to give his daughter this special gift.

'I'm thrilled, and it's going to be a big help with the business.' Kate grinned. 'Just wait until Pete sees it! The Webster Photographers will be tearing around London in style!'

'Webster's?' Her mother looked up sharply.

'Yes, we're going to name the shop after you, Mum, and I'm going to be Kate Webster for the business.' She smiled at her father. 'I hope you don't mind?'

'Not at all,' he exclaimed. 'I think it's a lovely idea.'

'Thank you, Kate,' Rose said, looking quite taken aback with pleasure.

10

There had been more work than Kate or Pete had anticipated in order to get the shop ready for business. However, not daunted by the task, the pair had pitched in with scrubbing brushes and pots of paint. Ten days later it was starting to take shape.

'If we work all this weekend we should be ready to open on Monday.' Pete stood back to admire the wall he'd just painted white.

'Do you think so?' Kate wasn't at all sure about that. There was still a heck of a lot left to do, and it was Saturday morning now. 'The darkroom isn't ready, the studio needs another coat of paint, and I haven't been able to get the toilet clean.'

'Yeah, that is a mess, but a new bit of lino will make it look better. The rest we can finish easily.'

'You're terribly optimistic.' Kate laughed at his animated expression. Pete was excited, and having the time of his life getting the shop ready. And so was she. There were no lingering regrets about leaving the paper now. This business venture was risky, but she was determined to make it a success.

'What's that?' Pete rushed over to the window as a large van pulled up outside. 'It's got the name of Grant Phillips on the side.'

Kate joined him and watched in wonder as her brother, James, got out, then her father and Reid. The back door of the van was thrown open and her Uncle Will jumped out, carrying a brand-new toilet.

'Wow!' Pete exclaimed, rushing to open the shop door.

'Where do you want this?' Will smiled at Kate's stunned expression and offered his cheek for a kiss, which he got.

'Through to the back, please,' Pete said.

'Oh, all my favourite men,' Kate cried, hugging each one in turn. 'Why didn't you tell me you were going to do this?'

'We hatched the plot last night when we realized you were going to have a job finishing in time for Monday.' Reid had already taken off his coat and rolled up his sleeves. 'Will's going to put the new toilet in for you and I'm handy with a paint brush . . .'

Kate slapped a brush in his hand, gave him an impish grin and pointed to the studio. 'The paint's already in there.'

Loud banging was coming from the back as Will began to rip out the old toilet. Kate turned to her father and brother. 'And what can we get you to do?'

'I'll finish your darkroom,' James said.

'And I'll make the tea,' her father announced, winking at Kate. 'I'm playing golf with Will tomorrow, so I can't wear myself out!' He disappeared into the small back kitchen, whistling happily to himself.

Pete was practically doing a jig of delight. 'We'll definitely be able to open on Monday now. What a smashing family you've got, Kate.'

'They are a bit special, aren't they?' Kate thought she would burst with love for them. When it seemed that they might not be ready for the planned date of opening, her marvellous family had arrived to help. She really was a lucky girl.

When opening day arrived, they were delighted with the shop. It was bright, inviting, and the display of photographs in the window was causing a lot of interest from passers-by. Kate hoped they would soon stop walking past and come in. They had flooded the area with advertising leaflets by tramping the streets and spreading the word. They'd also put an advert – designed by Pete – in one of the popular daily papers. The car had been a tremendous help and had enabled them to travel around without wasting time on buses and trains.

She gazed around the shop and smiled at her assistant. Pete was so happy, and she wondered why she couldn't match his mood. Everything was going well: things were improving at the children's homes, with offers of help coming in; the shop was ready to welcome customers. She should be feeling elated. But she wasn't! Her emotions were on a roller coaster – one day up and the next down. It didn't make sense and she was irritated with herself. The only time she'd ever felt like this had been towards the end of the war when her Grandpa George had been killed by a flying bomb. She'd only been eight at the time and it had taken her a long time to accept that he had gone. But they were at peace and there wasn't anything like that in her life now, so why was she so unsettled?

She was completely at a loss to explain her strange mood. It wasn't because she'd lost her job with the paper; that no longer bothered her. So what the devil was wrong? Her sigh was ragged.

'Don't worry, Kate.' Pete came and stood beside her. 'The customers will soon be flooding in.'

'A slow trickle would do for a start.' She gave herself a severe mental telling-off. This nonsense had to stop! She smiled at Pete, who was looking at her with a worried frown. 'I wouldn't mind coping with a flood, though.'

The bell on the door tinkled as someone came in. It was their first customer. Pete gave her a little shove and whispered, 'We're in business!'

'Good morning, madam,' Kate stepped forward, smiling warmly.

'Oh, morning.' The woman returned her smile and held out one of their leaflets. 'I'd like a picture done of my children and me, please. It's to be a Christmas present for my husband.'

'Certainly, madam.' Kate turned to pick up the appointments book, only to find Pete already had it open, pen poised.

After the customer had left, Kate grinned at Pete. 'If my Grandma Marj was here, she would say that called for a nice cup of tea!'

They had several more customers that morning. Christmas was only eight weeks away, and people were beginning to respond to their advert about giving portraits as presents. They even had bookings for a wedding and a twenty-first birthday party.

Kate pushed her earlier strange mood aside. Everything was going to be all right.

They closed for lunch, and when they reopened a tall man walked in and Kate rushed forward. 'Dad!'

'I've come to see how you're getting on.'

'We're doing fine, Mr Freeman.' Pete showed him the

appointment book. 'We've had all these customers this morning.'

'Well done. You're going to make a great success of this business, I can see.' Bill wandered into the studio and nodded approval. 'While I'm here, Pete, you can take a photograph of me. It's time Rose had an up-to-date picture.'

'Me, sir?' He looked startled.

Bill sat on the chair, faced the camera and nodded.

Pete was in his element and Kate stayed out of the way, not wanting to interfere with his first commission. Her father was a kind man, and she suspected that he'd taken a liking to Pete, and wanted to encourage him.

Bill left an hour later and Pete rushed off to develop his film. Kate had several more inquiries, so the afternoon passed quickly. Just before closing time, Pete emerged from the darkroom, flushed with pleasure. He handed her the prints of her father.

'Oh, these are wonderful!' The paise was easy to give, because they really were excellent. 'These are the best photos of Dad I've ever seen. He'll be delighted. Make out an invoice for him.'

He looked at her aghast. 'We can't make him pay for them.'

'Of course we can. We're in business now.'

They were just packing up for the day when the doorbell went again. Kate looked up from what she was doing. 'Terry! When did you get back?'

'Last Friday.' Terry gazed around the shop in obvious approval. 'It's lovely to see you again, Kate. We all miss you at the paper, but I'm sure you've done the right thing. This shop looks great – I'm so proud of you.'

'Thanks. How was the Congo?'

'Unpleasant.' He shuddered. 'You two got time for a coffee? And I'll tell you all about my dreadful trip.'

'Hello, Will.' Rose put her book aside when she noticed her brother's worried expression. Will had always been her favourite brother. He cared for other people and wasn't afraid to show it. 'What's the matter?'

'Where's Bill?'

'He's gone to see how they're doing at the shop.'

Will sat opposite his sister. 'I don't suppose Bill's told you, but when I played golf with him yesterday he had bad pains in his chest. We were on the twelfth hole and a long way from the clubhouse, so I was dreadfully worried. We sat down for ten minutes, then he said he was all right and insisted on playing the rest of the course.'

Rose was concerned. 'He didn't tell me. Did he overdo it when you were all at the shop on Saturday?'

'No.' Will couldn't help smiling, even though he was obviously worried about Bill. 'All he did was make the tea and offer me advice on how to fit the new toilet properly.'

'Was he all right yesterday after a rest?'

'I think so, but you ought to get him to see a doctor, Rosie.'

'He already has. He's got angina, but the doctor said it isn't too serious, as long as he doesn't overdo things. The hospital said it's all right for him to play golf – moderate exercise will be good for him.'

'How long has this been going on?' Will frowned.

'He had his first attack just over a year ago. That was the real reason he retired.'

'Oh, I'm sorry, Rose. Why didn't you tell us?'

'Bill didn't want anyone treating him like an invalid. He's determined that it isn't going to restrict his life.'

'I can understand that. Does Kate know?'

'No, we don't want her worrying.' Rose spoke firmly. 'Especially now when her life is unsettled.'

'She'll soon realize there's something wrong,' Will pointed out. 'She's always been tuned in to him.'

'I know, but let's leave it as long as possible before she finds out. James has already been told. He won't say anything, though.'

'I don't agree.' Bill came in and sat down. 'I've been thinking about this, and I don't feel it's right to keep her in the dark about my health.'

'I don't either,' Will said. 'Kate won't make a fuss, Rose, she's got more of you in her than you think.'

Rose held her hands up in surrender. 'Okay, you do what you think is best.'

Kate didn't arrive home until nearly eight. They'd spent some time listening to Terry's tale and looking at the photographs he'd taken, then she'd dropped Pete off before making her way back home. She drove the Mini up to the garage, got out and hurried into the kitchen. Her parents were just finishing dinner and she greeted them with a broad smile on her face, well satisfied with the first day's business.

'Do you want dinner? I've saved some for you.'

'Not really, Mum, we had something after we'd shut the shop.'

'I can't wait to hear about your first day.' Rose put the

kettle on. 'Sit down, have a cup of tea, and tell us all about it.'

'We had ten customers. Not bad for a first day, and if things go on like this we'll soon have a sound business.' She took the photos of her father out of her bag and handed them to him with a mischievous smile. 'You'll find an invoice inside.'

Bill chuckled, examined the pictures and gave them to Rose to look at. 'They're very professional and worth every penny. That boy's got flair.'

Rose was obviously pleased. 'They're very good.'

'There's something I think you ought to know, Kate,' her father said.

'Oh, what's that?' Then she saw his serious expression and her smile died.

'I retired because I haven't been too well. I've got a heart complaint called angina. It's only mild, and as long as I don't overdo things it shouldn't be too much trouble. It isn't serious, so I don't want you worrying about me.'

She reached out and took hold of his hand. Now she understood why her emotions had been so up and down lately. She had assumed it was because of the upheaval in her working life, but it hadn't been that at all. 'I felt something was wrong, Dad. Thank you for telling me. I won't make a fuss, but you must promise me you'll take care of yourself.'

'I promise.' He smiled and squeezed her hand. 'I've got another twenty years in me yet.'

'You make sure you have, and more!' she threatened, making light of the situation.

'Of course it would ease my mind considerably if you would find yourself a nice young man and get married.'

Her father's mouth twitched at the corners as Rose chuckled.

'Dad!' Kate jumped up and stood in front of him with her hands on her hips, just as her mother did when she was at her most commanding. 'You're not going to play on my sympathy and start badgering me, are you?'

His grin spread, well knowing how much his daughter disliked being told to settle down. 'Now would I do such a thing?'

'Yes, you would!' Kate tried what she hoped was a fierce expression. 'Mum, I'm sure he's trying to get rid of me!'

Both women looked at Bill, who was now roaring with laughter. 'My God, look at you, you're like two peas in a pod.'

Kate glanced at her mother with pride. What a compliment!

II

Closing the shop door against the icy wind, Kate blew on her fingers. 'Thank goodness we haven't any more outside assignments until after Christmas. It's freezing out there.'

Pete took the camera from her and ginned. 'Come to the kitchen and I'll make you a hot drink. What do you want?'

'Is there any soup in the cupboard?'

'Tomato?'

'That'll do lovely.' She sat in front of the single-bar electric fire they had in the back room, slipped her boots off and wiggled her toes at it. 'All I'm going to do the next few days is lounge by a blazing fire and eat.'

'Me, too; it's going to be a cold Christmas by the look of it.' Pete poured the steaming soup into two mugs and then produced some crispy rolls.

She took the mug, bit into a roll and groaned with pleasure. 'What would I do without you?'

'You'd manage very well on your own, Kate,' he said.

'I wouldn't.' She clasped her hands around the hot mug, and marvelled at how much he'd changed since they'd opened the shop nearly two months ago. He had grown in stature, confidence and skill, and was taking on more and more of the everyday running of the shop. This left her free to go chasing after pictures they could sell to newspapers and magazines. She'd been getting some decent commissions. 'Our business is doing well, and I could never have done it without you. You're the best manager anyone could have.'

He spluttered over a mouthful of soup. 'Manager?'

'Yep, I've just promoted you. I think you're ready for more responsibility.'

'Wow!' He cast her an amused glance. 'Does this mean a rise in pay?'

'Of course.' She drained her mug. 'How much do you want?'

'Another two and six a week.' He spoke with a touch of laughter in his voice.

'It's yours, starting this week. And I think you need a trainee assistant, so we'll advertise after Christmas.'

He was staring at her open-mouthed. 'Are you serious?'

She held out the mug. 'Completely. Is there any more soup?'

He filled it with the last of the soup from the saucepan and handed it back to her.

'Don't look so stunned. You've earned every penny, and the way the business is increasing, you're going to need help.'

'I can't thank you enough for giving me this chance.'

'We've got an ideal partnership. You enjoy running the shop, and I love roaming around looking for exciting pictures.'

Pete smirked. 'I'm a partner now, am I?'

She gave him a teasing smile. 'Play your cards right and I might make it official one day.'

He began to beg like a dog and they both ended up roaring with laughter. The tinkle of the doorbell stopped their foolery, and they went into the shop ready to greet another customer.

A stocky, smartly dressed man was standing there, and when he saw Kate he smiled. 'Miss Freeman?'

'Yes.' Why had he called her Freeman? She was known as Webster here. She didn't much like the look of him, even though he was totally respectable-looking. Pete could handle him.

'My name is Derek Howard. I work for your brother. He would like to see you urgently and he's asked me to collect you.'

Kate frowned. Why would James send for her like this? He could have telephoned if he'd wanted her . . .

'We're having trouble with the phones at Grant Phillips,' he said, as if reading her mind. 'Mr Freeman thought it would save time if I came for you.'

'Did he say what was so urgent?' Kate was worried now; this was not a bit like her brother. Had something dreadful happened, something with her father? She looked into the street and saw one of James's cars sitting outside, the dark blue Wolseley. She knew it well: it was the car in which they'd gone to the New Forest. Perhaps it was something to do with the trouble he'd mentioned, and he didn't want to alert their parents at the moment.

'Please hurry, Miss Freeman. Your brother is most anxious.'

She hesitated only for a moment, dreadfully worried by this unusual request from her brother. 'Very well, but I'll take my own car.'

'There's no need for that,' he insisted. 'Your brother was adamant that I should drive you, and it's more than

I dare to disobey him. Mine's right outside and I'll bring you back.'

This sounded like her brother; he could be a hard taskmaster if need be. She nodded and turned to Pete. 'I won't be more than an hour or so.'

'Okay. Do you want to take your camera with you?'

'No. I'll just get my coat.' She patted her pocket to make sure her purse was still there with some money in it, and, on impulse, she slipped a small camera into the other pocket before hurrying out to Mr Howard, who was standing by the car.

He opened the rear door and she slipped into the back seat, anxious to find out why her brother had sent for her.

Derek Howard drove as fast as the traffic would allow and never said a word. By the time the building came into sight they were travelling at speed. As they shot past the premises Kate gasped in surprise. 'You've gone past the building!'

'Sit back and relax, Miss Freeman, we're going for a little ride. I've fixed the doors and windows so they won't open,' he said smoothly, checking on her in the rear-view mirror.

She reached for the door and was horrified to find all the handles had been removed. Oh, what a damned fool! She should have insisted on using her own car, but the man had been plausible and clever. He'd played on her love for her family. She started to shake in terror as she realized what terrible danger she was in.

For about the first time in her life she didn't stop to think. In blind panic she lunged forward, leaning over the seat to try to pull his hands from the wheel. She had to stop him any way she could!

He swore. Took one hand off the steering wheel, turned slightly in his seat and aimed a punch at her head. It caught her a stinging blow, and at that moment he lost control of the car and hit the kerb. As Howard fought to gain control and get the car back on the road, Kate was thrown violently sideways, hitting her head on the metal part of the door . . .

'Sir.' James's secretary came into his office as he was packing up for the day. 'There's a young man downstairs, and he insists on seeing you. Says his name is Pete and he works for your sister.'

James stopped what he was doing. 'What's he doing here? You'd better send him up.'

Pete fell into the room in a state of agitation. 'Is Kate here?'

'No.' James frowned. 'What made you think she would be?'

'You sent a man for her nearly four hours ago. She said she wouldn't be long, but she hasn't come back!'

'I didn't send for her. I'd phone if I wanted to speak to her.' James was not unduly alarmed. He knew his sister lost track of time when she was taking photographs. Pete must have been mistaken about someone collecting her from the shop.

'But the man said all your phones were out of order.' Pete was becoming more distressed with every passing moment.

Now James *was* worried. He didn't like the sound

of this at all. He made Pete sit down. 'Tell me what happened.'

Pete babbled out the story, hardly able to keep in the seat. 'I shouldn't have let her go. I could see she wasn't easy about it, but she was worried about you . . .' He leapt to his feet, started walking to the door and then back again, gazing at James with frightened eyes. 'She didn't expect to be long. What's happened to her?' he whispered.

'Calm down.' James caught hold of his arm to keep him in one place. 'Tell me what this man looked like.'

Pete described him in detail, and James swore. 'Derek Howard.'

'That's his name. Do you know him, sir?'

'Oh, yes, I know the bastard!' James strode to the door, flung it open and called to his secretary. 'Get me all the information we have on Derek Howard, and find everyone who worked with him or knows him. I want them in here right now!'

'Should we call the police?' Pete asked, when James stalked back to his desk.

'It's too soon. They won't consider her a missing person yet.' He patted the distressed boy's shoulder. 'Thank you for coming, but you go home now. I'll deal with this.'

'I can't!' Pete shook his head, eyes wide with worry. 'Please let me stay, sir. I can't go until I know what's happened to her. I can help. I saw the man and know what he looks like.'

James could see the desperation in Pete's eyes and knew it wouldn't be kind to send him away. 'I understand.

Give my secretary your home address and she'll let your family know where you are.'

When Pete left the room, James gazed out of the window, not seeing the impressive view of London as dusk descended and the lights began to come on. He bowed his head as worry gnawed away at his insides. 'Oh, dear God, I'm so sorry, Kate,' he murmured.

'Sir?'

He lifted his head and turned at the sound of his secretary's voice.

'Everyone's here.'

'Send them in.' He sat behind his desk and made Pete take the seat next to him.

Most of the staff filing in to the office had their coats on ready to leave and didn't look too pleased about being delayed.

James didn't waste time. 'My sister has been abducted by Derek Howard, and I want each of you to tell me what you know about him.'

There were gasps of disbelief, but he evidently hadn't been well liked and they were only too ready to air their opinions. As James listened the fear for his sister grew until he could feel cold sweat running down his back. He was almost eight years older than Kate and he still looked upon her as his little sister, but she was a woman now – and in terrifying trouble. He forced himself to concentrate and to write down all the places Howard was known to frequent.

When they'd all had their say, he thanked them, and as they left his mind was already trying to sort out the fabrication from the truth. Howard obviously had upset a lot of people. He was sure that some of the tales had been motivated by malice, but, whatever the truth was, the man was clearly dangerous.

Fear swamped James. He shouldn't have sacked him. It would have been wiser to hand him over to the police straight away. But even if he had, Derek Howard would still have been out on bail until the case came to court. That thought didn't make James feel any better.

His secretary closed the door behind them and handed James a file. 'All Mr Howard's details are in there.' She paused. 'Have you taken out the dark blue Wolseley and left it somewhere, Mr Freeman?'

He looked up quickly. 'No. It should be in its parking space.'

'The doorman has just told me the keys are missing and the car isn't there. Shall I report it to the police as stolen?'

'Please – '

'It was a blue car that came for Kate,' Pete said, breaking in.

James swore under his breath again. 'She would have recognized it and assumed the message was genuine.'

'Is there anything else I can do?' the secretary asked.

'No, thanks, you go home now.' He let out a ragged sigh. 'This is up to us.'

'I hope you find her, Mr Freeman.'

'We'll find her,' he ground out through clenched teeth, then stood up. 'Come on, Pete, we need more help.'

In less than an hour, James screeched to a halt in front of the Roehampton house, jumped out of the car and ran indoors.

'James, what's the rush?' his mother asked as he burst into the kitchen with Pete right on his heels.

'Where's Dad?'

'Right here, son.' Bill was standing in the doorway.

James drew in a deep breath. His father looked calm as usual. His wartime years as a naval captain made him no stranger to danger, but he had a weak heart. James balked at telling him that a man out for revenge had abducted the daughter he loved – and his greatest fear was that she might already be dead.

'What is it, James?' His father spoke quietly but with firmness.

'Kate's missing.'

'For how long?'

'About six hours, we think. A man by the name of Derek Howard fooled her into going with him.'

'Howard?' Bill frowned as he sat on the chair James had pulled out for him. 'I know that name.'

'He'd only been with us for a year and worked in accounts.' James was alarmed at how white his father was becoming, but he appeared outwardly calm. His mother always claimed that nothing could ruffle his father's placid temperament, but this was going to hit him hard.

'I remember. So why has he kidnapped Kate?'

'I sacked him last week.' James hit the table with his fist in frustration and anger with himself. 'I should have handed him over to the police straight away. I was too damned soft with him and he's getting back at me for chucking him out.'

'What's he been up to?' Bill beckoned to Pete, who was still lurking in the doorway, and made him sit down. 'And why didn't you tell me about it?'

'I was going to as soon as I had a clearer picture, but

his crime was very clever and well hidden. It's taken weeks to unearth the extent of his fraud. He'd set up a series of fictitious building supplies companies and was invoicing us for non-existent goods. The money was paid into a special account only he had access to. We don't know the full extent of the fraud yet. The accountants are carrying out an investigation. If it turns out to be a substantial amount of money, then we'll prosecute. I warned him we would.'

His mother lit the stove to boil a kettle. 'Just how vindictive is this man?'

'I don't know for sure, Mum, but we must get Kate away from him as soon as possible.' He had no intention of telling his parents the full extent of Howard's brutal nature. One member of his staff had been forthcoming on the subject. He prayed the man had been exaggerating. His mother guarded her emotions but he could see she was blazing mad and worried as hell. This room was usually a happy and relaxed place, but now the atmosphere was tense.

Pete appeared more angry than frightened. 'If he's hurt her, then I'll kill him!'

Rose grimaced. 'That would be my instinct, but once we've found him we must leave this to the law.'

James opened the folder and handed the papers round. 'This is all the information I've been able to glean at short notice. I want every place checked out. Mum and Dad, you go together, and Pete will come with me. On no account take on Howard: we don't want to do anything to put Kate in more danger.'

'What about getting Reid and Will to help?' Bill asked.

James shook his head. 'I think it's better if we keep

this to ourselves for the time being. No point sending everyone into a panic; that won't help.'

There was a knock on the front door and James went to see who it was. 'Beth!'

'Hi, is Kate ready?'

'You'd better come in.'

Once in the kitchen, Beth looked at the strained faces. 'What's the matter?'

'Kate's been kidnapped by an ex-employee of Grant Phillips.'

Beth's face drained of all colour and her eyes filled with tears.

'We'll find her,' Bill said through stiff lips.

'Where were you going?' James asked.

'We've got tickets to see the Shadows in Hammersmith this evening.' A tear trickled down Beth's face. 'Kate would never have missed that. Is there anything I can do?'

'No, Beth,' Rose said. 'You go home and we'll let you know when we find her. Take young Steve with you tonight. Don't waste the tickets.'

Rose stood up after Kate's friend left. 'I'll report her missing to the police, then we'll start searching.'

'I hope they're still in London,' Pete murmured.

'Let's pray he'll stay on familiar ground.' Bill scribbled down the location he and Rose were going to check on.

James watched in concern as his father stood up and swayed for a moment. Shock was taking hold. 'Wouldn't it be better if you stayed here, Dad? Howard might phone in with a ransom demand, or something.'

Bills mouth tightened into a grim line. 'If money had

been his motive, then we'd have heard from him by now. And you're not keeping me out of this, James.'

'Let's get going.' Rose strode back with her own coat on and Bill's over her arm.

They filed out and got into their cars. No one spoke, knowing full well that they were taking on an impossible task. But they had to do something! James roared off towards London, and he knew there was only one thing on everyone's mind – was Kate still alive?

12

The next thing Kate knew was that she was being dragged from the car. It was dark now, her head was pounding, and she felt sick. She took some deep breaths to try to regain her senses.

'Move!' Derek Howard pushed her forward.

She stumbled over rough ground, losing her balance. A building site? No, there would have been lighting of some kind. A demolition site!

She was pulled upright again and made to take a few more steps. Her head was clearing now, and in the gloom she glimpsed a building in front of her. Once he got her there, there would probably be no chance of escape. She stumbled again, and, as she fell, she wrenched herself out of his grip, but he soon had a firm hold on her again. The camera she had in her pocket had her name and address inside the case, so while she was down on the ground she placed it beside a heap of rubble. It was an action born of desperation, because Derek Howard would probably see it when it was light. Her only hope was that someone would find it before he did – and that they were honest and would want to return it.

There was no more time to do anything. He was pushing her up some wooden stairs. Kate couldn't see a thing, but he obviously knew every inch of the building. She made it as difficult as possible for him to manhandle her, but he was incredibly strong. He unlocked a door at the top of the stairs and threw her inside.

'I'll deal with you later.' He was out of breath as he locked the door and hurried back downstairs.

The room was in pitch-darkness. Kate wrapped her arms around herself in an effort to stop trembling with a mixture of fear and cold. She listened to the footsteps echoing on the wooden staircase as Derek Howard left the building. She gave a ragged sigh – at least she was safe for the moment, but the wild look she'd seen in his eyes when they'd been in the car made her very frightened. He was a man under great stress and was not to be trusted; she was in grave danger. She made herself move and groped along the wall until she found a light switch. Nothing happened when she turned it on, and the thought of spending the night in total darkness terrified her. She began to explore the room by touch. There were strips of wallpaper hanging off the walls, and she jumped when a large piece of plaster came crashing down. Dust filled her nose and mouth. She whimpered in fright. More cautious now, she moved forward again. A floorboard creaked loudly, so she eased one foot forward, testing with her toe to see if it was safe. It seemed to be, and she inched her way along until her fingers curled around the icy metal of an iron bedhead. She found the mattress and sat on the edge. It appeared to be very worn, with springs sticking through in places. It was also very cold and damp in the room.

Easing herself further on to the bed, she huddled against the wall in an effort to keep warm, and away from whatever was scuttling around in the room. She felt so alone, and that was something she was not used to. She sat there trembling, unable to grasp what was happening to her. She felt herself start to crumble inside. She was supposed to be out with Beth tonight to see the Shadows. They'd had a terrible job getting tickets . . .

She scrambled off the bed and swore violently. If she allowed herself to fall apart, the chances of her coming out of this would be slim. Once morning came, she could try to find a way out. She bowed her head and prayed for sunrise.

Her eyes were becoming accustomed to the dark, and a sliver of pale light caught her attention. She edged her way across the room towards it and reached out her hand: she felt what seemed to be rough sacking. When she pulled it aside, she found herself looking out of a small window. It was a clear frosty night, and the sky was filled with stars. Kate was relieved to have something other than darkness to see as she gazed up at the twinkling lights.

She started to shiver violently. Was he going to leave her here to die of cold and hunger? Her family and Pete must be frantic with worry. How she loved them all. Would she ever see them again?

That thought snapped her alert. She began to stamp her feet and pump her arms up and down in an effort to keep warm. She couldn't do much, but she *must* get through this night.

She increased her activity, gritting her teeth in determination.

It was the worst night of Kate's life. She'd been grateful she was wearing boots, trousers and a warm coat. The cold had even seemed to penetrate her mind: it would have been so easy to collapse on the bed and sink into oblivion, but she fought the desire with all her might. She'd spent the long hours trying to keep her blood circulating, as she knew that hypothermia was a real danger. She ripped the old piece of sacking from the window and wrapped it around her head to help conserve body heat. The fact that it smelt disgusting didn't bother her. Her attention was focused on one thing: staying alive.

As soon as it was light enough to see, she checked the room. It was completely empty except for the old bed pushed up against the wall, and a bucket in the far corner. There was a thick layer of dust everywhere, and old newspapers were strewn across the floor. What was left of the wallpaper was hanging in shreds, like tongues sticking out and mocking her. An inspection of the door showed the frame had been repaired and a stout lock added. It was very secure. She turned round and gazed helplessly at the small room. Derek Howard had chosen well: only a mouse could get in and out of this room.

She went over to the window. Rubbing the glass to remove enough dirt so she could see through it, she gave a moan of despair: the whole area was uninhabited and appeared to be ready for demolition. She'd been banking on catching someone's attention, but the place was deserted. She tugged at the window. It had been nailed up and wouldn't budge.

She continued to peer through the window, her mind whirling. She had to get out of here! She'd been looking forward to the holiday season with her family. It was always such fun, and she'd promised to go to see the children at Wilkins House. She had presents for all of them, and Eddie was looking forward to her visit . . .

The sound of footsteps coming up the stairs made her spin round to face the door, her heart thumping against her ribs as the lock turned with a smooth click.

Derek Howard stepped into the room, took in her dishevelled appearance, and burst out laughing. 'I must have a picture of this. The mighty James Freeman will be horrified to see his elegant sister with an old piece of sacking tied round her head.'

Still chuckling in delight, he produced a camera – not hers, she was relieved to see. Kate guessed he intended to send pictures to her brother. Well, they weren't going to see her cowed by this brute, even if she was so terrified it was difficult to think straight all the time; it would only add to their worry. She struck an exaggerated pose she'd seen the models use many times.

'Cocky enough to play games, are you?' he said, after he'd taken several snaps. He was scowling now, angered by her defiance. 'We'll see what you're like after a few more days in here.'

'If you're going to keep me in this disgusting place, then I'll need some heating and a visit to the bathroom.' She wasn't sure where her bravado had come from, because all she wanted to do was to beg him to release her. She was disgusted with her cowardice!

Howard tossed a paper bag and a bottle of lemonade on the bed. 'There're a couple of sandwiches. That's all you're getting.'

'Very generous of you,' she remarked, as she tried to assess her chances of rushing past him to reach the unlocked door.

He guessed what she was thinking and gave an evil leer. 'Come on, then, try it. I guarantee you'll regret it if you do.'

Kate was now under no illusions about him; he was a big man and would enjoy hurting her. She stepped back. 'I need to go to the bathroom.'

He pointed to the bucket in the corner of the room and sniggered. 'You'll have to use that. See, I have provided everything for your comfort.'

She looked at it with disgust but lifted her head proudly. She wouldn't let him see that Rose Webster's daughter was scared. 'Thank you *so* much.'

'You would have had the pleasure of my company earlier, but by the time I'd dumped the car the trains had stopped running. But you appear to have survived the night without too much harm.'

'Would you have cared if I hadn't?' she snapped.

'You'd be less trouble to me dead, but I'm not ready to get rid of you yet.'

It was hard not to let her terror show. Her instinct was telling her that he was *not* going to release her once he'd had his revenge on her brother. This man was evil. Her stomach lurched.

'What are you intending to do with me?' She wanted to know what he had in store for her, praying that she was going to be brave enough to deal with it.

'Nothing yet.' His smile was malicious. 'It's your brother I'm after. If he doesn't agree to drop all charges against me, then I'll probably have some fun with you first.'

'First?' Kate's heart was hammering.

'Before I kill you.' His gaze raked over her as if he

relished the prospect. Then he dragged her into his arms and laughed. 'That's right, Miss Freeman, you're not getting out of this room alive. You're a beauty, all right. I think I'll change my mind about waiting.'

Kate was no weakling, but Howard was built like a rugby player. She brought her knee up and heard him grunt in pain, and when his grip loosened for a moment she tried to wrench herself free. He caught her a stinging blow across the face, laughing as he swung at her.

'Missed your target but nice try. Now I'll make you suffer for that.'

She was stunned by the punch, and all her efforts to stop him from ripping her trousers from her body were useless. The thought of this animal raping her was more than she could stand. She fought, kicked and even bit him in desperation.

His demented laugh caught her attention and through her terror she recognized the danger. This was just what he wanted!

'This is going to be fun. I really like a woman who struggles.' He pushed her on to the bed and came down on top of her.

It went against all her instincts, but Kate knew what she must do. She stopped struggling and became passive, turning her head away from his excited face.

He erupted into fury, hitting and shaking her, but she didn't respond – not by cries of pain or even a twitch of her hand; she remained frozen. That infuriated him even more, and she felt his hands tighten around her neck. The life was being squeezed out of her. She began to gasp and lose consciousness. Her ordeal would soon be over. She was going to die. The overriding feeling was one of great sadness at leaving her family and little Eddie . . .

Suddenly the pressure on her neck was gone and she took in great gulps of air to fill her empty lungs. She became fully conscious as he hit her hard.

'Lost your fight already, have you?' he snarled, getting off the bed. 'Well, I'll see you don't next time. I'll take everything your family owns until they're back in the gutter where they started – and then, as the final blow, I'll kill you.'

As soon as she heard the door lock behind him, Kate curled into a tight ball with a whimper of anguish; she wasn't capable of screaming, which is what she felt like doing. Slowly the cold started to seep into her body and she scrambled back into her torn clothing as quickly as she could, then huddled up again. The sheer terror she was experiencing was something beyond her understanding. She heard the downstairs door close. Howard had stopped this time, but she knew he would be back and then her torment would really begin. Rape first, and then death.

She pushed the terrifying prospect to the back of her mind, forcing herself to think clearly. All the time she was alive there was hope. He'd dumped the car some distance away, by the sound of it, but where the blazes was this place? The only comforting thought she had was that her family would be looking for her . . .

Kate uncurled herself, wincing as she became aware of her bruises. The first thing she must do is eat. She hadn't had anything since the soup Pete had prepared for her. She must keep up her strength, so that if a chance came to escape she would be able to take it. She ripped open the paper bag, not caring what it was, but was shaking so much it took two hands to bring the food to her mouth. After finishing the sandwiches she allowed herself a few mouthfuls of drink to ease her sore throat, knowing that she must make this last as there was no telling how long it would be before she was given anything else – if he even bothered. And to be truthful she prayed he would never return. It would be better to die of hunger and cold, than at the mercy of this brutal man. She swore again at that defeatist thought. She couldn't die! There was too much to live for.

Kate eyed the bucket and knew she would have to use it. She picked up some old newspapers and placed them over the top of the bucket afterwards, and then went back and sat on the bed again.

Her eyes began to close, so she forced them open. She had to find a way of either escaping or alerting someone to her plight.

'Think!' she shouted at herself. 'Don't just sit here, do something!' This was not the time to size up the options in her usual careful way – this was a time for action!

She made her legs move and went over to the window. The wooden frame was rotten and she began to pick away with a small piece of broken china she'd found, loosening one nail after another until they were all out. The sash on the window was broken and it took a great deal of effort to open it, but she eventually managed to push her head through and have a better look at her surroundings. What she saw made her groan in despair. Although she was only on the second floor, there was a huge crater below the window, making the drop twice as far.

She was about to close the window again when a

movement caught her eye. There were some children playing in the ruins of another house, but they were too far away to see or hear her, even though she shouted as loud as her bruised throat would allow. Perhaps the place wasn't as deserted as she'd first thought. She leaned right out and looked sideways, first one way and then the other, but there was nothing but ruins.

She was thoroughly chilled by now, so she closed the window. That line of action was obviously useless. She'd have to find another way. If she could throw the mattress out of the window it might cushion her fall, but the window was much too small to push the bulky mattress through. Another useless idea!

The only thing that might help her family was the camera – but would anyone find it? Her mother was well known in London, and it would have a chance of reaching her. Providing Derek Howard hadn't taken her out of London of course. Her head bowed as she sent up a silent prayer, hoping that there was someone up there who was listening to her plea, because she just didn't know what else she could do. Kate wasn't used to feeling helpless, but she did now. She felt utterly alone and very frightened.

That was all she could do for the moment. She must sleep now; she was exhausted.

'Why don't you try to get some rest, Bill?' Rose told her husband. 'I expect James and Pete will soon be back. I'll wait for them and wake you if there's any news.'

Bill turned away from the window, looking haggard and every one of his sixty-seven years. 'I feel so bloody helpless, Rose!'

'So do we all.' She clenched her hands. 'I swear that if I could get hold of that man at this moment I'd knock him into next week.'

'I couldn't be responsible for my actions either.' Bill ran a hand over his eyes. 'Howard's hit our family in the most effective way by targeting Kate. He must have known that was how to hurt us the most.'

Rose was incandescent with rage and sick with worry about their daughter, but she mustn't give vent to her anger. It had been a long night, and Bill was liable to have a heart attack if he didn't rest soon. She wouldn't add to his burden by erupting like a volcano.

'Go to bed, Bill,' she ordered in a firm tone. 'We can't do any more at the moment. We've given the police all the details. They'll have more chance of finding Kate than us.'

He sighed and dropped into an armchair. 'You're right of course. I'll rest here until the others return.'

Rose watched in concern as his eyes closed; he looked so ill. She allowed her mind to drift, remembering all the years they had been married, and she thanked the Lord for every one of them. Bill was a quiet placid man, but could be tough when necessary. But this disaster was tearing him apart.

She sat in another chair and rested her head back; eyes wide open, remembering the attack on herself when she'd been only fourteen. She hadn't given it a thought for years, but now she prayed that her daughter wasn't suffering the same fate. If that man Howard raped Kate, then she would see he spent a very long time in prison!

She didn't dare consider that he might have already killed her.

13

Eddie ran over to the window for the umpteenth time, peered out and then came back to sit in front of the fire again. He was more dejected with every visit.

'What are you looking for?' Jon asked him.

'She said she'd come and see me today.' The child appeared to be utterly dejected.

'Who?'

'The pretty lady.' Ed's bottom lip trembled. 'She promised she'd come this morning, but it's nearly dark now. I've drawed her a picture and I wanted to give it to her for Christmas, but she don't care about me any more.'

'I'm sure that isn't true, Eddie,' Mrs Green told him. 'She's very busy and I expect she's been delayed.'

'Who are you talking about?' Jon asked Mrs Green. He'd only arrived back from the Congo last night and was puzzled by Ed's distress. He was usually excited when he came home, but when he'd arrived this afternoon Eddie had been too preoccupied to show much enthusiasm. And that wasn't a bit like him!

'Mrs Freeman's daughter, Kate, she's been coming regular to see the twins and talk to the rest of the boys. Eddie's become very fond of her.'

'I didn't know Rose Freeman had a daughter.' Jon was trying to picture her in his mind. 'Is she anything like her mother?'

'Oh, yes, she's a lovely girl. She isn't quite as tall as

her mother, but she has the same dark colouring.' Mrs Green warmed to her story. 'She used to work for your newspaper as a photographer.'

'Really?' Knowing Andrew Stevenson's dislike of women, Jon found that hard to believe.

'She didn't stay long, though,' Mrs Green continued, 'because she had trouble with the boss. And when he refused to print a story about Standish and Wilkins that her and her mother had worked on, she left.'

'They did a write-up on the homes?'

Mrs Green smiled and nodded. 'Yes, did a lot of good as well. Kate and Mrs Freeman came one day, took loads of photos and put it in the paper, asking for volunteers to give the children a bit of their time.'

'Which paper did it go in?' Jon asked.

'Oh, yours, she won in the end.' Mrs Green stood up as one of the boys called her. 'Such a nice girl, and very determined.'

'She's ever so kind,' Eddie said.

'Ah,' Jon turned his attention back to the solemn-looking boy. 'You like her, do you?'

Eddie dredged up a small smile. 'I asked her if she'd be my mum when she gets married. She said she'd think about it – serious like,' he added.

Tom came and joined them, sitting on the floor next to Eddie. 'You can't take any notice of what people say. Nobody bloody wants us, you ought to know that by now.'

'Why?' Eddie spun round on his bottom to face Jon. 'Why don't nobody want us?'

Jon gave Tom a quick clip around the ear. 'Don't tell Ed lies, and watch your language. Mrs Green wants you,

I want you, and everyone who works here wants you.'

Tom rubbed his ear and scowled at Jon. 'Nobody adopted you and you're clever. He ought to see that a posh lady like that won't adopt him.'

'She would too!' Ed was angry now and Jon had to keep the two boys apart before they ended up in a fight.

Jon thought it was time to change the subject, as he knew the hopeless anger these boys were suffering. 'Will you show me your drawing, Ed?'

He scrambled to his feet, tore up the stairs, and, after much thumping of feet and banging of doors, reappeared with a sheet of paper in his hand.

Before looking at the drawing Jon gave Tom a warning glance as the kid started to snigger. Then he examined the childish drawing. 'This is very good, Ed.'

Eddie squirmed with shyness at the compliment. 'It's Kate.'

'Miss Freeman.' Mrs Green corrected him, coming back to join them.

'She said we could call her Kate,' Tom informed them.

'Oh, that's all right, then.' Mrs Green left them again to see why one of the babies was crying.

Tom sloped off as well, and Ed came and sat beside Jon on the battered old sofa. 'Do you think she'll like it?'

'She'll love it.' He studied the picture carefully. It really was rather good, except for one thing. 'Has she got wings?'

The boy giggled. ''Course not, but she's pretty enough to be an angel, so I drawed her as one. She's ever so kind and makes us laugh. I've got a special present for you on Christmas Day.'

Ed was about to go and look out of the window again but Jon stopped him. 'She'll come as soon as she can. Now, what's this present?'

'I'm not telling! You'll have to wait and see.'

He was pleased to see that the boy was brighter now, but *he* was angry with this woman for breaking her promise. Didn't she realize that these children had so little in their lives that every treat or visit was waited for with much eagerness? She couldn't be much like her mother, he thought. He was certain that Rose Freeman would never let anyone down.

Rose showed the two policemen out, closed the door and bowed her head as fatigue swept through her. There wasn't anything else they could do. It was the third day since Kate's kidnapping, and all their efforts to find her had proved fruitless. It was now up to the police.

She straightened up and walked back to the lounge, strain etched on her face. Christmas Eve was usually a happy time as they looked forward to the festive season, but not this year. It had been a job making the entire family stay away, but Rose hadn't wanted the house filled up; it would have only caused Bill more agitation. She was sick with worry for her daughter and her husband's health. She knew everyone was holding their breath waiting for news, and praying that Kate would be found soon, and alive!

Bill and James were staring at a photograph as if mesmerized. The picture had been found on the reception desk of Grant Phillips just before the offices closed last night. No one had seen who had left it there.

'That tells us she's still all right and in good enough

spirit to ham it up in front of Derek Howard.' Rose spoke briskly. Since receiving the photos, she found her admiration for her daughter had risen markedly. Of course she'd always loved her, but had worried that she might not be able to take the knocks life handed out from time to time. Now she knew her daughter could.

'Why's she got a piece of sack tied around her head?' Pete wanted to know. He had refused to go home until Kate was found, so he'd been living with Rose and Bill.

'I don't suppose there's any heating where he's keeping her and she's trying to keep herself warm.' Bill's voice was husky with tiredness and worry.

'James,' Rose turned to her son, 'why didn't anyone see who delivered the photos to Grant Phillips? You always have someone on duty in reception, surely?'

'The receptionist left her desk for only a few minutes to take a visitor up to the drawing office. The envelope was there when she returned.'

'You sure this is the only message with the pictures?' Bill asked his son.

'Yes, all it says is – I'll see the Freemans back in the gutter they came from.' James ran a hand over his eyes. 'Mum, let's cook a proper meal, and then we must try and get some rest. We've done all we can.'

'Can I help?' Pete asked. 'I'm good at peeling spuds.'

'You've got yourself a job.' Rose gave him a studied glance. Kate had been right to help him. It was already evident that there was something special about Pete. Her daughter would have seen that of course, she had an uncanny knack of seeing beneath the outward appearance of people. Her insides clenched painfully, praying that Kate was putting that talent to good use. It might increase her chances of survival.

Rose was about to go to the kitchen when there was a knock on the door. 'I'll get it.'

Standing on the doorstep in the fading light of dusk was a man of about thirty-five, holding firmly on to a girl of no more than nine or ten years old. She'd been crying and didn't look as if she wanted to be there.

'I'm looking for someone called Freeman.'

'That's me,' Rose said, trying to keep a weary note out of her voice. People had the habit of coming to her when they had legal problems, but she wasn't capable of dealing with anything at the moment. She had enough trouble of her own.

He held out a package. 'My daughter came home with this a while ago, and I think it belongs to you.'

Rose pulled aside the paper and saw a small camera. Although she didn't recognize it, Kate and cameras went together . . . 'You'd better come in, Mr . . .?'

'Sanders,' he told her, 'and this is my daughter May.'

She took them to the sitting room, introduced them, and held out the camera to Pete.

'That's Kate's!' he cried, taking it from Rose. 'She put it in her pocket when Derek Howard came for her. She never steps outside the door without a camera of some sort.'

Suddenly they were all on their feet talking at once.

Clearly frightened by the turmoil in the room, May peered from behind her father, eyes brimming with tears. 'I didn't steal it!' she shouted in panic. 'I didn't do nothing wrong! I want to go home, Daddy.'

Bill stooped down in front of her and smiled. 'We know you didn't do anything wrong, May. We have a daughter and she's in terrible danger, so could you tell us where you got the camera?'

May was calmed by Bill's gentle voice. 'What's happened to her?'

'A man's hidden her somewhere. That's her camera and we need to know where it was found.'

'I don't know, honest!' The girl was becoming agitated again and cast her father a beseeching glance.

'Tell Mr Freeman where you got the camera, May. No one's blaming you for anything.'

'I went to the shops for Mum. She'd run out of flour, and I met two girls and they had it. They said it wasn't any good but I liked it, so I swapped a film star magazine for it,' she informed the room. 'I'd just bought the new *Photoplay* with my pocket money.'

'Who were these girls?' James asked.

'Dunno. They said they didn't live in Hammersmith. Their mum and dad was doing some shopping for Christmas and told them to wait outside the shop.' May stopped and looked anxiously at Bill. 'They said it wasn't pinched; they'd found it where they play.'

'Did they say where that was?' Rose prompted.

The girl shook her head. 'I didn't have time to talk no more because their mum came out of the shop.'

'Thank you, May.' Bill stood up, his disappointment clear for anyone to see.

'I'm sorry I don't know any more.' May was looking more composed now.

'Mr Sanders, we were about to have dinner – would you like to join us?' Rose asked.

'Thank you, Mrs Freeman, but we must be getting back.'

'It was kind of you to return the camera,' James said.

'I couldn't do nothing else when I saw it was quite valuable. We don't want to be accused of stealing.'

Bill took a five-pound note out of his wallet and gave it to May. 'That's for bringing us Kate's camera.'

May's eyes opened wide when she saw the small fortune. 'Thank you, sir, but I didn't want to come. My dad made me,' she admitted.

'I hope you find your girl safe and well, Mrs Freeman. I'm sorry we couldn't be of more help.'

After Sanders and his daughter left, Rose and Pete went to the kitchen and set about preparing a quick meal. They worked silently, their thoughts and prayers with Kate.

Dinner was ready and Rose made everyone sit down. All they'd eaten during the search were sandwiches. They'd chased every lead, however flimsy, but to no avail. It was a silent meal, with everyone lost in their own thoughts.

James let out a ragged breath as he pushed his plate away, his appetite evaporating as he gazed at the photograph of his sister.

'Show me those pictures again,' Rose ordered, taking them from her son.

Bill leant towards her. 'That's obviously a room in a derelict house. Where can it be, Rose?'

She frowned. 'It isn't one of Grant Phillips's building sites, is it?'

'No, Mum, we've checked all of those,' James said. 'Howard wouldn't be daft enough to take her to one of ours.'

'The police haven't found the car yet,' Bill said, 'but that's hardly surprising. Howard would have dumped it miles away, if he's got any sense.'

Rose returned to studying the pictures. Her mind went over all the building developments taking place at the moment and she cursed silently. There was a time when she'd have known every one of them, but she was out of touch now.

'Rose.' Bill sat beside her. 'Isn't there any clue in the photos?'

She closed her eyes trying to visualize places where Kate might have been hidden, but there were hundreds of suitable sites in London alone . . . And then it came to her! 'James show me the note again!'

'*I'll see the Freemans back in the gutter they came from.*'

Rose surged to her feet. 'My God, he's taken her to Bermondsey! And I think I know the very place.'

She scribbled the location on the back of the photo-graph and thrust it at James. 'Take this to the police station. Kate might be there.'

James left at a run. Bill and Pete were scrambling into their coats when Rose stopped them.

'We are going to let the police handle this. If we go storming in, he might panic and kill her.'

That warning was enough to stop everyone, and they waited.

James was soon back. 'The police are mounting a raiding party. They've asked that we keep out of it.

Oh, and by the way, they've found the Wolseley in St Albans.'

Bill's mouth was set in a determined line. 'I'll leave it to the police, but I'm going to be right behind them.'

14

The waiting was terrible. It was dark again and Kate shivered. She had done her best to keep her circulation going, but now it was an effort to move. All she wanted to do was sleep. Derek Howard hadn't come up here for a long long time. Night had come, then morning, then night again. How many days was it? She couldn't remember. Time seemed to have stopped for her. She was past feeling hungry, but was glad she'd rationed herself to a couple of sips of lemonade now and again because she needed the liquid. Fear gnawed away at her as she vacillated from praying that he wouldn't come, to fear that she might be left here to die. Suppose he'd been arrested and wouldn't tell them where she was? How long could she stay alive without food and water? And yet, if he came, she would die for sure. What a choice!

She leant against the wall. It was so quiet she had the feeling that the world no longer existed and she was the only person left alive. She was even pleased to see a mouse, which turned up now and again. It was quite unafraid of her and she watched as it foraged around, feeling sad when it disappeared through a tiny gap in the floorboards. Her slim hope that the camera would find its way to her family had evaporated. It had been a crazy idea anyway. Had James been contacted, or was Howard trying to make him sweat by keeping him in the dark?

She gave an uncontrolled giggle. She was in the dark all right!

Her mind was starting to play strange tricks. She tried to work out again how long she'd been here. Was it two days . . . or three? Maybe more, she'd lost track of time. Was it two days ago Howard had tried to strangle her, or was it the day before that? Perhaps it was Christmas Day now? Kate realized she was confused and had tried hard to keep alert. She had sung all the popular songs she could think of, recited poems and her favourite Psalms from the Bible. But she really couldn't seem to concentrate now . . .

She drifted off to sleep, seeking release in oblivion.

The sound of heavy footsteps running up the stairs snapped her awake. She scrambled off the bed with a startled cry. Howard was coming for her, and he was in a hurry. She'd been asleep. Dear God, she'd been sleeping when she should have been trying to escape. She began to shake in terror; she didn't want to die! Panic ripped through her. He was almost at the door now. He would kill her this time!

The door burst open and with a scream of terror she squeezed herself behind the bed. A bright light blinded her and she heaved the mattress up, standing it in front of her for protection. He was saying something and trying to pull the mattress away. She was going to die!

'Steady, miss.' The man's voice was gentle. 'I'm a policeman. You're safe now.'

It was a trick. She was gulping in air.

It was bedlam as more people came into the room.

After the silence of a short time ago Kate became frightened and even more confused.

'Quiet!' someone ordered. 'She doesn't know what's happening.'

'Miss Freeman, I'm Detective Andy Green. We've caught Derek Howard and he's now in custody.'

She cautiously peered around the mattress she was using as a shield. They looked like policemen . . .

'It's all right, miss,' one of them said gently, reaching out for the mattress. 'Let me have that. You don't need it any more.'

She let it drop and stood there shivering, her mind not being able to grasp what was going on.

'Where are the ambulance men?' Detective Green asked. 'She's hurt. And let her family come up. She needs to see a familiar face.'

After the isolation, the room full of people was disorientating. She was dry-eyed but inwardly she was screaming in terror. It took every ounce of self-control she had to stop herself passing out. Was it over? Or was she hallucinating?

'Kate.'

The voice of her father was nearly her undoing, but when she saw his haggard face she knew it really was all over. She wrapped her arms around him, giving a dry sob. This was no trick of the mind. He was here. He was solid. Neither spoke. There was no need for words.

Rose appeared. 'Are you hurt, Kate?'

She stepped away from her father and hugged her mother. 'I'm all right.' In the torchlight she didn't miss the look of anger and concern that swept over her mother's face. Then James gathered her in his arms, his face wet with tears.

'I'm so sorry . . . I'm so sorry.'

'We caught the blighter,' the policeman informed her. 'You've got nothing to fear now, miss.'

'Thank you.' She swayed and her mother took hold of her arm to steady her. 'Can I go home now please?'

'You must go to the hospital for a check-up first.' A police officer beckoned the ambulance man over. 'Take Miss Freeman now.'

'Can you walk, miss, or would you like the stretcher?' He wrapped a blanket around her shoulders.

'I can manage,' she told the ambulance man, and hoped she was telling the truth, because her legs didn't feel as if they would hold her.

Kate sat on the edge of the examination table, her head bowed as the doctor wrote his notes. The check-up had been thorough, painful and embarrassing. The police had wanted photographs of her injuries. She hadn't realized how badly bruised she was after Howard's attack on her. But it was what that beast had done to her mentally that would be hard to get over.

'I'll give you a full medical report in the morning,' the doctor told the policeman, who had stayed the other side of the screen all the time. Then he turned his attention back to Kate. 'I would like to keep you in overnight.'

That made her look up. She wanted the sanctuary of her own room. 'No, I'm going home.'

He studied her for a few moments, then nodded. 'Very well, your parents are waiting outside for you.'

★

Kate awoke from a deep sleep feeling bewildered. For a few seconds she thought she was still in that cold dark room. She sat up with a cry of alarm.

'It's all right, my darling.' Her father sat on the edge of the bed and took hold of her hand. 'You're safe now.'

As she gazed at his face, her eyes clouded, but not with tears. She was so angry. Her father had suffered, and that odious man had no right to inflict such pain on him or on the rest of her family. She remembered James's tears and hoped Derek Howard burnt in hell for what he'd done. She had never before wished harm on anyone in her life, but now she did . . .

'Are you feeling better?'

She did her best to dampen down the fire of revenge raging inside her and smiled. 'I'm fine, Dad. What day is it?'

'Christmas Day.'

Kate laid her head back and wallowed in the luxury and warmth of her own bed, knowing that her family were all around her. 'What's the time?'

Bill glanced at his watch. 'Ten in the morning.'

Her gaze rested for a moment on the pile of presents in the corner of the room and she sat up straight. 'I was supposed to visit Wilkins House yesterday!' Or was it the day before? Damn, damn, damn! She couldn't think clearly. Her mind was skittering about all over the place.

'That can wait. We'll send someone round with the gifts.'

'No, no.' Kate shook her head. 'Eddie and the boys will be so disappointed if I don't turn up. I ought to pop into Standish House as well to wish them a happy Christmas.'

'Your mother's already done that, and we've sent each home a large Christmas tree and hampers of goodies.'

'That was a lovely idea.' Kate smiled warmly at her father. 'But I must go to see Eddie.'

'You're very fond of that child, aren't you?'

'Yes. He's a lovely boy and he yearns for a proper mum and dad.' Kate's expression was troubled. 'They all do.'

'You get yourself ready and I'll take you – after you've had some breakfast.'

'Thanks, Dad.' She watched him leave; he had aged ten years since she'd been kidnapped and she didn't think she would ever be able to forgive Howard for doing that to him.

She'd had a bath and washed her hair last night, but did the same again now. After the filth of that room it was lovely to feel clean. She chose her best suit, which was a lovely cherry-red, brushed her hair until it shone blue-black, tucked a silk scarf around her neck to hide the marks, then put on shoes with the highest heels in her collection. Now she felt ready to face the world, outwardly at least, but she knew she was going to have to give the performance of her life to fool everyone.

As soon as Kate walked into the kitchen, her gaze fixed on Rose's face, and she realized with dismay that her mother was also showing the strain. Kate had always considered her mother to be the tough one of the family, but this had caused her much anguish.

'You look better.' Rose smiled at her daughter. 'What would you like for breakfast?'

Kate thought for a moment. She hadn't wanted anything last night except a cup of hot cocoa, but now she was hungry. 'A fried-egg sandwich please, and a strong cup of tea.'

'I'll have the same, Mum.' James strode in and squeezed Kate's shoulder, then he sat next to her. 'I'm so sorry, Kate. I should have handed Howard over to the police as soon as we had any suspicion that he was involved in defrauding the company. I was too bloody soft on him!'

'It wasn't your fault.' Her smile was forced. 'As you can see, I survived.'

'Thank God, but it must have been a terrible ordeal for you.'

She wasn't going to let him blame himself. 'I'll get over it. How did you find me and what's happened to Derek Howard?'

'Your camera found its way to us, though it wasn't much use, but it was good thinking, Kate. When Mum realized that Derek Howard was talking about Bermondsey, we alerted the police and they got there just before Howard arrived. They arrested him at once.'

'After being kept so isolated, I was confused when the room was suddenly full of people and bright lights.' She grimaced at the memory, ashamed once again of the terrible fear she'd fought with all the time. 'Howard said he was going to demand that you dropped all charges against him. Did he do that?'

'No. He sent us a photograph of you but no demand.' James pulled the picture out of his pocket. 'If he had done so, we would have carried out his instructions immediately.'

'I know you would, but I don't believe he would have let me go anyway,' she admitted, picking up the photo.

There was something in James's voice that hinted he wasn't telling the whole truth. It was probably her imagination, though, and she immediately dismissed the notion. 'He's a terrible photographer, isn't he?' She was relieved to hear her family laugh at the comment.

James put the picture back in his pocket. 'I think I'll have this framed. It's a fetching pose. I've brought your car from the shop; I thought you might need it over the holiday.'

'Oh, thank you.' She turned to her father. 'I can drive myself to see the boys now, and after that I must visit Pete. I know he was at the hospital last night but I was too confused to thank him, and all of you for what you'd done.'

'I can still take you,' her father insisted.

'No, Dad.' She spoke gently. 'I'm feeling fine. I need to get my life back to normal as quickly as possible.'

'I understand.'

Kate bit into the sandwich and rolled her eyes in pleasure as the egg yolk oozed out. As children they had always loved these, but she hadn't had one for years. 'I've never tasted anything so delicious. Now tell me where everyone is.'

James swallowed the last of his sandwich. 'Annie and Reid are spending Christmas Day in Thatcham with his parents and then coming to us on Boxing Day. Will and Dora are coming this afternoon. I've already sent Charlie and Madge a telegram with the good news, and Sam of course.'

'What about Beth? I was supposed to go out with her.'

'We've told her you're safe,' James said. 'She's spending

Christmas with Steve's family, but she'll see you after Christmas.'

'Do you want a party tonight?' Her mother looked doubtful. 'Or would you rather keep it quiet for a couple of days?'

'Definitely a party.' Kate knew she'd said the right thing when some of the worry left their faces.

'Right.' Bill grinned. 'We'll throw the best damned party we've ever had.'

'I'll look forward to that. A bit of noise is just what I need.' She stood up. 'Now I must go and see the boys. They'll be wondering where I've got to.'

James helped her carry the parcels out to the car. 'You sure you want to drive yourself? I could take you.'

'I must do this,' she told him, her mouth set in a determined line. 'Mum and Dad must believe I'm coping, and the sooner I start acting normal the sooner they'll stop worrying.'

'It isn't going to be easy, though, is it?' he said perceptively.

'No, but that's just between us, James.' She clenched her fingers around the car keys until it hurt. 'I won't have them worried any more.'

'I agree. This has taken a terrible toll on both of them.' He kissed her on the cheek. 'You sure you're okay?'

'I'm such a coward, James.' The words came out in a whisper and she dipped her head in shame, not able to look at him.

'Don't think that,' he said, a deep frown on his face. 'You come to me if you need anything.'

'I will.' She got in the car, started the engine and set off towards Wandsworth.

*

Jon watched the tall elegant woman walk in and, as cries of delight came from Eddie, saw her lift up the boy and spin around on her high heels. The sight was stunning: bright red suit, short skirt and long shapely legs. Her hair shone black against the scarlet. She was unmistakably Rose Freeman's daughter.

Eddie had his arms around her neck and the rest of the boys gathered round.

'You said you were coming two days ago,' Tom said, accusingly. 'Ed thought you'd forgotten about him.'

'I wouldn't do that.' She smiled at Eddie and put him down. 'I couldn't get here.'

'Were you sick?' Eddie asked.

She stooped down in front of him. 'Yes, but I'm all right now.'

Mrs Green was all smiles. 'Jon, this is Kate.'

'I'm pleased to meet you,' she said in a distracted way.

As he shook hands with her, he looked into her eyes for the first time and was shocked. They were just like her mother's, so dark they were almost black, but there the similarity ended. This woman's eyes looked empty, the only emotion showing a deep simmering anger. She was the most beautiful girl he had ever seen, but there was something wrong with her.

'Mr Devlin, I have a car full of parcels and could use some help bringing them in.'

With a slight inclination of his head he followed her out. When they staggered back, loaded with brightly wrapped parcels, the boys went wild and wanted to open them right away.

'No,' Mrs Green told them firmly. 'Put them round the tree for us to open after lunch.'

'Where are the twins?' Kate asked, looking around the room.

'We've got the most amazing news. They've been taken home for Christmas by a very nice couple who are thinking of adopting them. They can't have children of their own and are happy to have them both. I would have been very upset if they'd been split up.'

'That's wonderful, Mrs Green. I hope everything works out.' Kate nodded approval.

'I believe it will. They're a well-off couple and fell in love with the twins as soon as they saw them.'

'It's quieter without them,' Tom said, pulling a face. 'They couldn't half grizzle!'

Eddie scrambled to his feet as soon as all the packages were in place and tore up the stairs, returning out of breath with the picture he'd painted for Kate. He smiled shyly and handed it to her. 'I drawed this for you.'

Jon watched carefully to see what her reaction would be. The boy had put a lot of love into that picture.

She studied the painting for some time, then gathered Eddie into her arms for a hug. 'Thank you, Eddie, it's beautiful and the best present I've ever had.'

Her voice was husky and, when she looked up, Jon was sure he saw tears welling up in her eyes. Then the emotion vanished, and he thought he must have been mistaken.

She stayed for about two hours and then left, promising to come again in two days' time. He went with her to the car. After putting the drawing carefully on the back seat, she shook hands with him again, and then drove off.

He wandered back indoors, where the boys were all

excited about her visit, and shook his head in bewilderment. He was sure she'd been touched by Eddie's gift,
and she did seem to care for the boys – but there was a
detached look about her, as if she were walking in
a dream. No, it wasn't that. There had been a tortured
look in those lustrous dark eyes.

Kate breathed a sigh of relief as she drove to Pete's house.
She'd been in danger of unravelling when Eddie had
given her his painting, and it had taken a supreme effort
not to collapse on the floor and cry her eyes out. It had
been a struggle when she'd seen how Eddie had depicted
her as an angel with jet-black hair and wings, but she
wouldn't break down in front of strangers. Jon Devlin
was a severe-looking man and not at all how she'd
imagined him. She'd only ever seen black and white
pictures of him and his colouring had come as a shock:
his hair was the colour of wet sand and he had the
greenest eyes she'd ever seen.

As soon as she pulled up outside Pete's small terraced
house, he rushed out to greet her. 'Kate! I'm so happy
to see you. The police wouldn't let me come up to the
room when they found you. Only close family were
allowed, but I was right there all the time. Are you okay?
Shouldn't you still be in hospital?'

'I'm fine, Pete; I've come to thank you. James told me
it was you who told him I was missing, and you wouldn't
leave until you knew I was safe.'

'I was so worried,' he admitted.

Kate reached into the car for the last present and
handed it to him. 'Happy Christmas, Pete.'

He smiled. 'It will be, now that you're safe. I've got

something for you indoors. Will you come in and meet my family?'

'I'd love to.'

Pete's parents welcomed her with warm smiles, ushering her into the front room. The furniture had seen better days, but it was spotlessly clean and comfortable.

'Do sit down, my dear,' Mrs Sheldon urged. 'We were all that pleased to know you were safe. Would you like a cup of tea?'

'No, thank you, Mrs Sheldon.' Kate sat in one of the imitation leather armchairs, suddenly feeling very drained.

Pete's father was obviously not in good health, moving slowly as if in some discomfort. He was beaming with pleasure, though. 'It's lovely to meet you at last, and know you're safe. Our Pete's been worried sick about you.'

Kate looked at Pete with affection. 'I know, and my family have been so grateful for his help and support. This kidnapping has been very hard on them.'

Pete's four young brothers and sisters watched her with interest as they talked, and Kate forced herself to join in the conversation. She had been too stubborn to realize just how tiring this morning would be, and she was beginning to feel quite unwell.

It was an hour before she could politely leave. There was the party to get through. And for her parents' sake, she must shine tonight!

15

'Happy New Year, Pete.' Kate walked into the back room of the shop, glad to be at work and occupied. 'Sorry I'm late. I popped in at Wilkins House and had breakfast with them.'

'You don't have to apologize to me,' he laughed. 'You're the boss. You can come and go as you please.'

A plan had been forming in Kate's mind all over the Christmas holiday, and she'd decided to put it into action without delay. She would talk to her parents tonight. Her view of life had changed dramatically during her captivity. Her dreams of working abroad had vanished, but she would root out cruelty and injustice in her own country and expose it. Everyone had been telling her how brave she'd been. She knew that wasn't true. She'd been terrified, and, apart from that one effort with the camera, she'd just sat there and done nothing. She should have tried harder to escape! It was no good berating herself. Her nature had always been to wait and see how things turned out. If she had done something silly in panic, then she might not be here today talking to Pete. It was during the dark lonely hours she'd realized just how much he meant to her. He was more than her assistant – he was a loved and respected friend. It had worried her that if she had died he could have been left with nothing, and that wasn't fair, after all the hard work he'd put into the shop. She was determined to put that right.

'I think 1961 is going to be a good year for us.' Pete's eyes shone with excitement. 'The phone hasn't stopped ringing this morning. I've taken bookings for three weddings and two portraits and it's only eleven o'clock.'

'Wonderful.' Kate put the kettle on to make tea. 'We must get you an assistant. I'll be off chasing stories a lot of the time.'

'I know that's what you want to do, so I've already put an advert in two local papers,' he told her. 'And they should be out today.'

She studied him carefully as he put out biscuits for their elevenses. There wasn't a trace of the timid boy who had started working with her last year.

'Did you have a good Christmas?' she asked.

He looked up. 'Oh, yes, and my mum and dad haven't stopped talking about your visit.'

The bell on the shop door jangled and Kate went out to see who was there, fighting down the panic she was feeling in case another Derek Howard came in the door. A girl of around Pete's age was standing by the counter and clutching a newspaper.

'Can I help you?' Kate asked.

'Er . . . I've come about the job.' She looked uncertain. 'But I don't suppose you want a girl.'

'What's your name?' Kate rather liked the look of her. Petite was the right way to describe her. She had short light brown hair, and lovely clear blue eyes. Her smile was hesitant but engaging.

'I'm Susan Richards. I'm very interested in photography, but I'm afraid I haven't had any experience.'

'That isn't important; we'd be willing to teach you.

Come and have a cup of tea, meet my partner and tell us about yourself.'

Half an hour later Susan Richards left, and Kate asked Pete, 'What did you think of her?'

'She seems a nice girl and very keen.'

'You don't have to take the first one,' she told him. 'I expect there will be others applying.'

'Sure to be.' Pete chewed his lip. 'Do you think she'd do the job okay?'

'Yes, I do, but it's your decision.'

'Mine?' He looked startled.

'Yep.' Kate grinned. 'I've just promoted you again. You're now in charge of the hiring and firing of staff.'

'The last time you promoted me you gave me a rise,' he said, chortling. 'Does this mean I'll get another one?'

'You've just had one,' she teased, 'but I'll think about it later.'

Pete tipped his head back and roared. 'Fair enough, boss.'

'Now, what about this girl?' Kate said.

'I think we'll give it a couple of days and see who else applies, but she's definitely at the top of the list.'

'Very sensible.' She picked up her camera and headed for the door, stopped and looked over her shoulder. 'Can you drive?'

He shook his head.

'Right. Apply for your provisional licence and I'll find someone to teach you. Then we'll see about buying you your own car.'

'Really?' Pete squeaked. 'That'll be great!'

Kate packed up early from work and found her parents

in the sitting room, both reading by a blazing fire. They looked much better and she was glad she'd been able to convince them that she was all right after the abduction. Only James knew what a difficult time she was having coming to terms with it – but it was early days yet. No doubt the memory would fade in time. The nights were the worst. Often she was afraid to fall asleep in case the nightmares came. And they did.

Her father looked up and smiled. 'Had a good day?'

'Yes. We're taking on someone else to help with the shop and the bookings have been pouring in today.'

'I knew you'd make a go of it.' Her father didn't try to hide his pride in her achievement.

'Well, most of it is due to Pete. He's turning out to be an astute businessman. And that's what I'd like to talk to both of you about. I want to do something special for him, so I'm going to give him a 40 per cent share in the business.'

'That's very generous, and I do approve,' her father said, 'but wouldn't 25 per cent be enough?'

'No.' Kate was adamant. 'Pete would have been left with nothing if things hadn't worked out so well before Christmas. I know that isn't going to happen again,' she added quickly, 'but I want to give him security. He deserves it.'

Bill's face clouded at the mention of Derek Howard. 'You're right of course, and it's your decision.'

'I think it's a fitting way to thank him for his prompt action in going to James when you didn't come back,' Rose said. 'If the business thrives he'll be set up for life.'

'That's what I want, Mum. Would you draft out an agreement for me and I'll take it to a solicitor tomorrow?

Now I must get ready to go out. Beth has somehow managed to get more tickets to see the Shadows. They're at Hammersmith again.'

The cinema being used for the concert was packed with loud teenagers, and when the performance began the noise was even worse. Kate watched Beth's animated face and felt like crying. That animal Derek Howard had done something to her inside. She should be on her feet shouting and cheering like everyone else . . .

'Aren't they great!' Beth sat down as the group left the stage, then she took Kate's hand. 'Are you all right?'

'I'm fine and really enjoying it. I'm just not as noisy as you,' she teased, as her earlier gloom vanished when Beth punched her arm playfully. 'It's the interval, so let's see if we can fight our way towards the ice-cream.'

'Good idea.' Beth started to carve her way through the jostling crowd.

Kate laughed; her friend might be small, but that didn't stop her pushing and shoving.

They bought the ice-cream and returned to their seats.

Beth looked anxiously at Kate. 'Are you really all right? I thought a noisy night out would do you good.'

'I'm struggling, Beth,' Kate admitted. 'I keep waking up in the night drenched in sweat and crying out in panic. Mum and Dad are always beside the bed, trying to calm me. I'm putting them through hell and I'm so ashamed of myself.'

'You mustn't feel like that.' Beth gave her arm a friendly squeeze. 'They love you and understand. You'll get over it in time.'

'Of course I shall.' Kate smiled. That was enough

gloomy talk; they were here to enjoy themselves. Beth had gone to a lot of trouble to arrange this night out for her, and she damned well wasn't going to spoil it! Normally she hated noise, but now she welcomed it.

Two weeks into the New Year and Jon was feeling restless and couldn't work out why. Would he ever settle down, he wondered. He'd thought that he would by marrying Jane, but when it came to it he'd realized that the wanderlust in him was too strong. It would take something, or someone, special to keep him at home. That proved he couldn't have loved Jane enough. He'd had a talk today with Andrew Stevenson, and with the continued unrest in Algeria they'd decided that he should go out there next month. It looked as if General de Gaulle hadn't been able to resolve the conflict, as the country tried to decide whether to secede from France or to remain integrated. It should be a lively assignment.

He picked up the photograph Eddie had given him for Christmas. Kate Freeman had caught the boy as he'd laughed up at her, and it was an excellent picture. Ed had asked for a photograph of him, so he'd promised to have one taken before he left for Algeria.

He replaced the picture on his bedside table. Might as well have Kate Freeman take the photo, as that would please Eddie even more. Mrs Green had told him where the shop was, so he grabbed his coat and hurried out, closing the door of his flat with a thud. It wouldn't shut if you didn't give it a real tug.

A bus to Kensington arrived just as he reached the stop and he jumped on. There was something troubling him about that beautiful woman, yet he couldn't for the life of him decide what it was. She appeared to have everything in the world going for her, but . . .

He paid his fare and stared out of the window. Perhaps seeing her one more time would solve the mystery of Kate Freeman.

There was a young girl in the shop, and she gave him a welcoming smile. 'Good afternoon, sir.'

'I'd like a portrait of myself. Could it be done today? Right now if possible?'

'I'll find out. I only started here this week and I don't know how things work yet. Excuse me, sir.' She disappeared into the back of the shop.

He walked around looking at the many photographs lining the walls. They really were excellent. He'd heard the story about Andrew Stevenson's treatment of her – the man had been a fool to lose her.

'I can do the portrait for you now, sir.'

Jon turned from gazing at a stunning photo of trees with the sun filtering through the branches with misty fingers. The young man standing beside him was tall and had a bright smile on his face.

'Thank you,' he said. 'Is Kate Freeman around?'

'She isn't here at the moment. My name's Pete and I do most of the studio work, but if you'd rather have Miss Freeman take the pictures, then I'll make an appointment for you.'

'No, that isn't necessary. Did you take any of these?' Jon swept his hand around the room.

'Most of them are Miss Freeman's work, but four are mine. The one you were looking at for instance.'

'Really.' Jon regarded him with renewed interest. 'I think it's stunning.'

Pete smiled, a touch of shyness surfacing at the compliment. 'Thank you, I've had an excellent teacher in Miss Freeman, and I was lucky with the light.'

They were about to go to the studio when the shop door opened and Kate came in, followed by five others.

Rose smiled when she saw him. 'Hello, Jon, let me introduce you to everyone. This is my husband, Bill, my son, James, my sister Annie and her husband, Reid.'

'You'd better put the kettle on, Susan,' Pete said.

'Don't bother with that,' Bill said, as he and James held up bottles of champagne. 'We're going to have a celebration.'

Pete was wide-eyed with amusement. Then his expression turned to astonishment as a taxi drew up and his parents got out and came into the shop. He rushed forward to greet them. 'What are you doing here?'

'Mr Freeman sent a taxi for us,' his father told him.

Pete spun round and looked at Kate. 'What's going on?'

'You'll see in a moment. Susan, there's a box of glasses in my car, would you get them for me, please?'

Jon watched the proceedings with something akin to pain. What must it feel like to belong to a close-knit family like this? The security and outpouring of love was something he had never known – would never know, and the loneliness of his life hit him with force. He didn't belong here!

'I can see you're busy,' he told Pete. 'I'll come another time.'

'No.' Rose touched his arm. 'Stay and enjoy this moment with us.'

'I'll take your photos now,' Pete told him.

'I'm sure Mr Devlin won't mind waiting a while.' Kate stood next to Pete and smiled at his parents. 'Thank you for coming, Mr and Mrs Sheldon; we wanted you to be here.'

The couple looked rather overwhelmed, and Jon knew exactly how they felt. He could handle riots, strife, war and flying bullets, but finding himself in the middle of the Freeman family was something quite out of his experience.

The young girl came back with the glasses. James lined them up on the counter, popped the champagne corks and filled the glasses. Then Bill and Reid passed them around.

As Jon gazed at the bubbling liquid, he wondered what the devil he was doing here. This wasn't anything to do with him, but he'd been included without a second thought.

'Quiet everyone,' James said, calling them to order. 'Kate has something to say and a presentation to make.'

Holding a large envelope in her hand, she moved to stand beside her friend. 'Pete, you took a big chance when you left the *World Explorer* to stay with me, and by your hard work and enthusiasm this shop is turning into a good business.' She paused. 'We're also very grateful to you for going to James so quickly before Christmas, and staying with Mum and Dad through that dreadful time. I know your family rely on your salary, and it has worried me very much to realize that you didn't have any job security should things have turned out differently.

My family would have looked after you of course, but I wanted to do something more for you.'

She handed him the envelope and kissed his cheek. 'Welcome, partner.'

Jon was too busy trying to make sense of Kate's words to notice Pete's reaction. She was talking as if she could have died and left the boy high and dry, but that didn't make sense: she was in perfect health, as far as he could see. He frowned and turned his attention back to the boy, who was nearly in tears as he looked at the document.

Bill raised his glass. 'Let's drink to Pete and wish him every success in the future.'

Jon sipped his champagne and found Reid standing beside him. 'What's this all about?' Jon asked.

'Kate's given Pete a 40 per cent share in the business.'

'But he's so young!'

'He'll be twenty this year and has a good business head on his shoulders. Kate wanted to make him secure for the future.'

Jon took another mouthful of his drink. 'Well, she's certainly done that, but why?' He never received an answer, because Reid moved away.

Pete recovered his composure and began to speak, his voice husky with emotion. 'I couldn't believe my luck when I was ordered to be Kate's assistant at the paper. She taught me with such patience and didn't laugh when I told her I wanted to be a photographer like her. In fact she gave me a camera and encouraged me to go out to take pictures. I had no hesitation in coming with her when she left the paper. She's often joked with me and called me her partner, but I never expected anything like this.' His voice broke, and he paused to give Kate an affectionate smile. 'I'll work hard for the success of our business. Especially now that I really am your partner!'

Laughter and a round of applause followed this last remark, as the glasses were refilled.

Kate came over to Jon and held out her hand. 'Hello. Pete said you've come for a portrait?'

'It's for Eddie,' he told her, as Pete joined them.

'Is that the little boy at the home?' Pete asked.

'Yes.' Kate gave a fond smile.

'Why don't you have one taken together, then?' Pete urged. 'I'm sure Eddie would love a picture of you both.'

'What a good idea.' Jon took hold of Kate's arm, and they followed Pete into the studio, where all the portraits were taken.

He arranged them sitting side by side. 'Put your arm around Kate's shoulder, Mr Devlin.'

He did as ordered and said quietly to Kate, 'Smile for Eddie.'

She did so while the pictures were being taken. When the photography was finished, he stood up, holding out his hand to help her from the chair. What he saw in her eyes in that unguarded moment rocked him back on his heels. It was an emotion he'd seen many times in his line of work.

Kate Freeman was traumatized. Something had happened to her, or someone had hurt her. What was it? He couldn't ask, but he damned well wished he knew.

16

'Have you seen these?' Bill slapped two papers on to the garden table. 'What's our daughter up to? Why's she writing about who's sleeping with whom, and scandals like that? She doesn't need this kind of money.' He gave a weary sigh, sat down and lifted his face to the warm spring sunshine. 'I don't understand what she's doing, Rose.'

She studied her husband's worried face. He was finding it difficult to understand what Kate was going through. 'She's coping with the horror of the abduction in the only way she knows. Give her time, Bill.'

He sat up and frowned. 'What do you mean? That happened three months ago, and she didn't seem terribly distressed once she was released.'

'She disguises it well, but I understand the turmoil she's experiencing.'

Bill's expression softened. 'Yes, you would. How long did it take you to come to terms with the attack on you?'

Rose looked thoughtful. 'I don't think I really did until I married you. As you know, I was only fourteen when I was raped. I was ashamed of myself and somehow felt that it was my fault. It wouldn't have happened if I hadn't walked through the park at that time of the evening – I should have fought harder . . . You know, all things like that. I felt guilty and I believe Kate is suffering in the same way.'

He was leaning forward in his seat. 'But the situation she found herself in was completely different from yours. She assured us that she wasn't raped, and I believe her. She's never lied to us, Rose. Has she talked to you? Do you have any idea what she's struggling with?'

Rose was well aware that Kate hadn't lied to them, but she hadn't told them the whole truth either. Whatever had really gone on in that room, their daughter was keeping to herself. 'She hasn't discussed it with me yet, but she will when she's ready. From her attitude and a few unguarded remarks, I'm pretty sure she believes she's a coward.'

He groaned. 'That isn't right; anyone would have been terrified. But surely reporting and photographing every scandal she can find is not the way to deal with this.'

'No, it isn't, but we must leave her to find that out in her own time.'

'Hi.' Kate breezed into the garden and sat next to her father. 'What a gorgeous day.'

'You've finished early,' Rose said.

'It's Susan's birthday, so Pete and I are taking her out for a treat.' Kate's grin was amused. 'She's turning out to be more than Pete's assistant. I think they're rather attracted to each other.'

'Are you going to the pictures?' Bill gave his daughter a thoughtful look.

Kate helped herself to a glass of home-made lemonade from the jug on the table. 'No, we're going to see one of those new groups. Pete says they're great.'

'If Pete's dating Susan, won't you be in the way?' her father asked.

'This is my treat, so I'll stay with them for a while and

then come home. Beth and Steve are coming as well.'

'Isn't it time you found yourself a boyfriend?' Bill asked hopefully.

'I don't want one at the moment. I'm too busy.' She dismissed the suggestion with a shrug.

'Doing things like this?' He pointed to the papers on the table, not hiding his distaste.

Kate picked up an evening paper. 'I'm writing my own articles now as well.'

'But why are you writing mindless gossip pieces? You've never been interested in that side of journalism. There must be plenty of worth while stories to photograph and write about. Are you proud of this?' Bill asked.

She bent down to stroke a neighbour's cat that had come to wind itself round her legs, begging for a fuss. She ran her hand along its back, scratching behind its ears as it rumbled with pleasure. Rose recognized the stubborn set of her daughter's mouth and knew she didn't want to answer that question. It wasn't often you saw this in Kate these days, but it had happened quite a lot when she'd been younger.

'Answer me,' her father prompted.

She sat back again and stared across the garden. 'No, Dad, I'm not proud of the work I'm doing, but it pays well and it's helping to expand the business.'

Bill sighed, perplexed. 'You used to have such high standards. I know how much you wanted to work for the *World Explorer* and the respect you have for its lack of sensationalism. That was important to you once. And you're leaving Pete to take care of the shop. You only go there when there's too much work for him to handle.'

'Pete doesn't need me there all the time. If he did, he'd

tell me. The success of the business is very important to him – and to me!' She gave him an anguished glance. 'I don't want to argue with you, Dad. I'm doing the best I can.'

He leant forward and took her hands in his. 'I'm worried; this just isn't you. From the time you could walk you've had a love of people. Many times I've watched you help them in a loving and understanding way. These people you're writing about have made their own problems. You're wasting your talent, darling.'

Kate looked down at their clasped hands, released her grip and shook her head. 'I don't know what all the fuss is about. I'm twenty-four years old now, so surely I'm allowed to live my own life?'

Bill started as if he'd been stung and sat back, his expression one of sadness. 'Of course you are. I'm only concerned about you, Kate.'

She stood up calmly. 'I don't know what you're worrying about; I'm perfectly all right. Now I must change, please excuse me.'

Rose watched her walk away. She was obviously bottling up strong feelings, and it was even making her snap at her father. That was something she'd never done in her life. 'We must try not to worry. She'll see sense eventually.'

'I hope to God you're right, Rose.' Bill tossed the papers aside in disgust. 'I've never heard her speak like that before. She's always been such a caring girl, but this abduction has changed her.'

Rose stood up and kissed her husband on the top of his head. 'She's fighting inner demons and we must be patient. Howard has been charged with kidnapping and attempted murder, so more happened in that room than she's told us, but she's our daughter, darling, and she'll come through this.'

The noise was deafening and Kate covered her ears. This was even noisier than the concert she'd been to with Beth. The more racket the audience made, the louder the band seemed to play. She liked Elvis, the Everly Brothers and bands like the Shadows, but that was when she played them at home on her Dansette record player, and she could control the volume. She had inherited her mother's aversion to loud noises; she wished she'd inherited more of her strength of character!

But even the ear-splitting noise couldn't drive out the memory of that spat with her father. She shouldn't have snapped like that, but she had to keep herself busy every minute of the day and was taking any commission that came her way. It wasn't work she liked, but it gave her little time to think. She had been irritated at the censure. Still, she had been in the wrong – again – and would apologize the moment she saw him. She turned her attention back to the seething throng of dancers.

Pete, Susan, Beth and Steve were thoroughly enjoying themselves, as was everyone else. Kate glanced at her watch: another half an hour and she would leave them to it. Her twenty-fourth birthday had been last month and she was too old for this. She fanned herself with her hand; it was unusually warm for the beginning of April and it was hot in here.

She was just about to say she was leaving when she saw Pete rush over to greet a young man who'd walked in. He was now being dragged towards her.

'Kate!' Pete yelled. 'This is my cousin Jim.'

The family connection was obvious, but Jim was several years older than Pete. She smiled, shook hands, and mercifully at that moment the music stopped.

'Hello,' Jim said. 'The famous Kate. Pete never stops talking about you and your shop. Would you like to go somewhere quieter and have a drink?'

He certainly didn't waste any time, she thought, noticing the gleam of appreciation in his eyes. He was a presentable man, but since the abduction she'd become wary of being alone with anyone she didn't know. 'I was thinking of going home,' she told him.

'Just one quick drink in the pub across the road.' He glanced at the stage. 'I'd like to leave before they get going again.'

Kate laughed at the expression on his face, and, after waving farewell to the others, they left just as the noise started.

The pub was crowded, but Jim found her a seat and went to fight his way to the bar. While he was away, she had to repulse more than one attempt to chat her up.

'Phew!' Jim plonked a pint of beer and the lemonade she'd asked for on the table. 'That was worse than a rugby scrum.'

He was big enough to play that game, she thought, as her insides heaved, remembering what another large man had planned for her. Would this fear never leave her?

He squeezed in next to her and gave an engaging smile. 'I know a lot about you, but you don't know anything about me. I'd better introduce myself properly. My name's Jim Sheldon and I'm Pete's cousin, as he told you. I'm twenty-two and work in a factory as a toolmaker. I'm not married and I don't have a girlfriend at the moment.' He sipped his beer, and when he put down the glass the corners of his mouth twitched in amusement. 'And I'm considered quite respectable.'

'By whom?' she asked.

'Oh, just about everyone.' He wiggled his eyebrows. 'I hope you're impressed?'

His light-hearted banter made her laugh. 'Does it matter what I think?'

'It does, because I want to persuade you to come to the pictures with me tomorrow evening.'

He was Pete's cousin, so . . . She remembered her father's remark about her having a boyfriend. He'd been angry with her for the kind of work she was doing, and she couldn't remember when he'd ever been like that with her. It had hurt dreadfully . . . and her reaction had been disgraceful. 'What's on?'

'There's that creepy film *Psycho*. I've seen it once, but if you'd like to go . . .'

'No, thank you!' Kate exclaimed in horror. 'I've heard about that and I definitely don't want to see it.'

'Hmm.' Jim looked thoughtful. 'Well, there's *Spartacus* on at the Odeon, Leicester Square.'

'That's better. I wouldn't mind seeing that one.'

'Does that mean you'll come?' he asked.

Why not, she decided. It was no good shutting herself away from life; she had to start living normally again, if only to put her parents' minds at rest. 'I'll meet you outside. What time?'

'Can you make it six o'clock and we can have a bite to eat before the show?'

'That sounds nice.' She finished her drink and stood up. 'See you tomorrow, then.'

It was three o'clock in the morning, and Kate was still wide awake. She was watching a finger of moonlight casting a river of silver across the ceiling. The conversation she'd had with her father was still worrying her. Her parents were obviously concerned about her, and she knew they had every right to be; she was concerned about herself. Of late she'd become disgusted with her aimless pursuit of a story – any story. She wasn't a journalist, for heaven's sake, she was a photographer, and her father was right when he said she was wasting her talent. Where had her zeal gone, her dream to give something back to society for all the good she had in her life?

She rolled over and thumped her pillows into shape, and, as she did, her attention became focused on the photograph by her bedside. Eddie's little face was laughing at her, and she reached out to touch it tenderly. Her twice-weekly visits to Wilkins House were always a joy. Since her pictures and article had appeared in the news, conditions had improved considerably for the children in both homes, but that was the only positive thing she'd done in months.

She heard a sound downstairs and swung her legs out of bed. Her mother was a poor sleeper and was probably making tea. She headed for the kitchen.

'Ah, I thought I smelt tea.'

'Can't you sleep either?' her mother asked, as she walked in.

'Afraid not.' Kate sat down and watched her mother warming the pot. 'I hope I didn't wake you.'

When the tea was ready, Rose poured two cups and handed one to her daughter. 'Your nightmares aren't so frequent now.'

Kate sipped the hot brew and waited until her mother was sitting. Her terrible nightmares were fading, thank goodness. 'I'm sorry I've been worrying you and Dad. That's the last thing in the world I want to do.'

'We understand that. But it's frustrating watching you act out of character. I know you've got to work it out for yourself, but it would help if you could talk about it.'

She knew well enough that her parents had given her room to sort herself out, but she wasn't making a very good job of it. She was still crying out in the night and waking up her parents. She'd send them back to bed, then bury her head in the pillow and sob quietly. She really was quite pathetic.

'I'm so *angry* with Derek Howard and myself.' The words began to tumble out. 'I'm lost, Mum, and I don't know how to find my way back. Nothing seems important any more. I think this all started when I left my job with the paper – it was a bitter disappointment – and then the abduction . . .'

'We know you've given the police the full story but you've never told us what really happened.' Rose poured them both another cup of tea.

'I can't talk about it. I'm so bloody furious!'

Rose looked at her thoughtfully. 'A very wise lady once told me that you must be the master of your anger and not let it control you, then you can put it to good use.'

'Wise words,' Kate agreed. 'But how do you put it into practice?'

'That's what I used to wonder as I fought my way through the early years of my life.'

'You learned, though.' Kate had enormous respect for her mother. She was still a lovely woman, and the wisdom gained through many harsh struggles shone in her dark eyes.

'It took me years, and it was only the strong but gentle nature of your father that finally brought me to my senses.'

'I hope I meet someone like him one day.'

'You will, Kate, but be prepared to wait, don't settle for second best. Annie never considered marrying until she met Reid during the war, and she was in her early thirties then, so you've got plenty of time.'

'I'm in no rush. In the meantime I'll try to master my anger.' Kate gave a helpless shrug.

'Derek Howard's trial is next month,' Rose pointed out. 'That isn't going to be easy for you but once it's over you'll probably feel better.'

'I hope you're right. That's hanging over me like the sword of Damocles.'

'I'll be beside you the whole way through, and so will your father. You know that we love you very much?'

Kate gave her mother a grateful smile, tears very close to the surface. 'What would I do without you both?'

'You'd manage.' Rose gave her daughter a studied look. 'I believe you've convinced yourself that you're a weakling. You are not!'

Her head came up in surprise. She'd been under the impression that she was hiding her disgust about herself quite well. 'That's very perceptive of you, Mum. But you're wrong. Not only am I a mental weakling, but I'm also a coward.'

Rose sat back with a faint smile on her face. 'Your character has always been a mixture of my determination and fire, tempered by your father's gentleness and quiet strength. The last thing you are is a coward, but you'll have to discover that for yourself.'

'Have you seen the papers, Kate?' Pete rushed up to her as soon as she walked in the shop. She'd managed to sleep last night for a while after her talk with her mother, but she felt just as troubled this morning. 'I overslept and didn't have time for anything this morning.' She took the newspaper he was waving around excitedly. It was today's date – Thursday, 13 April – and the headline read MAN IN SPACE. She sat down and read the story with a mounting sense of awe. What an achievement!

'A Russian, Yuri Gagarin,' Pete pointed out, looking over her shoulder. 'I'll bet the view of the earth from up there is fantastic.'

'Absolutely breathtaking, I expect.' As Kate thought about it, her mind lifted away from the earthly doubts and fears. If you could view the earth from a great height, it must make the wars, heartaches and struggles seem very small in comparison with the vastness of space. For the first time in nearly four months, Kate began to feel the grip of confusion ease a very little bit. But the anger still remained. She hoped Howard was put away for the rest of his life! However, she'd been wrong to keep all the hurt inside and let it fester. Instead of sitting down and talking about it with her parents or James, she'd been behaving like an idiot! She'd tried to speak to her mother several times but somehow the words just wouldn't come. Even last night, although she had tried very hard to get the words out, she had kept the real horror of that room to herself.

'Are you all right?' Pete bent down in front of her. 'You look upset.'

She smiled at him. There would be a time to talk about it, but it wasn't now. Perhaps it would be easier after the trial. 'I'm fine. Let's have a cup of tea and toast Yuri Gagarin's flight, shall we?'

'Susan's already put the kettle on.' Pete stood up, still with a concerned frown on his face. 'Is the thought of the trial next month playing on your mind?'

Kate grimaced. 'I must admit I'll be glad when it's over.'

'Try not to worry.' He sounded very mature now. 'We'll all be there for you. No one's going to let that man harm you again.'

'I know, but it's going to be an ordeal.'

17

When Kate met Jim that evening the talk was all about the first man in space. The café they went to was a buzz of excited chatter, and later, at the Odeon in Leicester Square, there was a special newsreel. Once the film started she sat back and watched the epic *Spartacus*. The outside world faded as she became completely absorbed in the story, and she didn't even protest when Jim put his arm around her.

When they came out, it was drizzling and Jim hurried her across the road. 'Let's have a drink.'

She agreed readily enough. It had been a pleasant evening, and she was not eager for it to end just yet. She became edgy when night fell, and welcomed the bright lights of town and the sound of people enjoying themselves. The worst time for her was the middle of the night, when the house was still. She would wake suddenly with a cry, believing she was back in that awful room and feeling that animal's hands on her . . .

She drew in several deep breaths to try to calm her racing heart. Was she ever going to be able to put this nightmare behind her? She was still sleeping with the bedside light on and was deeply ashamed of herself.

'What would you like?' Jim asked, when they were in the pub.

'An orange juice, please.'

He gave her a disgusted glance. 'Come on, Kate, have a sherry or something like that. I can afford it.'

'Not sherry, get me something light.'

'Such as?'

'I'll leave it to you.' Kate watched a bad-tempered frown cross his face, and she sighed inwardly. 'Oh, just get me a lemonade.'

While he was at the bar, a sense of unease crept over her. She'd caught a brief glimpse of something in Jim she hadn't noticed before. She was normally good at sizing people up, but she hadn't been paying attention lately.

When Jim returned, the teasing smile was back in place. 'I asked the barman what he thought I should get you, and he said beer if you were common, and white wine if you were posh. I told him you were posh.'

Kate fixed her gaze on him and demanded, 'I am what?'

'Posh.' He sat down and pushed a glass towards her. 'So I got you a white wine.'

'I'm not posh!' She was thoroughly irritated now.

He laughed as if it were a huge joke. 'Of course you are. Your family's loaded.'

The alarm bells were really clanging now, and Kate studied him carefully, trying to delve beneath the affable façade – for she was sure that was all it was. Why the devil hadn't she noticed it before? 'Is that why you asked me out?'

'No, you're beautiful as well, which is a bonus.' The look he gave her was sly. 'Though I wouldn't mind a car like the one you've just bought Pete.'

That was breaking point for Kate. She surged to her

feet, knocking the table so that the drinks sloshed over. 'Pete's car is for our business.'

She pushed her way through the crowded bar and made it to the street before he caught up with her and took her arm.

'I didn't mean it, Kate. I was only teasing. I thought you'd take it as a joke.'

The drizzle had turned to a steady downpour now, and the cool rain ran down her face as she looked at him. That remark about her beauty being a bonus infuriated her. He was a man on the make. She should have guessed that as soon as she'd spoken to him for a while. She was a blasted idiot.

He tugged her arm. 'Come back and finish your drink; we're getting soaked out here.'

Without speaking, Kate shook herself free, removed a couple of pound notes from her purse and shoved them into his hand. 'I wouldn't want you to be out of pocket for the evening.'

'Kate!' he called as she walked away.

She didn't turn round. Perhaps she was being oversensitive, but she wasn't going to put up with anything like this. She felt utterly miserable. This wasn't the first time she'd been asked out because her family were considered rich.

By the time she reached her car her self-esteem had dropped another notch. She got in, locked the door and wiped her face with a handkerchief. She wasn't some spoilt rich kid; she and James hadn't been brought up like that. At the thought of her brother, Kate started the engine and headed for Richmond. It was late, but James wouldn't mind.

She drove past her home and on towards Richmond Green. James had bought himself a beautiful house there, and she loved this elegant area. Although it was nearly midnight, the downstairs lights were still on. Kate had her own key to his house, but didn't use it in case he was entertaining. She knocked on the door.

'Kate!' he exclaimed when he saw her. 'What are you doing here at this time of night? Is anything wrong?'

'I wondered if I could talk to you.'

'Of course.' He ushered her into the lounge. 'Why didn't you use your key?'

She glanced around the room and, seeing he was alone, grinned. 'I thought you might have company.'

He pulled a face. 'I don't bring girlfriends here, Kate. It gives them ideas.'

I'll bet it does, she thought. One look at this place and the only thing on their minds would be marriage. Not only was her brother a successful businessman, he was also a very handsome man.

'Do you want a drink?' he asked, holding up the brandy decanter. When she shook her head, he poured himself one and sat down. 'What's on your mind?'

She explained about Jim and how she'd misjudged him at first. Because he'd been Pete's cousin she'd taken him at face value, and that was something she didn't usually do. Her sigh was heartfelt. 'I don't know what's happened to me, James. I seem to be looking for ulterior motives all the time, and I don't think I can cope any more.'

James sipped his drink, studying his sister intently, then he put the glass down. 'Did Howard sexually assault you?'

The sudden shift in the conversation startled Kate. 'I've told you he didn't.'

'I don't believe you. I think you concocted that story to save Mum and Dad more anguish,' he told her bluntly.

'I didn't come here to talk about this.' She started to stand up, but he stopped her.

'All right, Kate, but you realize this is all going to come out at the trial, don't you?'

'I know.' She settled back in the chair again and dipped her head. 'I'm dreading it.'

'So am I, because before it starts I've got to tell Mum and Dad something they don't know.'

She looked up quickly at the weary tone in her brother's voice. 'Oh, what's that?'

'When Howard sent me those photographs of you, there was something else in the envelope. A demand that all charges against him be dropped . . . and a ransom of a million pounds.'

'That's preposterous!' Her mouth opened in disbelief. 'Why didn't you tell Mum and Dad?'

James leant forward, elbows on knees. 'Because if I had, Dad would have frantically tried to scrape the money together, and I believe the stress would have been too much for him.'

Tears welled up in her eyes. 'You mean it could have killed him?'

'Yes.'

'Oh, God.' She'd always loved and respected her brother, and her heart ached for him. While she'd been locked in that room, she'd been afraid of the strain this was putting on their parents, but she'd been removed from the problem by her isolation. James hadn't! 'What were you going to do?'

'Try to raise the money myself.' He took a large swig of brandy. 'People think that because we own Grant Phillips we have a great deal of money floating around, but that isn't the case. The Freemans' wealth is tied up in the business.'

Kate knew this, so she nodded and waited for her brother to continue.

'I immediately set about seeing how much this house and all my possessions would raise. Then I contacted the bank for a massive loan . . .'

Kate's sharp intake of breath stopped him. 'You'd have beggared yourself trying to raise that kind of money.'

'It would have been worth it to get you back safe and sound.' He gave her a wry smile. 'You were a *weird* kid, but I've always loved you dearly.'

He'd called her that when she'd been little, and the tears flowed unheeded down her cheeks. What unselfish love. 'But you'd never have been able to raise a million pounds.'

'No, I wouldn't, but I was hoping I could negotiate a more reasonable ransom with Howard.'

'This will come out at the trial.' Her insides cramped at the thought. It was going to be even more of an ordeal than she'd imagined. 'You haven't got much time to tell Mum and Dad.'

'I wanted to after you were released, but you haven't been yourself, and they've been worrying about you. I didn't want to upset them any more. Sort yourself out, Kate,' he added gently. 'The trial is only three weeks away.'

'I will, I'll spend more time at the shop. I won't cause Mum, Dad or you any more worry.' She looked at her brother in anguish. 'I'm *so* sorry.'

'None of this is your fault,' James assured her. 'Howard's responsible, and I'll see he pays for it. But I'm worried about Dad's health. If he saw you involving yourself in something worth while – acting more like your usual caring self – then I'm sure he would feel easier. Couldn't you do another article on the orphans?'

'That's an excellent idea,' she agreed, a bit of her old enthusiasm springing into life. 'I could show how much the children long to belong to a family, and perhaps it would make couples come forward ready to adopt.'

Some of the worry eased from James's face, and he smiled affectionately at her. 'Go for it, Kate!'

It had been a good idea talking to James last night, Kate thought as she drove to Kensington the next day. Much to her surprise she'd slept well and had even reached out and switched off the bedside light. She knew she had a long way to go yet, but that had been a small step in the right direction. Although her date with Jim had ended badly, it had helped to clear her mind of some of the confusion and doubt. The kind of mood she was in at the moment made her want to argue with anyone, even her father. She was dreadfully sorry for that and knew she was causing her parents a lot of worry. Perhaps it would be better if she moved out for a while until she came to terms with the horror Derek Howard had put her through. The idea of leaving her home was not a welcome one, but she couldn't go on like this. She needed to be alone without someone watching her every mood. The play-acting was becoming difficult to maintain. She was still ashamed of the abject terror she'd experienced and her lack of action to try to free herself.

After parking the car, she walked into the shop, and, finding Pete and Susan busy with customers, went out to the back and put the kettle on.

'Lovely, just what I could do with,' Pete told her as he walked into the room. She handed him a cup of tea. He sat down and stretched out his long legs. 'As soon as I've finished this I must run. I've got a wedding at Caxton Hall at eleven and another at two.'

'How busy are you?' Kate perched on the end of the table.

'Rushed off my feet. It's the wedding season and bookings are pouring in.' He drained his cup and stood up. 'We need another photographer, Kate, because if it wasn't for the car you bought me, I'd never be able to manage.'

'Will I do?'

He'd been making for the door but stopped and spun back to face her. 'Are you serious?' He beamed with pleasure when she nodded. 'Ah, that's wonderful. I've missed working with you.'

'I'm sorry I've been so bloody difficult, Pete.' She'd been putting everyone under unnecessary pressure, all because of one man – Derek Howard – and by doing that he was still getting his revenge. Well, it wasn't going to continue. She would not allow him to win!

A measure of strength and determination began to surge back into her. After the trial she *was* going to put it all behind her.

'Grab your camera,' Pete told her. 'I can do with your help at once.'

They went in Pete's car, and she couldn't help noticing again how changed he was. The boy Andrew Stevenson had given her as an assistant because he didn't know what to do with him had turned out to be a treasure. There wasn't a vestige of the timid, awkward youth left. He was tall, confident and one hell of a photographer. One day he was going to be better than her – if he wasn't already. The time she'd spent teaching him had been one of the best things she'd ever done. And she'd gained a stalwart friend and business partner in the process.

'I wish I'd known you had a date with Jim,' he said, casting her a quick glance while they waited at traffic lights.

So his cousin hadn't wasted time telling him about last night.

'He's a nice-enough bloke, but there's only one thing in this world he wants, and that's money, or someone who has money.'

'I realized that too late,' Kate admitted, 'but I was too harsh with him. I'm looking for ulterior motives in a lot of people these days.'

'You were quite right to put him in his place.' He continued driving as the lights turned green. 'I believe he only turned up at Susan's party so he could meet you. I should have warned you about him.'

'There wasn't any harm done.' Kate smiled at him. 'He said you'd told him all about me.'

'The liar!' Pete exploded. 'When he found out who I was working for, he went and did a lot of research into your family. He must have thought that as he was my cousin he might be in with a chance.'

'Well, he wasn't.'

'That's a relief.' Pete shook with silent laughter. 'He said you'd sussed him out much more quickly than most girls, and that was a shame, he told me, because he really liked you.'

They reached the Register Office just as the wedding guests were arriving, and from then on there wasn't time to talk.

The day swept by in a flurry of activity. Kate enjoyed working with Pete again, and they returned to the shop about four thirty – tired but pleased with the work they'd done.

Before walking in the shop, Kate glanced up at the flat above the shop. It had been empty for weeks, and there was still no sign of a tenant. She handed her camera and bag to Pete. 'Start on the developing – I won't be long.' Then she headed for the estate agents'.

Half an hour later she was back with the keys to the flat in her hand. 'I've rented the flat above the shop,' she told Pete and Susan. 'I'm going to live there.'

'You're leaving home?' Pete's eyes were wide with surprise.

Kate watched Susan hurry off to serve a customer and turned to Pete. 'I'm worrying the life out of my parents. I need to be on my own for a while.' Her laugh was dry and devoid of humour. 'I never thought I'd say that, but the nearer the trial gets, the more unbearable I become. I know everyone loves me and wants to help, but I feel stifled. I need some space to be myself.'

'What's the matter, Kate?' Pete asked gently.

'I'm frightened,' she admitted. 'Frightened of facing

Derek Howard again, and terrified about the things I'll have to reveal when I'm called to testify.'

'We'll all be supporting you, but if it makes you feel better, then go ahead and move in upstairs.' He gave her an understanding smile. 'Susan and I will help you make it comfortable.'

She felt her spirits rise and knew she was doing the right thing. Most women of her age were either married or out on their own, and it was time she became more independent. The kidnapping had made her realize that she mustn't reply on other people so much. She must become more self-sufficient, more able to stand on her own. Telling her parents was going to be hard, though.

When they closed the shop, she headed for Wilkins House to see Eddie before he went to bed. She stayed to read him a story, and then, as his eyes began to close, she tucked him up. This was a treat he loved, so after kissing his cheek she watched him fall asleep with a blissful smile on his face.

Kate stood up and gazed at the little boy with affection. This was the only time she felt at peace, and she came as often as she could now. As she turned to leave the room, she saw the photo of herself and Jon Devlin on the cupboard beside his bed. This was Eddie's most prized possession. She gave the boy another gentle kiss to see him through the night.

Her parents were clearing up after dinner when Kate arrived home.

'Do you want something to eat?' her mother asked.

'No, thanks, I had tea with the boys.' She gave her

father a silent hug to say that she was sorry for the way she'd snapped at him, and was relieved when he squeezed her shoulder to let her know he understood.

'Had a good day?' he asked.

'Very good.' Her smile was genuine as she remembered the fun it had been working with Pete again, and Eddie's little face in repose as he'd fallen asleep; it had been balm to her troubled soul.

She told them all about it as they sat at the kitchen table drinking tea, and the worry gradually eased from their expressions as she chatted away. Now she was going to hurt them again, but there was no putting it off. 'The flat above the shop is empty, so I've rented it. I'm going to move in there tomorrow.'

There was absolute silence for a few moments, and Kate cursed herself for telling them in that abrupt manner. When neither spoke, she gave them a beseeching look. 'I need to do this.'

Her mother recovered first. 'That will be handy for you, Kate. No more travelling back and forth.'

'What's it like?' Her father sounded falsely bright.

'Small but clean. There's one bedroom, lounge/diner, bathroom and a tiny kitchen, and it's already furnished.' She knew this was the last thing they'd expected, but they were doing their best to sound pleased for her. 'I could use some help with moving in the morning.'

'We'd love to help you settle in, wouldn't we, Rose?'

Her mother agreed and Kate knew she'd done the right thing to involve them. It would have been cruel to do otherwise. She loved them too much to do that.

*

Packing her things the next morning was painful, knowing she was leaving the home she'd lived in all her life. The tears were streaming down her face when her mother walked in.

'You don't have to do this,' Rose told her.

'Yes, I do, Mum.' She wiped her face and summoned up a smile. 'I need to be on my own.'

Rose sat on the edge of the bed. 'You'll always have a home here if you want it, but, for what it's worth, I believe you're doing the right thing. I'd feel exactly the same as you in this position. Don't hide yourself away, though, that won't solve your problems.'

'I don't intend to. I'll phone every day and come to lunch on Sundays.'

'Good.' Rose stood up. 'You'll get through this bad time, but you've got to do it in your own way, so having a place to call your own might help. We understand that, Kate.'

She kissed her mother for being so understanding, but if anyone knew about hard times, it was Rose Freeman.

18

Kate kept her word and over the next couple of weeks she found a measure of contentment. She had never liked being alone but now she welcomed the solitude. At night, in the privacy of her own home, she could rage or cry without distressing her parents, so that by the time the trial arrived she felt stronger, both mentally and physically.

She'd had to go through everything with the prosecuting barrister, and James, whose constant love and support was a blessing. Much to her relief, she'd managed quite well, but there was no use kidding herself, she was dreading it.

The night before the trial she packed her overnight bag and headed for Roehampton. She was going to need all the help and support her family could supply. This would be an ordeal for all of them, so they would band together and help each other, as they had always done in any difficult situation.

Her parents were delighted to see her, and both gave her a hug.

'Can I stay until the trial's over?' she asked.

'You don't have to ask,' her mother said. 'Your room's always there when you want it.'

'This house is empty without you and James,' her father said, sighing.

'How about putting your other wandering child up

for tonight?' James strode in with his bag. 'I'll take the spare room, as Kate's turned my old room into a darkroom.'

She'd planned this with James, and when she saw how pleased their parents were she nodded to her brother.

'Right, let's have a drink,' Bill said. They all trooped after him into the sitting room.

They had a brandy each, even Kate, who knew she was going to need it.

Rose sipped her drink and studied her children. 'You can tell us what this is all about now.'

James smiled ruefully. 'You don't miss a thing, do you, Mum?'

'I know you two well enough to guess when you're up to something, and there's more on your minds than keeping us company before the trial.'

James glanced anxiously at his father. 'You'd better have another drink, Dad, because we've got something to tell you.'

'We know you've been keeping secrets,' their father said. 'So you'd better start talking, because we don't want any unpleasant shocks at the trial.'

'Who's going to start?' Rose put her glass down and waited.

James glanced at Kate, and when she indicated that he should go first, he launched into the story of the ransom demand.

'My God!' Bill gasped. 'The man's mad. We'd never have been able to raise that kind of money. Why the blazes didn't you tell me, James? You shouldn't have tried to shoulder the burden on your own.'

'I thought I could handle it, but if I couldn't I'd have

come straight to you. I would never have put Kate's life at risk, you know that.'

'I should damned well hope not,' Bill exploded. 'You had no right to keep anything from me.'

Kate watched anxiously. She'd never seen her father lose his temper before, and she glimpsed the extent of his love for them both. It was humbling.

'James was trying to save you from more worry,' she told them. 'He was ready to give everything he owned and was hoping for a chance to negotiate, but Derek Howard had no intention of letting me live. He would have taken the money and then killed me. I suspect James realized that.'

'I did.' James swallowed his brandy in one mouthful. 'I was praying I could talk with Howard, and keep Kate alive until we could find her.'

Her father drew in a sharp breath. 'Tell us what really happened, Kate.'

She unburdened herself, knowing they would hear this during the trial, leaving nothing out, and by the time she'd finished she let out a deep sigh of relief. That had been difficult, but she *could* talk about it now without falling apart, and that gave her hope for the trial. If she could just hold her composure during her time in the witness box, then she might be able to put this whole thing behind her and start getting her life back together again. Her emotions were being tossed around like a piece of flotsam, and at times she felt as if she had no control over her life any more. How she longed for the calm, confident Kate Freeman of before to emerge from the turmoil.

Her mother handed her another small brandy and she sipped it gratefully.

Rose nodded at her husband. 'I think we've brought up a couple of children to be proud of, don't you agree, Bill?'

'I most certainly do.' He lifted his glass to James and Kate. 'Thanks for trying to shield us, but it wasn't necessary.'

She cast her brother a quick glance. Their father might say that, but he still looked drawn and ill. She knew James was just as worried as she was.

As Kate dressed the next morning, she was glad she'd taken trouble over her appearance. She'd chosen a classic suit in a burgundy so dark that it was almost black; this was teamed with black suede court shoes and a cream silk blouse. The effect was elegant in its simplicity.

She could hear voices downstairs, and gained comfort from the fact that she had much loving support. She headed for the kitchen. Reid and Annie had arrived and she hugged them, grateful to have them there.

James smiled in approval when he saw her. 'You look perfect.'

'So do you.' Her brother was wearing a beautifully cut suit in dark grey, with a tie almost the same colour as her outfit. She didn't miss the dark shadow of strain under his eyes, though, and knew that he was dreading this.

He touched her arm. 'Soon be over.'

She tensed at the thought of the next few days or weeks, or however long the trial took. Their barrister had warned them that they could expect some hostile questioning from the defence lawyers. No one was claiming that Howard was innocent, for he had been caught on his way up the stairs with a knife in his hand. After being told that, she knew he had been about to carry out his threat and kill her. Another ten minutes and rescue might have been impossible!

She knew she mustn't dwell on what might have been. She had to concentrate on seeing that Derek Howard was given a long prison sentence for his crimes.

A plate of eggs and bacon was put in front of her, and, when she hesitated, wondering if her stomach could take the food, her mother said firmly, 'Eat, Kate, it's going to be a long day.'

The food vanished from her plate, but she was hardly aware of eating it.

Because of the serious nature of the crime, the trial was being held at the Old Bailey. Her mother knew the building well and Kate followed her, not taking much notice of her surroundings. If Derek Howard had pleaded guilty, then this would have been less of an ordeal, but she knew that his lawyers were going to try for a lesser sentence than that for kidnapping and attempted murder, by showing that he was unbalanced at the time and had not been aware of his actions. That made her furious! He had known exactly what he was doing and it had been well planned.

They reached some seats in a corridor and her father gave her a reassuring smile. 'Sit here, Kate, while your mother finds out what is happening.'

'There will be a lot of hanging around,' her mother

explained. 'They've got to choose a jury and that might take a while. I'll see how they're getting on.'

Kate watched her mother walk along the corridor with her usual determined air. There were people hurrying along and in and out of the various doors, but they parted like the Red Sea to let Rose Freeman through.

'I wonder if we can get some coffee while we wait.' James stood up, and, as he wandered off, her father and Reid went with him.

The men were already restless with nothing to do, and she was left with her Aunt Annie. Her mother had run through the proceedings with her. She knew what to expect, and until she was called there wasn't anything she could do. Up to now she had not been greatly involved in the run-up to the trial. The hearing at the magistrates court had been brief, when it was decided that there was a case to answer. There would be a separate trial for the embezzlement. Grant Phillips was bringing that charge, and James had assured her that she wouldn't be needed for that.

Kate watched as Annie's hand rested over her tightly clasped ones. She looked up and grimaced. 'I'm so scared. I'm a coward, Aunt Annie.'

'Kate, we all have times when we're frightened, but that doesn't mean we're cowards.' She cradled Kate's hands in her own and smiled. 'You haven't anything to be ashamed of, sweetheart.'

Kate knew her aunt had parachuted into France during the war to find a man who was missing. She'd found him badly injured, and, although Annie had managed to get him back to England, he had died.

'Before I jumped out of the plane I was terrified, Kate,

but a strange thing happened as the order came to jump. My mind cleared, and I was completely calm and focused on the task of finding Jack Graham. That will happen to you when you go into the witness box. Waiting is the worst time.'

She prayed that would happen, yet she doubted it. Annie had extraordinary courage – but did *she*?

It was a wasted and anxious day for Kate. She wasn't called. James had been in court for quite a while, and her parents and Reid had been following the case carefully. Annie had sat with Kate all day, trying to take her mind off things by telling her about being in the WAAF during the war, and the antics she and Dora had got up to.

She was struck by the courage of everyone during the conflict. They had been perilous times, but they had laughed then, and still could. Her father had been a naval captain, Uncle Will in the Fleet Air Arm, Uncle Charlie in the Air Force as a mechanic, and Reid had been a Battle of Britain pilot. Her mother had risked her life in London during the Blitz, and Annie had gone behind enemy lines. All had been in grave danger, but they'd never hesitated to do what had to be done.

She lifted her head defiantly. She mustn't let them down!

It was ten o'clock the next morning when Kate was called to give evidence. Rose watched her daughter walk into the courtroom. She was wearing the same clothes as yesterday and looked composed and elegant as she went into the box, but she understood the turmoil that must be raging inside Kate. It was going to be terrible to stand in a public courtroom and tell everyone what that animal had done to her. Rose knew she would never have been able to do such a thing after the attack on her when she'd been a girl. She'd hidden the truth from almost everyone, and it had taken years before she'd been able to put the trauma behind her. She glanced at her husband sitting tensely beside her with his gaze fixed on his daughter.

As Kate answered the questions put to her by the prosecution lawyer in a clear steady voice, fury raged through her that their daughter had to face this ordeal. Her dark eyes glared at Derek Howard as he sat in the dock, and, as if sensing the scrutiny, he looked straight at her. Rose held his gaze, her black eyes leaving him in no doubt that he was going to suffer for his actions. He was the first one to break the contact, and he looked at the floor, appearing uneasy for the first time.

When questions came to an end, Kate took in a deep silent breath. That had been fairly easy; she'd known in advance what the prosecution lawyer wanted her to say, and he'd guided her carefully through it. But now for the cross-examination!

'Miss Freeman.' The defence barrister, Mr Holdsworth, came towards her with a smile on his face that didn't reach his eyes. 'Are you a virgin?'

'Objection!' The prosecution barrister, Charles Prendergast, was on his feet. 'Miss Freeman's private life is not relevant to this trial.'

'I disagree, my lord. I aim to show the court that, far from being the innocent victim, Miss Freeman was the instigator of this plot in order to get money from her family.'

Kate's head began to swim, and she gripped the witness box to steady herself. What was going on? The judge said something, but she didn't grasp it; the words sounded like a meaningless jumble.

'When did you meet Mr Howard?' Mr Holdsworth continued.

Kate fought for concentration. She looked towards the barrister. Should she answer? He nodded quickly at her. 'When he came to the shop just before Christmas.'

'Come now, Miss Freeman, remember you are under oath. You first met Mr Howard at a party given by Grant Phillips almost a year ago, didn't you?'

'No!'

He ignored her reply. 'You became lovers and decided that you needed money – lots of money – to give you a lavish lifestyle.'

'No!'

'And it was you who came up with the idea of a kidnapping – '

'No!'

'You deny it vehemently, Miss Freeman, but my client assures me it was your idea, and he only went ahead with it because he was besotted with you.'

'Then he's a liar!' Kate was so distressed by now that the courtroom had blurred around her. All she could focus on was the arrogant, unfeeling man who was accusing her of this crime. Wasn't this supposed to be Howard's trial? She was now the one in the dock, and her character was being torn to shreds.

'You knew your nasty little scheme had been uncovered when the police found your hiding place, so you concocted this ridiculous story against my client.'

'No, no!' Dear God, she was the one on trial now. This couldn't be happening; she must be having a nightmare. She was dry-eyed with shock and looked over to where she knew her parents were sitting. When their faces came into focus, she gazed at them as her mind cried: don't believe this, please. I would never betray you! I love you.

'You bewitched Mr Howard with your beauty, and forced him to go along with your scheme.'

'No.' The single word came out on a faint cry of despair. Derek Howard hadn't raped her – but this court just had!

'No further questions.'

Kate watched the man sit down with a smirk of satisfaction on his face, and wondered how he felt. Was he proud of what he had just done, or did he honestly believe she'd try to cheat her family? Either way she couldn't understand it.

'We will break for lunch and return here at two o'clock.' The judge stood up and left the court.

Kate remained where she was as the court cleared, unable to move.

'Come on, sweetheart, let's get you into the fresh air.'

Even the gentle voice of her father didn't completely penetrate the horror racing through her, but she allowed him to lead her out. They had just reached the door to the street when there was a flash. She looked towards it just as another one went off.

'Kate, I'm so sorry.' Terry from the newspaper was apologetic. 'The Chief has ordered Mike and me to cover the case . . .'

She hardly heard the words as her stomach heaved,

and she ran back through the door towards the nearest ladies' cloakroom. She only just made it in time, and was violently sick. Annie was beside her, holding her shoulders and talking quietly to her until the sickness eased.

'All over now.' Annie wiped her face with a dampened handkerchief. 'Stand up, Kate.'

She'd been on her knees and hauled herself upright with difficulty. Her mother was standing by the sinks with a glass of water in her hand. Kate reached for it, but was shaking so badly that the liquid spilled over the floor. Annie held the glass then so that she could take a drink.

'Better?' her mother asked.

She nodded, and with the help of her mother and Annie she was able to walk out of the cloakroom and join her family.

Mr Prendergast hurried towards them. 'I wouldn't go outside if I were you. The press are six deep out there. I've found you a private room and I'll see that refreshments are brought to you.'

'I would like to go home.'

The lawyer turned to her parents. 'I'm going to recall Kate. I want the jury to see how upset she is by the defence claims.'

'Upset?' Rose exploded. 'When this trial's over, I'm going to tear that arrogant little squirt apart with my bare hands. And I'll expect you to be quicker on your feet to stop any repeat of this morning's disgraceful episode, young man, or I'll bloody well take over the case myself!'

Anyone on the receiving end of Rose Freeman's wrath knew they were up against a force to be reckoned with.

He took an involuntary step back. 'I assure you it won't happen again. Now, if you'd like to come with me, I'll show you the room we've prepared for you.'

Kate followed with her father on one side of her and Reid on the other, only half aware of what was going on. There were plates of sandwiches, cakes and biscuits; tea and coffee were there for them. She sipped tea when a cup was put in her hands. There was only a slight tremor now.

'I didn't do what they said,' she whispered.

'Of course you didn't!' Everyone spoke at once.

'Kate.' Her mother sat beside her. 'I watched the jury's faces the whole time. They didn't believe it, no one did. They haven't got a sound defence. That was a last attempt to get Howard off. He's used the only weapon he had, but it won't help him – quite the reverse in fact.'

Reid squatted in front of her and took hold of her hands, a wry smile on his face. 'He's shot himself in the arse, darling.'

She squeezed his hands. How she loved this wonderful man. A fleeting smile touched her mouth. 'That was careless of him.'

A ripple of laughter echoed around the room and the tension eased.

At two o'clock sharp the trial resumed, and, although Kate was still in a state of shock, she knew this was something she had to see through to the end. An hour later her mother came out of the courtroom. 'I think they're going to call you again, but the questioning won't be hostile this time. They recalled the medical examiner and made him go over his findings in great detail. The photographs of your injuries leave no doubt that Howard was brutal with you, and *was* trying to kill you.'

Kate's name was called and her mother hurried back into the courtroom. Once in the witness box again she was relieved to see Mr Prendergast stand up.

'I would like to ask a few questions only.' He gave her an encouraging smile. 'When was the first time you met Mr Howard?'

'When he came to the shop to tell me that my brother wanted to see me urgently.' Kate spoke clearly, trying to make sure her voice didn't tremble.

'You had never seen him before that day, even though he worked for your father and brother?'

'Never.'

'I want you to think back to the room you were being held in.'

She tried to visualize the room, trying to remember every small detail because she sensed it was important. It had been cold, dirty and dark . . .

'I know this is distressing for you. Describe it to me. Take your time.'

'All it contained was an old bed with a torn mattress on it. No light and no heat. There was one small window and it had been nailed shut.'

'Was there anything to indicate that the room was ready for you?'

Kate was stumped. She knew her lawyer was trying to show that this had been a premeditated crime, but . . . Suddenly two points came to mind. They hadn't seemed significant at the time. She looked up eagerly. 'The building was derelict and yet the lock on the door was new; the key turned easily and silently. And there was a bucket in the corner to use as a toilet; that was also brand-new.'

Mr Prendergast turned to the jury. 'A new lock on a door in a derelict house; a lock already fitted before Mr Howard took his victim there.' He paused to let this fact sink in, then turned back to Kate with a smile on his face. 'Thank you, Miss Freeman, I have no further questions.'

'Do you wish to cross-examine again?' the judge asked the defence lawyer.

He half rose to his feet, not looking quite so smug now. 'No, my lord.'

She was dismissed, but how she managed to walk out of that courtroom without falling down she would never know. The sheer relief pulsing through her kept her step firm and her head up. She'd done her part. Now it was up to the barristers and the jury.

19

The trial had lasted for three days, and the evidence against Derek Howard was overwhelming. The jury retired to consider their verdict. Kate and her family waited.

'How long will they take?' she asked her mother.

'No one can say, but there can be little doubt in their minds of Howard's guilt.' Her mother smiled at her. 'All we can do is wait.'

It took the jury only four hours, and the family filed back into court to hear the verdict. When Derek Howard was convicted of kidnapping and attempted murder, Kate nearly passed out with relief. He would be sentenced in a week's time.

The journey back home was a blur to her. After the strain of the last few days she felt detached from reality, making it difficult to concentrate on anything at all. She was sensible enough to recognize what was happening to her: her mind was shutting down. But she mustn't allow that to happen. There was no escape from what had occurred in that courtroom and it would be better to face it now. She was vaguely aware that Terry and Mike had been outside the court, and she was sure she'd glimpsed Robert sitting in the court when she'd first walked in, which meant it would be in the papers. She was well known to most of them from her freelance work, and they wouldn't be able to resist such a sensational trial.

She felt her insides start to churn again. When she'd heard the verdict of guilty, she'd thought it was all over, but that was foolish and she should have known better. This would be headline news in the morning, and it was going to be uncomfortable being the subject of news stories. Derek Howard had been proved guilty, but how many of the accusations against her would stick?

'Nearly home.' Her mother spoke quietly as the car headed through Barnes. 'We'll have a nice strong cup of tea as soon as we get back.'

They were sitting in the back of the car, with her father driving. Reid, Annie and James were in the car just behind them. Kate dredged up a smile for her mother. 'You sounded just like Grandma Marj then.'

Rose sighed. 'I'm glad Mum and Wally weren't around to see all of this – it would have torn them apart.'

'It hasn't done us much good either.' Kate's laugh was forced and humourless.

'I agree.' She cast an assessing look at her daughter. 'I expect it feels as if the bottom has dropped out of your world, yet I can tell you that you'll get through this.'

She didn't know the whole story of her mother's life, but she realized that it had been harsh. Kate prayed that somewhere inside her she had a measure of her mother's strength, because she was going to need it. However, she was under no illusions about her own character, and was aware that she was going to have to dig deep for every ounce of courage. Her life, unlike that of her mother's family, had been happy and secure, and the kidnapping and trial had shaken her badly.

The cars pulled into the driveway, and as soon as they

were indoors the kettle was put on the stove even before Rose had taken off her coat.

'Thank God that's over!' James sat at the large kitchen table and ran a hand over his eyes. 'I'm desperately sorry you've had to go through this, Kate.'

She was upset to see her brother so distraught. 'It wasn't your fault, James, and, as you said, it's over now.'

'If I ever see that defence barrister again, I'll knock him flat on his smug face!' Bill declared. 'I know he had a job to do, but he didn't have to be so brutal about it.'

Rose gave a grim smile. 'You can leave him to me. After the sentencing I'll deal with him!'

'Poor sod!' It was unusual for Annie to swear and everyone gave her a startled glance. 'He doesn't stand a chance with Rose after his hide.'

A ripple of laughter went around the people at the table and Kate joined in.

Her father reached across and squeezed her hand. 'That's better, sweetheart. This has been a terrible ordeal for you and you showed great courage in the witness box. Your denials were short and convincing. No one believed you had been involved in the plot, as the unanimous guilty verdict showed.'

Kate realized that she had been silly to even entertain the idea that the defence would be believed, but in the shock and confusion she hadn't been thinking straight.

There was a sharp knock on the kitchen door and Pete came in all smiles. 'Sorry I couldn't be there when the jury came in, but I had a wedding to do. Your dad left a message with Susan about the guilty verdict. I hope they put Howard away for a very long time.'

'I'm pretty sure they will,' Rose told him. 'The judge

didn't like the defence tactics, and I've been told he's a tough old devil.'

'And Howard's still got to face the embezzlement charges next month.' James gave a satisfied grunt. 'He hasn't got any defence against that, so that should add a few more years. I think it will be a long time before he sees the outside world again.'

There was a knock on the front door this time and Reid went to answer it. He came back with Andrew Stevenson, Robert Sinclair and a man they didn't know.

James shook hands with the reporter who'd interviewed him a while back, and, as there wasn't room for everyone in the kitchen, Rose ushered them into the sitting room.

When they'd settled themselves, the stranger looked at Rose and Bill. 'My name's Joel Perkins, and I must say that neither of you has changed much in almost forty years. I'd have known you anywhere, Mrs Freeman.'

Rose studied him carefully. 'You would only have been a lad then. When did we meet?'

'I was six years old at the time. Our street was being demolished and my dad was refusing to move.'

'Of course!' Rose turned to her husband. 'Do you remember, Bill? The bailiffs were there and I persuaded them to hold off until I'd spoken to Mr and Mrs Perkins.'

Joel laughed. 'You took my dad in your car to see the new houses, Mr Freeman. He never stopped talking about you. You made a big impression on him.'

'You sure it wasn't the car that impressed him?' Bill joked.

'That too!'

'How are your parents?' Rose wanted to know.

'They're still alive and I'm able to keep them in comfort now.'

'You've done well for yourself,' Rose said, clearly admiring the smartly dressed man.

'I have, and it's all thanks to you. Once we were out of the slums I went to a good school, and then on to university.'

'And now you're the owner of the *World Explorer*.' Bill studied him carefully. 'It was you who ordered Mr Stevenson to employ our daughter.'

'I've always felt I owed you a great debt, so that's why I told Andrew to give her the job at the paper.'

Kate joined in the conversation for the first time. 'I wish you hadn't done that. It was a great disappointment to learn that I hadn't won the position on my own merits as a photographer.'

'Oh, but you had. I checked you out very carefully and knew you were an excellent photographer.' He gave a wry smile. 'I am a businessman and wouldn't have employed you if you'd been hopeless, in spite of my debt to your parents.'

This cheered Kate immensely and went a long way to clearing the self-doubt she'd experienced since leaving the paper.

'The job is still yours, and' – he turned to Pete, who was watching the scene with a frown on his face – 'you can also come back, young man.'

Kate watched Pete give a firm shake of his head. She went and stood beside him. 'Thank you, but we have a flourishing business going now and are set on making that a success.'

'Well, it's very nice to meet you again, Joel, and to see

that you've done well for yourself.' Rose eyed the three men perceptively. 'But I'm sure this isn't just a social visit.'

'This was my idea, Mrs Freeman.' Robert Sinclair looked angry. 'I was in court throughout the trial and was appalled at the treatment Kate received.'

'If you're going to suggest more publicity,' Bill said sharply, 'I believe we shall have more than enough of that when the papers hit the streets in the morning!'

'The trial will be covered sympathetically by us,' Andrew Stevenson told them, 'but we'd like to have something in addition to the report.'

'Such as?' James appeared wary.

Robert turned to Rose, speaking with enthusiasm. 'The *World Explorer* would like to run an article about the good you and Kate have done for the children's homes in Wandsworth, and' – he paused – 'perhaps a little about your past?'

Kate almost snorted out loud. Robert never gave up! She was sure he'd been trying to get this close to her mother for a long time. She almost giggled when he gave her a sly wink. He seemed a completely different man from the first time she'd met him.

'What do you consider a *little*?' Rose asked him.

'Just a mention about your struggles as a young girl to get better housing and education for those living in the slums.'

Bill looked at him in disbelief. 'My wife's life and achievements would fill several books, Mr Sinclair.'

'I know. And I'd love to do your whole life's story – '

Rose held up her hand to stop him. 'I will never agree to that.'

Robert sat back with a sigh of disappointment. 'I didn't think you would, but let me write the article: it will be further publicity for the children. The Bible says "To every thing there is a season, and a time to every purpose under the heaven . . . A time to keep silence, and a time to speak." I believe this is a time to speak.'

Rose's smile was one of approval. 'You know your Bible.'

'I consider it the greatest book ever written. It contains wisdom, history and some damned good stories.'

'And a lot that is difficult to understand,' Rose pointed out.

'I agree, but that makes it all the more interesting, don't you think?'

'Without a doubt. Now, about this proposal of yours. We'll do it, but you'll write the article here and let us see it before you leave. If we disapprove of anything, it won't be published. My daughter has a typewriter upstairs that you can use.'

'I agree.' Robert beamed.

Rose stood up. 'But first we must eat. We've had a long distressing day. You will all join us?'

Joel and Andrew shook their heads.

'We have to get back, but thanks for the invitation.' Joel smiled at everyone in the room and then turned to Rose. 'Perhaps another time?'

'Just give us a call.' Bill stood up and held out his hand to Joel Perkins. 'Remember us to your parents when you see them.'

'I will. They'll be so pleased to know I've met you again.'

When Joel and Andrew had left, Annie and Rose prepared a quick meal, and after that they set up the typewriter on the kitchen table. Then Rose, Kate and Robert settled down to thrashing out the article.

That must have been the most frustrating two hours Robert has ever spent, Kate thought, highly amused, as she watched him gather up his papers and rush out. He would only just make it in time for the morning's edition.

'Let's have a drink,' Rose exclaimed. 'That was damned hard work.'

They went into the sitting room, where her father and James were listening to the radio. They switched it off as soon as they came in.

'Reid and Annie have gone home,' James said.

'Finished?' Bill asked.

'Yes, thank goodness.' Kate laughed. 'That article would have taken up the entire paper if Robert had had his way, but Mum kept a tight rein on him.'

'Don't feel sorry for him, Kate.' Her mother poured them both a small brandy. 'I did make a few concessions and he was well pleased with what he had.'

'You didn't have to do it, though, Mum.' Kate was well aware of her mother's aversion to publicity.

'We're going to get a lot of media attention over the next week or so,' Rose admitted. 'So we might as well have something positive printed about us, because the trial was unpleasant stuff.'

'Your mother's right,' Bill said, giving a worried frown. 'The sentencing will be next Friday and after that things will quieten down. I hope you'll stay with us until then, Kate. If you go back to the flat, you might get pestered by reporters.'

She'd already thought of that and readily agreed to spend the next week with them.

20

It had been quite a restful night, much to Kate's surprise, but this was probably because of mental exhaustion combined with relief that the trial was over. When she went downstairs, her parents were in the kitchen reading the daily papers.

Rose opened the *World Explorer* and placed it in front of her daughter. 'What do you think of Sinclair's piece?'

She read it through carefully and nodded in satisfaction. 'He hasn't changed a word.'

'He wouldn't cross your mother, not with his boss, Joel Perkins, watching his every move.'

Her mother chuckled, and then became serious again. 'I'm afraid that all the other papers mention your grilling in the witness box. Do you want to read them?'

'Not today; keep them and I'll have a look later.'

'All right. Do you want a cooked breakfast?'

'No, thanks, Mum, toast and tea will do.' She made her mother stay in her chair. 'I'll get it.'

When she sat down again, her father pinched a slice of her toast and spread butter on it. 'What are you going to do today?'

'As it's Saturday, I thought I'd take Eddie out for the day.'

'Why don't you bring him here?' her father suggested.

'Oh, he'd love that, and I could show him the deer in Richmond Park.'

'That's settled, then.' Her mother began to clear the table. 'You go and get him and I'll make a nice suet pudding.'

When Kate walked into the home, Eddie raced towards her with a squeal of delight. Because of the trial she hadn't visited for a week. She laughed as he swung on her outstretched hands. She'd felt violated after the abuse she'd endured in the witness box, but seeing the joy on his face swept the pain away.

'Can I take Eddie out for the day?' she asked Mrs Green.

'Of course you can, my dear.' Then she whispered, 'I'm so glad that dreadful man was found guilty. What a terrible time this has been for you.'

Kate pinned on a bright smile. 'Thank you. It's all over now.'

It was a lovely day, so Kate parked the car and they wandered through the park. Eddie's pleasure was catching, and she revelled in his laughter. This was what life was about, she decided. Bringing pleasure to someone less fortunate than herself was more important than worrying about accusations that had no foundation in truth. Once the newspapers had lost interest in the story it would fade into nothingness.

They spotted some deer and Eddie hopped about with excitement. 'Can you take a picture of them?'

She slipped the camera off her shoulder. 'You go and stand by that small tree and I'll get you with the deer in the background.'

They spent time looking, walking and chatting, before

Kate took Eddie back to the car and headed out of the Roehampton Gate.

Her parents were in the back garden, where she took Eddie to meet them. 'This is my mum and dad.'

He stuck to her side and smiled shyly when they said hello.

Just then James strode into the garden. 'And this is my brother,' she told Eddie.

Rose and Bill stood up and Eddie spun round, looking at each of them in turn. 'Crikey, ain't you all big!' Then he clapped his hands over his mouth and gazed at Kate, wide-eyed.

She stooped down in front of the boy. 'What's the matter?'

He removed his hands. 'Mrs Green wouldn't 'alf tell me off for being rude.'

'We do come as a bit of a shock when we're all together.' James laughed at the boy's expression.

Sensing that no one was angry with him, Eddie giggled. 'You're all giants!'

Kate looked at her family and tried to see them through his eyes. She understood what he meant: her father was six foot four; her brother six foot two; her mother almost six foot. At five foot nine she was the shortest.

Eddie was studying James with interest. 'Do you play football?'

'I used to. I've still got a ball upstairs somewhere. Shall I find it so we can have a game?'

Eddie's little face lit up. 'Oh, please.'

James was soon back and Bill marked out a goal at the end of the lawn. When they began to kick it about, Kate grinned at her mother. 'I'll help you with lunch.'

All the time they were preparing lunch they could hear squeals of excitement and shouts of 'Goal!'

'Dad's letting him score quite a few.'

Rose stopped what she was doing for a moment to watch Bill and James playing with Eddie. 'The man never quite outgrows the boy, does he?'

'Obviously not.' Kate saw Eddie rushing towards her father in goal, only to be swept high into the air by James, who then scored the goal himself.

Eddie was screaming in delight. 'That's cheating! It was my goal.'

Rose called out of the window. 'Come on, children, lunch is ready.'

James tucked Eddie under his arm and marched into the kitchen with the boy giggling and kicking. 'What shall I do with this?' he asked his mother.

'Take him to the bathroom first,' Rose told him.

James disappeared, and Bill came in with a wide grin on his face. 'That takes me back a few years.'

Eddie was soon back, scrubbed clean and trotting along beside James.

It was a lively lunch. The little boy had obviously worked up an appetite, because he almost cleared his plate. There was complete silence as he tackled his pudding.

'Would you like some more?' Rose asked, as he scraped his plate clean.

He gazed at the empty plate for a moment, licked the last of the treacle from his spoon and sighed. 'Don't think I can; I'm full up to the back teeth.'

'In that case,' Bill chuckled, 'there won't be room for any more.'

Eddie solemnly agreed that that was so. 'That's the best plum duff I've ever tasted.'

Kate and her mother cleared up, while the others went back to the garden. When the last of the pots was stacked away, they went out to join them.

'Just look at that.' Rose stopped suddenly. 'The poor little dears have worn themselves out.'

Kate nearly doubled over with laughter. Her father and James were dozing in comfortable garden chairs, and Eddie was fast asleep on her father's lap. So they wouldn't disturb the sleeping beauties, they decided to sit in another part of the garden, under a tree, talking quietly.

'I'm glad you brought Eddie here today. It's done us all good to have a laugh and watch the little chap enjoying himself.'

'I agree, Mum. The last few months have been difficult, haven't they?'

'That's putting it mildly,' Rose remarked.

For the next hour they talked about many things, including the kidnapping and trial. Kate found her mother's sound common sense healing. She thought of Eddie and all children without parents, feeling sad for each of them. She had been in a prison when Howard had kidnapped her, but her captivity had been short and she had family she could lean on in the difficult times, but these children didn't have that kind of freedom.

'How can a mother abandon her baby?' she asked.

'I don't know, Kate, it's a mystery to me. When I was growing up in poverty, you could understand why they felt they couldn't feed another child, but help is available these days.'

They sat in silence then, Kate counting her blessings.

Eddie woke up, slid off Bill's lap, shook James awake and urged the men into another kick-about. At five o'clock they had tea in the garden, then Kate cleaned up Eddie and got him ready to return to the home.

Much to his delight, he received kisses from Rose, Bill and James. His grin was as wide as it could get. 'I've had a *luverly* day, thank you.'

Although he was obviously tired, he kept chattering on the way back to Wandsworth. 'What's it like, having a brother?' he wanted to know.

'It's very nice,' she told him, 'especially when he's as kind as James.'

Eddie's nod was one of approval. 'Is James married?'

'No, not yet.'

'He'd make a great dad.' Eddie cast her a sideways glance. 'Can you marry your brother?'

'No, I'm afraid not, it's against the law.' If she hadn't been driving, she'd have given him a hug and tried to assure him that everything would turn out all right for him, for he was obviously still yearning for a family of his own. Belonging, that's what these children wanted.

By the time they reached the home, he could hardly keep his eyes open, so Kate put him to bed herself, and watched him fall asleep as soon as his head touched the pillow.

He had a blissful smile on his face, even in sleep, and she had to agree with his summing-up of the day. It had been *luverly.*

Monday morning Kate found reporters and photographers congregating outside the shop, so she drove past, parked her car in the next road and hoped she could slip in the back door without being noticed. This was what she had expected: they were only doing their job. But this week would be difficult. There was going to be so much interest in such a sensational story. She wasn't reading the papers, but she could just imagine the headlines: BRUTAL KIDNAPPING AN ATTEMPTED MURDER OF ROSE WEBSTER'S YOUNG DAUGHTER BY SACKED EMPLOYEE OF THE FAMILY FIRM, GRANT PHILLIPS. Kate shivered. James had said that it might be better if she didn't go to work for the next few days, but she wasn't going to be kept a prisoner because of the avid interest in the case. She'd been confined once by Derek Howard, and she was damned if she'd allow anyone else to stop her going about her usual work.

As she walked up the alley towards the back entrance, she saw two men leaning against the wall. She gave a wry smile when she saw who it was. 'How did you know I'd even come here today?'

Terry took a photo and Mike had his notebook at the ready.

'Sinclair took over our story of the trial,' Mike told her, 'so we hoped you might give us a personal interview. Seeing as we're old friends.'

She unlocked the back door and held it open. 'Come on, then, I'm not in the mood to talk, but you can make the tea.'

Terry was putting the kettle on to boil when Susan shot into the back room, looking worried. 'I've had to keep the front door locked,' she told Kate. 'Those reporters have been trying to get in ever since I arrived.'

'Where's Pete?'

'He's out seeing a customer who wants family portraits

taken in their own home. He won't be here for a while.' There was a loud rap on the door, making Susan jump. 'Customers won't come in while they're outside.'

Kate picked up her camera and strode through the shop. 'Come on, Terry, we'll turn the tables on them.'

She threw open the door and stepped outside with Terry beside her, their flashes blasting into the crowd. Mike scribbled in his book with a grin of delight on his face.

'Pack it up, Kate,' someone shouted, but they were all laughing.

She had met quite a few of these men while working as a freelance. Lowering her camera, she said, 'You're all wasting your time. I've given the *World Explorer* exclusive rights to my story.'

There was a disgruntled mutter from the reporters. 'Oh, come on, Kate, give us something. We didn't bother you over the weekend.'

'I'll answer one question only.'

'How did you feel when you thought you were going to die?' someone called out.

'Bloody terrified! Now, will you all go away? I've got a business to run and you're making my customers nervous.'

'Were you telling the truth when you said Derek Howard didn't rape you?'

She glared at the man who was pushing his way towards her. He was from one of the more salacious rags. 'I wouldn't lie under oath!'

Mike stepped in front of her, protecting her from the eager crowd. 'You've had your question, so will you now leave? You can read Kate's story in the *Explorer* tomorrow.'

Seeing that they weren't going to get any more, they dispersed, and Kate went back into the shop, followed by Terry and Mike, who were looking pleased with themselves.

'You can leave the door open now, Susan, they won't be back today.' Kate turned and scowled at the men. 'And you can stop looking so smug. What makes you think I'm going to give *you* a story?'

'Because we're your friends' – Mike's grin spread – 'and you've just told the whole of Fleet Street that you are – exclusively!'

'Ah, I dropped myself into that, didn't I?'

Terry was loading another film into his camera and chortling quietly to himself. 'That was brilliant, Kate. Did you hear them laughing? There will be some amusing stories tomorrow, and all to your benefit.'

'Yeah.' Mike was still scribbling away in his own brand of shorthand. 'It took courage to go out there and face them. They liked that.'

Kate went back and finished making the tea. Everyone kept saying how brave she had been, but they couldn't see inside her. If they could, they'd know that she was a mess.

'Sit down.' Terry spoke gently, obviously sensing her troubled thoughts. Then he stooped down in front of her. 'You're strong. You'll get through this.'

'Maybe after the sentencing on Friday I'll feel better, but at the moment it's agony.' She gave Mike a warning look. 'And don't you dare print that!'

'I promise. However, that question they asked you out there is a valid one. We know from the trial what happened, but it's your reactions and feelings everyone's interested in.'

'I find it hard to talk about it,' she admitted.

'Will you try to answer one question for me?' Mike gave her an encouraging smile. 'If it's too personal or difficult, you can tell me to go to hell.'

'I'll do that all right.' She gave a wan smile. 'Ask your question, then.'

'When Derek Howard was choking the life out of you, was everything a blur, or were you aware of what was happening?'

She gazed into space, forcing herself to relive that moment. 'I was sad,' she whispered. 'As I started to lose consciousness, I was overcome with a sense of incredible sadness that I was leaving those I love.'

Mike leaned over and kissed her cheek. 'Can I use that, Kate?'

'If you want to.'

For the rest of the week Kate functioned, as each day that passed brought Friday closer. The reporters left her alone; she knew there had been articles in most newspapers, but she didn't read them, not even those in the *World Explorer*. Her parents were keeping them for her to read when she felt up to it, but in truth she didn't want to know what other people were writing about her. She was having enough trouble dealing with her own emotions. She knew she was being unduly harsh with herself by not facing up to everything that was going on, but she would when she felt stronger.

No one knows how they will react to a desperate situation until they are faced with it, and her thoughts went to her extraordinary family. How had they coped during the war? How had they handled the fear? One day she would ask them.

On the Friday afternoon they took their seats in court for the sentencing of Derek Howard.

The judge looked stern as he addressed the prisoner. 'You have been found guilty of a particularly brutal crime. I consider you to be a most dangerous man from whom the public must be protected. I am, therefore, going to impose the maximum allowed by the law. I sentence you to life imprisonment.'

Kate heard Howard gasp; she looked straight ahead, not wanting to see his face again. She had always had a compassionate nature but there wasn't a shred of pity in her for this man. This experience had certainly knocked off a few of her soft edges.

As Derek Howard was being led from the court, he started to shout. Then she looked at him. He was staring straight at her, and the hatred he felt was there for all to see.

'I should have killed you when I had the chance, you bitch! The high and mighty Freemans should be made to suffer . . .'

He was dragged out still shouting abuse at the entire Freeman family; the venom in his words reverberated through Kate. But for once she didn't mind the pain. He was going to prison for a very long time.

It was over at last!

2I

After finishing off his report, Jon wished he'd had a cameraman with him. You needed pictures to show what was really happening here. He'd run out of film for the small one he always carried and he couldn't get any more here. Not that he was much good with it; he was better with words, but it would have helped to show the violence and turmoil going on in Algeria at the moment. On 23 April, four generals opposed to de Gaulle's policy had taken command of the city and the port of Algiers. De Gaulle had acted swiftly, cutting off all supplies and pay to the rebels. There was a bitter struggle going on, and a state of siege had been proclaimed over the entire area of French North Africa.

He'd received a message from Andrew Stevenson telling him to get out, return to Paris and report from there for the foreseeable future. He would do so as soon as he could make travel arrangements. If he were based in Paris, perhaps he could fly to London once or twice to see the children and make sure Mrs Green wasn't having any more trouble. He took his commitment to the children and the home very seriously and would do all that he could to improve their lives. He was sure Rose Freeman and her daughter would be keeping an eye on the home, so he wasn't too worried. He frowned when he thought about Kate Freeman. She was incredibly beautiful, but something awful must have happened to her – she'd undoubtedly been traumatized when he'd seen her. Or was it just that there was always a flaw in every lovely thing?

An urgent knocking on his door broke his train of thought. His room was in a rough part of town, but he'd taken it because it brought him closer to the warring factions. He opened the door a crack; it paid to be cautious if you wanted to stay alive.

'Oh, thank God, you're home!' A German war correspondent, Gerhard Staddler, whom he'd met out here, slid in and shut the door behind him. 'I'm leaving in an hour on a military flight to Paris. I've got you on it as well. It will be quicker than sea and land.'

It only took Jon five minutes to collect his belongings – he always travelled light – and Gerhard hurried him to a waiting car.

Somehow the German had managed to get written permission for them to travel with the military, and Jon didn't ask questions. He was looking forward to a stay in Paris. After London, it was his favourite city.

It was an uncomfortable journey, with only bench seats in the old Dakota, but neither reporter minded that. In their line of work they often travelled in the oddest modes of transport, and this was luxury to them.

'Thanks for fixing the flight,' Jon told Gerhard when they arrived in Paris. 'Let me buy you dinner tonight.'

'Thanks. Do you know a decent hotel? I could do with a taste of luxury for a change.'

Jon knew just the place, so he hailed a taxi and told the driver to take them to the Hôtel Anglais. It was down a quiet side street in the Tuileries, and the food was excellent.

They checked in, and, after a long bath and change of clothes, Jon phoned Andrew Stevenson. 'I'm in Paris,' he told the Chief when he was finally connected.

'Good. Stay there and see if you can get near de Gaulle or one of his generals.'

'I'll do my best.'

'The stuff you've been sending back is marvellous. Enjoy your stay in Paris, within reason.'

'Are you paying?' He heard a chuckle from the end of the line.

'You know damned well I am, but do try to keep it modest, will you?'

The line started to crackle and fade. 'Andrew, are you still there?'

'Yes,' came the muffled reply.

'I haven't been able to get hold of any English papers for a while. Could you send me some from the last few weeks, so I can catch up on what's been going on?' He wasn't sure if his request had been heard because the line was now dead.

Gerhard was waiting for him in the bar, and after a quick aperitif they went to the dining room. The food was good, the wine superb, and the company stimulating. He'd liked Gerhard from the moment he'd met him – in a ditch as bullets whistled over their heads.

When they reached the coffee stage, Jon sat back and sighed with satisfaction. 'When are you going back to Germany?'

'Tomorrow morning.'

Jon was disappointed that he was leaving so soon. He raised his glass. 'I hope we meet again some time.'

'You might well be in Berlin soon.' Gerhard looked grim as he wrote his address on a napkin. 'Come and stay with me when you arrive.'

'You sound very positive. Are you expecting something dramatic to happen soon?'

'I hope to heaven I'm wrong, but I can't see the Russians allowing the situation to continue. East Berlin is almost paralysed by the mass desertion of bus and train drivers, factory workers, doctors, dentists and hundreds of professors. People are pouring into West Berlin every day.'

Jon was aware of this, as he kept his eye on all world events. 'I agree that the Russians are furious, but what can they do?'

'I've no idea, but I have a nasty feeling that something is going to explode soon.'

On that worrying note, they finished off another bottle of wine and then headed for the nightspots, to have what they considered a well-earned evening of revelry.

Over the next few days Jon gleaned as much information as possible out of those in power, all the time hoping to get to the men at the top of the heap. It was proving to be difficult, and after another long fruitless day he returned to his hotel.

'Package for you, sir.'

The receptionist gave him an enticing smile, but he wasn't in the mood to take up the invitation. 'Thanks.' He walked up the stairs, weighing the heavy package in his hands. He'd asked Andrew for some newspapers but hadn't expected him to send this many. When he reached his room, he tossed it on his bed. He'd have a bath first, then order dinner in his room and have a relaxing evening reading the papers.

Jon wasn't sure if Andrew would consider room service and the best wine justifiable expenses, but, after living in that hovel in Algeria, he didn't feel at all guilty about the expense.

After a leisurely bath, he devoured the meal, propped himself up on the bed and opened the parcel. He shuffled through the papers, muttering in irritation. Why had Andrew only sent their paper? He'd asked for English papers, meaning a selection.

He poured himself another glass of wine and settled down to read, picking up the oldest edition first, one dating back three weeks. When he reached the centre pages, he nearly sent his glass flying. He'd never seen such an expression of shock and despair on a face before, and, when he considered the atrocities he'd witnessed, that was staggering. Kate Freeman was being supported by her father, Annie was on the other side of her, and Rose was about to step in front of her daughter to protect her from the photographer.

He read the account of the trial, spelling out the details of her ordeal and the accusations thrown at her by the defence lawyers. After reading it through twice, including the excellent piece written by Robert Sinclair, he studied the picture again in disbelief. He then sat back and closed his eyes. Dear God, she must have come to see Eddie and hand out Christmas presents to the children a few hours after her rescue. What strength that would have taken!

Opening his eyes, he gazed at the picture again and saw Terry's name underneath it. The expression of utter dejection on a face so lovely gave the photo tremendous impact.

His heart reached out to the family he liked so much. How they must be suffering. He also now understood why Kate had given her young assistant a large share in the business. She was making his future secure in case anything happened to her. She had believed she was going to die!

There was a knock on the door, and a maid entered to remove the remnants of his meal. When she went to pick up the half-empty bottle of wine, he shook his head. 'No, leave that.'

Alone again, he reached for the next paper. Andrew had obviously thought he would want to see this, and he'd been right. This one was dated three days after the trial, and had him chuckling at the picture of Kate and Terry turning their cameras on the crowd of reporters. There was a gap of a week, and Kate was with her family after the sentencing of the man who had kidnapped her. He didn't laugh at this picture. The strain on each of them showed, but Kate's expression was the most worrying.

He recognized what she was doing. She was shutting herself off from the torment and pain – and she mustn't be allowed to do that. He reached for his notepad. He would write to Rose, give his support and ask if there were anything he could do. Then a letter to Terry: he wanted to know how the girl was coping with this, and everything about her that hadn't been printed in the papers.

With the letters finished, he went out, bought some stamps and posted them. Feeling restless now, he walked along by the Seine, watching the streetlights casting glittering splashes of light on the water. It would be the first of June tomorrow, and almost a year since he had been here last. Jane had broken off their engagement and his plans to have a family of his own had come to an end. And, to be honest, that wasn't a bad thing, because he could hardly remember her now.

His thoughts dwelt on Rose and her family. This must have been a terrible time for them, and still would be if Kate were unable to cope with the trauma. He sent up a silent prayer that the girl had inherited her mother's strength of character and her father's calm.

Resting his arms on a low wall overlooking the Seine, Jon gazed at the shimmering river, oblivious to the people walking slowly past, enjoying the lovely evening. Water always had a soothing effect on him.

'Kate. Why don't you take a holiday?'

'I can't do that when we're so busy, Pete.'

'If you went after the tenth, it would be all right. I saw Terry yesterday and he's got a couple of weeks off then. He'd be happy to help out.'

Pete had such an innocent expression on his face that she was suspicious. She knew they were all fretting about her, but really there wasn't any need. She was perfectly all right, and Terry seemed to be calling in rather a lot just lately – it was almost as if he were keeping an eye on her. 'Terry won't want to spend his holiday working.'

'He isn't going away,' Pete hastily assured her, 'because his wife's expecting and she keeps being sick, so they'll leave it until she's over that stage.'

Kate sat on the table in the back room of the shop and

swung her legs. 'Have you two been planning this behind my back?'

Pete looked sheepish.

'I thought as much.' She jumped off the table. 'I'm not going to run away, Pete!'

'Look, Kate, the papers have lost interest now, so no one's hounding you, but you're looking tired. Why don't you have a week of peace and quiet somewhere? It'll do you good after what you've been through.'

'You sound just like my dad. I'll tell you what I told him, I'll think about it.'

No more was said on the subject. When they locked up the shop, she said goodnight to Susan and Pete, then went upstairs to her flat. She had become quite fond of her little home. The flat and its furniture had not been looked after, but, with the help of Pete, Susan, several pots of paint and loads of polish, they now seemed quite presentable. She arranged the bunch of carnations in a vase and placed it on the sideboard. The flowers had been a thoughtful gift from James when she'd told him she was going back to the flat. They made a lovely splash of colour.

After Howard had been sentenced, she had insisted on moving back, although she knew her parents would have liked her to stay with them. However, she was twenty-four years old now, and it was time she stood on her own. The Freemans and Websters were a close family and couldn't understand her need to have a place of her own, but it was vital that she became more self-reliant. And she didn't want to worry her parents any more if she could help it. Since the trial her nightmares had returned, so it was better to be in a place where she could walk up and down during the night without the worry of waking anyone up. She was very disappointed with herself. She should be getting back to normal, but she just couldn't seem to put the whole rotten business behind her.

She'd had a decent meal at lunchtime, so she made herself scrambled eggs on toast and a pot of tea. The idea of going away was growing on her, but where, and with whom? Beth wouldn't be able to manage time off work at such short notice. Perhaps she could take some of the boys to the Haven in Wales. It was a lovely place. She and James had spent most of the war there. There was space for children to run around in . . .

But no, the boys still had a few days left of school, and she couldn't take them away from their lessons. Her thoughts turned to the happy and sad times during those war years, and especially to the frightened little French boy Sam had brought to them.

She sat up straight. Of course, she could go to France for a few days. It was some time since she'd seen Jacques. His cheerful company would be just the thing!

And thinking of cheerful company, if she hurried she could still catch Beth at her shop and give her a lift home. Kate grabbed her bag and car keys, hurrying down the stairs. Since her friend had been going steady with Steve, Kate hadn't seen as much of Beth as she would have liked, but that was life. People moved on and things changed. They still took any small chance to see each other, though.

The dress shop was just closing when she drove up. She threw open the car door. 'Hi, want a lift?'

Beth clambered in and grinned. 'Thanks. What are you doing here?'

'I know you're meeting Steve tonight, but I wondered if you'd have time for a coffee and a quick chat.'

'A quick chat?' Beth roared with laughter. 'When are our chats ever quick?'

Kate looked at her friend in amusement. 'Well, we'll make this a short one. I don't want to make you late.'

'Stop here!' Beth grabbed her arm.

Kate stamped on the brakes, much to the annoyance of the driver behind, who tooted his horn angrily.

'Don't do that when I'm driving,' Kate groaned.

'You'd have gone past the café if I hadn't stopped you,' Beth said, quite unperturbed about nearly causing an accident. 'A coffee is a good idea, 'cos I've had a rotten day at the shop. I hate that job! I'm just a dogsbody, fetching and carrying all day for the senior window dresser. He never lets me have a go at a display, or takes any notice of my ideas.'

Kate parked the car neatly down a side road and they went in and found a free table. 'Why don't you find another job?'

'I will one day, but Steve works near by and we can meet at lunchtimes.'

'Ah, well,' Kate nodded understandingly. 'Worth putting up with, then.'

'Yep. Now what's on your mind?' Beth asked perceptively.

For the next half an hour Kate told her about how much trouble she was having getting over the kidnapping and trial. 'I'm thinking of going over to France for a holiday with Sam and his family.'

'Good idea,' Beth agreed. 'A change of scene will do you good.'

'Yes, you're right.'

After their coffee, Kate dropped Beth at her home in Putney, and drove back to the flat. Her mind made up about going away, and looking forward to seeing Jacques again.

22

Three days later Kate was on the boat to Calais. Sam had received her letter and had phoned through to her father, saying that they would love to see her.

The sea was choppy so she stayed on deck most of the time. The weather had driven the majority of the passengers inside. Kate watched the churning water, enjoying the solitude. It was strange: she'd never liked to be alone, but since the kidnapping she wanted to be by herself at times. The boat lurched and rolled, and she felt as if the sea were a mirror of what was going on inside her. However, she knew that this was temporary and that the calm would come. She longed for that day.

Sam was waiting for her as the boat docked, and she rushed towards him.

He wrapped her in a fierce embrace, rocking her gently in his arms. 'Ah, Kate, it is good to see you. I am sorry we couldn't be with you during the trial, but Maria has been ill and we could not leave her.'

Kate looked at him in surprise. 'Oh, I'm so sorry, why didn't you tell me? Is she all right? I wouldn't have come if I'd known. I'll stay in a hotel – '

'Shush.' Sam stopped her outpouring of concern. 'We didn't tell you because you had enough to cope with. She's had a hysterectomy, but is now well on the way to full recovery and looking forward to having you stay with us for a few days.'

'If you're sure. I won't be any trouble. I just need a rest away from everything that's happened this year.'

His smile was gentle. 'You are never any trouble.'

He picked up her case, and they walked to where he'd parked the car. She knew she could be honest with Sam. She always had been, ever since she was a little girl. 'I've been nothing but trouble, Sam. I'm not coping well and worrying the life out of Mum and Dad.'

Sam put her case in the boot of the car, took her arm and guided her to a corner seat in a café on the harbour. Kate sat down and took a deep breath of fresh air. It was lovely to be somewhere else, away from the stress of the last few weeks.

After ordering coffee for them both, Sam studied her face, as if trying to see inside her. When he spoke his tone was firm.

'Rose and Bill have faced more problems than you'll ever know, and they will handle this with the same fortitude they've always shown. You must stop using that as an excuse and deal with your own problems. Your parents, with Annie and Reid, are among the bravest people I have ever met. So stop worrying about them.'

Kate was taken aback by his words and irritated by them. 'I know they're strong and brave, but I'm not like them!'

'You have their blood running through your veins, you can't help being like them. But you seem to have forgotten that.'

'You don't know what you're talking about.' Kate snapped at him, angry now. Sam was a close family friend, but what right did he have to pass judgement? She'd come here for a rest, not to be lectured to.

'Do I not?' He didn't seem at all put out by her sharp tone. 'That is strange, then, because I've known you since you were about five years old. Even then you showed great sensitivity to other people's troubles and did your best to help. Jacques would not be the well-balanced boy he is now if it hadn't been for you.'

'It wasn't just me.'

'I agree, it was your entire family, but it was you he clung to in his confusion; you who showed him you cared. That little girl is still there, even if you are trying to bury your true nature because you've had a nasty experience.'

She'd had enough of this and went to stand up, but Sam caught her hand. 'Sit down, Kate. Let's get this done with and then you can really enjoy your holiday. But, if after we've talked, you want to get the next boat back home, then I won't stop you.'

She'd never known him be this forceful before, and there was something about him that made it hard to disobey. Kate stirred her coffee, sipped it, then sat back. 'What are you up to, Sam? Why are you doing this?'

'We love your family. Everyone else might be tiptoeing around you, not wishing to cause you more distress, but I'm not willing to see you hurt yourself and everyone who loves you.'

What the devil was he talking about? She'd been behaving perfectly normally – outwardly anyway – hadn't she?

'Have you cried for yourself?'

His question threw her for a moment, and the words that came out of her own mouth shocked her. 'How can I cry for such a coward? I was so terrified when the police broke into that room. I fell apart. I didn't want to die and would have done anything at that moment to stay alive. I hid behind the mattress in blind terror.' She glared at him. 'How can I respect a person like that?'

'Ah, at last we have the crux of the problem.' He gave a satisfied nod.

She was furious now. How had he managed to wring that admission out of her? 'You're good at this, aren't you?'

'I had plenty of practice prising secrets out of people during the war.' He leaned towards her, ignoring the interest they were causing in the café. 'And I also know what it's like to have my world torn apart. When the Germans invaded, I fought them, was captured and managed to escape. When I arrived back in my village, I was told that the girl I was about to marry, and our unborn child, had been killed. I fled to England. I was consumed with grief and anger, until I met a gentle fragile-looking woman, who reached out in compassion and kindness. That was Annie, and you have more of her character in you than you have of your mother's.'

She gave him a sceptical look.

'I know you're thinking that gentleness won't get you through this, but let me tell you something about Annie you probably don't know. There was an agent named Jack Graham. He was a great friend of ours. One day we lost contact with him and, as Annie spoke fluent French and knew him, she was the logical choice to go in to try to find him. She never hesitated.' Sam paused, gazing into the distance, obviously remembering.

Kate waited, hardly daring to breathe.

'On the night she went, I watched her walking towards

the plane with her parachute on. She looked so small and fragile, and I knew that every step she took towards the plane revving up its engines was a tremendous effort. She was well aware that if she were captured it would most certainly mean death. She was very frightened, but that didn't stop her finding Graham and bringing him back. During the war death was our shadow. We were prepared for it, but you are living in a time of peace and would not have expected such cruelty to happen to you. Being terrified does not make you a coward, so stop judging yourself. You did what you had to do and did it well. You survived!' He slapped the flat of his hand down on the table. 'You're alive, Kate, and that is reason for rejoicing, not self-contempt!'

She was amazed by his vehemence and began to speak, her voice husky with emotion. 'I've always been so sure of myself. Secure and loved, knowing what I wanted in life and believing I would get it. It was a terrible shock to realize that I could lose control. I hated Derek Howard so much for destroying all my illusions, and if I could I would have killed him without a second thought . . .'

Sam didn't stop her this time as she rushed out of the café and began to walk along the road, head down, deep in thought. He was right. She was alive, and was lucky to have had so much support. Perhaps she was finding it so hard to come to terms with what had happened because she'd been over-protected all her life. So safe! Well, the kidnapping had uncovered the real her; she must learn to live with that and begin to find her own level in life.

She sat on a seat with the harbour in view and lifted her head. A hand reached towards her with a packet of cigarettes in it. Sam had followed her but had not said anything, leaving her to sort out her own feelings. 'No, thanks, Sam.'

He lit a fag for himself, his expression back to the likeable Sam she'd always known. Good heavens, he was like a chameleon, she thought, already feeling better for giving voice to her secret. She could just imagine him interrogating people during the war.

He took hold of her hand. 'Kate, you are many things, but you are *not* a coward. There is no shame in being frightened or terrified; it happens to us all at some time or other, so have some compassion for yourself.'

She felt the tears burning the back of her eyes. How she longed to believe that!

'When Jack Graham died only a few hours after Annie had got him home, I watched her bottle up all the emotion and grief. I told her then, and I'm telling you now, let the tears flow. This tendency you British have for hiding your feelings can be crippling. Don't do that to yourself, chérie. Don't let that animal win!'

Sam *was* right. She had been wrong to believe her fear was cowardly. The situation she'd found herself in had been terrible and would have frightened anyone, but she'd kept her wits about her and stopped Howard from raping her. With hindsight she could see that she'd dealt with it as well as she could. There was no shame in that! Derek Howard would win if she carried on the way she was now. The tears ran in floods down her cheeks, and Sam held her hand and waited for the storm to pass.

Eventually she wiped her eyes and blew her nose. 'Even if I can get my life back together again, I'll never be quite the same, will I?'

'No, you won't, you'll be a stronger woman, but you'll never lose your gentleness and desire to help other people. Your were born with those qualities, and you must never allow them to be buried under the debris of bitterness and self-doubt.'

'I'm glad I came. I needed someone to talk some sense to me.'

His smile was wry. 'Annie said I was the one to do it.'

'She knows you so well.'

'We went through a lot together.'

She smiled for the first time. 'I thought you would marry her.'

'That was my intention, but only because I needed a mother for my troubled son. We did not love each other as a husband and wife should, you understand? I knew Reid loved her, but I was prepared to be totally selfish. I could have ruined her life, and I'll always be ashamed of that. After I found Maria in a German labour camp and managed to get her back to the allied lines, I was relieved to see Annie and Reid marry.'

Kate thought of these two people she loved so much and gave a deep sigh. 'They are made for each other. Everything turned out right in the end, didn't it?'

'Perfect, and it will for you. Give it time and be kind to yourself.'

She looked at the man sitting beside her and understood something of the suffering he must have endured. Hers was small in comparison. She felt as if she'd walked through a long dark room into the light at the other end. The memory of the terror was still there, but it was bearable now. The inner turmoil had been debilitating, and she could now feel the strength seeping back into her body and mind.

'Do you want to get on the next boat, or shall we go home? Maria and Jacques are very excited about your visit.'

When they stood up, she gave him a hug. 'You're a wise old Frenchman, and I'm looking forward to my holiday.'

'Good, and not so much of the old!'

They were laughing as they reached the car, and for Kate it felt like the first real, natural laugh she'd had for months and months.

As Sam drove up to the lovely old stone-built house about five kilometres outside Saint-Omer, Maria rushed out and towed her inside. Kate was relieved to see her looking so well and just as lovely. She'd hardly had time to say anything when the door burst open and Jacques erupted into the room.

'Kate!' He was now taller than her, and she was lifted off her feet and swung round and round, making a strand of dark hair fall into his eyes. 'I'm almost finished for the year, and can take a few days away from my studies at university.'

'Can you do that?' she laughed, slightly breathless from his exuberant greeting. She was struck by how good-looking he was now.

He gave a very Gallic shrug. 'For you, I can do anything.'

'I have a few days free as well, so I thought we might all go to Paris for a couple of days,' Sam suggested.

'That's a wonderful idea,' Maria said, giving her

husband an amused glance. 'Kate and I can do some shopping.'

Both men groaned, but they didn't look too put out by the prospect.

'As long as you leave us time to show Kate the sights, Mamma,' Jacques said.

Maria considered this for a moment, then winked at Kate. 'Do you think one day will be enough to buy everything we need?'

Kate blew out through pursed lips and frowned. 'Well, my wardrobe could do with quite a few new things, but I suppose we might be able to manage with just one day.'

'We'd better make our stay three days.' Sam laughed and stood up. 'If you intend to buy up half of the Paris fashions, then you must both rest tomorrow.'

After they'd eaten their meal in the garden, they sat talking as the sun set. Then they lit candles and continued talking, enjoying a bottle of wine and the peaceful surroundings. Kate found the flickering light soothing and, for the first time since the kidnapping, she relaxed. In fact she was so relaxed by eleven o'clock that she found it almost impossible to keep her eyes open.

'Bed,' Sam ordered the women. 'You both need to get your strength up for Paris. And I need to see how much I have in the bank.'

This made them laugh, and Kate felt quite excited about their proposed trip.

She kissed Maria goodnight and hugged Sam and Jacques.

Sam spoke softly. 'Sleep well, chérie. No more nightmares.'

*

It was nine o'clock in the morning before Kate opened her eyes the next day. The sun was shining; the only sound was the chattering of birds in the large tree outside her window. She watched sunlight casting shimmering patterns on the wall and sighed with contentment. That had been the most restful and untroubled night's sleep, and she felt more like her old self. She hadn't enjoyed Sam's grilling when she'd first arrived, but he'd known what he was doing. He'd obviously been very well informed about the state she was in, and she could see her Aunt Annie's hand in this. Her aunt would know he was the right person to give her a jolt. Sam knew how to deal with trauma. She was glad she'd come.

'What do you want to do today?' Maria asked, when she finally wandered downstairs.

'We could go for a drive, if you like,' Sam said.

Kate broke open the light croissant and spread jam on a piece. 'Oh, that's delicious.' She swallowed and smiled at them. 'Would you mind very much if I borrowed one of the bikes? I'd like to ride around and enjoy a quiet day.'

'You do exactly what you want,' Sam told her.

'Of course you must,' Maria agreed. 'Jacques will be home around five o'clock, so we will have dinner at six.'

'I'll be back long before then,' Kate told them.

Kate kept away from the main road to Saint-Omer and headed for the open country she always visited with Jacques when she was here. After about two kilometres, she dismounted and walked along pushing the bike. She passed some farm workers who greeted her politely. After that it was empty countryside.

A movement in a field on her right caught her attention. Something was thrashing about in a clump of rough bushes. She propped the bike against the low wooden fence and clambered over. It was a scrubby piece of land and what she saw filled her with fury. A rabbit had one of its hind legs caught in an old piece of chicken wire that had been dumped there. When it saw her, the poor animal went frantic trying to escape. Afraid it would injure itself, she caught hold of it and held on firmly with one hand while she eased the leg free. When that was done, she examined the animal carefully to see that it wasn't badly hurt. After assessing that no great damage had been done, she released it. It shot off into the middle of the field, then turned to look at her as if to say thank you. It gave a little dance of joy and dived down a hole to safety.

Kate sat back on her heels and laughed. She agreed with the little animal – freedom was a wonderful thing, and so very precious.

Everyone was in a happy mood as they set off for Paris the next day. Maria had clearly made a good recovery from the operation and was looking forward to the trip, explaining what she intended to buy. Kate had made up her mind to find an outfit in the latest fashion. She would also keep her eyes open for something unusual for the boys. Although Ed was her special favourite, she never wanted the others to feel left out.

Kate enjoyed the journey – especially deciding what

kind of clothes she wanted. She had been brought up to be wise with money and was not usually a lavish spender, but for the next few days she was going to forget caution and, like that little rabbit, rejoice in her freedom.

23

After ordering coffee in a café on Boulevard Saint-Germain, Jon found himself a table outside on the pavement, underneath the shade of a small tree. It was a lovely day again, with just enough breeze to stir the air and add a touch of freshness. The café was busy with some people reading newspapers, while others, like himself, just watched the people walking by. He found the relaxed atmosphere restful, and that was what he needed after the party last night at the British Embassy. It had been some affair, he thought, gingerly sipping his coffee. He'd been surprised to find himself in his own bed, but how he'd managed to get back to his hotel was a mystery. He couldn't remember much after midnight, but the notebook in his pocket held copious notes, so at some point he must have been sober enough to get some work done. Thank goodness for that, he thought with a wry smile, the place had been crowded with politicians from all over and he'd have hated to have missed such a chance. He had enough material to keep him going for several days, so he intended to have an easy day.

He spent a lot of his time trying to interview prominent people and chasing around the city after politicians. It was a small price to pay for such a comfortable assignment. He hoped Andrew Stevenson didn't find him another war too soon.

The waiter refilled his cup, and he sat back with a

contented smile on his face. Suddenly he jerked upright, his gaze riveted on the girl walking on the other side of the street.

Kate Freeman?

He surged to his feet, threw some francs on to the table and ran across the road after the girl. Was it her? If she'd had a camera bag on her shoulder, he wouldn't have doubted it. If it was her, then she had obviously been shopping, because she was carrying packages and laughing with the petite woman beside her.

He followed, almost sure it was Kate. No one had hair that black, or such long shapely legs. He remembered those attributes very clearly from the first time he'd met her.

He saw them stop at a café further along the street, to be greeted by a middle-aged man and a young boy. He wished she would turn round so he could see her face . . .

At that moment she did just that and looked straight at him. It was her!

'Hello, Kate.' He walked forward, and she shook hands with him politely, not looking very enthusiastic about meeting him again. A little thing like that didn't bother him, though. He was so pleased to see her, and besides, he encountered that attitude every day in his work. 'Are you on holiday?'

'Yes, I'm staying with friends.'

The other three people were eyeing him with interest as she introduced him.

'This is Jon Devlin,' she told them. 'He's a war corres-pondent with the newspaper I worked on for a few months.'

'The one that kicked you out?' the boy asked, ducking quickly as she turned on him.

'Unfortunately I kicked myself out.' Then she smiled at Jon. 'These are my friends, Maria and André Riniou and their son, Jacques.'

Jon shook hands with them. The boy was slightly younger than her, and his arm was around her shoulder in a possessive way.

The man smiled. 'We were just about to have lunch – will you join us, Jon?'

'Thank you.' He didn't feel like eating, but he was curious about Kate's relationship with this young man, so he agreed readily. Maria obviously didn't speak much English. But his French was adequate for the occasion.

Jacques pulled two more chairs over to the table. 'Shall I take all those parcels back to the hotel?' he asked his mother.

'No, just pile them on a spare chair for the moment.'

'Be careful with that one, Sam,' Kate said, as he put one on the top of the heap, causing it to wobble. 'It's delicate.'

Maria took it from her husband and placed it carefully under the chair. 'Sit down everyone, we are hungry after all that shopping.'

'I should think you are.' Sam raised his eyebrows. 'I hope you've finished for the day.'

'Well, almost.' Kate burst into laughter. 'Don't look like that, Sam. We promised we'd only take one day to go round the shops.'

Jon was puzzled. 'Why does Kate call you Sam when she introduced you as André?'

'Confusing, isn't it?' Jacques said. 'All Kate's family call him Sam because that's what they knew him as during the war. It was his code name.'

'Really?' Jon thought this was getting more interesting by the minute. As a reporter he had an inquisitive nature.

'Yes.' Jacques continued, ignoring the warning look from his father: 'The only one who ever knew what he really did was Kate's Aunt Annie. They worked together through most of the war, and that's how we know the Freeman family.'

Jon was about to ask more questions when Maria stopped him. 'And what are you doing in Paris, Mr Devlin?'

'I've recently returned from Algeria, and I'm working from here for a while.'

'Ah, there is great trouble out there.' Maria shook her head sadly. 'One would have thought that the last war would have cured the world of fighting. However, it seems not.'

'If we all stopped fighting and learned to live in peace, this planet would become a Garden of Eden.' Jon grimaced. 'But then I would be out of a job.'

'I shouldn't think there's any danger of that for a long time to come.' Sam studied him thoughtfully. 'You have the reputation of a man who goes into places others are afraid of.'

'I go after a story that needs telling and the best way to do that is to be in amongst the fighting groups.'

'I agree that is often the only way to find out what is really going on.' Sam smiled. 'You have a more peaceful assignment at the moment.'

'Paris, yes.' Jon had almost forgotten his hangover in talking to this interesting man. He had the feeling there was a great deal more to him than you saw on the surface. He turned to Kate and said jokingly, 'Don't tell the Chief I'm enjoying myself, or he'll soon find me another trouble spot to visit.'

'I won't tell anyone I've met you,' she said, the corners of her mouth slanting upwards.

He looked deep into her eyes and was relieved to see her less withdrawn. The first time he'd met her there had been coldness in those glorious dark eyes. There was more warmth there now. She had inherited her mother's beauty, but he'd doubted that she had the same strength of character. Now he knew he'd been wrong. Kate Freeman had a lot of inner strength; he could almost feel it, and see it in her steady gaze.

'Have you seen Eddie lately?' he asked, and watched her expression soften. The change was so marked that he felt it go right through him, almost robbing him of breath.

'Yes, I took him home to have Sunday lunch with my parents and brother. Dad and James played football with him, and Mum filled him up with her suet pudding and treacle. He said he'd had a *luverly* day.' She chuckled softly at the memory.

'Give him and the rest of the boys my love when you see them, and please tell them that I'll take them all out when I can get home.'

'I will.' She gazed into space for a moment. 'We have a house in Wales and I did think of taking the boys there, but they haven't finished school for the summer yet, and it is a long way.'

'What, all of them?' Jon looked horrified. 'They'd wreck the place. How big is this house anyway?'

'A modest size,' Sam told him. 'But it was a haven during the war and always full. Everyone was welcome.'

'And there's a lovely cottage in the grounds.' Maria gave her husband a loving glance. 'We were married there.'

Sam slipped his arm around his wife's shoulder. 'They have been our dear friends ever since.'

'You were all there during the war?' Jon asked.

'No.' A brief moment of anger flashed across Sam's face, then it was gone. 'After I found Jacques and managed to get him out of France, Rose looked after him for me and I visited when I could. The war was almost over before I found Maria. Again Kate's family came to our aid. We all have so much to thank them for – they are a caring family.'

'You sound as if you had a rough time.' Jon looked at them with respect. He knew that after the war there had been thousands of displaced people, and the task of reuniting families had been enormous. Many had never found their loved ones.

'We did,' Maria agreed, 'but many were not as fortunate as us. We survived and are together.' Her expression was compassionate as she gazed at Jon. 'Don't be too eager to throw your life away for a story, young man. It is too precious.'

'I'll try to remember that the next time someone's shooting at me.'

That made everyone laugh, and Sam stood up. 'It has been a pleasure meeting you, Jon. Any friend of Kate's is welcome at our table. Now, if you will excuse us, Maria must rest before they set out on the second half of their shopping trip.'

Jacques dragged Kate out of her chair. 'Come on, let's go for a trip on the river while the old ones sleep.'

'Just a minute, what about all these parcels?' Maria scolded her son for wanting to dash off. 'You're not going to leave your *ancient* parents to carry them all, are you?'

'I'll help you.' Jon picked up the heaviest of the parcels.

'Thanks.' Jacques shook hands with him. 'It was good to meet you.'

Kate only had time to smile at him before she was towed away by the young man.

Sam watched them with a rueful expression on his face. 'He still treats her like the small girl he met during the war.'

'Do you think she'll be your daughter-in-law one day?' Jon asked in amusement, watching the two running across the road.

'Good heavens!' Sam tipped his head back and laughed. 'A lovely idea, but I doubt it. They are more like brother and sister.'

For some strange reason Jon was quite pleased with that piece of information.

The hotel where Sam and Maria were staying was only ten minutes away, and, while they made their way up to their room, Jon told them about the help Rose had given him with the children's home.

'Ah, you went to the right person,' Sam told him. 'If you want something done quickly, then Rose is the person to contact.'

Jon changed the subject. 'I've read what happened to Kate. It must have been terrible for her. She looks happy enough, but is that just a front? Do you think she'll be all right?'

'Yes, she'll come through it okay.' Sam sounded confident.

Jon helped them to their room with the parcels. He noticed Maria only carried a couple of very light ones and appeared rather tired. She clearly needed to rest, so he turned to leave.

'We shall be here for the next two days,' Sam told him, 'so if you have time, would you have dinner here with us tomorrow?'

'Thank you, I'd like that.' He was delighted with the invitation.

'Seven o'clock suit you?'

'That's fine. I'll see you tomorrow, then.'

It was more than two hours later when Kate and Jacques returned to the hotel, sagging under the weight of their purchases. They went straight to his parents' room, giggling like a couple of kids. It was impossible to open the door, so Jacques knocked with the toe of his shoe.

'What the blazes have you got there?' Sam exclaimed as two piles of parcels walked in.

Kate peered around the side of her stack and grinned. 'We've been shopping.'

Maria was now viewing the strange apparitions, with only the legs visible. 'We can see that. Come on, drop them on the bed and show us what you've bought.'

The top parcel was unwrapped and Jacques held up an orang-utan on strings.

'Puppets!' Sam quickly counted the boxes. 'You've bought twelve large puppets?'

Kate pulled out a cat with huge eyes and began to

make it dance. The monkey joined in as Kate and Jacques sang – very out of tune.

Sam and Maria were roaring with laughter at their antics.

'What on earth do you need those for?' Maria managed to compose herself enough to speak.

Kate stroked the cat and made it roll its eyes and shiver in excitement. 'They're for the boys at Wilkins House. There are twelve of them living there, so I had to get one for each of them. Do you think they'll like them?'

'They will love them,' Sam assured her. 'It will make them very happy.'

'How are you going to get them home?' Maria asked. 'You already have as much luggage as you can carry.'

Kate's eyes opened wide. 'Oh, dear, I was so excited about finding them that I never gave that a thought.'

'Ah, Kate,' Sam's look was full of affection. 'You've never done anything without first giving it careful consideration, and it's wonderful to see you act so spontaneously.'

She sat on the edge of the bed, the animal on her knee, and bounced it, deep in thought. 'You're right. I've always known what I wanted to do with my life, so sure it would go the way I'd planned. I know now that things don't happen like that. Life is unpredictable, like my job, for instance. For years I had one aim, and that was to work for the *World Explorer*. It didn't work out, and I can see that it wasn't the right place for me.'

'Have you decided where your right place is?' Maria asked.

'No.' Kate put the puppet back in the box. 'Since the kidnapping and that horrible trial, I've stopped planning.

I'll concentrate on my photography and the shop and see where life leads me.'

'Wonderful philosophy!' Jacques exclaimed. 'That's just what I intend to do. It will make life more exciting.'

Maria gave a sigh of resignation as she listened to her son. 'Finish your education first.'

'I'll contain myself until then.' He grinned. 'Now, that still leaves the problem of how Kate carries all these parcels.'

'Hmm.' Sam surveyed the huge amount of boxes. 'We'll stack everything in the car and I'll come back with you.'

'Oh, Sam, I can't let you do that. I should have thought before I went mad and bought the puppets. I never even considered it, all I could think about was how much the boys would love them.'

'I will drive you home; it's all settled.'

Kate knew from the firmness in his voice that it would be useless to argue, and really it was the only solution.

'Are you two ladies going shopping again?' Sam raised an eyebrow in query.

'Would you mind, Kate?' Maria asked. 'I don't get to Paris very often, and there are still one or two things I'd like to buy.'

'I'll be ready in fifteen minutes.' She stood up. 'Would you help me to my room with these parcels, Jacques?'

'I want you both to buy yourselves a special dress. We're entertaining a gentleman for dinner tomorrow,' Sam said.

'Who's that?' Kate asked.

'Jon Devlin.'

24

After knocking on Sam and Maria's room, Kate walked in. Jacques was already there and when he saw her he let out a whistle of appreciation.

'Wow! You look fabulous.'

The deep amber dress suited her to perfection, emphasizing her dark looks in a dramatic way. The neckline was cut away in a heart shape, exposing her flawless skin; the long sleeves were moulded to her arms and ended in a row of tiny gold and amber buttons at the wrist. She sketched Jacques a curtsy, making the delicate material flow around her ankles.

'That's beautiful,' Maria sighed. 'It looks even better than it did in the shop.'

'And so does yours.' Kate walked around Maria, inspecting her from every angle. The outfit she'd chosen was royal-blue with straight lines and a short jacket to cover her bare arms, if she felt the need for it. Both gowns had been wildly expensive and shouted Parisian chic.

Kate smiled at Sam. 'Doesn't she look stunning?'

'I can't argue with that. However, I'm about to have a row with you. Maria tells me that you insisted on paying for both of these lavish gowns.'

Ah, she'd thought this might happen. He was going to object.

'I can't let you do that.' Sam reached in his pocket.

'You can hold it right there!' she ordered, standing to

her full height and placing her hands on her hips. 'I wanted Maria to have that dress; it's my way of saying thanks to both of you, and it won't do you any good to argue.'

Jacques gave a yelp and shot to the other side of the room, his eyes wide in mock terror. 'You can't win, Papa. That isn't Kate standing there, it's Auntie Rose, and no one argues with her!'

They were all shaking with laughter now, but Kate managed to keep her expression stern. 'Am I going to have trouble with you, Group Captain Riniou?'

There were howls of laughter coming from Jacques. 'Now she's turned into Auntie Annie. I've heard her talk to you just like that.'

Sam raised his hands in a gesture of surrender. 'I don't stand a chance.'

'Accept defeat graciously, my dear,' Maria told him, 'or you'll have the whole Freeman family after you in the shape of Kate.'

'Thank you for buying Maria the dress,' he said meekly, kissing her on both cheeks. Then he whispered, 'Don't you ever believe you're not made of the same stuff as Rose and Annie.'

Jacques sidled back and looked at her cautiously. 'Is my Kate back now?'

'I'm not sure I want the old Kate back. I think I like the new one much better.'

'Bravo!' she heard Sam murmur under his breath.

They were in a happy mood as they went downstairs to meet Jon. Kate was just beginning to realize how much she had changed over the last few months, and she *did* prefer the new Kate Freeman.

Jon was waiting for them in the bar, and Kate's step faltered when she saw him. He was wearing a dark charcoal-grey suit and a subdued tie in grey with delicate splashes of maroon on it. He was certainly an impressive man. He stood up and smiled when he saw them, his startling green eyes resting on her with obvious appreciation.

Kate felt her heart rate increase. Before they'd even met she'd had a mental picture of him, but he was nothing like she'd imagined, and the last couple of times they'd seen each other she'd been too traumatized to take much notice of him. Now she did study him and what she saw made her uneasy. He was six feet or more, long legs and strong build. Her mind flashed back to Derek Howard, knowing that if Jon Devlin ever turned nasty, she wouldn't stand a chance against him either. She despised herself for her suspicions, but he was a tough man and she would do well to keep her distance.

After greeting each other, they stayed in the bar for a drink before the meal. The conversation flowed easily between the men, and Kate's mind drifted. It was then she realized that the only young men she trusted now were Jacques and Pete, and it was in their company she relaxed. That came as a shock, and she told herself off for being so stupid. Not all powerful men were violent or rapists! Her own father was an example of that truth – six foot four, strong, but so kind and gentle.

'Kate?' Sam's voice snapped her out of her musing. 'Do you want another drink?'

'No, thanks.' She shook her head and hoped the movement would dislodge her silly fears. If she wasn't firmer

271

with herself, then Howard could ruin her life. She could *not* allow that to happen!

'Let's go in to dinner, then.' Sam led the way to the dining room.

The hotel restaurant was renowned for its cuisine. The tables were generously spaced, so that you could have a conversation without being overheard; the lighting was subdued; and in the centre was a small dance floor with five musicians playing quietly.

Their table was right by a window with a good view of the Seine. Kate gazed out at the scene and breathed in deeply. It wasn't quite dark yet, and the lights were just beginning to come on. In the dusk people were strolling along arm in arm, talking, laughing, and boats were gliding along causing gentle ripples in their wake. Paris was a beautiful city. This was lovely.

Jon was laughing about something Jacques had said. It was a deep, enticing sound; the kind of infectious laugh that made everyone smile. She turned away from the window as Jacques touched her arm.

'What are you going to have to eat?'

She glanced down the extensive menu. 'What a choice! You decide for me.' When she noticed the gleam of mischief in his eyes, she hastily added, 'But not escargots.'

'Come on,' he teased, 'where's your sense of adventure?'

'Running like hell when it's faced with snails.'

'Okay, what about pâté, sole and then a steak? Is that English enough for you?'

'Sounds lovely.'

'What are you going to do after university?' Jon asked

Jacques, now that the problem of food was out of the way.

'I can't decide. Kate's brother, James, has offered me a job at Grant Phillips.'

'Has he?' She didn't know her brother had done that, yet it wasn't really surprising. Jacques was like a brother to them.

'Yes, some time ago.' His expression became serious. 'I appreciate it, but I don't want to live in London. I know Papa spent a long time in England, but I love France and wouldn't be happy anywhere else.'

'Then you must do what makes you happy. That's the most important thing, and James will understand.' Kate was a little disappointed about his decision. It would have been lovely to have Jacques come into the business, and her mother would have loved it.

'He does. I've already told him how I feel, Kate.' He finished off the last of his fish course and grinned at her. 'You and James will have to get a move on and have sons to carry on the family business.'

'Planning our lives for us now, are you?' Kate asked, giving him a stern glance.

'You two are working towards a fight, so you can stop that right now,' Maria said, not being able to hide her smile.

'I can't understand it,' Kate sighed dramatically. 'He was such a quiet boy.'

'Of course I was. I was whisked out of France by a man I didn't know, then there were two females with eyes as black as night, the big one ordered me around, and the little one . . .' He paused. 'Ah, how I loved the little one.'

Kate leant across and kissed his cheek. 'I hope you still do.'

'Always, chérie.'

'How long are you staying in Paris?' Sam asked Jon.

'As long as I can wangle it. I love the place.'

'The boys miss you when you're away,' Kate told him. 'Tom and Eddie are always talking about you. I think you're their hero.'

'I started life as an abandoned baby, so they look at me and think there's a chance for them.'

'You were abandoned?' Maria was shocked.

'I was just a few days old, evidently. The nurses at the hospital I was taken to gave me an estimated date of birth, and put names in a hat.' He grimaced. 'They pulled out Jonathan and then used the ward sister's surname, and so I became Jon Devlin.'

Maria's expression became sad. 'But how can a mother abandon her child and never want to see it again?'

'I don't know. Yet there are many who do. You only have to go into the children's homes to see that.'

At the mention of the children Jacques chuckled. 'You ought to see what Kate's bought for twelve of the boys.'

Jon turned to her, looking pleased. 'You've bought them all a present?'

'There was this quaint little shop full of puppets and I couldn't resist them.' Kate's chuckle was full of pleasure.

'They're about two feet high,' Sam explained, 'and Kate was so excited about them that she never gave a thought as to how she was going to get them home.'

'Papa will have to take her back in the car.'

'When are you returning to London?' Jon asked Kate.

'Five days' time – Sunday morning.'

'I'm popping over to see the boys then, so why don't you come with me?'

She wasn't sure she wanted to spend any length of time with him. It would save Sam an unnecessary journey, though. 'Well . . .'

'It's up to you,' Sam told her. 'I'm quite happy to come with you.'

'No, that's silly when Jon's going and will take me and all my parcels.' She smiled reassuringly at Sam. It was as if he sensed her doubts about being alone with Jon in the car.

'I can come with you,' Jacques offered, 'and catch the next boat back. I'm not due at university until nine on Monday.'

'Oh, no, I can't let you do that.' She turned to Jon. 'Thank you, I would appreciate a lift home.' Having accepted, she smiled at Sam and Jacques. This lingering fear was a damned nuisance.

'I hope you have a large car, Jon,' Maria said. 'Not only does Kate have the puppets, but she's also bought clothes and presents for just about everyone.'

Kate sat back, folded her arms and gave Sam an accusing look, or at least she tried to but was shaking with laughter. 'And who was daft enough to bring me to Paris?'

'Now it's my fault you spent so much money?' Sam raised his eyebrows at Jon. 'You sure you want to travel with her?'

'It will be a pleasure, and I'm sure I can fit all the luggage in.' Jon turned to Kate. 'Now, where shall I pick you up?'

Sam wrote down his address for Jon.

When Kate saw what Sam was doing, she reached out to stop him. 'That isn't necessary. I'll meet Jon at Calais.'

'No, no,' Maria said. 'Give him our address. He could collect Kate at around seven in the morning and load the car at our house, or' – she turned to Jon – 'you could stay with us on Saturday.'

'I'm afraid I shall be busy on Saturday. I'll have to pick Kate up at your house on Sunday.'

Kate was relieved he couldn't come the day before, but that still left her with the prospect of travelling in a car with him on her own. This was another fear she was going to have to conquer. Damn Derek Howard!

'Come and dance with me.' Jacques pulled her on to her feet. 'The music's a bit tame, but I'm sure we can manage.'

The band was playing a slow waltz, and she couldn't help wondering how he was going to deal with that. 'All right, as long as you don't jump about like a demented rabbit.'

'You are so behind the times,' Jacques teased. 'I expect I can manage a slow dance.'

What he meant was he could shuffle around the floor and tread on her toes far too often. When the dance was finished, she sat down and gave him a pitying look. 'That was supposed to be a waltz.'

'That's what I did.' He grinned, thoroughly enjoying himself. He did love to tease her.

Jon stood up and held out his hand. 'Will you risk a foxtrot with me?'

Kate felt it would be rude to refuse their guest, so she stood up again. He swept her on to the dance floor and, much to her surprise and relief, she found that he was an excellent dancer. Being this close to him, however, made her uncomfortable. She could feel the strength in his arms and wanted to run, but she forced herself to relax and smile. 'Are you enjoying your stay in Paris?' she asked, making polite conversation.

'Very much, but knowing Andrew Stevenson, he won't let me have an easy life for long.' Jon held her away from him, so he could look into her face. 'How's Eddie?'

'Oh, he's great!' The dance came to an end then, and Kate was rather sorry.

It was nearly midnight when Jon walked back to his hotel through the still busy streets. He whistled softly to himself. It had been a very enjoyable evening. Kate had looked stunning in that Parisian creation, and he was pleased she'd taken the trouble to buy the boys presents. She was obviously wary of all men now, unless she knew them. It would be understandable after what she'd been through, but he still hadn't been able to resist the challenge of making her accept his offer. It had been a spur of the moment thing, as he hadn't had any intention of going back to London just yet. She'd had a sheltered life, he guessed, and the kidnapping must have been a great shock to her.

Her friends had been aware of her unease, and he'd watched the older man's face as Kate had hesitated. When she'd accepted, Sam had given him a slight nod of the head, as if satisfied with her decision. And so was he. It would be interesting to see how she coped with her lingering fears, and perhaps he could help her to come to terms with what had happened. Not that he was interested in her, of course, just curious. The last thing he intended to do was get romantically involved with a girl again. But Kate Freeman was hard to resist.

Now, who could he borrow a big car from?

Before it was light on Sunday morning Jon was on his way. Sam's village was only about five kilometres from Saint-Omer and would be easy enough to find. He'd left in plenty of time, though, in case he lost his way.

The large Citroën purred along, and he chuckled in delight as he remembered Rupert Walsh's look of disgust when he'd seen the battered old Ford he was offering to lend him in exchange for this sleek beast. He'd had to throw in enough francs for a slap-up meal before he had given way. Rupert was an ex-public-school boy, and now secretary at the British Embassy. From one lavish lifestyle to an even more lavish one. It would do him good to rough it for a change.

He stopped for breakfast in Saint-Omer, then wasted another half an hour walking around the ancient market town. Sixteen years after the war and there was hardly a sign of the devastation caused by that conflict.

Judging that if he left now he would arrive at seven, he returned to the car to continue his journey. He was really looking forward to seeing Kate again. Not that he intended anything but friendship between them. But he found her intriguing, and this would give him a chance to spend some time with her.

25

'Oh, dear.' Maria gazed at the pile of luggage outside the door. 'I do hope he has a very big car.'

'I have rather overdone it,' Kate admitted. 'But I've had such a wonderful time.'

Jacques stacked the last box on top of the heap. 'You'd better ask him to take you straight to the children's home and get rid of the puppets first.' After issuing that piece of advice, he wandered off to see if Jon was coming yet.

Kate chewed her lip anxiously. 'I don't want to put him to all that trouble.'

'He won't mind.' Sam turned her to face him. 'I'm a good judge of character, Kate. Jon Devlin has a tight control over his emotions and would never allow his feelings to overrule his actions. You'll be safe with him. Had I believed otherwise, I would never have allowed you to go back with him.'

'I know.' She gave him a hug. 'You have helped me so much, but some things are still vivid in my mind.'

'They will fade in time. You must be patient with yourself,' Maria told her. 'It took me quite a while to overcome the horror of the labour camp. It did eventually fade and it no longer hurts me.'

Kate felt sad as she remembered what these dear people had been through. But they were happy, whole people, and she would be again!

Jacques was peering up the road and began to wave

eagerly, then he turned and hurtled back to them. 'There's a great big black car coming. It must be him.'

Jon drove up to the house, got out and was greeted warmly by everyone, including Kate.

Jon looked at the parcels and shook his head. 'Good Lord, you have bought a lot.'

'I'm afraid so,' she said apologetically.

Sam and Jacques helped him pack everything into the car, and she watched carefully. As a child she had been intuitive about people and seemed to know if they were nice, or someone she didn't want to know. That instinct had faded as she'd grown up, but it was still there and she now concentrated on Jon Devlin. What was he like as a man?

The feeling that swept through her was that he was calm, reliable, with controlled strength, tempered with kindness. Her doubts seeped away. There wasn't anything about him to be afraid of, in fact she could trust him. If only she'd made more use of her intuition last December, then it could have saved a great deal of anguish for herself and her family.

'That's the lot, then.' Sam closed the boot of the car.

It had begun to drizzle and a wind was whipping the trees into a frenzy. Maria looked up at the leaden sky. 'The weather is deteriorating. I hope you don't have too rough a crossing.'

'Let's hope so.' Jon grimaced. 'If you're ready, Kate, we'd better get going.'

She kissed them all. 'Thank you for a lovely holiday.'

'Don't leave it too long before you come again,' Maria told her. 'And you pay us a visit when you have time, Jon.'

'Thank you, I'll do that.' Jon started the car and headed down the road.

Kate waved until they were out of sight.

'They're fine people,' he remarked as they turned on to the Calais road.

'The best,' she agreed.

It was only about an hour to Calais, and they chatted easily all the way, mostly about the children. That was something they both had a great interest in and were in complete agreement about.

They drove straight on to the ferry when they arrived. The sea was choppy but not rough enough to delay sailing, and they were soon on their way. The rain had stopped, and they stood on the deck as they sailed away from France. It had been a wonderful week. Kate felt really relaxed. Bless Sam for his understanding.

She shivered and pulled her jacket around her. 'You'd never believe it was the first week of August, would you?'

There was no response from her companion.

'I'd like a cup of tea and something to eat,' she said. 'Shall we go inside?'

'I don't want anything. You go ahead.'

She was surprised by his sharp tone and wondered what she had done to upset him. But if he didn't want her company, then she'd leave him alone. He might not want anything to eat, but she was starving!

She enjoyed a pot of tea and a bacon sandwich, and, as there still wasn't any sign of Jon, she weaved her way back to where she'd left him, laughing to herself as the deck dropped from under her now and again. The weather was getting rougher.

He was still in the same place, so she stood beside

him, grabbing at the rail to steady herself. She was about to make a joke about the way the boat was rolling when she saw his face. He looked awful!

'You're seasick!' She was surprised that the big, tough man could succumb to a choppy sea. She put her arm around his shoulders in sympathy. 'Let me get you a drink.'

'I don't want anything.' He shook her arm loose, moving further along the rail. 'Go away!'

If he thought she was going to leave him in this state, then he was very much mistaken. He might fall overboard. The only concession she made to his request was to take two steps away from him. He could glower at her as much as he liked, but she wasn't moving.

They were only about half an hour from Dover when he straightened up. She was relieved to see he had more colour in his face.

He ran a hand through his wind-blown hair and glanced at her. 'All right, I'll have that cup of tea now.'

She walked beside him not speaking, resisting the urge to steady him by holding on to his arm. He obviously found sympathy unwelcome, so she wouldn't risk that again. Once this journey was over she wouldn't have to see him again. It was a comforting thought, because he made her feel very edgy.

'Sit down,' she ordered. 'I'll get the tea.' She was soon back and watched him drink two cups of sweet tea.

'You can stop looking at me with such disbelief,' he growled. 'Everyone has a weakness, and mine is the sea.'

'Then why didn't you fly back?'

'I was hoping it would be like a millpond.'

'And you'd promised to bring me back.' She was suddenly sure that the only reason he was on this boat was because of her.

'That too.' He managed a slight smile. 'Reckless of me to think I could make the journey without throwing up.'

The call came to disembark, and they were soon heading for London. Jon appeared to have recovered completely and was obviously happy now he was on dry land again.

'Do you want to go to the children's home first?' he asked.

'That would be lovely. Do you mind?'

'Not at all. I can't wait to see these puppets.'

There were squeals of delight as they staggered in with the parcels. After making sure the boys were all there, Kate lined up the boxes on the floor.

'There's one for each of you, so who's the youngest?'

'Me, me!' Eddie was beside himself with excitement.

Kate knelt on the floor behind the boxes. 'I want you to come up one at a time in order of age and choose a box. Whatever is in it will be yours.'

The boys shuffled along, kept in order by Mrs Green, and pounced on the parcels.

'I don't want you to open them until you've all chosen one,' she ordered sternly, as little fingers eagerly tore at the wrapping.

When each child had his parcel, she sat back on her heels. 'Now you can open them.'

It was bedlam as the puppets were pulled out of the boxes with screams of delight. Eddie rushed at her, knocking her flat on her back. It was a good job she was wearing trousers, she thought, as she rolled on the floor with not only Eddie but also Tom and the rest of them, all trying to thank her at once.

'They move!' Tom shouted as she extracted herself from the mêlée.

'How, how?' Eddie was clutching a white, long-eared rabbit with enormous eyes and a gleeful expression on its face.

They all appeared more than satisfied with the ones they had, particularly Tom, who had the orang-utan.

Jon was busy showing some of them how to manipulate the strings, and she made Eddie's and Tom's dance for them. She was enormously pleased to see that the older ones were as taken with the puppets as the younger ones.

'They're going to have hours of fun with those.' Mrs Green smiled as she looked at twelve happy faces. 'Would you stay and have lunch with us?'

Jon looked up. 'Can you spare the time, Kate?'

'Of course.'

Eddie and Tom were overjoyed that they were staying for a while, and had a hard time remaining quiet when they were eating – something that Mrs Green was strict about. Kate noticed that Jon must have recovered from his boat journey, because he appeared to enjoy his mince and dumplings.

They left half an hour after the meal, and Kate saw him slip some notes into Mrs Green's hand.

'Where to next?' he asked.

'Could you take me to Roehampton? I've left my car there.'

*

Her parents were in when they arrived. Her father shook Jon's hand.

'Thank you for bringing Kate home. I can see from the amount of luggage that she couldn't have managed on her own.'

'This is nothing,' Jon told him. 'You should have seen what she brought back for the children.'

Kate explained about the puppets, her face animated.

'You sound as if you've enjoyed yourself,' Rose said, pouring them all a cup of tea and slicing a freshly baked fruitcake.

'I've had a wonderful time.' She pulled a comical face. 'But I've spent a lot of money.'

'That's all right.' Her father didn't seem troubled by that fact. 'It isn't often you buy things just because they take your fancy.'

Her mother's expression told her that she didn't approve of reckless spending. Kate knew that as a child her life had been one of extreme poverty, never knowing where the next meal was coming from. Although they were now considered quite wealthy, her mother had, understandably, never completely lost her caution about money. To Rose it was a commodity to make life more comfortable, and to help others in desperate need. Squandering money did not sit easily with her.

'My biggest expense was the puppets,' she explained to her mother, 'and it was worth every franc to see the children so happy. I also bought Maria a beautiful gown.'

Her mother nodded her approval at those purchases, then said to Jon, 'Will you stay and have dinner with us?'

'I'm afraid I can't, but thank you for the invitation.'

He stood. 'I promised the children that I'd be back for tea.'

'Thank you for helping me,' Kate told him as they walked into the hall. 'I'm very grateful.'

'It was my pleasure.'

She tipped her head to one side and looked disbelieving.

'Except for the boat trip.' He picked up his jacket, grimacing at the memory.

'You travel all over the world and must have to go by sea sometimes, so how do you manage?' she asked. If he was ill like that every time, then he must dread such journeys.

'I try not to go by boat if I can, but you're right, it is unavoidable at times.' His mouth turned up at the corners in a wry smile. 'I throw up for a couple of hours and then I'm all right.'

'Well, pick a calmer day when you return to France, won't you?'

'I'll do my best.' Then he strode out to the car and roared off up the road towards Wandsworth.

'Are you staying?' her father asked her.

'No, sorry, Dad, I want to get back to the flat and then check and see what Pete has lined up for next week.'

Bill was in the sitting room watching his daughter drive away. 'She looks happier and more relaxed. That haunted expression is still in her eyes, but I think she's feeling more like herself.'

'The holiday has done her good.' Rose sat down and rubbed her temple.

'Have you got another headache?' Bill asked in concern.

'Yes, damned things. I thought I'd grown out of these, but they've returned just lately.'

'It's stress caused by everything that's happened, I expect.' Bill kissed her on the top of the head. 'Why don't you go to bed for a while?'

'It isn't that bad.' She settled herself in the armchair and closed her eyes. 'I'll rest here for an hour.'

Bill sat opposite her and gazed out of the window, deep in thought. After a while he looked back at Rose, who had opened her eyes.

'I can hear your mind working, Bill. What are you chewing over?'

'Jon Devlin seems to keep popping up everywhere. Do you think Kate is falling for him?'

Rose sat up straight. 'I don't think she's capable of falling in love at the moment. It might be a while before she can trust a man again.'

Bill was clearly saddened by that prospect. 'She's always been such a loving, sensitive girl, and I'd hate to believe she'll never have a family of her own because of one man.'

'For the first time in my life I wish she were more like me and would rant and rave, fighting everyone in sight, but she isn't like that. It is because she is so sensitive that I'm afraid the kidnapping and violence might leave scars too deep to heal properly.'

Bill looked deeply worried at this. 'Dear God, Rose, I hope you're wrong!'

26

On Monday morning, Jon went to see Andrew Stevenson before returning to France. There were rumblings of trouble coming out of Berlin and he wanted to see if Andrew knew anything.

'What's the news about Berlin?' he asked, when he was settled in the office chair with a cup of coffee in front of him.

'There's a great deal of speculation, but we do know that during July over 30,000 East Germans defected to West Berlin, and they're still streaming across. East Germany must be facing collapse. Khrushchev is becoming belligerent and talking about war.'

'I've heard there's a big build-up of Soviet troops in East Berlin. Do you want me to go out there and see what's going on?'

Andrew tapped the desk with a pencil, a frown on his face. 'I think you'd better. Something's going to happen soon. I'm damned if I can figure out what, though.'

'Khrushchev wouldn't be crazy enough to declare war on the West, surely?' Jon really couldn't see what the Soviets could do about the situation, but he had a nasty feeling that they would deal with it ruthlessly.

'Who knows what that man will do? He's volatile and unpredictable.'

'Right.' He finished his tea and stood up. 'I'll return

to France and finish up there, then I'll catch a train to Berlin.'

Andrew nodded grimly. 'Let me know where you're staying, and take a camera with you.'

'You sure?' Jon raised an eyebrow in query. The Chief had told him in the past exactly what he thought of his attempts at photography.

'I know you're no good with one of those things, so just do the best you can. I'm short of good photographers at the moment.'

'You should have kept Kate Freeman.' He couldn't resist the dig.

The only reply he received was a bad-tempered scowl as he headed for the door.

The journey back to France was calm and the boat hardly rocked at all, but he still managed to be sick. Still, at least he'd been a little more comfortable without having Kate standing about two feet away from him, watching anxiously. It was a relief to step on to dry land again, and the first thing he did after driving into Paris was to take the car back to Rupert at the embassy.

'I hope you've taken good care of it.' Rupert inspected every inch before giving a satisfied grunt. 'Looks undamaged. You can take that heap of junk you lent me and dump it somewhere. It's embarrassing driving around Paris in a wreck like that.'

'I'll get rid of it. I'm going to Berlin within the next couple of days.'

'Thought you might,' was the terse reply.

Jon recognized Rupert was on the defensive, so it was unlikely he would get any information out of him. He tried anyway. 'What news do you have about the situation there?'

'You know I can't tell you anything.'

'It isn't a secret, Rupert, there's trouble brewing. Khrushchev's threatening the West, and the East Berliners are defecting in droves.'

Rupert sighed in exasperation. 'You war correspondents are always looking for trouble. I agree that the Russians are becoming desperate, but they're impotent. There isn't anything they can do to stop the flow of people to the West.'

Jon's eyes flashed in irritation. 'I hope everyone in the British Embassy isn't that complacent. You can try to write off Khrushchev, but he's not that impotent. He'll do something!'

'And what the hell can he do? Nothing!'

As Rupert strode away, Jon shook his head in disbelief. If that was the general attitude, then God help the German people.

He drove the car back to his hotel and began making plans to leave.

That evening he did the rounds, knowing all of the haunts of those who might be in a position to hear confidential news. By midnight he was becoming increasingly concerned. It sounded as if Berlin were a powder keg just waiting to explode, with terrible implications for the rest of Europe. He'd better get out there as quickly as possible.

The next morning he gave his old car to a young waiter, who was delighted with the gift, packed his few belongings and headed for the station.

*

'Hi, Kate.' Pete greeted her with obvious pleasure. 'You look great. Did you enjoy your holiday?'

'I had a wonderful time.' She gazed around the shop. 'Where's Susan?'

'Taking a week off while we're not so busy. August will be a quiet month, as this is the height of the holiday season.'

'Now that I'm back, why don't you take some time off?' she asked him.

'No, I don't want a holiday. I enjoy my work too much.'

She didn't argue with him because she knew that was the truth. 'What bookings are there for this week?'

'Mostly portraits and passport photographs, but there's a twenty-first birthday party on Friday and a wedding on Saturday.' Pete placed a new photo in the window and then came and stood next to her. 'More people are going abroad for their holidays now, and they're all taking cameras with them, so what do you think about our running a developing and printing service?'

'That's a great idea. Can we manage it with only the three of us?'

'Yes, I've been thinking about this for some time. Susan is now good at developing films, and . . .' He hesitated. 'Terry enjoyed working here so much that he'd like to join us.'

'Terry?' Kate was astonished. 'He'd be willing to leave his job at the newspaper?'

'He talked to me about it and he's not happy there, Kate. The Chief keeps sending him away, and now he's married with a baby on the way he doesn't want to live like that. He's been looking for another job but hasn't found one he likes yet. Until he does, he'd be happy to work with us.'

She dragged Pete into the back room, opened the account book and sat down, drawing up a chair for her partner. 'We'd better grab him while we can. Let's see if we can afford him.'

An hour later they'd filled two sheets with scribbled figures. 'He'll have to take a cut in pay. Do you think he'd consider that?'

'I'm pretty sure he would.' Pete looked at her expectantly. 'He's very good.'

'I know he is.' Then she gave a mischievous grin. 'I don't think Andrew Stevenson will take kindly to our pinching his best photographer, do you?'

Pete shook with suppressed laughter. 'But I think he's going to leave anyway, so I don't think we should let that stop us.'

Kate studied the figures again and added a few more, as she made absolutely sure of her facts. 'We are doing very well.'

'That's because we're the best!' Pete lifted his head proudly. 'We've gained a good reputation.'

'If Terry joined us, we could think about opening another shop next year. And with a promise of a shop of his own we might be able to persuade him to stay permanently. What do you think of that idea?'

'I was thinking about that myself.' Pete's eyes shone with excitement. 'Do you think we really could?'

'Yes, we'll make Terry an offer.'

'He's at home today, so I'll go and collect him right now.' Pete rushed out of the shop.

When Pete arrived back with Terry, the three of them sat down and Kate explained their plans to take in people's holiday snaps for developing and printing. Then she told Terry what they could afford to pay him.

'Think about it very carefully, Terry,' Kate advised. 'We're planning to expand the business and would love to have you with us, but you'll be giving up a good job. And with a baby on the way – '

Terry stopped her. 'I'd already given it a lot of thought before I mentioned it to Pete. I know it will be a drop in salary but I could manage on what you're offering, and it would be a regular job without the fear of being sent away to heaven knows where. That last trip to the Congo was enough for me. I don't want to risk anything like that again.'

'We're thinking about opening another shop next year,' Pete said. 'Would you be willing to run it for us, if we do? Providing you decide to stay with us, of course.'

Terry looked thoughtful. 'That would certainly tempt me. I'd like that.'

'Great!' Pete exclaimed, as he and Kate shook hands with Terry to seal the appointment.

'I'll get my mother to draw up an agreement for you. As soon as you've worked your notice, come and join us.'

'I'll go and resign immediately.' Terry rose to his feet. 'Thanks to both of you.'

'I think we're getting the best of this arrangement,' Pete remarked. 'And with your help we'll be able to take on a lot more work.'

'My wife will be happy to have me around more while

she's pregnant.' Terry looked pleased about being offered the job.

As soon as Terry left, Kate and Pete hugged each other and did a little dance.

'There's no stopping us now!' Pete said. 'One new shop a year?'

She couldn't help laughing at his enthusiasm. He was turning into a dynamic businessman, but he wasn't reckless; he thought everything out carefully. By the time he was thirty, he would be a force to be reckoned with. It made her proud to know that she'd been able to help unlock his potential. 'Hold on,' she laughed. 'Terry might only be with us for a few months.'

'Oh, once he settles in he won't want to leave.' Pete sounded sure of this.

'Your confidence, Pete.' Kate rolled her eyes at him.

'Have I been wrong up to now?' he asked.

Kate pretended to give this deep thought, then said, 'Actually I don't think you have.'

'What are you going to do this week?' he asked her, changing the subject. 'I can handle everything here until Saturday, then I'll need your help.'

'I think it's time I did another article on the children's homes. Quite a few helpers have come forward, but they still need more. Standish House in particular.' She didn't visit there as often as she should because it upset her too much to see the babies without parents to love them. Wilkins House was different: the boys were older and she could talk to them. But the babies just watched with large soulful eyes, making her feel so blasted useless.

'I'll nip round to the café and get us something for our lunch, then you'll have the afternoon to go visiting.'

Pete disappeared. Kate checked her camera and loaded a film. She was ready for the first pictures.

It was Wednesday when the article and the photos for the children's homes were ready. She walked through the door of the *World Explorer* wondering what kind of a reception she was going to receive from Andrew Stevenson. It was strange to come back.

The newsroom was in uproar when she arrived. The atmosphere was tense. She grabbed Mike as he shot past her. 'What's going on?'

'There's speculation that the Russians are going to blockade Berlin again. Troops in the West are on full alert. We're desperately trying to find out exactly what's happening out there.' He dived for a phone that was ringing incessantly.

Kate went to the Chief's office and found him in a state of agitation, shouting down the phone. 'Well, bloody well find out!'

Joel Perkins was also there, standing quietly as if untouched by the sense of urgency running through the place. 'Hello, Kate, how are your parents?'

'They're fine, thank you. I think I've chosen the wrong moment.' She grimaced as Andrew Stevenson swore again and slammed down the phone.

'What do you want?' he growled. 'Are you after more of my bloody staff?'

'Not at the moment,' Kate told him quite seriously, which only seemed to infuriate him more. 'I've done a follow-up article on the children's homes.'

'My God, we could be heading for World War Three and you want me to print that?'

Joel took the envelope from Kate. 'Leave it with me. I'll see it's included in Saturday's edition.'

'We won't have room for that,' the Chief snapped.

'You'll make room, Andrew. This is important as well.' Joel placed the envelope in front of Andrew. 'The welfare of these poor children is something I want this paper to be concerned with.'

The Chief gave a resigned sigh, realizing that if the boss wanted something printed, then he had little choice in the matter. He gave Kate a malicious glare, obviously not caring what Joel Perkins thought. 'All right, you've got what you came for, and, as you've stolen my best photographer, you can try doing something useful.'

The phone jangled again and he snatched it up. She waited. Was he going to offer her an assignment?

He crashed the instrument down again. 'You still here?'

'You suggested I do something useful, so I'm waiting to see what you had in mind.' She nearly laughed out loud at his expression, and suddenly realized that he didn't intimidate her any more. She kept her eyes fixed on Andrew as she heard Joel chuckling softly.

'Young woman, you're just like your mother,' he murmured.

That remark filled her with joy. Yes, she was! And she'd fight anyone who said she wasn't. It had taken the trauma of the last few months to bring it to the surface, but the strength and determination had been there all the time.

'Well,' she said, 'what do you suggest I do?'

The Chief snorted. 'Don't tempt me, Kate Freeman, you may be a friend of the big boss here, but I'm under pressure and I don't give a damn if he kicks me out. So, if you're such a wonderful photographer, why don't you go to Berlin and get some pictures?'

Why not? 'All right, I will.' As she walked across the newsroom, Andrew bellowed, 'I want exclusive rights to them.'

'It will cost you,' she called back.

'If they're any good, you can name your price, as long as we're the only paper with them.'

Joel gave her a thumbs-up sign and she left with a grin of delight on her face. She'd get his pictures, and make him pay for their new shop.

Pete couldn't hide his worry about Kate's plan. Although she appreciated everyone's concern for her, it was time she came out fighting. She wouldn't budge in her resolve to do this, and Pete had to admit that it might bring in enough money to open the other shop sooner than next year.

'How are you going to get there?' he asked, sensing that it would be useless to argue with her.

'Fly if I can. I want to get there as quickly as possible, and, as we're busy on Saturday, I'll see if I can get a flight on Sunday.'

Pete considered this carefully. 'I'm sure Terry would help out if you want to go sooner.'

'Do you think he would?' Now she had made up her mind she was eager to get going.

'He told me on Monday he'd be around if we need him.'

'That's great!' Kate opened her purse to see how much money she had. 'I'll pop along to the bank and draw out some cash and then see if I can book a flight for tomorrow.'

'You take care,' Pete told her, 'it might be dangerous.'

'I'll be careful.' She gave a slight shrug. 'I doubt if anything could be as dangerous as being in that locked room with Derek Howard.'

Pete nodded grimly. 'Nevertheless, I wish I could go with you.'

'Don't worry. I'm just going to take some pictures, make Andrew Stevenson pay an exorbitant price for them, and then we'll open another shop. You can start looking for a suitable place.'

27

It was Wednesday the 9th of August, when Jon arrived in Berlin. The year 1961 was certainly proving to be busy for him. There was still turmoil and conflict in the Congo and Algeria, and now it looked as if a highly dangerous situation was developing in Berlin. It was late afternoon and people were hurrying along, heads down, not talking or smiling. Was Khrushchev going to declare war on the West, or was it just posturing on the part of the Soviets?

He could feel the tension in the city as he walked the streets looking for Gerhard's address. When they'd spent a couple of days together in Paris, Gerhard had said Jon could stay with him if he came to Berlin. He hoped the offer was still open.

He usually arrived somewhere when fighting was already going on, but this was different: the atmosphere was one of worry and waiting. Everyone was sure something was going to happen. But what? The question was so strong in the minds of Berliners it was almost audible. The only ones who didn't seem overly concerned were the politicians.

Ah, this must be it. He walked up to the front door of a large, rather dilapidated building, hoping Gerhard was at home; if not, he would have to find a hotel. This place would be more convenient, though, as it was only about twenty minutes' walk from the Potsdamer Platz, which was the busiest East–West crossing point. He knocked and waited.

He heard someone running down the stairs, and Gerhard opened the door.

'Jon!' He shook his hand. 'I've been expecting you. Come in.' He led the way up two flights of stairs and opened a door. 'I rent an apartment here, and you're welcome to use the sofa if you want to stay.'

'Thanks. I hoped your invitation was still open.' Jon walked into a spacious sitting room with a small kitchen area on one side, partitioned off with a row of low units. The sofa was well-worn leather and huge. He'd be very comfortable on that; he'd slept in far worse places.

'Coffee?' Gerhard asked.

'Love one.' He sat down on the sofa. 'It's good of you to put me up.'

'No trouble.' He put two mugs of coffee on a small table and sat down opposite Jon. 'I expected you days ago.'

'How bad are things?' He took a mouthful of coffee and studied Gerhard's worried face.

'People are pouring out of the Russian sector, and there's an air of desperation about them. From the stories I've heard from those coming to the West, things are pretty bad in the East. People are frightened. They are being watched by the secret police. They can bring very little with them, as coming across with cases would only arouse suspicion and they would be stopped. No one can hazard a guess at what the Soviets are going to do about it. It's obvious they can't sit back and let this go on for much longer.' His expression was haunted. 'My parents are still over there, but I can't make them leave their home. My old dad always has been a stubborn devil. I was seventeen when the Russians fought their way into Berlin. When I found out that the city was going to be divided up, I came to the British and American zones. I've been able to go across and see them regularly, but things are getting difficult now. The Soviets must be desperate to stop the flow of people leaving the East. They are losing all their skilled labour and professionals, like doctors, nurses, university lecturers and even train drivers.'

Now Jon understood Gerhard's worry. This wasn't just about his city – it was personal as well. 'I'm sorry. Don't worry. Perhaps all Khrushchev's threats will come to nothing.' The words sounded hollow even to his ears, because if he believed that he wouldn't be here.

Gerhard ran a hand distractedly through his hair. 'That's what I hope, but my gut feeling is that something is about to explode. There's growing panic in the air. Families are coming across one at a time so as not to alert the East German police. They can't let it go on. They just can't!'

That was exactly what Jon thought as well, yet he didn't voice his fear because this man was worried enough. 'Is there any chance of talking to some of the refugees?'

'Sure.' Gerhard drained his cup and stood up. 'I'll take you to the Marienfelde Centre – the place is crowded with the poor devils.'

For the next two days Jon prowled around the border crossing points, talking to as many people as he could and standing for hours watching the troop movements on the other side. His unease grew, though he wasn't sure why. There wasn't anything concrete to indicate that war between East and West was about to break out. But his years working in war zones had made him sensitive to trouble, and the atmosphere here was making the hair stand up on the back of his neck.

He was wondering if he was wasting his time when everything changed on Saturday, the 12th of August. People were streaming across the border carrying what possessions they could. Jon studied the faces as they reached the West, and, although there was relief that they'd made it, there was also grief that they'd left their homes and everything behind. His heart ached for them. By the evening he reckoned that several thousand had come into West Berlin that day.

There was no sign of Gerhard when he arrived back at the flat, so he settled down to try to get some sleep, knowing that the Russians were not going to allow this to continue. They could not afford to, and whatever they intended to do it would be soon.

It was a hot night on Saturday, the 12th of August, and Jon had trouble sleeping. He'd been wandering around all day, watching hundreds of worried, frightened-looking people come through the main crossing points between East and West.

Jon tossed in the stifling heat of Gerhard's sitting room, thumping his pillow. Eventually he drifted off to sleep.

'Jon!' Gerhard was shaking him. 'Wake up and get dressed. Something's happening!'

He was instantly on his feet and when he looked at his watch he saw that it was two in the morning, Sunday, the 13th of August. He didn't ask questions and was ready in a couple of minutes. They hurtled down the stairs and ran towards the Brandenburg Gate.

They watched in disbelief as the crossing point was sealed completely with barbed wire.

'Oh, my God!' Gerhard was clearly distressed. 'Are they going to put a barrier around the whole sector? They won't be allowed to do that, surely?'

As dawn began to lighten the sky, only a handful of people watched the work, silent with shock. East Germans drilled into the road to put up concrete posts, then they strung barbed wire across to make a fence. Soon barbed wire and armed guards stretched for miles across the centre of the city.

Jon placed his hand on Gerhard's shoulder. 'Let's get some breakfast. Once Berliners wake up to this, all hell is going to break loose.'

Kate forced herself out of bed after a restless night. She hadn't been able to get a flight to Germany until late on Friday evening, and on arrival she'd been lucky enough to find a small hotel quite close to the border. This had been the first time she'd flown and she hadn't cared for the experience much, but it was certainly faster than going overland. The view had been quite beautiful, though, when she'd forced herself to look, and she had taken some photographs of wonderful cloud formations. As she had gazed at the countryside below, she'd suddenly been able to grasp what great courage her Aunt Annie had shown when she'd parachuted out of a plane during the war. Then they had been fighting the Germans. Now she was here because of her country's concern for the residents of Berlin.

She looked at her watch. It was just six o'clock, and, as it was Sunday morning, she hoped it wasn't too early for breakfast. There was a busy day ahead: she'd allowed herself only a couple of days for the assignment; she was due to catch a flight at nine o'clock tonight back to London. She wanted to get the photos to Andrew Stevenson in time for him to include them in Monday's edition.

She had some good ones and was sure he'd be pleased. After a few hours' sleep on Friday night, she had set out the next morning with her camera. She had toured the crossing points and was astonished at the number of people coming over to the West. She could have cried for them. How desperate they must be to leave their homes with only what they could carry. She had followed one group to the Marienfelde Refugee Centre, where one of the helpers who spoke good English helped her to interview some of the people. She would be able to add personal stories to the pictures.

She made her way downstairs, planning the day. When she'd left the Marienfelde Centre last night they had been preparing for a huge influx of people today, so she would go there first . . .

The sight that met her when she stepped into the dining room stopped her. She hadn't expected many people to be up this early, but the room was crowded and people were talking in hushed voices, some crying and others standing around looking helpless.

'What's happened?' she asked Bernhard, the waiter she knew who spoke English.

Before he could answer, a woman came up to her with tears streaming down her face. She pointed at Kate's camera slung over her shoulder and said something to her in German.

'I'm so sorry,' Kate apologized, 'I don't speak your language.' She held the woman's hand in sympathy; she was obviously dreadfully upset.

'It's the Soviets,' Bernhard informed her. 'They have sealed all the border crossings during the night and her daughter is over there. She was going to come out today but now she will not be able to.'

Kate held the woman, who sobbed on her shoulder, telling her all about it. Even though she couldn't understand a word, the anguish was all too evident. Her own eyes filled with tears. 'What was she asking me when I came in?' Kate said, looking up at the waiter.

'She asks that you take pictures to show the world the suffering this barbarous act will cause.'

'Tell her that's what I'm here for.'

When he translated, the woman kissed Kate on the cheek and stepped back, now composed enough to give a brief smile of thanks.

Her instinct was to go out there at once to see what was going on, but Bernhard stopped her. 'You will eat before you leave. It might not be easy to buy food today.'

She knew he was right, so she sat down and ordered coffee and toast, as that would be the quickest. She didn't want to waste more time than was necessary.

The main crossing was the Potsdamer Platz, so after a hasty breakfast she made for there. West Berliners were staring at the barbed-wire barrier and the line of soldiers guarding it. Kate was stunned. How could they slice a city in half, separating family and friends? Her anger was rising as she took pictures of people over on the other side, standing around helplessly. Some were crying and trying to talk to loved ones just a few feet away, but with no hope of reaching them. Kate could feel her own tears clouding her eyes. This was terrible! Others were trying to get to their jobs in the West. When the guards turned them away, they looked bewildered and frightened, gazing in disbelief as workmen unloaded fencing and barbed wire.

She stayed there as the residents, now alerted to the barrier, began to arrive. It seemed as if thousands of people were there. It was raining, but no one appeared to notice. She caught a glimpse of the mayor of Berlin, Willy Brandt, walking among the crowds, but she couldn't get near him. There was utter disbelief that a great city could be cut in half. Surely it would be stopped?

By five that afternoon she was tired and saddened beyond belief, as the implications of the Soviet move dawned on her. One distraught man had just told her that the whole of West Berlin had now been sealed off. Those in the East were prisoners, with no hope of seeing loved ones who lived in the West. To her that was an unforgivable crime. If she were separated from her family in this way, the pain would be unbearable. She had been told that even the telephone lines had been cut, so contact that way was also impossible. The heart-rending scenes of people calling across the wire and being driven away by the East German police were almost more than she could bear.

She returned to the hotel and booked in for another week. There was no way she could leave now. With that settled, she found Bernhard. 'I need somewhere to develop film and make prints, then a way to get them back to London as quickly as possible.'

He gave hurried instructions to another waiter to stand in for him, then took her arm. 'Come with me, I know a man who has a photography shop. I'm sure he will help.'

The shop was only ten minutes away, and, although the owner was just leaving, he tossed the keys to Bernhard and hurried away saying something over his shoulder.

'Mr Braun said you can use anything you want,' Bernhard told her. 'He has an elderly mother in the East and is trying desperately to see if there is any chance of getting her out, though I fear that is impossible now.'

The darkroom was a shambles, but Kate soon saw that everything she needed was there.

'Why do you not just send the films to London?' Bernhard asked as she set to work.

'I don't want to risk losing them, so if I send prints only I can keep the film with me.'

'Ah, yes, that is sensible. May I be of some use?'

He was, but it was just after six when they finished. She found a card-backed envelope on a shelf and addressed it to Andrew Stevenson, then put the photos and her report she'd written the night before inside and sealed it. Now how on earth could she get this to London quickly? Then she remembered her return ticket. 'Do you have a passport, Bernhard?'

'No, but my brother Franz does.'

'I have a ticket for the nine o'clock flight tonight – do you think he would take this to London for me and deliver it by hand? I will, of course, pay all his expenses.'

'I'm sure he would. The world must know about this,

Fräulein. It appears that no one is doing anything about it. Now they have cut the city in half!'

She heard the anger and frustration in his voice. He was right! Why wasn't anyone putting a stop to this?

They left the shop and ran the two blocks to Bernhard's brother. He listened, nodding his head all the time, then took the packet and with rage burning in his eyes said in perfect English, 'I shall see that this is delivered safely.'

Kate gave him enough money for his return flight and any other expenses. She was glad she'd had the sense to bring a lot of Deutschmarks with her, as well as sterling.

He already had his passport in his hand. 'I will let Bernhard know when the photos are in the hands of the editor.'

She looked at her watch anxiously. 'Nearly seven o'clock – I hope you make it in time.'

'I will, do not worry.' Then he left at a run, jumped into a car outside and roared off.

Kate breathed a sigh of relief; she'd done all she could for the moment. 'Thank you for your help,' she told Bernhard. 'I intended to go back tonight, but I don't want to leave now.'

'I understand. You must have a meal and try to rest. By tomorrow the realization of what the barrier means will have sunk in, and the city will erupt, I think.'

'I agree. The reaction has been one of numb disbelief today. That will soon turn into fury.'

They made their way back to the hotel, each one silent with their own thoughts.

At breakfast the next morning the receptionist came to Kate's table. 'There is a phone call for you, Miss Freeman.'

She hurried to take it, hoping it was news that the photos had arrived safely.

'Kate!' Andrew Stevenson bellowed. 'That you? I've had a hell of a job getting through.'

'I'm not surprised,' she told him. 'Did you get the photos?'

'Yes, and they're damned good. You've captured the emotion of the people. You're one great photographer.'

Praise indeed, she thought wryly.

'I want you to stay there and work exclusively for the *Explorer*. I'll pay your fare and hotel bills.'

'All right,' she agreed, then frowned as the line began to crackle. 'Are you still there?' Then she held the phone away from her ear as a stream of bad language came down the line.

'Can you hear me, Kate?'

'Yes, I said okay.'

'Good, good, stay as long as you need to.'

Kate put down the phone and gave a disbelieving shake of her head. She'd achieved her ambition after all. She was now working abroad taking photos for the *World Explorer*. She had thought that dream lost.

28

On Monday, Jon and Gerhard joined the huge crowd at the Hindenburg Platz on the west side of the Brandenburg Gate. Everyone was quiet at first, then they became more agitated as questions were asked. West Germany was now completely sealed off. How could this be allowed to happen? Why wasn't someone doing something about it?

Jon brought Gerhard's attention to large concrete blocks being unloaded from lorries.

'The bastards!' Gerhard spat out. 'They're going to build a permanent wall!'

At the Brandenburg Gate some people began to throw stones, and the whole atmosphere became highly charged.

'My God!' Gerhard gasped. 'Look at that girl – she'll get hurt or even killed if she doesn't move away from there.'

Jon looked in the direction in which Gerhard was pointing and could not believe his eyes. He surged into action, pushing his way through the crowd. He had a reasonable repertoire of German swear words and he used them as he fought his way towards the barrier. He could hear Gerhard behind him adding a few invectives of his own as he hauled people out of the way so they could get through.

The girl had a camera to her eye and was right against the barrier, with stones flying past her head and guns pointing in her direction, but she appeared to be oblivious to the danger.

Once Jon was close enough he lunged, grabbed her around the waist and hauled her off the wire. She lashed out with her free hand and kicked her feet, catching him a nasty blow on his shin. It was a good job she was hanging on to a camera, because if she had let loose with both hands she could have done some damage. This was no weakling he was grappling with, as he used all his strength to drag her to a safer spot.

Gerhard caught hold of her legs to stop her kicking, and between them they managed to get her away from the seething crowd. They stood her on her feet and a fist shot past Jon's head; he ducked only just in time.

As she glared at him, he could see she was incandescent with anger. 'What the hell are you doing here?'

'Working!' She began to push her way back into the crowd and both men caught hold of her again.

She lashed out in fury and Gerhard caught a well-aimed punch on his chin.

'Stop it, Kate,' Jon growled.

Gerhard checked his chin for damage. 'Do you know her?'

'Oh, we know each other,' Kate snapped at Gerhard. 'Have you seen what's going on over there?' She didn't give him a chance to answer. 'Have you seen people trying to talk to their families, and crying as they're driven away from the border? I'm going to get close-up pictures of the soldiers' faces and show the world what these unfeeling beasts are doing. Those people are prisoners now. You've no right to stop me!'

Jon studied her through narrowed eyes. He'd never

have guessed that the quiet controlled girl he'd met before could be so explosive. It was clear now that, like her mother, she cared about other people, but this one cared too much and allowed her emotions to get the better of her. He doubted Rose had ever been like that, or acted so recklessly.

'I know exactly what is going on,' Gerhard told her icily. 'My parents are still over there and I haven't any idea when, or if, I'll see them again. So don't you lecture me, Fräulein!'

The fire drained out of Kate and she appeared contrite. 'I'm sorry.'

'You could have been killed,' Jon said.

Her glance turned to one of contempt. 'Don't be ridiculous!'

He badly wanted to shake some sense into her but he tried to make allowances for her inexperience in this kind of a situation. 'Those soldiers are as jumpy as hell – it won't take much for them to start shooting.'

'They won't do that!'

Just then a shot rang out somewhere further along the border. Jon raised an eyebrow in query. 'You think not? Now, who are you working for?'

'Your newspaper.' She was edging back into the crowd, but Gerhard blocked the way.

'Exclusively?' When she nodded, he said, 'Then we'll work together and you'll do as you're told.'

She bristled, offended at being spoken to in that abrupt manner. 'Stop ordering me around. It's none of your business what I do!'

'You never know what a crowd this angry is going to do. It's dangerous, damn it!' he ground out through clenched teeth, not caring how much he upset her. He wasn't going to allow her to roam around this volatile city on her own. He would have a few choice words to say to Andrew when he saw him!

'I never thought you were a coward!' she snapped.

'Call me all the names you like, but you're going to do as I say!' He was furious with her and curled his large hands around her upper arms, making her look straight at him.

'Don't you touch me!'

Jon released his grip and took a step back. He'd never seen such animation in her face. Her eyes were smouldering like burning coals.

'I need pictures that show the suffering this barbarous act is causing and' – she looked him up and down in derision – 'I can't do that if I have to stay in the background and view it from a distance.'

Gerhard stifled a laugh, and Jon said to him, rather belatedly, 'Meet Kate Freeman.'

Gerhard shook hands politely. 'You would do well to heed his advice, for he does know what he's doing.'

'Advice? That was an order.' Kate's tone was scathing.

Jon clenched his jaw in exasperation – what had happened to her? During their meeting in France and the journey back, he had begun to find her appealing, but this wasn't the same woman. For her family's sake and for Eddie's, he wasn't going to let her run into danger. 'You'll get your pictures, but you'll stay with me and do the job as safely as possible.'

He watched her struggling to accept his restrictions on her movements. He'd seen plenty of photographers in war zones and they all seemed to have one aim, and that was to take their pictures, whatever the situation. When they had a camera to their eye, danger was forgotten in the need to capture the scene. She had the same compulsion, he realized. The only one he knew who had shown any caution was Terry, and he wished to heaven that Andrew had sent him instead. Kate was going to be a blasted nuisance because he felt he had to protect her.

She was obviously determined to get her photos, and this was a story crying out to be told in pictures, as well as in words. 'You tell me what you want and I'll see you get it.'

Her dark eyes were still smouldering, but she had calmed down at last. 'What I'm trying to capture is the pain and despair of the people of Berlin, East and West. I want to show not only the brutality of the act, but also the sheer inhumanity of separating family and friends.'

Gerhard nodded approvingly. 'This is not the place – come, we shall go to another part of the border.'

They walked for about fifteen minutes. There were people all along but not as many as at the main crossing points. Gerhard stopped and pointed to a street now cut in half by the barbed wire. 'You see the third house down?'

'Yes.' Kate held the camera to her eye, framing the shot.

'That is where my parents live.' He couldn't hide the anguish in his voice.

Kate swung round, her fingers moving quickly to adjust the camera, and took a photo of Gerhard's face before he grasped her intention. Then she photographed the street and the soldiers guarding the barrier.

She knew what she was doing by turning the camera on Gerhard at that moment, Jon realized, as he watched her working. Alerted, by the German's tone of voice, she had caught him when his despair was visible.

It was mid afternoon before they decided to find somewhere to eat. The demonstrations were growing in size and spreading throughout the city. The first shock had faded, and fury was taking over. Gerhard took them away from the main streets to a quiet area where he knew of a small family-run café.

After the meal Kate stood up and slung the camera bag over her shoulder, then, after thanking Gerhard, she turned to walk out of the café.

'Just a minute.' Jon beat her to the door. 'Where are you going?'

'I don't think that's any of your business, but, as you asked, I'm going to develop my films, make prints of the best, then try to find a way to get them back to London.'

He noted her sharp tone and knew he hadn't been forgiven for dragging her away from the barrier. He really wished she wasn't here; it was a distraction he could do without. 'Why don't you take them back yourself? I'm sure I could arrange transport for you.'

'I'm not going. You needn't worry, though, I'll keep out of your way.' She eyed him up and down disdainfully. 'I know how much you hate commitment of any kind.'

He lowered his head until they were eye to eye. 'As I've already said, you're wasting your time throwing insults at me. You'll stay with me all the time and we'll work together, or I shall dump you on the first mode of transport I can find out of this city.'

'You really are not a very pleasant man,' she snapped.

'And you, *Miss Freeman*, are a pain in the backside, so are you going to do as you're told, or do I have to demand that Andrew recall you?'

She gave him a triumphant smile. 'That won't make any difference. I'll simply sell to another paper and that won't please the Chief. I'm freelance, *Mr Devlin*.'

Gerhard hustled them outside. 'There is enough anger in this city without you two sniping at each other. Now, where are you staying?' he asked Kate.

'The Hotel Saxony.'

'I know it; we'll collect you at eight o'clock tomorrow morning, and all three of us will work together. As reporters, it's our job to let the world know what's going on here.' He turned to Jon. 'Are you in agreement with that?'

'Perfectly.' He was quite amused at the way Gerhard had stepped in and defused the situation. He had been right to do so. For some reason he and Kate had begun to strike sparks off each other, and that was something new for them. 'Where are you going to develop the film?'

'There's a photographer's near the hotel. The owner let me use his darkroom yesterday, and I'm sure he will again.'

Gerhard wrote his address on a piece of paper. 'When you have the photos ready, bring them to me and I will see that they are delivered to London at once.'

'Can you do that? I'd be very grateful.'

Jon noticed the way her smile charmed Gerhard. She really was a beautiful woman, but he'd be a fool to let that influence him. She was stubborn, argumentative and trouble!

'Yes, I'm an expert at moving information around the

world.' He returned the smile with warmth. 'I'm on my home ground. I've got excellent connections in Berlin.'

'I'll do the prints right away; it shouldn't take me more than two hours,' Kate said. She hurried away, eager to get on with the job.

Gerhard and Jon both had reports to write and file with their respective papers, so they returned to the apartment.

'Okay.' Gerhard gave Jon a quizzical glance over the rim of his coffee cup. 'Who is she?'

Jon settled comfortably on the sofa and told him about Rose, the Freeman family, and as much as he knew about Kate, including the newspaper reports of her kidnapping and the trial.

'No wonder she fought so hard when we grabbed her. That experience must still be vivid in her mind.'

'I expect it is.' Jon put his cup down and gazed into space for a few seconds. 'I'm damned if I can make her out. Every time I meet her she's a different person. She's wonderful with the children at the home – so warm and caring – and then she turns into the wildcat we met today. I just can't fathom her.'

Gerhard laughed. 'I can tell you exactly what I think of her. She's the most beautiful woman I've ever seen.'

'Fancy her, do you?' Jon studied Gerhard with fresh eyes. His friend was good-looking in a rugged way, with fair hair and blue eyes. He was well educated and able to turn on the charm when necessary. Jon guessed he must be in his mid thirties.

'Yes, I like her. Do you mind?'

Jon looked surprised. 'Why would I mind?'

317

'You show such concern for her safety that I thought you might be after her yourself.'

'Oh, no.' He held up his hand in horror. 'After the fiasco with my last romantic attachment, I've sworn off women.'

'The field is clear for me, then.'

'I wouldn't have thought she was your type. She'll be difficult to handle.' Jon didn't like the look in Gerhard's eyes when he talked about Kate.

'I've never looked for an easy life.' Gerhard grinned and set to work on his report, and said without looking up, 'Jealous, Jon?'

Jon ignored that last remark and picked up his pen. He lost track of time, as he always did when he was writing. He was just making the final alterations to the report when there was a knock on the door.

'That will be her.' Gerhard was on his feet and making for the front door.

Jon listened to them coming up the stairs, talking and laughing. So Gerhard was going to work straight away in his effort to charm her. When they came into the room, he couldn't help noticing how tired she looked. The distressing day had taken its toll. His protective instinct came to the surface once again. He pushed it away. She was a grown woman and responsible for her own life. His only obligation was to keep her safe while she was here.

She acknowledged him with a slight nod of her head, then she handed Gerhard the package. 'There's a photograph of you in there. I hope you don't mind?'

'Not at all. Is it good?'

'It's front-page stuff.' She still appeared uncertain. 'I've also put in a short piece about your parents, but I'll take it out if you object.'

'You can leave it in,' he told her as he smiled sadly. 'The world needs to be shown what anguish this division is causing.'

'Thank you. I've also put in a couple of personal letters. My parents and business partner will worry if they don't hear from me.'

'I'll get this on its way tonight. I will walk you back to your hotel and you must rest.'

'Oh, you don't have to do that, I'll be quite all right.'

'I will be happier if I see you safely back.' He smiled again. 'Berlin is explosive, and you should not be out on your own in the evening.'

'All right, thank you.'

She accepted without further protest, and Jon wondered if she would have been that docile if he had suggested the same thing. His mouth twitched in amusement. Given the mood she'd been in today, she would probably have thrown another punch at him.

'I'm just taking Kate back to the hotel, then I'll deliver this package to my courier friend,' Gerhard told him. 'I shouldn't be more than a couple of hours.'

He watched Gerhard take Kate's arm as they left the room together, and wondered why his stomach felt sour. It must be something he'd eaten.

29

When Kate arrived back at her hotel, Bernhard was waiting for her. 'Franz has returned and said the trip went well. He asked me to give you this.' He handed her the morning's edition of the *World Explorer*.

She took it, eager to see what coverage Andrew Stevenson had given to the crisis in Berlin. She wasn't disappointed. There were two of her pictures on the front page showing the distress of the people as they realized that they were separated from their loved ones. The scenes she had caught were poignant, and underneath was a report by Jon. The inside pages were full of her photos. The whole of the centre contained a long detailed account of events from the time the barrier started to be put in place to the moment the people awoke to find the city divided.

As she was reading, the tears were brimming over. Jon Devlin's skill as a writer could not be denied. What a pity she had seen another side of him today. Who the hell did he think he was, ordering her around like that? Andrew Stevenson had given over almost the entire paper to this one story, and she had to admit that the combination of Jon's words and her pictures was a potent force. She hoped the paper would help to wake up the world to the plight of Berlin and its suffering inhabitants.

She wiped away the moisture from her eyes and folded the paper carefully. This was what she had always dreamt of doing, and she felt an overwhelming sense of gratitude that, in this instance, she might have been able to make a difference.

She was collecting her key when the phone rang. The receptionist handed it to her. 'It is for you, Miss Freeman.'

'Kate, we've been trying all day to catch you.'

'I've only just returned to the hotel, Dad.' She was so pleased to hear her father's voice. 'How are you?'

'I'm fine but worried about you being there at this time.'

'You needn't be,' she laughed. 'I have two protectors in Jon and his German friend, Gerhard. They're making sure I keep out of trouble.'

'That's all right, then.' By the tone of his voice he obviously approved. 'When are you coming home?'

'Not for a week at least,' she told him. 'I want to see what happens. It's terrible. The people of East Berlin are now prisoners, without any way of contacting their families.'

'That's barbaric,' her father said. 'We've read all about it. Your pictures are stunning, Kate.'

'Thanks. I've managed to get even better ones today. Dad, will you see Pete and explain why I'm staying longer than planned?'

'I'll do that first thing in the morning. You take care of yourself, my darling. Your mother wants a word now.'

She waited until she heard her mother speak. 'Hello, Mum. Dad's going to see Pete for me, but would you go to the home and explain to the boys that I'll come and see them as soon as I get back?'

'I was going there tomorrow anyway, so I'll bring Eddie home for a couple of hours.'

'Oh, thanks. He'll love that.'

'Is it very bad out there?' her mother asked.

'It's heartbreaking,' she told her, and explained about the anguish and desperation of the people.

Her mother uttered a well-chosen expletive, then said, 'You're doing a good job. Goodnight, Kate, we'll try to phone you again. I'm proud of you.'

As she put the phone down, those words, 'I'm proud of you', echoed through her mind. That meant more to her than bags of gold.

'Miss Freeman.' Bernhard appeared beside her. 'It is not too late for a meal if you are hungry.'

'I am, thank you.' She followed him to a table and sat down. The dining room was nearly empty now. There were only two local couples and they were silent, lost in thought about what was happening to their city. She smiled at Bernhard. 'Please thank your brother for going to London for me.'

'He was pleased to be able to help bring the news of our trouble to the world.' He handed her the menu. 'He said we are fortunate to have such a fine photographer here at this time.'

She acknowledged the compliment with a slight nod of her head and a smile, then studied the menu. After choosing a simple meal of soup and fish, she watched Bernhard walk to the kitchen. There was a vase of flowers on her table and she leant forward to smell a beautiful rose in full bloom. The delicate yellow and subtle perfume was a sign of beauty and peace in the bewildered city. She would be the best damned photographer she could be while she was here.

★

On the Wednesday an enormous mass protest took place at City Hall. The mood was one of anger. The people were looking for countermeasures, but nothing was happening and their frustration was showing.

'What do the placards say?' Kate asked Gerhard.

'They are asking where the Americans are and why the West is doing nothing.'

Protected by Jon and Gerhard, Kate was able to take photos without being jostled too much. The atmosphere was threatening, and it was with reluctance she realized that Jon was a help and not a hindrance.

On Friday, Gerhard disappeared on some mission of his own. Jon stuck by her. It was a good working relationship; both were dedicated professionals with respect for each other and the story they were reporting. She felt sure this was the only reason he tolerated her. His attitude made it clear that having a woman around was a damned nuisance.

Things got worse as people tried anything to get to West Berlin. There were houses in the Eastern sector right on the border, forming part of the solid wall now rapidly being built. People were leaping down into the waiting hands of eager rescuers.

'Oh, look at that!' Kate cried in horror. A woman was hanging from an upper window, being pulled from the top by East German guards who were trying to drag her back. A vivid picture of her own captivity flashed into her mind and she gasped in pain at the memory. She could feel the desperation of these poor people, feel their panic and fear.

Kate started to run forward, but Jon caught hold of her. 'It's all right. She's down.'

'Oh, dear God!' Kate was so upset she was shaking. She gripped Jon's arm, looking up at him wide-eyed with anguish, and moaned, 'This is too awful.'

Jon guided her away from the distressing scene. 'People won't be able to do that much longer. The soldiers are already boarding up those windows.'

She was speechless at the sheer inhumanity of this act.

On Saturday she saw her first death, as a man jumped from a house while trying to escape.

'Why did he take that chance?' Kate was horrified.

'People are desperate,' Jon told her, 'and there will be more deaths. If you don't think you can take it . . .'

She glared at him. 'I'm staying. If you don't like it, then you can slope off and do your own thing. I can look after myself.'

But he didn't go, and, although she hated to admit it, she was relieved. He knew what he was doing and always seemed to steer her towards the action. He appeared to have a built-in instinct for trouble; it was almost as if he could smell it. She wondered if his harsh upbringing had given him that talent.

They were walking along the Teltow Canal on the following Thursday when they heard gunfire. Jon grabbed her arm and started running towards the sound. Suddenly he halted.

'What's happened?' she gasped, out of breath after trying to keep up with his long strides.

'They've just shot someone trying to escape by swimming the canal.'

'Are they all right?' She couldn't see a thing, as he was blocking her view.

'I think he's dead.' Jon spun her away as she began to

shake with a combination of sadness for the unnecessary loss of a life, and fury at the outrage.

'Go home,' he told her firmly. 'You've done a damned good job but there's nothing else you can do.'

He was right. She was sickened by everything that had happened since she'd arrived in Berlin. She longed to see her family and friends again. That was more than the people here could do. She didn't think she could stand another moment of this. 'I'll make travel arrangements right away.'

'Good.' He glanced at the scene over her shoulder. stay here,' she told him, 'and find out what you can.'

'Oh, I will! You let me know when you're going.'

As she went to turn away, he caught hold of her arm and pulled her towards him, holding her in a silent embrace. She looked up at him in surprise. 'What did you do that for?'

'I just felt like it.'

With another puzzled glance, she turned and walked away. He was a very complex man. Tough, outspoken and uncompromising, yet, as that embrace had shown, he was capable of tenderness as well. He'd known just how shattered she was now. It was just as well she was going home because if she spent much more time in his company, her growing respect *might* turn to liking.

Jon watched her move through the crowds. She was a good photographer; she cared and it showed in every picture. It was as if there were a little of her in each shot. Her emotions made her the artist she was with a camera, but it also made her vulnerable, and he was relieved she had agreed to leave Berlin.

When he had gathered all the information he could, he returned to the flat and set to work on the story.

He'd been back about an hour when the door opened and Gerhard came in, looking weary and dejected. Jon set about making him a strong cup of coffee. His friend sat down and bowed his head in defeat. 'No luck, then?'

'No, it's bloody useless. The border's too well guarded, and when someone does find a way through, they plug that route as well. Once they finish building the permanent wall that will be the end of any escapes, though I fear that many will die trying.'

'I'm so sorry.' Jon liked this man who was fast becoming a firm friend, and he knew that he'd been trying to find a way to pluck his parents out of the East.

'There are some crazy schemes being plotted by relatives over here, but I can't risk my parents' lives.'

'I don't blame you. It's too risky,' Jon told him.

Gerhard slammed down his mug. 'The bastards are shooting at anyone who tries to escape. Dear God, Jon, we've spent our time in war-torn countries, but I never dreamt I would be doing the job in my own city!'

Jon refilled Gerhard's mug and placed it in his hands. 'Would you like me to see if I can do anything about your family?'

Gerhard smiled for the first time. 'I know you are expert at slipping behind enemy lines, but I wouldn't want you to risk your life. Even if I can't talk to my parents, I do know they are alive and I must be content with that. I'll keep my eye on things, and if there's any chance of getting them out in the future I'll do it.'

Jon could only guess at the torment his friend was going through. He'd never had a mother or father to worry about, but if he had, then he knew he would be as frantic as Gerhard.

His friend stood up. 'Now I must have a bath and a change of clothes.'

It took him only half an hour. He returned looking refreshed and more relaxed. He tucked into the sandwiches Jon had prepared for them.

'I heard about the killing at the canal. Did you see it?'

'We got there just after the shooting. Kate was badly shaken, and I've told her to go home. She's done enough.'

'And she told you to get lost,' Gerhard said, with a hint of a laugh.

'No, she agreed.'

'She must have been very upset, then, because I can't imagine her allowing you to order her about without a fight.'

'I chose my moment well.' Jon put the empty plates in the sink. 'I only hope she hasn't changed her mind, now that she's had time to think about it.'

'Do you think she will?'

'I don't know. She's unpredictable.' He drew in a deep breath. 'She's had a tough year and I'd like her to go home to her family.'

Gerhard gave him a studied look. 'You do care about her, don't you?'

'Of course I do. Her mother's a wonderful woman, and one of the boys at the home adores her. Eddie'll be devastated if anything happens to her.'

'And?' Gerhard waited.

'And what?'

'For a man who is expert with words, you are skirting around the issue with great inefficiency.'

'What the hell are you talking about?' Jon frowned.

'Why don't you just admit that you are more than a little in love with her?'

'Don't be daft!' Where on earth had Gerhard got that idea? Just because he wanted her away from any danger didn't mean he'd fallen for her.

Gerhard's expression was amused. 'I think you protest too much, but just to be on the safe side I will drop my plans to pursue her.'

'Please don't hold off on my account. I've no intention of falling for anyone again.' Jon began to laugh. 'How did we get on to this ridiculous subject?'

Gerhard joined in. 'I'm in an emotional state and perhaps I'm looking for something happy in this awful mess. But of course, you wouldn't be interested in an affair of the heart. How many times did you miss your wedding date?'

'Only once, but that was enough for Jane. I really did try to get back in time, but no one believed me.'

Gerhard produced a bottle of whisky and held it up. 'Shall we drink to the single state?'

'Good idea.' Jon found two tumblers and they sat down determined to try to numb all feeling with alcohol.

They were halfway through the bottle when there was a knock on the door. Gerhard hauled himself upright and went to see who it was. He came back with Kate.

'I promised to let you know when I'm leaving,' she said to Jon. 'There isn't much more I can do here. I'm sickened by the suffering this division of Berlin is causing.'

Jon stood up politely. 'You managed to arrange everything?'

'Yes.' She eyed the bottle and the two men who were still standing. The corners of her mouth turned up slightly and she sat down, allowing the men to do the same.

'I'm leaving at six tomorrow morning. It wasn't easy, as almost all the flights were booked, but I have managed to get one to Paris. I'll catch a train from there and a boat at Calais.'

'Will you stop off to see Sam and his family before you catch the boat?' Jon asked.

'I might.'

'If you do, remember me to them, won't you?'

'I will.' She reached out, picked up Jon's glass and took a sip, then pulled a face. 'I don't know how you can drink this stuff.'

'It's an acquired taste,' Gerhard told her, his eyes already taking on a glassy look.

'Are you two drunk?' she wanted to know.

Gerhard shook his head. 'Not yet, but we soon shall be.'

That amused her, and she rose to her feet. Good Lord, Jon thought as he watched her elegant movements, she's even more beautiful tonight. Or was that the drink playing tricks with his eyes?

'I won't disturb your valuable drinking time,' Kate said with a smile.

Both men stood up again as she prepared to leave.

'You take care of yourself, Kate. If I'm ever in London, can I come to see you?'

'Of course, Gerhard, it would be a pleasure to buy you a meal to thank you for your help while I've been here.'

329

'Why wait until then?' He held his arms out. 'Come and give me a hug.'

She laughed as she wrapped her arms around him, and he kissed her cheek. 'It's been lovely meeting you.'

'And you.'

She then turned to Jon. 'Thank you as well, you've been very patient.'

Much to his astonishment, she slipped her arms around his waist and held tight for just a split second, then stepped back. He'd been quite tough with her as he'd tried to keep her in line, so he'd expected a good riddance kind of farewell, not that show of genuine affection. It had been a completely spontaneous gesture, but he was sure she had meant it.

He was still standing in the same position when Gerhard returned after seeing Kate out.

'She had a taxi waiting for her, sensible girl.' Gerhard shook with silent laughter. 'You look as if you need a drink, my friend.' He filled Jon's glass, then sat down. 'That is a wonderful woman.'

The whisky burnt a fiery path down Jon's throat. 'I'm beginning to think you might be right, so I'm obviously not drunk enough yet.'

30

When Kate arrived in Paris, it was only mid morning and she wasn't sure what she wanted to do. It was tempting to go to Sam's while she was here. She could probably get a train to Saint-Omer and a taxi from there, but her overwhelming desire was to get home as soon as possible. She bought herself a cup of coffee while she decided, and, as she gazed around the airport, her attention lingered on the booking desk. It was worth a try, she thought, finishing her drink quickly. It would be quicker than going by train and boat.

She was in luck: there was a spare seat on a flight to London, leaving in half an hour. She hurried, as they were already beginning to board the plane.

During the short flight her mind was busy making plans. If she went straight to the shop and worked on the last films she'd taken, then she might be able to get them to Andrew Stevenson in time for tomorrow's edition. She was sure these would earn her enough to open another shop for Terry to run. She would see her parents tonight and the boys tomorrow.

She closed her eyes, suddenly feeling drained. It had been a difficult time, yet she felt as if she had grown in that time. Self-doubt had faded and her confidence had increased. The kidnapping and trial were behind her now. She could look forward to the future. And another important thing was that she had not felt any revulsion as Gerhard and Jon had hugged her. It was a relief to realize that a man's touch no longer frightened her. A huge step forward indeed!

When Kate arrived at the shop, Susan broke into a smile. 'Kate, you're back! Oh, Pete will be so pleased you're here.'

'It's good to be here. Where is he?'

'He's doing a wedding and Terry's at another one.'

'Is Terry already working for us?' She was surprised he had been able to start so soon.

'He's been here for five days now and we're already taking on more work.'

'That's wonderful.' Kate headed for the stairs. 'I'll take my case upstairs, then I'll be in the darkroom for a while.'

'Shall I make you a pot of tea?' Susan asked.

'Please, I'm gasping for a cup of English tea.' Coffee was all right, but she'd been brought up on cups of tea. Her Grandma Marj had always had the kettle on the boil. Kate went up to her bedroom and left the case there – she would unpack later. Gathering all the films from her camera case, she went back downstairs.

Susan was busy with a customer, but the tea was ready, so Kate poured a cup and sat down to enjoy it. There was nothing as refreshing as this favourite home brew. After nearly draining the pot, she poked her head in the shop. 'I'll be in the darkroom if you need me.'

Susan nodded and carried on serving her customer. She really was very conscientious, Kate thought, and they'd been fortunate to find someone like that. It was funny to think that only sixteen months ago she'd been so excited about starting at the *Explorer*, and now she owned her own business and it was proving to be successful. There was much to look forward to. Now they had Terry, it would be exciting to expand, providing they could keep him, of course. She would have to work on him, try to persuade him not to look for another job on a newspaper. She put on the red light and started work, singing to herself. That was something she hadn't done for some time. For a while, Derek Howard had taken her joy of life away, but thank heaven it was coming back.

She was just hanging up the last of the prints when there was a rap on the door. 'You can come in,' she called.

Pete tumbled into the room, and gave her a big hug. 'It's lovely to have you home.'

'It's good to be here.' She put the main light back on.

Immediately Pete was examining the rows of pictures. He whistled softly. 'Wow, these are wonderful.' He pointed out several photos. 'You must let the paper have those. Andrew Stevenson will be ecstatic.' He perched on the stool, his eyes fixed on the prints. 'How many more have you got?'

'About ten rolls,' she told him.

'Then I think you ought to put on an exhibition. People will flock to see what's really happening in Berlin.'

The idea came as a complete surprise to her. 'Put on an exhibition?'

'Do it, Kate.' Pete was now pacing the small room in excitement. 'We'll all help.'

'Oh, I don't know.' She was very doubtful; only famous people had exhibitions.

Just then Terry came in and Pete grabbed him. 'Come

and look at these. Kate's got loads more and I'm trying to convince her to put on an exhibition.'

'Hello, Kate.' Terry grinned at her.

'Hello, Terry, great to have you here with us.' Kate gave him an impish smile. 'Any chance of persuading you to stay permanently?'

'I'll think about it. I must admit that I'm enjoying the work. It's a relief not to have Andrew Stevenson yelling for me all the time. Now let's see what you've got here.' Terry studied the prints for quite a while, working his way slowly along the line, then he turned to Kate, his expression serious. 'These are some of the most moving photographs I have ever seen. An exhibition will help to highlight the plight of the German people.'

Now that was something she dearly wanted to do. 'Well – '

Pete didn't give her a chance to say anything else. 'I'll find you a gallery and make all the arrangements. You just concentrate on making large prints of them and we'll choose the best to show.' He was halfway through the door when he glanced back. 'Ask Andrew Stevenson if we can use those he's already bought from you. Tell him we'll give the paper plenty of publicity.' Then he disappeared.

Kate raised her eyebrows. 'Looks as if that's settled, then.'

'He's right,' Terry said, 'and you found yourself a gem when you plucked that young man out of the newsroom. It's hard to believe it's the same person.'

'I know. He deserves it, though, he's very talented.' The prints were now dry, and she selected half a dozen of the best to take to the newspaper.

'Make Andrew pay a lot of money for those,' Terry advised. 'No one else will have anything of such emotional quality. That man was crazy to let you go.'

She was heartened that Terry thought so highly of her work, because he was an experienced and expert photographer himself. 'I'm glad now that he did, because it's opened up new possibilities for me. Working as a freelance is more exciting and profitable.'

'Hello, Kate,' Mike called as she came into the newsroom later that afternoon.

She waved. It was strange. She felt more at home here now than she had ever done when she was an employee. The disappointment had been awful when she'd had to leave this job; now she could see that it had all been for the best. As much as she'd wanted to work here, it hadn't been right for her.

'What have you got for me?' Andrew Stevenson came out of his office to meet her when she stopped to speak to Mike.

He took the envelope from her and marched back into his office. She followed and watched him spread the prints across his desk and lean over to study them.

'Good,' he told her. 'I'll take them all. Jon's report arrived today and he mentioned that you had these.' The Chief gave her a quick, calculating glance. 'Would you like to come to work for me again?'

'No, thanks.'

'I promise not to shout at you,' he persisted, his mouth twisting in a wry smile.

That made her laugh. She couldn't help liking him, now that she knew why he'd been so against her at the start. 'You know you couldn't keep a promise like that.'

'No, you're right. So what are you going to do now? I hope you're not thinking of stealing more of my staff?'

That was a mild rebuke from such a volatile man, she thought. Being careful to keep off the subject of Terry, she explained about the exhibition, and asked if she could use the photographs he had bought from her.

He considered this for a moment. 'I shall expect the relevant editions of the *Explorer* to be on display as well. In a prominent position.'

'We'll be happy to do that.'

'Then I agree.'

That was easy, she thought, wondering why she'd ever found him intimidating. 'So how much are you going to pay me for my work?' She sat down, expecting this to take some time, but the figure he immediately gave made her gasp in amazement.

He actually laughed. 'That took your breath away, didn't it?'

She was speechless and merely nodded.

'Our sales have shot up and it's a lot to do with your photographs and Devlin's reports. You were a good team.'

'Yes,' she agreed, 'but I think he was glad to get rid of me.'

'I expect he felt responsible for you, and you being there would have restricted his movements a bit. He likes to get right in amongst the action.'

'I'm sure he does.' She stood up. 'When will I receive your cheque?'

'Within the next four days.' He gave one of his rare smiles. 'I shall expect an invitation to the show.'

'You're first on my list.' She stifled a yawn, suddenly feeling tired after her travelling.

'Oh, by the way, Robert Sinclair wants to interview you.'

Now why didn't that surprise her? 'I'll send him an invite as well.' She left, and once in her car headed for Roehampton.

Kate was delighted to find James with her parents, as they were about to sit down for a late dinner. They were all pleased to see her, and she didn't miss the look of relief on their faces.

'Are you staying for dinner?' her mother asked.

'I'd love to, thanks.' She didn't hesitate, because she knew her mother always cooked more than enough for second helpings if wanted. Her father often joked that it was a hangover from her childhood, when there had never been enough to feed the Webster family.

It was lovely sitting around the large kitchen table with her family. They wanted to hear all about her time in Berlin, what it was really like to be there. It was a relief to talk about it with those who knew and understood her. It had been a very upsetting time, and she didn't have to hide her feelings from her family. Afterwards she told them about the exhibition.

'That's a marvellous idea.' Her brother was obviously pleased. 'Where are you going to hold it?'

'We don't know yet. Pete's going to try to find somewhere.'

'What about using the foyer of Grant Phillips?' her father suggested. 'If we cleared it out, there would be plenty of room.'

'Wow, that would be perfect.' Kate could just imagine

her pictures there. The lighting was very good. She glanced at James, who was nodding his head in agreement.

'You let me know when you're ready to put on the show, and I'll have the place set up for you.'

'That's wonderful, James.' She yawned and stood up, now that the meal was over. 'Do you mind if I leave now? It's been a long day.'

'It sounds like it. It's wonderful to have you home again, sweetheart,' said her father, obviously happy to see her so enthusiastic about something again.

Kate promised to come and spend more time with her parents as soon as she could. She hugged them all and went out to her car. As she drove towards Kensington, her mind was already planning the exhibition. When Pete had suggested it, she hadn't been enthusiastic; now she was. It would be great fun to organize, and people would be able to come in off the street and see graphic pictures of the outrage in Berlin.

After parking the car, she went up to her flat, cleaned her teeth and fell into bed, her case still unpacked. She was asleep as soon as her head touched the pillow.

'That was more like my sister,' James said later that evening, as he sat in the sitting room with his parents.

'It certainly was.' Bill savoured his nightly glass of brandy. 'I was afraid that the trouble in Berlin might have made her withdraw into herself, but it seems as if quite the opposite has happened.'

'Perhaps she's fallen in love at last.' James grinned at the thought.

Bill glanced at Rose. 'Do you think she might have?'

'You men,' Rose scolded. 'Why are you so eager to see Kate tied down with a husband and family? At the moment I don't think that's what she wants.'

'I would like to see her settled and happy, that's all,' Bill protested.

'I expect she will be one day, in her own time.' Rose's expression softened as she considered her husband. He worried so much about Kate, and since the kidnapping his concern for her happiness had grown. 'Our daughter is a giver, Bill, always has been, but she's taken some hard knocks and must have time and space to recover.'

'We don't have to worry about her, Dad.' James poured another small measure of brandy into his father's glass. 'I'm sure she's back to normal now.'

Bill swirled the golden liquid around in the glass, then the deep frown smoothed out. Rose gave an inward sigh of relief. His angina attacks were becoming more frequent, and he'd had to slow down quite a lot. She knew that inactivity frustrated him, but she didn't want too much stress in his life. A ripple of fear went through her – she couldn't imagine life without him.

'I think Dad might have something, though, Mum. I've noticed that Jon Devlin's name comes up quite a lot in the conversation.'

Rose was sceptical. He was a fine man, but when she had seen Jon and Kate together there had been an unmistakable tension in the air. They weren't easy in each other's company. Stranger things had happened, of course. Look at her and Bill. But she'd always thought that perhaps Jacques might be the one . . . Look at her! Now she was getting as bad as the men! She shook herself.

Bill's voice interrupted Rose's train of thought. 'She mentioned someone else.'

'Yes, Gerhard,' James said. 'Now, she does seem to like him.'

'Will you two leave the girl alone?' Rose laughed. 'Kate's a grown woman, and she'll make her own decisions.'

'Quite right, Mum.' James got to his feet. 'You and Dad have brought us up to think for ourselves, and I've no right to interfere in Kate's life. Trouble is, I keep thinking of her as a little girl – loving, sensitive and damned stubborn.'

Bill chuckled. 'She was a handful, wasn't she? I remember your telling me how stubborn she'd been when you'd tried to persuade her to go to Wales in the war. She flatly refused until George bribed her with a puppy, a cat and two donkeys, no less.'

Rose rolled her eyes as she remembered the incident. 'She seethes and rages deep inside, whereas I used to shout and fight anyone who got in my way.'

'I wish she'd do the same. At least then we'd know what she was thinking and feeling.' Bill sighed and shook his head. 'I'm turning into an interfering old man.'

'Never!' Rose said in mock horror.

James headed for the door, laughing.

When their son had gone, Rose and Bill made their way upstairs.

'I think I'll pop along to the office tomorrow and see what needs doing with the foyer for the exhibition. Good idea, isn't it, Rosie?'

'Very,' she agreed.

Rose didn't sleep until she heard Bill's steady breathing,

then she allowed herself to drift off, her mind still working. She'd had doubts about whether Kate was going to be strong enough to cope with the hard times in life. Her daughter had proved her wrong.

31

After a good night's sleep, Kate was eager to get going the next day. There was a lot to do today, and by seven thirty she was on her way to Wilkins House to have breakfast with the boys.

She was nearly knocked flying when Eddie threw himself at her with a squeal of delight.

'You're home! You're home!'

She stooped down and hugged him, as the other boys crowded round, asking where she'd been.

Eddie swung on Kate's hand. 'While you was away, your mum and dad took me to the big park and we had tea there – real cream cakes.' He sighed blissfully. 'I was sorry you wasn't there too, but it was luverly.'

'My goodness.' Kate smiled down at his upturned animated face. 'You did have a good time, didn't you?'

'Breakfast is ready, boys.' Mrs Green arrived and smiled at Kate. 'Are you going to join us?'

'Yes, please.'

Once the meal was over, they went back into the big room and everyone talked at the top of their voices. Kate settled back to listen to each one tell of the things they'd done.

Suddenly Eddie jumped up. 'I nearly forget, I bought you a present.' He shot out of the room as fast as his little legs would carry him, thundering up the stairs.

There was much thumping and crashing coming from

the room above them and Tom giggled. 'He's hidden it so we couldn't get at it. I expect he's forgotten where he put it.'

There was silence for a moment, then he was running down the stairs. Eddie burst into the room breathless but triumphant. He held his present out to her. 'I bought that in the park tea place for you.'

'Is that for me?' She looked suitably impressed and took the bright pink gobstopper from him, giving him a kiss on the cheek. 'I am a lucky girl. Thank you, I love those.'

'I knew you would.' His smile couldn't get any wider.

'Time for your swim.' Mrs Green began herding the children out through the door.

Eddie looked downcast, although a visit to the baths was a great treat. 'You've only just come and now I've got to go.'

'I'll come back this evening to read you a story before you go to sleep.'

'Oh, yes, please!' His face was wreathed in smiles again. 'I haven't seen you for *such* a long time, and James gave us some new storybooks.'

She watched him run to catch up with the others. It sounded as if her brother were taking an interest in the boys, and that made her very happy.

'A couple of weeks seems an age to them.' Mrs Green sat beside her.

'I expect it does.' Kate put the gobstopper in her bag. 'Is there anything you need, Mrs Green?'

'No, thank you, my dear, Mr Devlin sees we have a few luxuries, and your mother keeps an eye on us.' She patted Kate's hand. 'We have much to be thankful for.'

Kate glanced at her watch and surged to her feet, knowing that *she* had much to be grateful for as well. It had been a dreadful year, but she was through it now, thank goodness. Her heart went out to all those poor souls in Berlin; what anguish they were facing! 'I must be going, Mrs Green. I'll come back before the boys go to bed.'

Pete was in the shop when Kate arrived, and she told him about the offer of using the foyer of Grant Phillips for the exhibition.

'That's wonderful! I noticed how nice it was when we went there with Robert Sinclair. If I remember rightly, it's large with plenty of wall space.' He flicked through the appointments book. 'I haven't got anything lined up for a couple of hours, so shall we have a look at it now?'

Leaving Susan in charge, they headed for Knightsbridge and Grant Phillips. When they entered the foyer, Kate was delighted to find her father and James already discussing the proposed exhibition.

'Ah,' James said, 'I thought it wouldn't be long before you two tumbled through the door.'

'This is very good of you.' Pete shook hands with the men, and then spun around, examining the area. 'This will be great! The lighting's good, and look at the lovely plain walls. We'll be able to get fifty or sixty people at a time in here.'

'Fifty!' Kate exclaimed. 'We'll never get that many turning up.'

''Course we will,' Pete said with his usual optimism.

'We can move the reception desk,' James told him. 'Where would you like it?'

Pete paced around making a rough map on a piece of paper he'd pulled out of his pocket. 'Over by the far wall, I think. Would you mind if we used it for drinks and snacks?'

Kate watched them as they worked, and slipped her arm through her father's, smiling up at him. 'I think it will be best if I leave everything to them and just do as I'm told. Pete is a marvellous organizer, so I expect he's already got it planned in his mind.'

'Hmm, let them get all the mundane arrangements out of the way, and that will leave you free to deal with the artistic side of things.'

Kate chewed her lip. 'Do you think anyone will come, Dad?'

'Of course they will,' he declared. 'They'll be flocking in.'

She sincerely hoped he was right. She still had her doubts that people would bother to come to see the work of an unknown photographer. But everyone else was enthusiastic about it, so it was worth a try.

'Kate,' James said, striding over, 'are you going to sell the pictures?'

'Oh, no.' She was shocked at the idea. 'They're not the kind of pictures someone would want in their homes.'

'Well, why don't you use the alcove just inside the door for some of your other works and put those up for sale?'

Pete rushed over to inspect the area and came back nodding vigorously. 'We could do that, Kate. It won't interfere with the main exhibition on Berlin.'

She considered this for a moment and decided that it would be an opportunity for Pete and Terry to show some of their work. 'All right, but only if you and Terry contribute.'

'This is your exhibition,' Pete protested.

'I won't agree unless you both put some of your best pictures up for sale.'

Pete didn't look too sure. 'Terry, perhaps . . .'

Kate was adamant. 'All three of us or none at all.'

'It's a good idea,' her father said. 'Try to choose prints with a lighter side to them. Kate, you could show that marvellous photo you have of Eddie laughing.'

The discussion became more animated, with much laughter as they decided on suitable photos.

'Do it.' James was equally keen on the idea. 'It will be a light-hearted contrast to the rest of the exhibition.'

'Yes, you're right.' Pete agreed without further objections, obviously seeing the sense of the idea. 'Now, we must fix a date; a Friday evening might be best. Say, two weeks' time?'

'Pete!' Kate was horrified. 'We'll never be ready that soon.'

'I suppose that is pushing it a bit,' he agreed with reluctance. 'We'll need to advertise it as well, so better make it three weeks.'

Kate pulled a face as she thought of what a rush even that would be. 'He's a slave driver.'

It was agreed. James would have the foyer cleared the day before; they would get the pictures up the next morning; her parents would see to the food and drink, Annie to the invitations. And they would open to the public at seven o'clock.

'Does Aunt Annie know you're volunteering her?' she asked her father.

He gave a dismissive wave of his hand. 'She'll love to help. In fact, once the family hears about this, you'll probably have more help than you need.'

'Right, now that's settled, are you all coming up for coffee?' James asked.

Kate glanced at her watch. 'Sorry, James, we've got to get back now.'

'I'll have one with you.' Bill kissed Kate and went upstairs with James.

Kate felt bemused as they drove back to the shop. This had been arranged so quickly, and she still wasn't sure anyone would come. There was one photo she knew had to be included, though.

Later that evening, in the quiet of her flat, she wrote a long letter to Gerhard, asking for permission to use his picture.

'What's grabbing your attention so much?' Jon asked Gerhard, as they ate a hastily prepared lunch.

'It's a letter from Kate, asking if she can use the photo of me in an exhibition she intends to put on showing the pictures she took here.' He put the letter down for a moment.

'When?' Jon asked.

Gerhard continued reading and then exclaimed, 'What date is it today?'

'The 12th of September. Why?'

'Oh, hell, this letter has taken an age to reach me. The exhibition is on Friday the 15th.'

'I might go back for that,' Jon said thoughtfully. 'I want to see the boys anyway.'

'I think I'll come with you.' Gerhard flicked through

his diary. 'I'll only be able to stay a couple of days, though. It would make a good story for my paper. The people of Berlin would like to think that somebody cares about them.'

Quite frankly Jon would rather have gone back alone in the hope of seeing Kate on her own, but he took Gerhard's point. There was a belief in Berlin that no one cared that the city had been cut in half. A very solid wall was being put up in place of the barbed wire. It was 2.4 metres high, ugly and depressing, topped with barbed wire. The border guards in the East had orders to shoot to kill. The chances of people escaping to the West were slim now, but some were still trying.

'That's settled, then.' Gerhard stood up. 'I'll go and see if we can get a flight.'

Jon watched Gerhard leave, and began pacing the room, stopping to gaze out of the window. The street was almost deserted except for a few people hurrying along, head down. The residents of Berlin now knew that this was not a temporary gesture of defiance by the Soviets; they were going to have to live with the wall for the foreseeable future.

Jon continued to stare outside with unseeing eyes. He'd been jealous when he'd found out that Kate had written to Gerhard and not to him. It was not an emotion he was familiar with, and it was then he realized that he was in love with Kate. He would stay in London for a week or two to be near her, and perhaps he would get a chance to tell her how he felt about her.

Friday, the 15th of September, was overcast. The evening had turned damp and drizzly, but that hadn't deterred people from attending. The place was crowded when Jon and Gerhard arrived.

'My goodness,' Gerhard said, as they pushed through the crush. 'This is causing quite a stir.'

'Jon.' Rose appeared, shook hands with him and then studied his companion. 'And you must be Gerhard. I recognize you from Kate's photograph. It's very good, by the way, have you seen it?'

'No, we've only just arrived and it isn't possible to get near the pictures. There must be nearly a hundred people crammed in here, Mrs Freeman.' Gerhard pulled a notebook out of his pocket and began to scribble in it. 'It's wonderful to see so much interest.'

'The poor bloody people of Berlin must be worried sick about their future.' Rose's dark eyes blazed. 'I'd like to get my hands on some of these politicians!'

Gerhard looked up from his writing and smiled at Rose. 'You and me both, Mrs Freeman!'

Jon chuckled, remembering how she had dealt with the officials when sorting out the trouble at Wilkins House. 'I'd love to have seen you when you were younger, Rose.'

'Oh, no, you wouldn't, Jon.' Rose grimaced. 'I was a blasted menace. The politicians used to run and hide when I appeared!

'Well, come and have a drink first, it will thin out later and you can see the photos in comfort.' Rose led the way, carving a passage through the people.

'She's everything you told me, Jon,' Gerhard said quietly, 'and she is still beautiful.'

'I never said she wasn't.' They were nearly at the refreshments when Jon saw Kate for the first time. People surrounded her. She was wearing the amber dress she'd bought in Paris, but he was not prepared for the impact the sight made on him. He wasn't the only one, though, because he heard Gerhard take in a deep breath.

He leant towards Jon. 'I take back what I said in Berlin. If you want her, then you are going to have to get past me first!'

'I've told you I'm not interested.' If there were such a thing as divine retribution for lying, then Jon Devlin would have been struck by a bolt of lightning at that moment. It was a real corker. He did want her! More than he'd ever wanted anything in his life. This wasn't merely a physical attraction, although that was potent enough; it was a deep, undying love. And that frightened the hell out of him!

It came to him with such shattering force that his instinct was to run out of there, and he knew this was the first time he'd ever shown cowardice in the face of danger. But this was a danger that could tear him apart mentally, and, if he couldn't make her his own, the pain would be intolerable.

'Aren't you supposed to be in Berlin?'

Jon turned at the sound of Andrew Stevenson's voice behind him. 'I'm just on a flying visit to see the exhibition. What are you doing here?'

Andrew dragged him over to a wall where the *World Explorer* was mounted with a circle of photographs round it.

'Good, don't you think?'

'Very impressive.' And it was. No wonder the Chief was smiling. It was marvellous publicity for the paper and highlighted the intelligent coverage it had given to the crisis. 'I'm surprised she let you through the door after the way you've treated her.'

Andrew looked smug. 'That's all behind us now. That girl knows what she's doing with a camera.'

'Pity you didn't recognize that sooner,' Joel Perkins said over his shoulder.

Andrew groaned. 'The boss never misses a chance to rub my nose in it. I admit I did make a mistake, but I managed to get her to work exclusively for us this time, and I'm sure she will in the future.'

'So you did,' Joel conceded, taking hold of Jon's arm. 'Come and have a drink and then you can tell me how things are in Berlin.'

They made their way over to the table, and Jon couldn't help noticing the smile Kate was bestowing on Gerhard. His friend hadn't wasted any time getting close to her, and by the way she was leaning towards him as he spoke, she obviously didn't mind one little bit. Of course you had to be near someone to hear what they were saying above the constant chatter, but that was of little consolation to him in this mood – he was jealous! He called himself a stupid bloody idiot and turned away from the sight. It didn't help when he saw the way Robert Sinclair was sticking to her side. This was only a temporary aberration; he would soon get over it.

Annie and Reid were serving at the makeshift bar and smiled when they saw him.

'It's good to see you again.' Reid shook his hand. 'What are you going to have?'

Jon eyed the bottles on the table. 'Something strong?'

Annie was apologetic. 'We've only got red or white wine.'

Reid winked at him, dived under the table and came up with a double whisky in a wine glass. 'Sacrilege, I know, but we've only got wine glasses. Bill smuggled in the whisky.'

'This will do just fine.' Jon took the drink and noticed that Reid, James and Bill had the same. He lifted his glass in a salute and grinned. The men in the family were quite clearly not wine drinkers.

He spent the next fifteen minutes or so telling Joel Perkins the unedited story of the Berlin crisis.

'I'm pleased you looked after Kate. I would hate anything to happen to one of Rose's children.'

He looked sharply at his boss. 'Do you know Rose, then?'

'Yes. I was only around six when she swept into our life. I remember it as if it was only yesterday. Our street was a slum and was being knocked down, but my father was refusing to move. The bailiffs were at the door ready to burst their way in and throw us out. We were all terrified. It was then Rose Webster strode in, got the bailiffs to hold off while she persuaded my father to move to the new house. She was successful and my family never looked back after that. Without her help I don't know what would have happened to us. And it wasn't just us she helped: she was tireless in her efforts to get rid of the slums.' Joel gazed across at Rose with obvious affection. 'Decent living conditions, education and rights under the law for women were her goals in life, and I know she has never stopped working for the under-privileged.'

Jon listened in fascination. The more he learnt of Rose and her family, the more he loved and respected them.

'What she did that day opened the way for a better life for all of us, and I'm so grateful.'

Things were becoming clear to Jon now. 'Is that why you gave Kate the job on the paper?'

'When I saw her application I knew who she was and checked up on her credentials. When I found that she was a good photographer, I ordered Andrew to take her on. We had the most almighty row about it, but in the end he knew he didn't have a choice.' Joel's sigh was sad. 'That was a big mistake because you know how Andrew hates women around the workplace.'

Jon emptied his glass, Reid quickly refilled it, and he nodded his thanks. 'I bet he made her life difficult.'

'No doubt, and she was right to leave, but it's all turned out for the best.' Joel chuckled. 'She's got her own back by pinching Terry. He's working for her now.'

'What?' Jon burst out laughing. 'Good for her.'

His boss helped himself to another glass of red wine. 'Andrew has found out the hard way that you don't mess with a member of that family and get away with it. Not even the quietest and most docile one. There's something in them that makes them rebel against injustice of any kind.'

'I saw that in Berlin,' Jon agreed. 'When I first spotted Kate, she was furious and trying to beat down the barrier.'

'Separation from family and any kind of imprisonment would be two of the most heinous crimes to Kate.' Joel sipped his drink. 'I'm relieved you were there at the time.'

Jon glanced across at the woman they were discussing, seeing her surrounded by family and friends. They were very important to her, and so must freedom be after her kidnapping. He was glad he'd had this talk with his boss; he felt as if he understood Kate better now.

'Beautiful, isn't she?' Joel said affectionately. 'But you should have seen Rose as a young woman. She was something to behold, even to a snotty-nosed kid.'

Joel Perkins wandered off then to talk to someone else, and Jon caught sight of Terry, busy taking photos with Pete. He beckoned Terry over. 'I hear you've jumped ship.'

'Couldn't get out quick enough.' Terry took a picture of him, and then shook his hand vigorously. 'Glad you could come tonight. Your friend seems to be staking his claim to Kate, but he's wasting his time.'

'What makes you say that?'

Terry looked at him in amazement. 'She almost died at the hands of Derek Howard. If you were a woman, would you trust a man again?'

Jon merely shook his head. That was so sad. Kate was a person who should love and be loved, with a family of her own around her. He only had to picture her with Eddie to know that. He spent too much time in dangerous situations not to understand what violence would do to a young woman like her. She would have been very badly shaken by the experience. He wasn't usually a religious man, but he prayed now that the damage would not be permanent.

But his fears soon passed when she looked him straight in the face. Her eyes were shining with happiness, without a shadow of the trauma or sadness he'd seen in them before. Clearly everyone was worrying unnecessarily. She was fine. He acknowledged her with a nod of his head and began talking to James, who had just joined him.

Kate was surrounded by people, so he decided not to fight his way over to her. His chance to see her would come later, he hoped.

'Someone wants to buy one of your pictures.' Beth touched Kate's arm to gain her attention. 'They'd like you to sign the back for them.'

'Oh, right.' The two friends walked over to the alcove where the other photographs were on show.

When the transaction was completed, Beth looked up at her. 'This is a great success. I wish I had a more exciting job.'

Kate laughed at her friend's disgusted expression. 'I've already told you to leave and find something else.'

'I'm sticking it out because I don't want to be out of work.' Beth waved her left hand in front of Kate's face. 'I'm saving up.'

'You're engaged!' She hugged Beth in delight. 'When did this happen?'

'Only yesterday.'

'Why didn't you bring Steve along? We could have turned this into a celebration.'

'He's got a rotten cold and didn't want to spread it around.'

'What a shame. Never mind, when he's better we'll open a bottle of champagne.'

'I'll keep you to that,' Beth laughed as she looked across the room. 'Jon Devlin's a stunning man, isn't he? It's time you got yourself a steady boyfriend.'

'He'd be anything but steady!' Kate snorted inelegantly. 'And don't you start. I've already had Dad and Aunt Dora on at me.'

Beth giggled. 'I'll go and talk to James. It's about time he got married as well.'

Kate groaned theatrically. 'Have you been talking to my Aunt Dora?'

'Of course.' Beth waved and disappeared into the crowd.

32

On Monday, Kate, Pete and Terry were back in the shop, elated with the success of the exhibition. Not only had it served to highlight the fate of Berlin, but they had all sold a few of their personal photographs. And it hadn't done their business any harm: bookings were flooding in. They were in good spirits and planning their next shop. Things couldn't be better, but underneath her happiness Kate could feel a knot of disappointment.

Gerhard had come straight over to see her, but Jon hadn't even bothered to talk to her. Apart from a quick acknowledgement from across the room, he'd spent the entire evening with other people. In Berlin she had believed they'd come to understand each other a little. It would have been lovely to discuss the pictures with him, and ask what he thought of the exhibition. She would have valued his opinion. Though why she should let his offhand conduct upset her was a mystery. He was obviously unsociable as well as unreliable.

'Where shall we start looking for a new shop?'

Pete's question cut through her musing. They were sitting around the table in the back room with mugs of tea in front of them. Pete had joked that this was their first board meeting. 'Have you any ideas, Terry? You're the one who'll be running it.'

'Well, I live in Putney, so what about there?'

'What do you think, Pete?' she asked.

'Sounds good. We'll have a look and see what's available.'

'You'll need a good assistant like Susan.' Kate gazed into space thoughtfully. 'My friend Beth is looking for a new job.'

'Oh, ask her if she's interested, then,' Terry said.

She grinned. 'She's just got engaged, so I'm not sure how long she'll stay, but she's just the cheery sort you need in a shop.'

'She sounds perfect.' Pete rubbed his hands in excitement. 'You see your friend and we'll start on this right away.'

Kate finished her tea and put the mug down, grinning at the men. 'We can afford really good premises with the money Andrew Stevenson paid me.'

Terry held up his mug in a mock salute. 'I never thought I'd say this: good old Andrew.'

Kate and Pete roared at his comical expression. At that moment the shop bell tinkled, and Kate, knowing Susan was busy, stood up.

'I'll get it.' She walked into the shop, and when she saw who it was didn't know if she felt pleased or angry. 'Can I help you?' she asked politely.

Jon's gaze swept over her in a strictly masculine appraisal.

'I've come to congratulate you on the exhibition.'

'Really?' Her eyebrows rose in query. 'And you couldn't have told me that on Friday evening?'

He frowned at her sarcastic tone. 'I would have, if I could have got anywhere near you.'

'Gerhard didn't have any trouble.' She still couldn't understand why his silly behaviour rankled so much.

'Ah, well, he wouldn't have done.'

'And what does that mean?' She was irritated now by his attitude.

He sighed and held his hands up in surrender. 'I don't know what I've done. Can we start again? When I arrived I could hear you laughing, but one look at me, and you're spitting like a feral cat. I'll just go outside the door and come in again, eh?'

She watched him go out, close the door, wait for a couple of seconds, turn around twice and then come back in.

'Hello, Kate,' he said with a cheerful smile. 'I just came to congratulate you on that marvellous exhibition.'

This was ridiculous! Laughter bubbled inside her; the man was a fool. She had the grace to be ashamed of her sharp tongue; it wasn't like her to snap at people. But then, she was doing a lot of things she'd never done before.

'That's very kind of you,' she replied, fighting to keep a straight face.

'Go on, smile, it won't hurt you,' he teased.

Her mouth turned up at the corners. 'Sorry I was so waspish, but I was disappointed that we didn't walk around and discuss the pictures. Most of them were taken while I was with you and I wanted to know what you thought of them. By the time the crowd had thinned out, you'd gone.'

'I looked at them. They were excellent. You get so much feeling into your photographs. You have a lot of emotional sensitivity when you're taking photos, and it comes out in the finished pictures.'

'Thank you.' She was pleased with the compliment, for she knew he didn't say anything he didn't mean.

'Now that's settled and we can talk politely, will you have lunch with me?'

When she didn't answer, he raised an eyebrow in query. 'Does that smile mean yes?'

'I'll get my bag.'

As they walked up the road to the restaurant, she asked, 'Is Gerhard joining us?'

'No, he's had to return to Berlin. He's still looking for some way to rescue his parents, so he doesn't want to be away too long.'

'It must be dreadful for him.' Kate could understand his worry. 'It was good to see him again anyway.'

'Hmm,' was the only reply.

'Are you returning there soon, or going on somewhere else?' she asked.

'I expect I'll go back to Berlin eventually, but I've decided to take a couple of weeks off now I'm back. I've earned a rest.'

It was an enjoyable meal. They talked about the children, Berlin, his job, her work, and a wide variety of subjects. By the time he walked her back to the shop she was completely relaxed in his company.

'Thank you for lunch,' she told him when they reached the door.

'It was my pleasure.' Keeping his hands to his sides, he leaned down and touched his lips to hers in a brief kiss.

It was an intoxicating feeling and she closed her eyes for a moment. The kiss had been so soft and fleeting, but it had also been warm and sensual – and completely non-threatening. Her heart seemed to swell inside her. With the right man, there wouldn't be anything to fear.

After giving her a searching look, as if trying to gauge her reaction, he smiled and walked away.

Kate watched him stride towards the high street. He walked straight, with his head up, and even from here she could sense his strength, not only in body but also in character. This was a man you could rely on, but not one to fall in love with. If she did eventually marry, she would want a man who was around most of the time, not one who kept chasing wars.

He turned the corner and disappeared from sight, but she still stood in the same spot, deep in thought. It would be foolhardy to love him, because he was as transitory as the wind, moving from place to place all the time. Touching the lives of others briefly, and then off again.

The next week flew by. Beth had jumped at the chance to work at the new shop; Terry had interviewed her and was quite happy. And to make things even better, Terry had just told them that as there was a new shop for him to run, he was going to stay with them. There was no sign of Jon, so Kate assumed he'd gone back to Berlin. After their lunch together, followed by a sleepless night, she had to acknowledge that she was attracted to him. Her feelings for him had begun to change in Berlin, so slowly that she hadn't realized it was happening. It was hopeless, of course – he wouldn't stay in one place long enough to put down roots. His work was the most important thing to him, and whoever fell in love with him would have to accept that. She wasn't sure she could. Anyway, she told herself firmly, he was not the settling-down kind, and, although he was showing some liking for her, she doubted if he would ever love a woman enough to make him change direction. He was obviously used to walking alone, and that was the way he seemed to like it. She smiled when she remembered how he'd looked after her in Berlin. What a nuisance she must have been to him.

All her careful reasoning didn't change one fact, though: she was greatly attracted to him and would love to get to know him better. However, there was little chance of that.

Taking firm control of her thoughts and emotions, she sang to herself as she worked in the darkroom. They'd found a perfect shop in Putney, and it would be ready for Terry and Beth in a couple of weeks. Pete was in his element arranging everything, and it made Kate happy to see them all so enthusiastic.

But there was one thing above all else that made her buoyant with hope for the future. That kiss Jon had given her had been wonderfully liberating, for she now knew that she could fall in love. Jon had shown her that the past really was behind her.

Kate's sigh, although one of contentment, also carried a hint of sadness. She could love a man, need his touch, want his body close to hers, and long to hold his child in her arms, and that was cause for enormous relief. She could only be happy about that, but sad that it wouldn't be Jon. However, the events of this year had made her stronger, more able to cope with disappointment. Jon Devlin had been an angel in disguise, waking her from a nightmare, and she would always love him for that alone. It was a mystery when her feelings for him had changed to love, for there was no denying that now. One minute she had been fighting with him, and the next she had wanted him near her.

She switched on the main light and went to put the kettle on for a cup of tea. It was a surprise when her brother came into the back room. She had never seen him so grim and upset.

'What is it, James?' She touched his arm in concern, and he placed his hand over hers.

'You have to come with me, Kate.' His voice was husky, as if he found it difficult to speak. 'Dad's had a heart attack. They've taken him to St George's Hospital at Hyde Park Corner.'

She could feel shock and disbelief surging through her, making her legs shake.

'We must hurry,' James urged.

'How bad?' She had found her voice at last.

The despairing shake of his head told her all she needed to know, and she was running out of the shop towards his car.

The journey was accomplished in silence, except for the muttered expletives from James every time they had slow traffic in front of them. They swept up to the main entrance and, leaving the car where it was, hurried into the hospital.

'Where is he? Where is he?' Kate spun in a complete circle, her insides tight with panic. There were so many different ways to go!

James took her arm. 'I know, come on.'

As they hurried along a seemingly endless corridor, Kate stopped as if she'd hit a solid wall, wrapped her arms around her middle and doubled over.

'What's the matter?' her brother asked in alarm.

She wasn't sure. It wasn't a physical pain; it was as if something had left her, leaving an empty space inside her. She gave James a tortured look and shook her head in denial, not wanting to believe what her instinct was telling her. She had always been tuned in to her father, and it felt as if he had just touched her. She straightened up and ran the rest of the way. She had to get to him!

The first bed in the ward had the curtains pulled around it, and she knew that her father was there. She pulled aside the curtain. A doctor was bending over the bed and her mother was sitting there, head bowed and absolutely still. The doctor moved back and she saw her father. His eyes were closed, and there was such a look of peace on his face that it took her breath away. But the man she had loved so dearly all her life was not there. He had left them – and she hadn't been here. She should have been with him!

Her mother looked up as they came in, her face a mask of self-control. 'He's gone.'

Kate went to the other side of the bed and sank to her knees, taking hold of her father's hand and cradling it to her cheek. 'I'm so sorry I wasn't here,' she whispered, her voice husky. 'If there's any way you can hear me, then know that I will always love you.'

James placed his arm around her shoulder. 'Let me take you and Mum home. I'll see to everything.'

They walked out of the hospital, one on each side of their mother, and Kate was so numb she couldn't even shed a tear. Life without her father was something she couldn't grasp, and she suspected that her mother and James were struggling with the same disbelief.

When they arrived back home, Annie and Reid were waiting for them. James had phoned everyone as soon as he had heard, but he'd asked them not to come to the hospital until they knew how Bill was. One look at their faces as they walked in told them the bad news.

'Oh, dear God.' Reid gathered Rose and Kate to him. 'I'm so sorry.'

Annie then hugged them, obviously fighting to keep the tears at bay. Then Annie put the kettle on and Kate laid out the cups, her hands shaking from the shock, but she was glad of a feeling of numbness, because when she thawed out the pain would be intolerable. Her life had turned around just lately and she had been happy again, but even her worst nightmare could not be as devastating as this. There still weren't any tears, but they were just underneath the surface now and fighting to spill out. She looked around at the solemn faces of her family and hoped she could keep control until she was alone. Her mother was her usual stoic self. Kate knew her well enough to recognize that the protective front was firmly in place. She mustn't break down and put more strain on her mother.

They sat around the table talking sadly about the man they had all loved and admired, but Kate hardly heard a word. All she could hear was her tortured mind screaming that the man who had been the pivot of her life was gone! The pain of loss was intolerable.

James stood up. 'I'll go back to the hospital, Mum, and deal with everything.'

'Thank you, James.' Rose was looking ready to drop with fatigue and shock. 'I'll just go and have a rest.'

'We're going to stay,' Annie told Kate when Rose had gone upstairs. 'What are you going to do?'

'I shall move back. I don't want Mum to be alone here.'

'I was hoping you would do that.' Annie's tears were falling quietly now. 'I'll stay until after the funeral, but Reid will have to leave tomorrow.'

Her own grief surfaced now. 'Why did this have to happen?' Kate gasped. 'He was such a good man.'

'Yes, he was,' Annie agreed, holding Kate in her arms and rocking her gently, 'but he was also sick and very tired.'

Kate dried her tears, knowing that however great her personal loss, her father was now at peace.

33

Jon walked into the shop; he was looking forward to seeing Kate again. After their amicable lunch together and her acceptance of the brief show of affection, he guessed she was beginning to feel more than liking for him. He had stayed away, not wishing to push his company on her, giving her a chance to think things over, and he hoped she would spend more time with him. They needed to get to know each other and he was determined to bring that about, if she would allow it.

'Hi, Pete, is Kate around?' The expression on Pete's face made his heart leap in alarm. 'What's the matter?'

'Her father died yesterday.'

'Bill?'

Pete swallowed and nodded. 'He had a massive heart attack.'

'Oh, my God! Where is she?'

'With her mother in Roehampton.'

Jon was out of the door and running for the bus – they would be devastated. When he'd realized how much he cared for Kate, he had called himself all the names he could think of for falling in love with her. At first he'd thought he was attracted to her because she was Rose's daughter, but that wasn't true. The feelings he had for Kate were like nothing he'd ever experienced in his life. He wanted to be with her all the time, to touch her, love her and make her a part of his life. He'd fallen in love with her because she was Kate, a unique personality, funny, sensitive, stubborn and volatile at times, and he loved her deeply. He'd been agonizing over what to do, but this disaster settled it. He wasn't going to leave her now, and he didn't give a damn if she wanted him around or not. He was staying. There was also Rose, and if there was anything he could do for her, then he would. For the first time in his life he was ready to commit himself wholeheartedly.

He sprinted and jumped on a bus going to Fleet Street as it was pulling away from the stop. Once at the newspaper he ran up the stairs to Andrew's office, taking them two at a time. He wanted this sorted out, so he could get to Rose and Kate.

'Ah, Jon,' Andrew greeted him, 'had enough lounging around? You can return to Berlin whenever you like.'

'I'm not going back. In fact, I'm not going abroad again. I want to work in London.'

The Chief frowned as if he couldn't believe what he was hearing. 'But you're a war correspondent. There isn't a war here.'

He was fast losing patience; he didn't have time to stand around arguing the point. 'I can bloody well start one if you like.'

'Calm down.' Andrew was clearly concerned about his favourite reporter's strange mood.

'Sorry, but I mean it, I don't want to go abroad again for a while, if ever. I have to stay here. If you don't like it, then I'll find another job.'

Andrew was on his feet in alarm. 'There's no need for that; you're due a long break. You're the best reporter

I've got and I can find you work in this country at any time.'

'Good.' Jon glanced at his watch. 'Why don't you send Mike or Robert to Berlin? I'm sure either would jump at the chance.'

'You're right, I'll do that.'

He glanced at the time again, anxious to be on his way. 'Did you know Bill Freeman had a heart attack yesterday and died?'

'No,' Andrew said, reaching for the phone. 'That's a damned shame. I'd better tell Joel Perkins, he'll want to know.'

'I must be on my way. I'm going to see if there's anything I can do for them. We'll discuss my job some other time.'

Andrew nodded his agreement. 'Tell them I'm very sorry. I only met Kate's father twice but he seemed a fine man.'

Annie opened the door to Jon and she looked so very sad. 'Hello, come in.'

He was taken into the kitchen, which he had soon learnt was the hub of this house, and was greeted warmly by Reid.

'Good of you to come,' Reid said.

'How are Rose and Kate?'

'They are stunned,' Annie told him, 'just like the rest of us, but they'll be pleased to see you. They're in the sitting room.'

Jon wasn't sure if he should be intruding on this family's grief, but he felt he *had* to be near Kate and Rose. Both women meant a great deal to him.

When he opened the door of the sitting room and walked in, they were around an open fire talking quietly. The room was very warm, but they looked frozen. He could almost feel their pain.

Rose looked up. 'Hello, Jon.'

'I'm so sorry.' The words were inadequate. He didn't know what else to say. 'I came to see if there's anything I can do for you.'

'Thank you for the thought, but we have everyone tripping over each other trying to help. They won't let us do a thing.' Rose stood up and tried to smile, without much success. 'I'll go and get us some tea. At least Annie will let me do that. You talk to Kate.'

He watched her walk from the room, tall, straight, and in control of her emotions. In the circumstances it was an impressive sight. Then he turned his attention to Kate. She was pale, which made the dark smudges under her eyes look like livid bruises.

He knelt in front of her and pulled her towards him. She wrapped her arms around him and rested her head on his shoulder. She was silent and dry-eyed but accepted the comfort he was offering.

For the moment that was enough for both of them.

It was a wet cold October day. The crematorium at Roehampton was packed with people. Kate was glad they didn't have to stand around a muddy hole in the ground. She couldn't have dealt with that.

Watching the curtains close around the coffin, she felt detached. Her father wasn't there; he'd gone days ago, she was sure of that. What they were doing today was honouring the life of a good man and disposing of the empty shell. She didn't know why she felt this way, but there was a certainty about this, and it gave a little comfort. Her personal grief was harder to deal with. She kept looking for him, listening for his tuneful whistle, expecting him to be in the kitchen or tending his garden. But he wasn't and never would be again . . .

After the service they filed outside. The ground was covered with a blanket of flowers, and everyone was looking at them, talking in hushed tones. Kate watched the huge gathering of people; her father had been a well-liked and popular man. All the family were here, including her Uncle Charlie and Aunt Madge, who had come from Scotland, and many friends and employees from Grant Phillips. Sam, Maria and Jacques had come over from France, and Joel Perkins with an elderly couple Kate didn't know. Even Andrew Stevenson had come. She wondered if he had been ordered to attend, but she quickly dismissed that cynical idea. Actually they got on quite well now, and she continued to warm to the man. Pete, Susan, Terry and Beth were also here, having closed the shops for the day. Her mother was talking to the couple with Joel Perkins, and she realized they must be his parents, who had known her mum and dad from a long time ago. She let her gaze roam idly around the scene. Her eyes met Jon's. He was standing a little way off, and she was pleased he was here; he'd been a tremendous support to her over the last dreadful week. She lifted her head and smiled at him; he nodded, returning the smile. Why did he have to go back to his job, she thought. Where would he be going? She knew she would miss him. His quiet strength had been such a help, not only to herself but to her mother as well. Kate didn't want him to leave, but he never seemed to stay in one place for long, that was the nature of his job. She gave a weary sigh and walked slowly along the rows of lovely flowers – beautiful tributes for a very special man.

The crowds began to thin out. Many were coming back to the house, but those who weren't took their leave of the family and drove away. Her mother, Annie and James came over to Kate.

'I'm walking back to the house,' her mother said. 'Do you want to go with James in the car?'

'No, I'll come with you, Mum.' It was only about fifteen minutes' walk from the crematorium, and it would be good to have a short time to themselves before facing everyone again.

'I'll come with you as well,' Annie told them. 'Everything's ready back at the house. The men can look after everyone until we arrive.'

They walked through the gates and up the road, each one lost in the sad realization that the man they loved would not be waiting for them with his usual ready smile. It was going to be hard to live without him.

'That went well,' Kate said, wanting to break the silence.

'Yes.' Rose walked slowly, obviously not eager to reach their home. 'It was good of everyone to come.'

Annie slipped her arm through Rose's. 'What are your plans, Rosie?' she asked. 'You're welcome to come and live with Reid and me, or just stay for a while if you want to.'

'That's kind of you, Annie, but Bill built that house for me and the only way I'm going to leave it is feet first.'

Kate's heart leapt in alarm to hear her mother talk of

dying. She dredged up a falsely bright smile. 'That's all right, then, because you've got at least another thirty years.'

As soon as the words were out of her mouth she knew she'd said the wrong thing. The look of pain in her mother's eyes was quickly controlled, but Kate had seen it. The thought of spending so long without her husband was like purgatory to her mother. She changed the subject quickly. 'Who were the elderly couple with Mr Perkins?'

'His parents.'

'Oh, it was nice of them to come.'

'Yes, it was. I'm glad to see they've done so well for themselves.'

Kate knew her mother was just making polite conversation. They had now reached the house and braced themselves to face the next few hours.

At last the house was empty except for Annie and her mother. Kate had found the funeral an ordeal, but her mother's tight control had made her fight to keep the sobs at bay. Silent tears had trickled down her face; she hadn't been able to stop these, and nor had Annie. She knew that Annie had first met Bill when she'd been a young child and had loved him dearly.

'I'm going to have a rest.' Rose stood up. The front she had erected to get her through this day was starting to disintegrate. 'I won't want any dinner, Annie.'

'All right, Rose.'

Kate and Annie watched her leave the kitchen and listened to her slow steps on the stairs.

'I'm worried about her,' Kate told Annie.

'So am I, but she's very strong-willed, and she'll eventually recover.' Annie began to wash the cups and glasses. 'I just wish she wouldn't keep it all bottled up inside.'

'But that's the way she is, she's never been demonstrative.' Kate picked up the tea towel and started to dry the dishes, packing them away as she went.

'That's the result of growing up in the slums, where every day was a struggle.' A brief smile touched Annie's face. 'You should have seen her then.'

'But you grew up there as well,' Kate pointed out, 'and you don't keep your feelings hidden.'

'Ah, but you must remember, your mum was the eldest in a large family and she took on the responsibility for us. Our mum, Marj, was always too worn out having babies to be able to look after us properly. I was very poorly, and Rosie used to see that I had some treats and a bit of decent food whenever she could get it. She looked after me and protected me from the worst of the squalor and violence.'

'Violence?' Kate was shocked.

'Oh, yes, my dad was a brutal man and he didn't like Rose because she wasn't his child. She was the only one with the courage to stand up to him, and if she hadn't we would have ended up in the workhouse. She took some beatings from him.'

'I didn't know that,' Kate whispered.

'You wouldn't, she never talks about those days. If it hadn't been for Rosie, I wouldn't be here today, and it was Bill's great unselfish love for Rose and all of us that made it possible for us to leave that disgusting place.'

'He was a wonderful man.' Kate's eyes misted again.

'He was.' Annie's smile was sad. 'And he'll never die while we hold our love for him in our hearts.'

Her aunt was absolutely right and a little of the pain lifted. 'That's a lovely thought.' Kate hugged her in gratitude. Annie was almost as wise as her mother, but then they had both lived extraordinary lives. And now the funeral was over they must all start to get back to normal – or as normal as possible without her father. He would have wanted that. 'Is it just going to be us for dinner,' Kate asked her, 'or is anyone else coming back?'

'No, it's been a difficult day and we thought it would be better if Rose had a quiet evening. Sam and his family are staying with James tonight; Charlie and Madge are next door with Will and Dora.'

Annie glanced around the kitchen. 'What are we going to do about dinner?'

Kate was about to say that scrambled eggs on toast would do her when someone knocked on the front door. She went to see who it was and found Jon standing on the doorstep with his arms full of packages. There was a wonderful aroma coming from them and she realized that she hadn't had anything to eat all day.

'I thought you might not feel like cooking tonight, so I've brought you fish and chips.' He held them out to her.

'Oh, thank you.' She stepped aside. 'Please come in.'

'Jon's brought us fish and chips,' Kate told Annie when they walked into the kitchen.

'That's so thoughtful of you.' Annie took the packets from him. 'My goodness, there's a lot here. You must stay and help us eat it.'

'I won't if you'd rather be on your own . . .'

'No, no.' Annie unwrapped the meals and popped

them in the oven to warm. 'We'd be glad of your company, wouldn't we, Kate?'

'Yes, we would,' she told him, and it was the truth. She wanted him to stay.

He accepted their invitation with a slight nod of his head.

'Kate, go and tell Rose to come down. She loves fish and chips and we might be able to persuade her to eat.'

She went up the stairs and opened her mother's door quietly. If she was asleep, she didn't want to wake her.

The sight that met her eyes tore the very heart out of Kate. Her mother was standing in the middle of the room, clutching one of her husband's jackets to her and sobbing into it. The material was muffling great wrenching cries. She closed the door as quietly as she had opened it and started back down the stairs. She had to hold on to the banister because her legs wouldn't support her properly.

When she staggered into the kitchen, Jon surged to his feet as soon as he saw her and reached out, pulling her into the shelter of his arms. She went gratefully, seeking comfort. It had been a terrible shock to see her strong, controlled mother like that.

Kate turned her head and gave Annie a tortured look. 'Mum – she's crying. I've never seen her like that before.'

Annie got up. 'Most people haven't. I did, just once. Bill and Rose had been married about two years when they had the most almighty row. Bill left her, but he came back.' Annie got up and ran a hand over her eyes. 'Only this time he won't be coming back. I'll go to her.'

34

It was past midnight when Jon drove away from the Roehampton house, the scene of so much pain. Rose had soon pulled herself together and had even managed to eat some of the fish and chips, but he suspected she'd used all of her considerable willpower so as not to cause her family any more upset. The grief in every member of that family was of a depth he had never encountered before. It showed what great love they all had for Bill. He was glad he'd bought himself this old car yesterday, as nothing on earth was going to make him leave Kate now and he would need his own transport.

Annie had asked Reid and Sam to come back at once, and he understood her choice. Jon only knew snatches of their life stories, but it was obvious they had been through so much during the war, as had Annie, and they were all used to dealing with trauma. Rose and Kate would be safe with them at their sides. He was pleased Jacques hadn't come, though. Kate was vulnerable at the moment, and he was afraid Jacques would upset her even more. He was also uneasy about their relationship. They were close – too close. He gave a disgusted snort and admitted to himself that he was jealous. He loved and wanted Kate, but was sure he wasn't the only one after her love. His gut feeling was that both Jacques and Gerhard were in love with her, with the French boy having the greater claim on her. Well, they'd have to get past him, for he was sure he could love her and protect her better than they.

Early the next morning, when Jon popped into Wilkins House, he was surprised to find Kate having breakfast with the boys. He knew she often did this before starting work for the day, but he hadn't expected her there today.

She was smiling at something Tom was saying, and Eddie was watching her in adoration. He accepted a cup of tea from Mrs Green before joining them at the long table. Kate appeared perfectly normal and relaxed until she looked at him and he saw the anguish in her eyes. She was putting on a great show, and his heart bled for her.

Kate knew that she must tell Eddie about her father, because he often chatted about the game of football he'd had with him, and he was bound to ask about him sooner or later. She stooped down. 'Eddie, I want you to know that my daddy's gone to heaven.' He was always smiling when she came; now the smile vanished from his face. He obviously knew what that meant. Kate was conscious of Jon coming to stand beside her and she was grateful for his silent support; it strengthened her.

'Is he with the angels?' Eddie whispered.

'Yes, and I expect they're having a lovely game of football.' She kept her tone light-hearted with great difficulty, but she must have been successful, because Ed's smile flickered into life again.

'Yeah, he's nice and I bet the angels are glad he's there.'

'I'm sure they are.' Eddie had only met her father twice and he had clearly liked him. Much to her relief, he'd accepted her explanation without any fuss. She stood up and had to hold on to a chair because she was trembling. As Eddie rushed off to collect his lunch box for school, her shoulders sagged as if all energy had been drained from her.

'Well done.' Jon placed his arm around her shoulder. 'You handled that perfectly.'

'Thanks.' She leant against him for a moment, glad of his closeness and understanding. 'I suppose it will get easier.'

'It will,' he reassured her. 'You will always miss him but the pain will ease with time.'

Kate kissed his cheek. Her life had been a battleground from the moment she had walked through the door of the *World Explorer*. The conflict had started in a small way with Andrew Stevenson's hostility, gathering intensity with the kidnapping and trial, now she was in the middle of the hardest fight of all – the loss of her dear father. How was she ever going to come to terms with that?

Jon took her hand in his, watching her long delicate fingers curl around his large hand. She felt icy cold.

'I didn't expect to see you here today.' He placed his other hand over hers in an effort to bring her some warmth and comfort.

'I must get back to work as quickly as possible. Dad would want me to carry on with my life.' Her eyes clouded. 'And I didn't want to worry Mum. She's having a hard-enough job coping without me adding to her grief.'

'How is Rose this morning?'

Kate looked down at their clasped hands and gave a

helpless shake of her head. 'I'm so worried about her. So is Aunt Annie and she knows Mum better than anyone.'

'Shall I go and see her, or do you think she would rather be alone?'

'I'm sure she would be pleased; she likes you.' She gave him a grateful smile. 'Annie, Reid and Sam are there, and the rest of the family will be in and out all day, but do go if you have the time.'

He raised her hand to his lips and kissed it gently. 'Your mother's a special woman. I'll always have time for her.'

'Thank you. She needs a lot of love and support to get her through this.'

'She'll get it, and so will you.'

Kate gave him a rather wistful look. 'Are you going back to Berlin soon?'

'No, I've told Andrew I want to work here from now on.'

'What, stay in London?' She couldn't hide her surprise. 'That's a sudden decision, isn't it?'

'I felt it was time for a change.' He wasn't going to tell her the real reason – that he was in love with her. She wasn't ready for that yet. He raised an eyebrow in query. 'Why, do you want to get rid of me?'

'Oh, no,' she said hastily. 'I'm glad you're staying.'

Her response gave him hope. She needed time to come to terms with the death of her father, and he would give her that. He reluctantly released her hand and stood up. 'I'll go to see Rose now.'

'Thank you.' She stood up as well. 'I must go to the shop. I've left Pete on his own for too long.'

He watched her leave, get in her Mini and drive away.

What a terrible few months that family had had, and the final blow was losing the man they all loved so much. He couldn't help wondering how much the kidnapping had contributed to Bill's death. Quite a lot, he suspected.

'Sad business, but she has a lot of courage and seems to be coping well.' Mrs Green joined him at the window. 'I wish I could help. You feel so helpless at times like this, don't you?'

He merely nodded, his mind focused only on Kate and Rose. Kate would be all right, he thought resolutely; he'd make sure of that. Now he must go and see Rose – the other woman he loved.

Sam opened the door when Jon arrived at Roehampton.

'It's good to see you, Jon, come in.' Sam shook hands with him. 'We've stayed on for a few days. Maria and Jacques are next door with Will and Dora.'

There was no sign of Rose when they went into the kitchen. Annie and Reid were clearing up the breakfast things, and both smiled when they saw him.

'Hello,' Annie said, 'would you like a cup of tea?'

'No, thanks, I've just had one with the boys. I saw Kate there.'

'How did she seem?' Reid's brow was furrowed in concern.

'In control.' He was aware that Kate was special to Reid and Annie. 'How's Rose?'

Annie's hand shook as she placed a cup on the drainer. 'Devastated. She's in the garden. Why don't you go and have a talk with her?'

He stepped through the kitchen door and into the garden Bill had tended so lovingly. The sun was shining, and it was pleasantly warm. He found Rose at the end of the lawn with a hoe in her hand, prodding at a weed in the vegetable patch.

'You missed one,' he pointed out as he stood beside her.

'Hello, Jon, thanks for bringing us fish and chips last night.' She continued with her hoeing.

'My pleasure.' He watched her tackle the weed he'd mentioned and hoped to coax her into a normal conversation. 'That's it – not an intruder in sight.'

She rested her arm on the hoe and surveyed the plot. 'You're right. I've dealt with all the little buggers.'

A smile touched his mouth. That sounded more like Rose. 'I saw Kate this morning, and she said you wouldn't mind me calling.'

'You're welcome here.' She turned her dark eyes on him. 'Jon, are you in love with my daughter?'

The question had come out of nowhere and threw him for a moment, but he didn't hesitate. 'Yes.'

'Are you going off to some war zone any minute now?'

'No, I'm not a war correspondent now. I'm staying here.'

'Does Kate know that?'

'Yes.' He couldn't fathom where this was leading. If she was about to tell him to leave her daughter alone, then she had a fight on her hands.

'Do you intend to marry her?'

He braced himself to meet Rose's disapproval. 'Yes, if she'll have me.'

'Good.' Rose gazed at the flowerbeds again. 'Bill loved this garden.' She spoke softly and then turned back to him. 'You take good care of her.'

The look in those almost-black eyes rocked him back on his heels. It was a look that said the greatest love of her life had gone, and with it her reason for living. She had given up fighting. Rose Freeman no longer had any use for this life!

'I will . . . we both will.'

'Of course.' Her eyes cleared. 'I shall be watching you, young man.'

He almost collapsed in relief. That had been the most frightening thing he had ever witnessed, but thank God, it appeared to be only a momentary lapse. He'd seen something like it before when he'd been reporting on some trouble spot in the world, but never in a woman as strong-willed as Rose. He'd seen people just give up and die for no apparent reason, and he was absolutely certain that if she decided she didn't want to stay here without her husband, then she *would* die. It was a terrifying thought.

'I'll make her happy – that's if she chooses me and not Gerhard or Jacques.'

'Jacques is like a very loved brother. Gerhard doesn't stand a chance.'

'And you think I do?'

'That is something you'll have to find out for yourself; I'm not omniscient.' Rose rammed the hoe into the ground until it stood up on its own. 'Now, let's go and see if there's any tea in the pot.'

James arrived just as they walked into the kitchen, and, after kissing his mother and greeting everyone else, he said to Annie, 'Put the kettle on, I'm gasping for a cup of tea.'

'I'll make it.' Sam picked up the teapot.

Rose moved swiftly and took it out of his hands. 'No, you won't, you still can't make a decent cup of tea.'

Sam leant against the sink, a glitter of amusement in his eyes. 'I remember the first time I made you tea, you told me it was too weak to struggle out of the pot.' His shoulders began to shake in silent laughter when he explained. 'It was during the war and I'd brought Annie home for a rest after her trip behind enemy lines in France. I was on my own in the kitchen when Rose swept in and threatened to box my ears if I didn't tell her who I was.' He was laughing now at the memory. 'I fell in love with her then and I've adored her ever since.'

Rose raised her eyebrows at Annie. 'He hasn't changed much, has he?'

'Well, Rosie, he is a Frenchman, so what else can you expect?'

Laughter rippled around the room and Jon marvelled at the camaraderie and love between these people. They had obviously shared a lot of good and bad times together.

Sam became serious and reached out to hug Rose. 'They were tough years, Rose, but we survived, and you *will* recover from this tragedy.'

'Of course I shall.' Rose gazed around at them all. 'I know I gave you all a fright last night, but you can stop fretting. I'm going to find it damned hard to live without Bill, but we had a good life together and I'm grateful for that. I might even go back into business – part time, of course.' Then she looked pointedly at James. 'I expect to have some grandchildren for me to watch grow up.'

The feeling of relief that swept through the room was palpable to Jon. No one in this family, apart from Annie, had ever seen this strong-minded woman lose control. It had obviously shaken them badly.

'Aha, that's our Rosie talking.' Sam spoke with a pronounced French accent, and Annie grinned.

'And you can cut that out,' Rose declared. 'You didn't fool me with that fake accent in the war, and you're still not too big for me to box your ears.'

The room erupted into laughter. Sam usually spoke English without the trace of an accent, so this was obviously some game they had played in the past. He must get Kate to tell him about it some time.

Annie poured the tea and everyone sat around the large table. This was a strange feeling for Jon, as they seemed to include him without the slightest hesitation. It must have been wonderful to have grown up in a loving family circle like this. But it was incredibly painful now, when they had lost one of their loved ones.

'Reid, you needn't stay any longer. I know you have a business to run, but I would like to have Annie with me for a few days, if that's all right with you.'

'Of course, she can stay as long as you need her.'

'Thank you.' Rose turned to Sam. 'It's time you took your family home; Jacques mustn't miss any more of his education.'

He nodded agreement. 'Maria is anxious to return to France. However, you must promise to phone me every week, Rose, or I shall be over here invading your kitchen again.'

'I promise.' She smiled at everyone. 'The worst is over, eh?'

Jon wondered if it was; he couldn't forget that glimpse of defeat he'd seen in her eyes a short time ago. But if she was feeling like that now, it was being expertly hidden.

In the relaxed atmosphere the conversation flowed and laughter came more readily.

Feeling better about Rose, Jon left, and, as he drove to London, he hoped she would go back into business again. She was going to need something to fill the void in her life.

That afternoon Kate was in the shop mounting photographs in a wedding album when James arrived. 'How's Mum?' she asked anxiously.

'She's all right, and talking about going back to work.'

'Oh, that would be wonderful.' She was so relieved; her mother was thinking about the future and that was a good sign.

'How long are you going to stay with Mum?'

'I'm moving back permanently.' Kate worried her bottom lip. 'I don't want her to be alone in the house; it holds so many memories.'

'I agree.' James squeezed her shoulder. 'But they're all good ones, aren't they?'

She looked up at her brother and smiled gently. 'We've been very lucky in life.'

'Don't I know it.' He sat on the edge of the table. 'What are you going to do with the flat?'

'I'll take it over,' said a voice from the doorway.

Kate looked up to see Jon standing there, feeling a sense of pleasure, as she always did now when he was around. 'Well, if you want it, but I thought you had a place near Wilkins House.'

'I do. My digs are a dump, and as my rambling days are over I'd like something better.'

'Go up and have a look at it, then, and see what you think.'

She watched him race up the stairs, taking them two at a time. It only took him five minutes and he was back.

'Perfect. When can I move in?'

'At once, and it comes with the furniture as well.'

Jon was already heading for the door. 'I'll go and get my things – and thanks, Kate.'

35

Later that afternoon, Jon, with Pete's help, began moving his few possessions into the flat. It was a great improvement on his other dingy place. This was clean and tidy, and the furniture sparkled with polish that left a faint smell of lavender. He was just arranging some of his books in a tall bookcase when there was a knock on the door. He opened it to find Kate standing there.

'Come in.'

'Thanks.' She stepped over a box of books – the only thing Jon had in abundance – and smiled. 'I had a five-year lease on the flat, and the agent was quite happy to transfer it over to you. Those are my spare keys.'

He didn't have time to thank her, as someone was thundering up the stairs calling her name.

'Kate!' Jacques erupted into the room and gathered Kate to him in a bear hug.

Jon watched the scene. The love and affection was there for all to see. He was rocking Kate in his arms and raining kisses all over her face, and she was laughing while trying to duck out of the way. When they'd all been together in Paris, the rapport between them had been clear, but now he saw something else. Jacques knew every mood and thought of Kate's, and he was here now because she was hurting badly. She needed love, companionship and affection at this moment, and Jacques had come to give her those. Jon was deeply curious about this friendship. He'd love to find out the whole story.

'What are you doing here? I thought you were going home.'

'I have a few days free from studying, so I thought I'd stay and spend them with you.'

Kate's expression said she understood. She hugged him again, her face serious this time. 'Have you told Mum?'

'I phoned her and she said I can stay with her.' He draped a protective arm around her shoulder and greeted Jon with a nod of his head.

Jon didn't miss the questioning look in Jacques's eyes as he saw him in what he believed to be Kate's private flat. 'Kate is moving back with her mother and I'm taking over the flat.'

'Jacques.' Kate took hold of his arm. 'I can't pack up work for a couple of hours, but if you don't mind waiting we can go home together. It will be good for Mum to have lots of people around her for a while. It's hard for her. They loved each other so much.'

'She's had plenty of practice at hiding her feelings, though, hasn't she?' Sadness flashed through Jacques's eyes for the woman he thought the world of. 'Can I wait for you downstairs? I won't get in your way.'

'Why don't you stay here?' Jon suggested, deciding that he mustn't be jealous of Jacques. He was a nice boy and meant a lot to the Freeman family. 'You can help me unpack.'

'Oh, thanks.' Jacques smiled at Kate. 'Will you phone my beautiful Rose and ask her if I can have some of her suet treacle for dinner please?'

They both doubled over with laughter at the private joke.

The unpacking didn't take long and Jon produced two bottles of beer. Then they sat around the table talking, ignoring the boxes littering the floor. The atmosphere was relaxed, but Jacques appeared a little distracted.

'Have you got time off from university?' Jon asked Jacques, as he poured them a glass of beer.

'Not officially, but we are worried so I've taken a few days off.' He looked at Jon over the rim of his glass, his eyes showing the pain he was feeling. 'You can't have any idea how much we love this wonderful family.'

'I know there's something special between you, so why don't you tell me about it, and then perhaps I'll understand.'

Jacques looked into space for a moment, as if gathering his thoughts. 'It started during the war. When the Germans invaded France, my father left our village to help destroy communication and transport lines in an effort to hamper the advance. He and my mother were about to be married, but when he finally made it back he was told that my mother had been killed, along with their unborn child. With the SS hunting him down, my father fled to England, where he joined the RAF and began working to recruit agents to be dropped into France. That's when he met Annie. She was a wireless operator who spoke French and German. They worked together for the rest of the war.'

When Jacques hesitated and sighed, Jon said, 'Take your time. We've got a couple of hours.'

'Well, Dad would only let Annie go into France once,

and that was because an agent was missing and she knew him. She found him and got him out, but he died soon after they arrived back in this country.'

Jon couldn't help picturing the lovely woman Reid was married to, and marvelled at her courage. 'Go on.'

'Then my father heard that a young child and his grandmother were with someone who sounded like his sister. He came for us.' Jacques emptied his glass and turned it round and round with his fingers. 'I was put in a small aeroplane with my grandmother and a man I didn't know. I was terrified.'

'How old were you?' Jon asked.

'Only about three but I remember it as if it were yesterday. My grandmother died soon after we arrived. I couldn't understand a word anyone said, except Annie, and she kept going away with the man I'd been told was my father. I was frightened and bewildered. There were these three people with almost-black eyes who seemed to care about me – Rose, Kate and James. Rose would pop food into my mouth, wait for me to swallow, and do the same until I'd finished it all up.' Jacques gave a chuckle. 'I wouldn't have dared refuse to eat.'

Jon grinned as he remembered how Rose had swept through all objections and sorted out the trouble at the children's home. Anyone who disobeyed her would have to be very brave indeed.

Jacques continued. 'James played with me and gave me his toys, but Kate reached out with love and understanding. She has great sensitivity to others' suffering, and I believe she feels what they feel. So, surrounded by their love, I began to settle down.'

'I can see why you think so much of them,' Jon said.

'But I'm confused. You said your mother had been killed along with her unborn child.'

'My father hadn't been told the truth. You must understand that the country was in turmoil, and many people never knew what had become of their loved ones. It seems that I had been born while my father was away, and given to my grandmother to look after. My mother was taken to Germany to a labour camp.'

Jon drew in a ragged breath at that piece of information, as he pictured the anguish this family must have gone through.

'My God,' Jon murmured. 'How you must hate the Germans.'

'No, no,' Jacques hastily assured him. 'Rose says that we shouldn't lump a whole nation together as being good or evil. Everyone is an individual, and most are decent people; only a few are beasts. It is those we hate, not an entire nation. Such evil is hard to comprehend and even harder to forgive, but some of those responsible were brought to justice at Nuremberg.'

Looking intently at the boy sitting opposite him, Jon saw past the youth who laughed and teased Kate. Jacques and his family had suffered a great deal, and, perhaps because of that, he understood what the death of Bill meant to the Freeman family.

'You have a wise head on your shoulders.'

'You can't live with Rose and not question what life is all about.' Jacques laughed quietly. 'She is the wisest person I have ever met.'

'I agree with that.' Their glasses were empty, so Jon said, 'Do you want another beer?'

'No, thanks.'

'What happened then?' Jon prompted, eager to hear more.

'As the allies began to move inland after D-Day, my father returned to France, and was told by someone who knew us that my mother was still alive. He took a great risk and crossed into Germany, found the camp, and managed to snatch my mother as she returned with a working party at the end of the day. She was emaciated and barely alive, so my father had to carry her most of the way. They moved at night and hid by day. When they reached the allies' lines again, they were shipped back to England. Rose and her family nursed my mother back to health.'

'And do you intend to marry Kate?' Jon asked.

'I have a very nice girl at university, but if that was what Kate wanted, then I would spend the rest of my life trying to make her happy.' Jacques gazed into his glass, then looked up, his expression earnest. 'Kate, James and Rose mean the world to me, and we loved and admired Bill. He was such a gentle man. Kate and Rose have always been caring and unselfish in their desire to help other people, but they are the ones who need help now – '

'Jacques.' Kate looked in the door. 'I've finished now, we can go home. Mum's got the pudding on the boil.'

With a wave of his hand, Jacques followed Kate. 'Thanks for the beer.'

'Nice boy.' Pete came into the room as they left. 'If you need help, I'll be free in an hour.'

'Thanks, Pete, but I can manage.'

Laughter from Kate and Jacques echoed up the stairs as they left the shop.

'Kate's pleased to see him,' Pete said.

'Hmm.'

A smile tugged at the corners of Pete's mouth. 'She won't marry him, you know.'

Jon looked up sharply. 'Why are you so sure?'

'I just am. I've listened to her talking about him. They're like brother and sister. If Jacques tried to make love to her, she'd collapse in helpless laughter. Marriage between them would never work.' Pete turned and left with a wave of his hand.

'How long can you stay?' Kate asked Jacques, as they set off for Roehampton in her car.

'Three days. Are you in love with Jon?' he asked bluntly.

Kate pressed her lips together as she thought about that. Her feelings for Jon went deep now, but she wasn't going to admit that to anyone just yet. 'I like him; he was helpful when I was in Berlin. He's a bit bossy, though.'

'Not a bad thing.' Jacques chuckled. 'You need someone who will keep you in line. I'd marry you myself, but I'm not sure I'm up to the job.'

Kate took one hand off the steering wheel to hit him. He ducked just in time.

'Hey! Keep your eyes on the road.'

'We've stopped at red lights, you fool.' Kate glanced at his smiling face and felt her spirit lift. She was so pleased he'd stayed. It was going to be a real tonic having him around for a few days and just what she and her mother needed.

'Well, they've turned green now,' he said, as the driver behind them tooted his horn.

'Have you fallen in love yet?' Kate kept a straight face as she put the car into first gear and drove on, much to the relief of the impatient man behind them.

'I've got a girl I met at university – Claudine. She's bright, intelligent and good fun.'

'That's great. I'd like to see you marry a nice girl, but you make sure she's the right one.'

'I wouldn't dream of asking her to marry me until I've run her past you.' His laughter rumbled through the car. 'But don't think you're getting rid of me yet. She's just a friend. Nothing serious.'

She pulled into the driveway, and Rose was waiting at the door for them. Her mother had lost a little weight since her husband had died, but she was smiling with pleasure as she greeted Jacques. Kate knew that her mother had been prepared to adopt Jacques if anything had happened to Sam during the war. That hadn't been necessary, though. Nevertheless, she knew her mother loved him as her own.

Dinner was ready, and they were soon sitting around the kitchen table laughing as Jacques told about some of his escapades at university.

After the meal they went into the sitting room to continue their talk and enjoy the coffee. The evenings were chilly now, and there was a lovely coal fire burning, making the room warm and cosy.

'I found myself a job today,' Rose announced as soon as they were settled. 'It's only three days a week.'

Kate was thrilled by the news. She'd been so worried about her mother, and because of her concern, there had hardly been time for her to grieve properly for the loss of her father. No doubt that would hit her some time when she wasn't expecting it.

'That's marvellous, Mum. What are you going to do?'

'I'm starting on Monday with a firm of solicitors. They've got offices on Richmond Green.'

'Oh, posh,' Kate joked.

Her mother's smile was wry. 'I expect the clients will be different from those I had at Garrett Street. But it will give me something useful to do. I also thought I'd like to get more involved with Standish House.'

'That would be a great help to them.'

Rose nodded thoughtfully. 'I've already had a word with them and they said I could come along any time I like. Bill wouldn't like it if we didn't get on with our lives, would he?'

'No, he wouldn't.' Kate blinked away the film of moisture covering her eyes and smiled. 'I can just hear him saying, "What do you think you're up to, Rosie?"'

It was a happy memory, making them all laugh out loud as they pictured him standing there and shaking his head.

Kate sighed inwardly. Living without him was so damned hard, but perhaps they were beginning to turn the corner at last.

36

Over the next three weeks Kate took little notice of the passing of time. She plunged into each day, taking portraits, doing weddings, the accounts, ordering stock, serving customers, in fact anything to keep herself fully occupied, longing for the pain of loss to ease. The horror of the kidnapping faded to a mere shadow beside this new disaster.

Jacques had stayed for almost a week while he'd done the rounds to see every member of the family. His cheerful presence had been a balm to them all.

The business was flourishing and Kate had been kept busy, throwing herself into each day. Terry and Beth were working well together and her friend was ecstatic about the job. Jon, with his vast knowledge of world affairs, was now a political correspondent, and she'd been out on a couple of assignments with him when he'd needed a photographer. He wouldn't take anyone else. She considered that a fine compliment, and she enjoyed watching him refuse to let the politicians evade his probing questions.

And as each day passed, she watched anxiously as her mother began to fill her days with work. It had frightened Kate when she'd seen her strong-minded mother fall apart after the funeral, albeit briefly. It was a blessing that her Aunt Annie had been there at the time, for of all people she understood her sister and knew how to help.

James, like Kate, was numb, but there was an echo of Bill about him – strong, dependable and with a calm outlook on life. And, in the background, supporting with love and understanding, were Annie and Reid – her pretend parents.

Kate's mouth turned up in a smile as she thought about the time just after the war, when she'd offered to be their pretend daughter until they had one of their own. They'd never had a girl, so they'd always called her their daughter, and she was turning to Reid more and more as the days passed. She spoke to him two or three times a week on the phone and he listened to her ramblings about work with patient good humour, just as her father had always done. No one could ever replace her father, of course, but she'd always considered Reid as her second father, so she naturally went to him in difficult times.

She pulled into the parking space at the back of the shop and walked round to the front to have a look at the display in the window. It was excellent as usual, and she counted her blessings at having found Pete and Susan. It looked as if there was a real romance blossoming between them and she was happy about that.

Opening the shop door, she walked in, feeling better than she'd done for some time. Her mother told her not to forget to be grateful for the good they had, and she was right, because that kind of thinking gave a more positive outlook on life.

'Hi!' she said to Susan, as she walked through to the back room. 'Sorry I'm late, Pete,' she called, seeing the red light on and knowing that he was in the darkroom. 'I popped in to see Terry and Beth first.'

'The Putney shop's doing well, isn't it?' The heavy curtain across the developing-room door muffled Pete's voice.

'It certainly is. Terry's enjoying the work as well.'

Pete's head came through the curtain. 'I've nearly finished here. Put the kettle on, I'm gasping.'

She filled the kettle and noticed lots of parcels and shopping bags on the table. She moved them out of the way and made room for the cups. 'Who's been going mad in the shops?'

'Oh, they're mine.' Susan came in and tucked them under the table out of the way.

'What on earth have you been buying?' Kate asked.

'Christmas presents.' Susan took over the making of the tea. 'It's only two weeks away now.'

'Two weeks?' Kate's eyes were wide in astonishment. Good heavens, she hadn't given it a thought. A long list of things she needed to buy began to form in her mind, and with such a short time it was going to be a rush. There were presents for all the family, then for the children in both homes. Had her mother done anything about them?

Pete came out of the darkroom and washed his hands in the sink.

'I've forgotten Christmas,' she said, shaking her head in disbelief.

With the holiday being so close, they were very busy in the shop and Kate didn't get a break until two o'clock. After pinching one of Pete's cheese sandwiches, she dashed up the road to the high street and began to buy presents. She was gazing in one shop when she saw a beautiful bronze statue of a golfer in full swing. Oh, she must buy that. Her father enjoyed his golf and he would love it.

Her hand was on the door when the realization hit her that he wasn't going to be there this Christmas – or ever again. She reeled back as if someone had punched her in the stomach. 'Oh, dear God,' she gasped, struggling to stand on shaking legs.

Kate didn't know how she got back to the shop. It took every ounce of strength she could muster, but somehow she did make it and lurched through the door, making for the sanctuary of the darkroom. Once inside, she gripped the edge of the bench and cried, great sobs shaking her body.

'Kate, what's the matter? Are you ill?'

Strong arms were around her, holding her up, and she clung on to Jon, thankful he was there.

'Pete's not here, so Susan came up to the flat for me.' He held her close, cradling her head on his shoulder. 'Come up to the flat and let's get you a cup of tea.'

The pain was so intense that she was unable to speak, as tears filled her eyes and clogged her throat.

Jon held her firmly and urged her forward. 'Just put one foot in front of the other, Kate. I won't let you fall.'

Once in the sitting room he made her sit on the sofa, gently pushing a strand of black hair away from her eyes.

'You rest there while I make the tea. Or would you like something stronger?'

'Tea will do fine.' Kate closed her eyes and listened to Jon moving around in the kitchen. She'd stopped shaking, but her breathing was erratic and it seemed difficult to get enough air into her lungs.

He soon returned with a steaming cup of sweet tea. She took it and began to gulp it down, watching him all the time in bewilderment. What the hell had happened?

He stooped down in front of her, and when she'd drained the cup he took it and placed it on the floor. 'Better?'

She nodded.

'Are you ill?' He held her cold hands in his, gently massaging them.

'I saw a statue of a golfer and I was going to buy it for Dad . . .' She stopped, unable to go on.

'And you finally realized he'd died.'

'Yes.' She dipped her head and looked down at their clasped hands. 'I don't understand. Why now?'

'It's delayed reaction.' He sat next to her and gathered her into his arms. 'You've been so worried about your mother that you haven't fully accepted his passing until now. I suspect you've kept a rein on your own grief in an effort to support Rose. Seeing her so upset shocked you, didn't it?'

'Yes, it did, and you're right, I've tried to keep reasonably cheerful for her sake.'

'Well, you don't have to worry about her any more.' Jon gently kissed her eyes and smiled. 'I saw her yesterday at Standish House, and I believe she's beginning to enjoy being back in the fray again. They're being reorganized, whether they like it or not.'

Kate's expression brightened. 'The posh solicitors she's working for are being urged to take on a few *worthy* cases as well.'

Jon held her away from him so he could look into her face. 'There's nothing to worry about, then, is there?'

She relaxed in his arms, feeling as if a burden had been lifted from her. She yawned, suddenly very tired.

'Sleep for a while.' He stood up. 'You'll feel better when you wake up.'

'Oh, I can't do that, we're so busy . . .'

He stopped her from getting to her feet. 'I've got the rest of the day off, so I'll go and give them a hand. You stay here.'

Kate tucked her feet up and laid her head back. He was right, she felt absolutely drained. As she heard the door close behind him, the tears began to flow unchecked down her face again, and for the first time she let her pain surface.

When there were no more tears left, she settled down. Jon was such a good man. She drifted off to sleep, grateful that he'd taken care of her and had the sense to leave her on her own . . .

It was just over an hour later when Kate woke up, feeling more herself. Her reaction in the high street had been unbelievable. What a blessing Susan had gone upstairs for Jon, because he'd handled the situation with calm understanding. She really must thank him properly, and Susan, for she must have been very worried to see her in such a state.

Now she must put the whole dreadful year behind her. It was impossible to change what had happened, but she must see that it didn't cloud her future. Jacques had had the most awful start to life but he'd grown into a well-adjusted happy person. Her life, until this year, had been one of love, happiness and security. And it would be again.

A line from the twenty-third Psalm came to her . . .
'Yea, though I walk through the valley of the shadow of
death, I will fear no evil.' The important words here were
'walk through'. Keep walking, she told herself firmly,
don't linger, move on.

She stood up, her head at a determined angle. That is
what her father would have wanted and expected of her.
She wasn't about to let him down, or any of her family
and friends.

With her mind clear, she headed down the stairs with
a smile of relief on her face. The shop was crowded, and
she looked around as if seeing it for the first time. Over
the last few months they had expanded, selling cameras
and everything for the enthusiastic photographer. Jon
was busy showing a man one of the best cameras, talking
and laughing with the customer. She fought down a
smile; he didn't know one end of a camera from the
other, but seeing him now you'd never have guessed it.
When the man nodded and said he'd take it, Jon glanced
across at her and gave a sly wink, making her chuckle.
He was enjoying himself. Pete and Susan were both
busy with customers. In came two more people, quickly
followed by Terry.

For the next hour they didn't have time to draw breath,
and when the last customer left, they all grinned at each
other.

'Put the kettle on, Susan,' Pete said, rubbing his hands
together with pleasure. 'Let's have a cuppa while there's
a lull.'

Jon came over to Kate and squeezed her hand, then
spoke quietly. 'You look better now. I didn't tell
Pete you'd had a bad turn and neither did Susan. I just

403

said you needed another hour to finish your shopping.'

'Thank you.' She reached up and kissed his cheek. He was so thoughtful not to worry Pete. 'Did anyone tell you that you're a very kind man?'

His extraordinary green eyes glittered with amusement. 'I don't think so.'

'What are you looking for, Terry?' Pete came from the back room carrying a tray of tea and biscuits.

'I've got a customer asking for the latest Leica. Have you got one in stock?'

'Well, I sold one yesterday. Have we got any more, Kate?'

She got down and opened a small cupboard under the counter, rummaging through the boxes, then grunted in satisfaction and emerged triumphant with it in her hand.

'Great!' Terry took it from her. 'May I have it? My customer's coming back in the morning. He's desperate to have it before Christmas.'

'Just sign the stock book to say you've taken it so we can order again.' She leant against the counter and sipped her tea.

'Hey, Kate, can we employ Jon? He can sell anything. His customers never leave here without buying something!' Pete chortled.

They were all laughing when the shop door opened and another two customers came in. Terry grabbed the camera, and with a wave left to go back to his own shop in Putney.

Jon stayed for the rest of the afternoon, and then bought them all a meal in the café up the road.

When they were all tucking into their steak and kidney

pie, Pete said to Jon, 'Are you enjoying your new job as political correspondent?'

A deep chuckle came from Jon. 'I am, much to my surprise. It's a real challenge interviewing politicians, for it's damned hard to get a straight answer out of them. I think they must go to a special school that teaches them how to evade answering questions.'

As soon as he'd finished his meal, Jon was on his feet. 'I must dash. I've got an appointment.'

'Some poor politician to grill?' Pete joked.

'Of course.' Jon squeezed Kate's arm and looked deep into her eyes, obviously searching to see if she was all right now. When she smiled, he nodded and left the café.

Susan left as well, leaving Kate and Pete to enjoy a quiet few moments.

'I've just heard that the shop next door is closing after Christmas.' Pete couldn't hide his excitement. 'We need more room, and the owners would be happy for us to take over the premises.'

'I agree that we are cramped now.' She studied him carefully. He had an innate ability for business that far exceeded his years, and during this year he'd had to take on a lot of extra responsibility, as she'd struggled with one disaster after another. He'd grown up quickly and was obviously thriving on the challenge. 'If you think it's a good idea, then we'll take it over. See if we can have permission to knock a door through to connect the two shops.'

'We can, I've already asked.'

'Right.' She held out her hand and they shook on the agreement, as they did with every joint decision.

★

Later that evening, when the meal was cleared away and Kate and her mother were in the sitting room in front of a lovely fire, she told her mother about nearly buying her father a Christmas present. She explained how the shock had hit her, and how good Jon had been.

'It won't be easy this Christmas,' her mother said, 'but I'm determined to see that we have the usual lively family gathering.'

She smiled at her mother. 'I hope you've made lots of puddings.'

'I've made eight big ones, that should do, plus a couple of Christmas cakes. I'll leave the mince pies to last, then you can give me a hand with those. Will and Dora are going to friends on Boxing Day, Charlie and Madge won't be coming until the New Year, so why don't you ask Jon, Eddie and Tom to come on Boxing Day?'

'That would be lovely.' Kate got to her feet. To have them over for the day would be wonderful. 'I'll phone Jon now. He had a phone put in the flat as soon as he moved in.'

She hurried to the hall, where they had their phone, and dialled his number. It rang for quite a while before it was answered.

'Devlin.' He sounded as if he'd been running.

'This is Kate . . .'

'Oh, hello, I heard the phone ringing as I opened the door and I tore up the stairs. How are you?'

'I'm fine now, thank you. I'm phoning to ask if you, Eddie and Tom would like to come to us for Boxing Day.'

'We'd love to; the boys will be over the moon. I might go over there now before they go to bed.' A deep chuckle came down the phone. 'You sure you want Tom? He could do a lot of damage in a whole day.'

'Mum will keep him in line; it was her idea.' She joined in the laughter. Tom was a real handful but it would certainly liven up the day.

'Ah, well, Rose knows what she's doing. And thanks for the invite. We'll look forward to it.'

As she put the phone down, she was so pleased her mother had suggested this. It would be good to give Jon and at least two little boys a real family Christmas.

Her mother was reading when she returned to the sitting room. She put her book away and looked up. 'What did Jon say?'

'They'd love to come.'

'Good. That's Christmas settled. Now all we've got to do is buy presents for everyone.' Rose gazed into the fire, a look of utter sadness on her face. 'It's going to be bloody painful without Bill, but it's happened and we've just got to get on with it!'

37

Christmas Day was much more relaxed than Kate had dared to hope. The house was full all day. Will, Dora, James, Annie, Reid and their boys had arrived early in the morning. After one of her mother's enormous lunches, the family crowded into the sitting room, full of good food and a drink or two. The empty space left by her father's death was, of course, on all their minds, but they had been determined to make it a good Christmas. As they sat around drinking their coffee, Rose and Annie began to talk about the first time they'd met Bill just after the First World War. The laughter flowed easily as Rose told how infuriating she'd found his unruffled calm, and Annie explained about the outings they'd had. She'd fallen in love with Bill at once, she said, although she'd only been around eight at the time, but it had taken her big sister longer to realize what a wonderful man he was.

Kate listened to the tales with eager interest, gaining a new perspective on Annie's and her mother's early life. They very seldom talked about it, but she knew it had been harsh for them in the slums of Bermondsey. Her love and admiration for her mother grew in leaps and bounds. Through her sheer determination not to accept the limitations of such an existence, she had dragged herself and her family out of that dreadful place. After marrying Bill, the door had opened to give them all the comfortable life they now enjoyed.

The conversation was animated as each related their personal memories of Bill. It was then Kate realized that he would always be with them. Their memories would keep him alive in their hearts.

At teatime Beth and her boyfriend Steve joined them, then Pete and Susan popped in for an hour in the evening. Pete and Susan were constantly together now, and Kate couldn't have been more pleased for them.

The next morning Eddie burst into the kitchen, arms full of parcels and a wide grin of excitement on his face. Tom followed more sedately, clutching a pot plant and looking embarrassed to be carrying flowers.

'Have you got a tree to put the presents round?' Eddie asked, hopping up and down. 'We've got more in the car.'

Rose placed her hand on top of his head to stop him jigging around. 'We've got one; it's in the other room.'

Looking as if he were holding a bomb, Tom thrust the plant at Rose. 'That's for you. Thank you for asking us today.'

It was obviously a well-rehearsed little thank you, because Kate saw Jon give Tom a nod of approval.

'Thank you.' Rose took the plant and arranged it in the middle of the kitchen table, then stood back to admire it. 'That's lovely, and it's just perfect there.'

After bending to kiss Tom's cheek, Rose took hold of Eddie's hand and led him into the sitting room.

'Bloody hell!' Tom touched his cheek. 'What did she do that for?'

'Watch your language.' Jon glared at the boy. 'If you don't behave yourself, I'll take you back to Wandsworth. Go and help Ed put the presents around the tree.'

Tom shot out of the room with a smirk on his face, not at all put out by the reprimand.

Reid was leaning against the sink, chuckling quietly. 'He's a bit of a tearaway, by the sound of him.'

'He sure is.' Jon shook his head in exasperation. 'He's rebellious, but he's a damned bright kid and worth trying to help.'

'How old is he?' Annie asked.

'Coming up to nine and he thinks it's big to cuss.'

Paul and David were standing beside their father and smirking. 'Don't you try copying him,' Reid said, but had great difficulty keeping his expression serious.

'No, Dad,' Paul said, edging away from him. 'Anyway that wasn't so terrible. You and Auntie Rose know worse words than that.'

As Reid pushed himself away from the sink, his sons tore out of the room, shrieking with laughter. 'They're getting very nifty on their feet. I would have a job catching them now, and they know it.'

'Kate!' Eddie erupted back into the kitchen, grabbed her hand and started to pull her forward.

'Where are we going?' She laughed at his antics. He did get so excited and loved being with lots of people.

'You'll see. Come on.' Once he'd dragged her into the sitting room, he made her stand in a certain spot, making absolutely sure she was in the right place; then he pulled up a stool and clambered on to it so he could reach her face by standing on tiptoe.

She knew what he was up to but pretended to look very puzzled. He giggled and planted a kiss on her cheek.

'You next!' Eddie swivelled round to look at Rose, and, as she took Kate's place, she also received a smacking kiss.

Annie was next in line. 'Hey, I'm not missing out on being kissed under the mistletoe.'

'That kid's daft!' Tom looked absolutely disgusted.

'No, he isn't, Tom.' Rose stooped down in front of him. 'He loves affection. Annie was like that when she was a little girl and I never could understand it, but I do now. Some people are more outgoing than others; there's no harm in it.'

'Suppose not. Still, I hope you don't expect me to kiss everyone.' He looked scandalized by the very idea.

'Not if you don't want to.' Rose stood up and lifted Eddie off the stool.

Once his feet were on the floor, he ran over to Jon. 'You've got to kiss Kate and her mum, because they're giving us this smashing day.'

Showing no reluctance to carry out Eddie's demand, Jon hugged Rose and kissed her on the cheek, then reached for Kate.

She was surprised when, instead of the expected peck everyone else had been getting, he eased her into his arms and kissed her full on the lips. It was a gentle embrace, and she was disappointed when he finally broke away. She had enjoyed his touch and nearness. Of course she had! She was hopelessly in love with him. Amid the heartbreak and suffering she had fallen in love. And like a fool, she hadn't admitted it to herself until now. She felt like shouting for joy as she gazed up at Jon and smiled. She had found the man she wanted to spend the rest of her life with.

'I don't think you're supposed to do it like that!' Eddie's whisper broke through her thoughts.

'That was a grown-up kiss.' Jon ruffled his hair and winked at Kate. 'And it is Christmas.'

Eddie still appeared a trifle worried and looked up at Kate. 'It's all right at Christmas, then? You didn't mind?'

'Did you?' Jon raised an eyebrow in query.

'Not at all.' She held his gaze for a moment and then gave Eddie a thoughtful look. He'd never had parents and seen affection between them, so it wasn't surprising he was puzzled by what he'd just witnessed, and yet he was a naturally affectionate child, longing to be loved. Her heart ached for all these unfortunate children who had to grow up without a family of their own . . .

'Come on everyone,' Rose called. 'Lunch is ready.'

There was a stampede for the dining room, which was being used for this special occasion.

James arrived just as they were sitting down, and it turned out to be a lively meal.

Eddie and Tom chatted away to Paul and David, whom they had obviously taken a liking to.

Afterwards the dishes were piled in the sink and left for later, then they all went into the sitting room to open the presents. It was clear that Jon had bought the gifts, but he made Tom and Eddie hand them out as if they came from them. The floor was soon littered with wrapping paper. Whoops of delight were coming from the young boys as they opened Meccano sets, boxes of toy soldiers and other wildly exciting things

'Wow! Look what Kate's bought me.' Eddie scrambled

to his feet to thank her, and then rushed around the room showing everyone the box camera. 'I'm going to help Kate when I've growed up.'

'That's a good idea,' James said encouragingly; then he looked at Tom, who had so many presents around him it seemed as if he couldn't believe his eyes. 'What would you like to be when you grow up, Tom?'

'I'm going to be a pilot,' he declared, the expression on his face defying anyone to laugh.

James sat on the floor beside him. 'Well, you'd better have a talk with Reid. He was a Spitfire pilot during the war.'

Tom spun round on his knees to face Reid, his eyes wide with wonder. 'Were you one of the Few?'

'Yes, I fought in the Battle of Britain. What do you know about it?'

'Everything!' Without standing up, he shuffled forward until he was kneeling in front of Reid. 'Jon gets me books from the library. I never spoke to a real pilot before.' He began to bombard Reid with questions, hanging on to his legs and gazing into his face so he didn't miss a word of the answers.

James stood up. 'Mum, where did you put all my stuff when you cleared out my room?'

'In the loft, I think.'

'Right, I'll go and have a look.'

As James left the room, Kate watched Tom with great interest. Reid had made room for him to sit next to him and was explaining what it was like to fly a Spitfire.

'He's found a hero.' Jon sat beside Kate. 'We won't get any more trouble from him today.'

'He's potty about aeroplanes,' Eddie said, 'but I'd

413

rather have my camera. Will you show me how to use it, please, Kate?'

'Of course, and I've already put a film in it for you.' She spent the next ten minutes explaining the workings, and then she turned to Jon with a smile of devilment. 'It's so simple even you could use it.'

'I doubt it.' His chuckle was deep as he put his arm around her shoulders. 'You photographers stand your ground when working, but I spent my time diving for cover.'

'But not any more?' she asked quietly. She knew he said he'd given up being a war correspondent, but she was still expecting him to get bored and disappear at any moment.

'No.' He pulled her towards him slightly. He'd never had any sense of belonging before, but he'd found that with Kate, Rose and the rest of the family. They had welcomed him, and he felt as if he had a family for the first time in his life. 'I've found everything I want right here.'

'You going to kiss her again?' Eddie tugged at his free hand.

'Not just yet.' He removed his arm, and there was a clear question in his eyes when he looked at her.

She held his gaze and smiled. No, she wouldn't mind being kissed by him again, and hoped she was reading the signals correctly.

James came back just then carrying a book and a large battered box. He put them down in front of Tom, who was still gazing at Reid in adoration. The book caught his attention, and he dived to open it, shuffling through the pages. It was all about wartime aircraft, and he found a large coloured photograph of a Spitfire. He held it out for Reid to see. 'Was yours like this?'

When his idol agreed that it was, Tom looked up at James. 'Smashing book. This yours?'

'Yes, but you can have it now. I know you'll look after it.'

'Gee, thanks, I'll slosh anyone at the home who touches it.'

'There's something else for you in the box.' James blew off the dust and watched as the boy opened it.

Jon leant forward. 'What's he got in there? I've never seen him so quiet, or lost for words.'

The box was familiar to Kate. She'd seen it when they were children during the war . . . then she remembered. 'James has just given him his model Spitfire.'

The plane was lifted out very carefully, and lovingly examined. Kate was sure she saw a glimmer of tears in the tough little kid's eyes, but they were quickly banished.

'Wow!' He ran his fingers over the wings, and gave James a rather watery smile. 'Thanks. It's the best blo . . . blooming present I've ever had.'

Kate blew her brother a silent kiss for his thoughtfulness. James grinned and then hit his forehead in mock disbelief as he looked at Eddie. 'I nearly forgot. I found something else in the loft.'

He went into the hall and was back immediately with a football and a locomotive and two carriages. These he gave to Eddie.

Everyone had to admire the special gifts, and the boys spent the rest of the afternoon sitting in front of the fire with Paul and David, chatting excitedly and playing with the toys. Tom, however, kept a sharp eye on Reid all the time and made sure he was never out of his sight.

*

There were two tired blissfully happy kids in the car as Jon drove them back to Wandsworth. He was quite pleased himself. He wanted Kate – until death us do part – and the signs were hopeful. When she looked at him now, her lustrous dark eyes gleamed with warmth. If Gerhard dared show his face again, he would send him straight back to Berlin, though he doubted if he would return here to pursue Kate because the last he'd heard he was back in Algeria.

'That pilot . . .' Tom, sitting in the back, leant forward. 'He said he'd come and see me but I don't suppose he will.'

'If Reid said he'd come, then he will,' Jon said, hearing the doubt in Tom's voice. 'He'll keep his promise.'

'Yeah.' His tone brightened at that assurance. 'He said he'd take me flying when the weather's better. In the spring, he said.'

'That's something to look forward to, then.'

'Yeah. When will it be spring?'

'In about four months.'

'That long?' Tom sighed but the excitement was soon back. 'We can't go in a Spitfire, but he told me how to fly it and how they'd had to dive, roll and turn quick like, during the dogfights.'

Jon smiled. Tom knew all the flying expressions.

'Smashing bloke. Paul and David are great too.'

'Yes, they're nice boys and very proud of their dad.'

'I should bloody well hope they are!'

'Tom!'

'Sorry.'

Well, that was a first. He couldn't remember a time when he'd heard Tom apologize.

'Reid said I've got to do well at my lessons if I want to be a pilot.'

'Good advice, Tom; I hope you're going to do that.'

'Oh, I will.' The boy fell silent then.

Eddie, who'd been nearly asleep all this time, woke up. 'Did you get another grown-up kiss?' he asked.

'No, but I'll make up for it later.' He glanced at Ed clutching his precious football and fighting to keep his eyes open. Tom would go flying in the spring; he would marry Kate in the spring . . . and then they'd see about Eddie.

But he was jumping ahead too far. He had to win that beautiful woman first. And that was something he was determined to do.

38

It was warm for March, and Kate sang as she drove to Wilkins House. The sky was clear, the sun bright, and there was a feeling in the air of nature's impatience to burst forth into glowing, vibrant life. And that was a mirror of her feelings.

Since Christmas Jon had been by her side every spare moment he had. They'd been dancing, walking, to the cinema, and one evening he'd taken her to Covent Garden to hear *Tosca*. She'd loved every moment of the glorious opera. It had been a total surprise and not something she'd expected he would like, but over the last few weeks different facets of his character had shown themselves. Jon Devlin was a complex man, and, like her mother, his upbringing had made him tough. Fortunately it hadn't destroyed the vein of warmth, gentleness and compassion. Also, like her mother, that side of him was kept under control and hidden, but he was now relaxing in her company. She'd watched each quality surface and loved him more every day.

The sun glared through the windscreen, so she slipped on a pair of sunglasses and sighed with happiness. At one time she had wondered if she would ever feel like this again. Last year had been terrible. But, with hindsight, she could see how Jon had supported both her and her mother. Without him, the journey back would have been longer and more difficult. She was so lucky to have found such a wonderful man, and he did love her, she was sure. Unless it was lust!

That made her laugh out loud as she pulled up at some traffic lights. If that had been true, he'd have persuaded her into his bed a long time ago. He was a passionate man but was the first one to back away when their loving became too heated. She sometimes cursed his iron self-control, for there had been many times when she wouldn't, or couldn't, have resisted.

The lights turned green and she took a left to Wilkins House. She was looking forward to this. The boys were putting on a show with the puppets. It was lovely to see how much enjoyment they were still getting from them.

As soon as she arrived, she went to the kitchen. Her mother was already there, helping Mrs Green to prepare the food – they were going to have a little party after the show as a treat for the boys.

'Can I do anything?' she asked.

'No, it's all under control.' Her mother piled sandwiches on another plate.

Kate's eyes opened wide when she saw the amount of food on the table. 'How many are coming?'

'Lots.' Mrs Green beamed. 'Your family, the older children from Standish House, together with some of the staff and helpers.'

'In that case you'll need another plate of sandwiches, because I've asked Pete, Susan, Terry and his family, Beth and Steve to come as well.'

'Oh, lovely.' Mrs Green couldn't have looked more pleased. 'We shall have a jolly time, shan't we?'

'James is already here helping Jon with the stage.' Her mother looked up from slicing another loaf and smiled. 'Why don't you see if they need any help?'

'Okay.' It was bedlam in the front room, with all the boys being given jobs to do. The furniture had been cleared out of the way, with rows of chairs in front of the stage. A small wooden platform had been erected at the far end of the room. There were bright red curtains to pull across, a black sheet at the back for the boys to stand behind and work their puppets without being seen too clearly . . . She was impressed.

'Kate!' Eddie rushed up, beside himself with excitement. 'We're nearly ready. Jon wrote the story and it's smashing!'

'I didn't know that.' She grinned as Jon came over.

'I'm a man of many talents.' He leant down and kissed her. 'Hmm, you look and smell delicious.'

'Bring my sister over to give us a hand.' James laughed. 'You can continue that later, because this whole bloody lot is going to collapse in a minute.'

They laughed and ran over to James, who was struggling with the frame to hold the curtain in place. Eddie came as well, still grinning. He thought it was great fun to see Jon kissing Kate.

It took them only ten minutes to put the finishing touches to the platform. As they were surveying their handiwork, the door opened and Tom erupted into the room, followed by Reid, Annie, Paul and David.

'I've been flying!' He yelled at the top of his voice, not wanting anyone to miss this momentous news. 'We went right out over the sea. We climbed, dived and did a somersault. Didn't we?' He tore back to Reid. 'Didn't we?'

'At least two somersaults,' Reid said in his clearest voice to the crowd of boys now clustered around Tom.

'Yeah, two.' He gazed up at his idol. 'You're a smashing pilot and I've had a smashing day!'

'I enjoyed it too.'

Tom threw his arms around Reid's waist and then Annie's, looking rather pink and embarrassed about showing so much affection. He grabbed Paul and David. 'Come on, let's go and tell Mrs Green. There'll be grub in the kitchen,' he added as an incentive.

Kate watched them leave and hugged Reid and Annie; then James and Jon came over.

'Two somersaults?' Jon raised a brow in query, making Reid chuckle.

'Not quite, but I threw the plane about a bit and he loved it. He squealed in delight and every time I levelled off he yelled at me to do it again.'

'So you think he's got the makings of a pilot?' Jon asked.

Reid looked thoughtful, then nodded. 'He could, and he certainly wants it enough. I'm going to keep my eye on him and see how he turns out.'

'That's good of you, Reid.'

'It will be a pleasure.' Reid smiled. 'He's like me when I was about his age.'

Annie had disappeared into the kitchen, so Kate stood back a little and watched Reid and Jon together. They were both at least six foot tall, strong, powerful men. Now in his early fifties, Reid was still handsome, with a special aura about him that hadn't dimmed with age. It wasn't hard to recognize the calm determination that had made him an outstanding pilot during the war. Then there was Jon, younger by more than twenty years, and yet with the same qualities. She drew in a deep breath. She hadn't noticed it before, but they were cast from the same mould, and she loved them both so much. Reid had always been like a second father to her, but her feelings for Jon were very different indeed. She prayed that he was her future.

The show was a riot as the audience screamed and hollered at the antics of the puppets. It was just as well the kids were making so much noise, because it muffled the helpless roars of laughter coming from the adults. Kate thought Pete was going to fall off his chair several times as he doubled over, and Reid was helpless with laughter.

It was impossible to tell what the story was as the boys got quite carried away in their enthusiasm to have their own particular puppet in the thick of the action. Audible whispered instructions were coming from behind the black curtain by Jon and James, but it was a hopeless task, and after a while they obviously gave up trying to control the show. No one minded. The children in the audience thought it was fabulous, and the grown-ups hadn't laughed so much for ages. Terry and his wife had brought their young son along; although too young to understand, he was wide-eyed and making as much noise as everyone else.

The curtain came down to thunderous applause, and the boys emerged from the back flushed and beaming. James made them all take a bow, then Kate yelled for the author. Jon stepped forward looking dishevelled from the struggle backstage, and gave an elaborate bow. James was next as the stage manager. Then, after one more round of cheers for the puppet masters, it was a stampede for the food.

'My God,' James said, mopping his brow, 'that was a shambles. What was the plot supposed to be, Jon?'

'Don't ask me. I only wrote it, but I lost track after about ten minutes.'

'Well, don't bother next time, just let the kids make it up as they go along. Which is exactly what they did tonight.'

A look of absolute horror crossed Jon's face. 'Good grief, you're not thinking of doing this again, are you?'

Kate exploded when she saw their expressions, laughing until the tears ran down her face. When she could speak again, she said, 'Come on, let's get something to eat before it all goes.'

They stayed until the boys were in bed. Eddie was too tired to listen to a story, and was asleep almost before she pulled the covers over him. Tom received a kiss from Reid and Annie without a murmur of protest. Everyone agreed that it had been a highly successful, if exhausting, show.

Nearly everyone had gone when Jon touched Kate's arm. 'Come back to the flat. I want to talk to you.'

They both had their own cars, so she followed him to Kensington. Once in the flat, he gathered her into his arms and kissed her, lingering as if he never wanted to let her go.

After a while he held her away from him and looked into her eyes, sighing deeply. 'That's better; I've been longing to do that all evening. I know I don't say it often enough, but you know I love you so much, don't you, Kate?'

'I know.' She reached up and ran her fingers over his lips. 'And I love you too, in fact, I do believe I adore you.'

'Good.' He held her tightly for a while, not speaking, then said suddenly, 'Would you like tea, coffee, or something stronger?'

'Tea, please.' She watched him walk over to put the kettle on. The easy laughter of earlier had gone; now he was serious, as if he had something on his mind. Was he going to tell her that he was going away again? She always had the worry at the back of her mind that he would return to his former life as a war correspondent. If he was going she wouldn't try to stop him, but what would she do without him? He had become the love of her life over the last three months.

He returned with two mugs of tea, and they sat on the sofa. She sipped her drink and gazed at him over the rim of her mug, steeling herself for whatever he was going to tell her. 'You said you wanted to talk?'

Reaching out, he took the mug from her, placed it on the floor, and took her hands in his, examining her delicate fingers, his head bowed. When he looked up, his serious gaze held hers for long silent seconds. Her heart raced. He *was* going away and didn't know how to tell her.

'My darling Kate,' he murmured. 'I can't bear to think of my life without you. Will you marry me?'

Relief was the first emotion to surge through her, and then joy. She tumbled into his arms laughing and crying at the same time. 'I thought you were going to leave me. Yes, yes, I will marry you.'

It was quite a while before they were able to talk and, as always, it was Jon who put a rein on their overflowing passion. He held her away from him until their breathing returned to something like normal. 'I'm never going to leave you. I'm not a rich man, my darling, but I'll make you happy.'

'We'll make each other happy. Grandpa George left me an inheritance in trust until I reached twenty-five or married – whichever came first. I don't know exactly what it's worth now, but I'm sure it will be enough to buy a small house.'

'Well, we'll see about that. We can always live here for a while.'

She guessed he wasn't too happy about having his wife provide for him, so she dropped the subject. 'Of course we can. I don't care where it is as long as we're together.'

'That's just how I feel. And stop trying to get close,' he laughed, 'we've got decisions to make first.'

'First?' she teased.

'Yes, I can't promise I'll be able to control myself tonight. Now, how soon can we be married?'

'As soon as possible.'

'Four weeks, then. Church or register office?'

'Church, the family will want . . .' Suddenly her eyes clouded and the familiar ache was back in her heart. 'Dad should be here to give me away.'

'I know, my love, he will be missed.' He gently caressed her cheek. 'But you'll have Will, Charlie or Reid to choose from for that honour.'

'Of course.' She was so lucky to have a family to share this day with. Jon didn't have anyone. If she couldn't have her father by her side, then there was only one other man she would want. 'I'll ask Reid.'

'I'm sure he'd love to do it.'

She laughed then, her sadness disappearing. 'Do you think we could get him to wear his old uniform? Tom would love that.'

'I don't suppose he would for a moment and it might not fit him now.'

'He's hardly changed over the years, but he'll look just as good in a morning suit.'

'Heavens,' he exclaimed, 'you're not expecting us to wear top hat and tails, are you?'

'Not if you don't want to,' she teased, 'but I might try to get Eddie and Tom into satin breeches.'

'You'd be wasting your time with Tom.' He roared with laughter at the thought. 'But Eddie might. He'd do anything for you.'

She looked down and chewed her bottom lip, remembering her promise to him. But did she have the right to expect Jon to take on a child so early in their marriage?

'Say what's on your mind, Kate.'

'Eddie asked me to adopt him when I married and I promised to think about it.'

'And what would you like to do?'

He was speaking softly, not putting any pressure on her, and she knew that the decision would be hers to make. 'I'd love him as our son . . . but if that isn't what you want – '

He stopped her with a kiss, then said, 'It *is* what I want.'

'That's wonderful!' She hugged him in delight, her

happiness complete. 'I'll get Mum on to the legal part straight away.'

'She's already set the wheels in motion, but Eddie mustn't be told until it's settled.'

Kate was surprised. 'You've talked this over with her already?'

'Of course I have.' He grinned. 'I'm not brave enough to ask you to marry me without Rose's permission. And she was sure you'd want to adopt Eddie.'

She tipped her head to one side, keeping her expression serious with difficulty. 'You were sure I'd accept you?'

'No, but Rose was. She told me to stop wasting time and bloody well get on with it.' He stood up and pulled her to her feet. 'Now that that's all settled, my self-control is torn to shreds. If you're going to make me wait for our wedding night, then you'd better go now.'

'I'm not going anywhere,' she said, wrapping her arms around his neck as he swept her up in his arms.

39

The 28th of April, 1962! Kate slipped out of bed and watched the sun rise in a cloudless sky. It was her wedding day, and it was going to be glorious.

The bedroom door opened, and her mother came in. 'Thought I heard you moving about. Do you want breakfast in bed?'

'No, thanks, I'll come downstairs.' When her mother had left, she sat on the edge of the bed and sipped her tea. She was feeling nervous, but couldn't wait to become Mrs Devlin. It had been a real scramble to get everything arranged in time, but neither of them wanted to wait any longer than necessary.

She put on her dressing gown and wandered down to the kitchen. There were two hours yet before anyone began to arrive, so this would give her a chance to have a quiet time with her mother. It had worried Kate that her mother would be living here on her own after today, but Rose had pointed out very firmly that she was quite capable of looking after herself. She hadn't gone soft in her old age!

Kate smiled to herself. Rose Freeman certainly hadn't gone *soft*. Without the gentle restraining hand of her husband, she was back to her old battling self and fast becoming the terror of the local magistrates court.

'Do you want a cooked breakfast?' her mother asked, 'or just toast and marmalade?'

'Toast, please.'

This was soon prepared, and with a fresh pot of tea in front of them they sat down.

'When are you going to tell Eddie that you've adopted him?' Rose buttered the toast and poured them both a cup of tea.

'At the reception. We would have liked to tell him sooner, but, as the papers only came through yesterday, we decided to leave it until we were married.'

'He'll want to come on honeymoon with you.' Her mother laughed.

'He won't have long to wait; we're only going for two days and we'll collect him as soon as we're back.'

'He can stay with me for that short time if you like.'

'Oh, that would be lovely.' Kate was thrilled with the suggestion. Not only would it please Eddie, but it would mean that her mother would have someone with her after the wedding.

'Reid and Annie want to foster Tom and have asked me to deal with it for them.' Rose poured them both another cup of tea. 'If things go well, they might consider adopting him.'

Kate stopped with a piece of toast almost at her mouth. 'That's wonderful! They've kept that quiet.'

'They didn't want to say anything until they were sure they would be allowed to do it.'

This day was already full of good news. 'He's a tough little kid, but Reid and Annie are the perfect couple to handle him.'

'It won't be an easy job, they know that, but they think he deserves a chance in life. They would have liked more children, but they left it rather late to start their family. I hope you and Jon will soon have a brother or sister for Eddie.'

'We intend to, Mum. This will be the first time in their lives that both of them have had a family of their own.'

'I can't imagine what that's like.' Rose shook her head sadly. 'Even when I lived in Bermondsey, fighting and struggling to exist, there was always the family. That was a good idea of yours, not to segregate the bride and groom's guests in the church. It would have been insensitive to have our side full to overflowing and only a sprinkling on Jon's side. It's much better to mix everyone up.' Rose smiled. 'We're all one family now, and I've gained a grandson already.'

'Eddie's going to love that.' Kate joined in with her mother's laughter.

'You won't be able to stay in that small flat for long, Kate. Eddie will need a garden to kick about in.'

'We've decided to look for a house as soon as we come back from Bournemouth.'

'I was talking to Mrs Ellis yesterday, and she told me she's going to live with her daughter and is selling up.'

'That's perfect!' Kate leapt to her feet. 'It's next to Will and that means we would have three houses in a row. I'll go and see her now.'

'It's only eight o'clock and she won't be up yet. I've already told her you might be interested. She said that she won't sell to anyone until she's spoken to you. I said you'd come and see her towards the end of next week.'

'Wonderful, you think of everything.' Kate sat down again and reached for the teapot.

At that moment, Reid, Annie and the boys, Paul and David, arrived. Annie immediately took charge.

'Have you had your bath yet, Kate? Time's getting on.'

She smiled at her mother and gave an amused shrug. Their quiet time was over, but she was pleased they'd had this precious hour together.

The kitchen door opened and the family poured in, all dressed in new clothes and ready early for this big day. The room filled quickly with Will and Dora, Charlie, Madge, and teenagers, all jostling for space and looking at Kate and her mother in disbelief. Right behind them were James, Sam and his family, who were staying with her brother in Richmond, quickly followed by Beth and Steve. Beth was going to be her bridesmaid, and it was a cause of amazement to Kate that she was marrying before her friend. Beth's wedding was set for July and would be another celebration.

'Kate, Rose!' Dora exclaimed. 'What the devil are you doing still in your dressing gowns?'

'There's plenty of time –'Rose was cut off with howls of protest.

Annie and Madge took charge of Kate, hustling her towards the stairs, leaving Dora to deal with Rose.

Half an hour later Kate was being eased into her dress. She had insisted that it be kept simple, and Annie had done a wonderful job with the design. It was in oyster satin, with a wide neckline to emphasize her lovely shoulders, tapering to a point at the waist, with the skirt falling almost straight to the floor. Long slender sleeves added to the elegant dress. Her mother's veil was attached to a crown of apple blossom, and satin shoes completed the outfit.

'Oh my,' Dora sighed as she came into the bedroom,

'Jon isn't going to know what's hit him when he sees you.'

Annie laughed as she smoothed the skirt down. 'Terry's best man, so I hope he keeps a tight hold on the groom. We don't want him collapsing with ecstasy at the altar.'

The thought of Jon being so overcome made Kate chuckle, though he had revealed a very passionate nature over the last few weeks . . .

Rose came in looking wonderful in a royal-blue dress and jacket and holding an old velvet case in her hands. 'This is for you. I'd like you to wear it today, Kate.'

Inside was a beautiful string of pearls with a diamond clasp. 'Great Grandma Gresham's necklace,' Kate gasped. She'd only ever seen it once and that had been on Annie when she'd married Reid just after the war.

'I wore it on my wedding day and so did Annie.' Rose fastened it around her neck and then stood back to admire the effect. 'Perfect. It's yours now, Kate, but I'd like your promise that you'll keep it to hand on to one of your own children.'

'I'll never sell it, Mum.' She ran her fingers over the pearls, knowing how much they meant to her mother. Rose was the illegitimate daughter of Sir George Gresham, and had lived all of her young life in the slums of London with her mother, Marj. Marj had been in service when she'd been seduced by the man of the house, only to be thrown out on the street when she became pregnant. Rose had finally met George when she was sixteen, and, both being of a fiery nature, they'd fought. George's mother, Lavinia Gresham, had been a dear, though, and eventually they'd all become friends.

After Lavinia's death, George had become a part of the Freeman family, and Kate had loved him so much. It had been a terrible shock when he'd been killed by a flying bomb just as the war was coming to a close . . .

Beth floated in wearing a long pale lilac bridesmaid's dress, with a circlet of white roses in her hair, and spun round for Kate to see the finished effect. 'Will I do?' she asked.

'Perfect.' Kate grinned at her friend. 'This will be a rehearsal for your own wedding.'

Reid peered in the room. 'Everyone out. The bridal car will be here in twenty minutes.'

There was a stampede as they headed for the cars to take them to the church in Putney.

When they'd all gone, Reid came and took her hands in his, smiling down at her. 'This is a very proud day for me, to be giving away my pretend daughter to such a fine man. And it's a day for happiness – not sadness, isn't it?'

She squeezed his hands and leant forward to kiss his cheek, knowing that he was talking about her father not being here. 'No sadness, I promise.'

'Good.' He handed her the bouquet of white roses. 'That sounds like the car.'

The church was packed, and, as she stood in the doorway waiting for the organ to play the wedding march, Pete gave her a thumbs-up sign. Gerhard was there, so were Mike, Robert, Andrew Stevenson and Joel Perkins from the *World Explorer*, also Mrs Green, the helpers and children from Wilkins House. Eddie was down the front, firmly under her mother's control.

433

Kate paused for a moment in the doorway to remember those who wouldn't be with them. Her dear father, Grandpa George, Grandma Marj and Grandpa Wally. Each one very dear, and she knew that all the family would remember them this day.

The organ burst into life and Reid urged her forward, smiling affectionately at her. How glad she was to have his strong support and love. After a few steps she fixed her gaze on Jon and everything else faded into the background. For a brief moment it looked as if he were going to dash up to meet her, but Terry held him back.

Jon didn't take his eyes off her the whole way through the ceremony, and as soon as they'd signed the register he gave an audible sigh of relief. As they began to walk up the aisle, she smiled at him. 'Was the service an ordeal?'

'Oh, no. I was just terrified you were going to change your mind at the last minute. I didn't feel it had really happened until we'd signed the register.'

'What on earth made you think I wouldn't marry you?'

'Well, I couldn't come up with one reason why you would want to be my wife.'

She stopped, reached up and kissed him. 'There's a very good reason why I want to spend the rest of my life with you. I love you.'

They stepped out into the sunshine, both smiling, and patiently obeyed as Pete and Terry ordered everyone around so they could get the pictures they wanted.

The reception was being held in a local hotel where they had taken over the large dining room. After speeches and the cutting of the cake, Kate and Jon took Eddie out into the garden.

She sat on a bench and pulled the child towards her. 'Do you remember the promise I made you when we first met?'

Eddie nodded, his eyes flitting from one to the other, saying nothing. Kate suspected that he was expecting a rejection.

Jon took some papers out of his inside pocket and held them out for Eddie to see. 'It says here that from today you are our son.'

The boy still didn't speak, waiting for a moment to let this momentous news sink in, then he threw himself at them, trying to hug them both together. There were great sobs of joy coming from his little body, making him shake in their arms.

They left him to get it out of his system, and when he hiccuped and gave them a watery smile, she wiped his face. 'Does this mean you're happy about it?'

He nodded and the tears vanished, his eyes now clear with happiness. 'I knew you wouldn't forget. Tom said you would and I mustn't say anything to you. You're my two most favourite people in the whole world. Where are we going to live? I must pack my things.'

'Mrs Green's already done that for you.' Jon knelt down in front of him. 'Your Mum and I are going away for two days on what's called a honeymoon, but while we're away you're going to stay with your Grandma Rose. When we get back we'll be together for always. We'll be living in the flat until we can buy a house.'

Eddie was wide-eyed. 'Can I call you Mum and Dad?'

'Of course,' Kate said. 'That's what we are now.'

'Is it all right to call your mum Grandma?' He didn't seem at all sure about that.

'She would love you to.' Kate was so happy it was difficult to keep her own tears at bay. 'And you don't mind staying with her for two days?'

'No, I like her.' He jiggled about a bit, far too excited to be able to stand still. 'Two days isn't long, but you won't be more than that, will you?'

'We promise.' Jon ruffled his hair. 'Why don't you go and tell Grandma Rose how happy you are to be her grandson?'

They both got trampled on as he kissed and hugged them. Then he tore off to find his new grandma.

40

After two blissful days on their own, Jon and Kate returned. They were not starting out like most newlyweds, for they had an instant family, but they were both so happy about it. As far as Jon was concerned, never having had a family of his own, it was a wonderful way to start married life. They had decided to have a child as soon as they could and give Eddie a brother or sister.

A house was a necessity, so they'd gone straight round to have a look at the one next door to Will and Dora's. It was perfect, very similar to the two Freeman houses, with three bedrooms and a good-sized garden at the back for Eddie to play football in. Kate had used part of the money her Grandpa George had put in trust for her, but Jon insisted on paying for all the furniture. His generous wife would pay for everything if he let her, but he wasn't going to have that. He would provide for his own family.

Within two months they were settled in their new house, Eddie was attending a local school and making friends, and Kate was pregnant. Pete and Terry were quite capable of running the business, and he helped whenever he had some spare time, giving Kate more freedom.

More good news was that Tom was now being fostered by Reid and Annie, and he visited them often. The difficult boy was making a big effort to reform and obviously adored his foster parents.

The Freemans had welcomed both himself and Eddie into the fold, and they now felt a part of this wonderful loving family. Jon had never believed he could be so happy.

As the year passed, their excitement grew. Eddie was so happy and proud of his mum and dad, and Jon made sure he never stopped showing Kate how much he loved her. The baby was due at the end of February, and the birth was eagerly awaited by all of them.

'It's a girl!'

At that delighted cry from her husband, the pain of the last few hours vanished, and Kate tried to sit up. 'Show me. Is she all right?'

Jon's grin spread as he gazed at their just-born daughter, his shoulders shaking in silent laughter. 'I'll say she is. Her hair's jet-black, and from the racket she's making I'd say she's furious about being thrust into the world.'

The nurse held up the baby for her to see. 'Oh she's beautiful!'

'Just like her mother.' Jon kissed Kate gently. 'Well done, my darling.'

'You must leave now, Mr Devlin, so we can make your wife comfortable,' the nurse ordered. 'You may return in half an hour.'

Kate watched her husband leave the hospital room and her heart soared with love. He now had the one thing he'd lacked all his life – a family of his own.

She was hardly aware of what was being done to her, but she welcomed the cool flannels being wiped over her hot and tired body. Then she was given a cup of tea and, after drinking it, laid her head back against the clean pillow and closed her eyes. She was so tired.

'I believe some of your family are waiting to see you, Mrs Devlin.' The nurse picked up the empty cup. 'Shall I ask them to come back when you're more rested?'

'Oh, no.' Kate couldn't do that to them. 'I'll sleep once they've all seen the baby.'

'I'll see they only come in two at a time.' The nurse hurried out of the room.

Almost immediately the door opened again and in came her mother, Jon and Eddie. She held her arms out to Eddie as he rushed over to the bed.

'Dad says I've got a sister,' he said in hushed tones.

'That's right.' She kissed him. 'She's in the cot on the other side of the bed. Go and have a look.'

He scampered round and peered at the baby. 'Cor, ain't she little.'

Jon stood behind Ed and held his shoulders as they both examined the small bundle in the cot. 'Don't wake her, she's got a powerful pair of lungs on her.'

Eddie giggled. 'Is she going to keep us awake, then, Dad?'

'I would think that's a certainty.' He didn't sound at all perturbed by the thought.

Kate reached out to kiss her mother. 'She weighed in at nearly eight pounds and has loads of black hair, Mum.'

'Has she now?' Rose went over to the cot. 'I better have a look at her, then.' She reached in and picked up the sleeping baby, who muttered a protest at being moved.

'Don't wake her up, Grandma,' Eddie whispered.

Rose settled her new granddaughter in her arms and

sat on the edge of the bed. The baby wriggled about until she had one hand free from the shawl, opened her eyes and shook her fist at Rose. 'I see, it's going to be like that, is it?'

With determination the other hand came free, the fist clenched.

Jon and Kate laughed and said together, 'Rose, we'll call her Rose.'

Kate's mother nodded in agreement and looked down at the baby. 'Well, Rose Devlin, I shall watch you grow up with interest. I have a feeling I might have met my match. If I'm not mistaken, this little one has inherited the Gresham fire. We shall, no doubt, have some great fights as she grows.'

She placed the baby in Kate's arms, kissed them both and left, her chuckle echoing around the room as she strode out.

Kate watched as the door closed behind her mother, and tears welled in her eyes. She would never get over the loss of Bill, but now she had someone else to live for. Rose Devlin.

Eddie sat on the bed and snuggled up to her. As she saw the happiness on his face, and on her husband's, she knew the baby was a blessing. Jon and Eddie had the family they'd always longed for, and her mother now had a granddaughter who, if early indications were correct, was going to be a replica of herself. And with the past behind her, Kate was blissfully happy, with a wonderful husband and a growing family of her own. Their time of peace had arrived.

She laid her head back with a smile of contentment and closed her eyes.

'Come on, son,' she heard Jon say, 'let's leave your mother to have a rest.'

When they'd left the room, Kate opened her eyes again and gazed at the baby in the cot bedside the bed. Rose Devlin was a new generation for the family, and an addition to the Webster Women. Rose, Annie, Kate and now another Rose. They had come full circle. The end of one era and the start of another.